ALSO BY TAYARI JONES

*An American Marriage*

*Silver Sparrow*

*The Untelling*

*Leaving Atlanta*

# KIN

TAYARI JONES

# KIN

*Alfred A. Knopf New York 2026*

A BORZOI BOOK
FIRST HARDCOVER EDITION
PUBLISHED BY ALFRED A. KNOPF 2026



Published by Alfred A. Knopf, a division of Penguin Random House LLC, 1745 Broadway, New York, NY 10019.

Knopf, Borzoi Books, and the colophon are registered trademarks of Penguin Random House LLC.

Library of Congress Cataloging in Publication Data
LCCN 2025037334
ISBN: 978-0-525-65918-1 (hardcover)
ISBN: 978-0-525-65919-8 (ebook)
ISBN: 979-8-217-20871-5 (open market)

penguinrandomhouse.com | aaknopf.com

Printed in the United States of America

7th Printing

The authorized representative in the EU for product safety and compliance is Penguin Random House Ireland, Morrison Chambers, 32 Nassau Street, Dublin D02 YH68, Ireland, https://eu-contact.penguin.ie.

*For*
*June McDonald Aldridge*
*Spelman College, Class of 1953*

*we are each other's*
*business:*
*we are each other's*
*magnitude and bond.*

—GWENDOLYN BROOKS

# KIN

*Chapter 1*

# VERNICE

My first word was "mother," spoken out loud and with texture. MOTHER. There was a host of witnesses, including Aunt Irene, who called out for God and considered running down the block to fetch the pastor. But before she could even straighten her skirt, she decided that this wasn't a pot to be stirred by any man's spoon. It was August, canning season, and the women were gathered to put away snap peas and pole beans. It was Louisiana hot, but even more so, due to the water boiling to purify the mason jars. Aunt Irene, never at home in the kitchen, busied herself plaiting my hair while everyone else hulled and cut up the harvest. The Ward Sisters sang out amid the thick radio static as Aunt Irene added her colorful soprano to the arrangement. Sitting between her knees, I rested my face on her thigh, still as stone and just as quiet. Sharp against my scalp, a rat-tailed comb created precise parts.

After the death of my parents, I had shown myself to be a peculiar child. No one could say if I was born that way or if I turned that way. I walked early and would do so in my sleep, escaping my crib. I once found my way to the front porch, where I was discovered humming with my face resting on the matted fur of a stray puppy.

At two and a half, I had yet to speak. Folks worried that I was slow. My cradle friend, Annie, was already talking up a storm. She even gave me my nickname, because Vernice had been too many letters for her to hold in her mouth at the same time. "Niecy!" she called, determined to shake loose a response. When shouting didn't work, she tried kindness, breaking her shortbread cookie in two. I smiled in gratitude, and sometimes offered sloppy baby kisses in return, yet I didn't say a word.

Annie's grandmother joked that Aunt Irene should be grateful for my silence. Annie never shut up, not even when she was asleep. Shut eyes quivering, she mumbled the name of her own mother, Hattie Lee.

"This baby will talk when she has something to say." Aunt Irene knew there was quickness in my eyes but feared that seeing my mama shot dead had shocked the words right out of my mouth. Others worried that I had been taken over. Spirits can be hardheaded and hold grudges—purposely missing their ride to the next place. When this happens, they might just set up house in a defenseless body. Aunt Irene shut that conversation down, dismissing it as "hoodoo"—her catchall word for anything not of this world that didn't involve our Lord and Savior. That said, even though there could be substance to that hoodoo talk, she knew her dead sister, my mother. When Aunt Irene held my face to hers, she didn't see Arletha staring back.

Because of this, but not only this, my aunt didn't indulge any gossip. She knew what it was to be whispered about and couldn't bear loose tongues lashing an orphan baby. But she was worried for a colored girl who seemed slow, even if she wasn't, a girl who couldn't say what had happened to her. I made people nervous, which is probably why no one objected when Aunt Irene ducked out from the canning kitchen and sat on the couch to fix my hair. I had been touched by blood, and not the blood of the lamb.

There I was, this haunted child, not even whimpering as Aunt Irene raked the comb through the thicket at the nape of my neck.

"Mother," I said, softly at first. As I raised my voice to a bellow, every heart in the house contracted, vulnerable as a scalded tomato gripped in a tiny greedy fist.

Only three women stood in that tight kitchen, but nearly the entire congregation would let the story play on their lips, sharing details as vivid as those of any eyewitnesses. Some say their throats closed to hear me call for Arletha, dead by then just over two years. They lost their breaths, the way you choke in your sleep when witches ride your dreams. Annie's granny said she heard wonder in my voice like I gazed into the eyes of an angel. Aunt Irene said she understood it as a command, her dead sister telling her that I was hers for life. Only Mrs. Ola Mae, the midwife, attended to me. Scooping me into her stout arms, she cooed, "I hear you, baby." Annie, who had been in the kitchen yapping away, toddled up to Mrs. Ola Mae, arms raised to be held as well. We were both crowded onto her lap. I kept saying my new word over and over, but Annie was quiet for once, sucking my thumb as though it were her own.

---

Women in my family have never been particularly fruitful. My grandmother had only the pair of daughters to show for some thirty years of marriage. She never gave Granddaddy a son, though word on the street was that there was a boy down in Bogalusa who shared his middle name and narrow feet. Four years in the marriage bed, and my mother hatched only me, and I hadn't come gently. (Mrs. Ola Mae told my mother to name me Miracle but instead, she called me Vernice up top, and Irene just after—like all the women in our family.)

Aunt Irene was what the old folks called "barren" but what she called "lucky." She figured this out when she was just a teenager, the summer a revival came to town. Aunt Irene heard that altar call and what was done, was done. When the tent came down and the saints moved on to Jacksonville, Aunt Irene had joined the choir. She also joined the associate pastor in whatever accommodations were available for colored travelers who happened to be servants of the Lord. "Have mercy, he was a pretty man," she said. "Listen. If you ever get a chance in life, grab you a preacher—but just temporarily. Don't fool around and end up being somebody's First Lady." She laughed at the memory, grinning into whatever was on the rocks. "I was wild when I was a girl."

Eight months later, she returned home slender as a daisy. Granddaddy flogged her like she was a runaway slave, so that the neighbors would be sure to hear her crying and know what was and wasn't allowed in his house. My mother, just nine, passed on the words whispered by the ladies in the parlor. These were grown women who dared not lift a finger while a skinny girl was beaten like a man.

"They say you must can't get pregnant, after all the you-know-what you been doing."

Aunt Irene lay on the narrow bed that would end up being mine. "They just jealous," she said. "All these heifers got nine-ten kids pulling at their titties."

"Not Mama. She just got us."

"So what?" Aunt Irene said. "It's the worst when you resent your own daughters."

My mother said, "I'm going to have me a whole bunch of babies."

Aunt Irene said, "You're not. But have yourself a lot of fun trying."

As soon as she was healed enough to sit on a bus for four days running, Aunt Irene left Honeysuckle. She had some money that the reverend had given her and also the cash her mother squirreled away in a crystal candy dish. She left a note. In those days folks wanted to make things plain, putting it all in writing. She didn't write "Dear" because what she had to say was addressed to everyone on God's beautiful earth. *You can't stay where they beat you. I don't care who they is.*

She ended up in Ohio, just over the Mason-Dixon, where she lived for eleven years. No babies, no beatings.

"Don't let nobody sprinkle dirt in your pocketbook." She shook her head at her folly. "There I was sneaking off in the night and Mama was two steps ahead of me. When I opened up my bag and I felt that grit and saw that crop soil in the corners, all I could do was laugh. But that was because I didn't have sense enough to believe in bewitchment."

By the time Aunt Irene entertained me with her stories, I had grown into a normal-seeming little girl, bubbling with wonder. "How come you didn't put Ohio dirt in your suitcase, so it could pull you back up there?"

She gave a little nod to let me know that I had asked a good question. "First off, I don't practice none of that hoodoo. I don't believe in it, and I don't *not* believe in it. Second, it's only home dirt that can pull you back."

Up in Ohio, as the purple cornflowers and lemon puffs were doing their thing, Aunt Irene had received a letter saying her mama was on her deathbed and wanted to make amends for letting her daddy whip her like that. Saying she understood why Irene didn't come back for his funeral. Services are for the dead anyway. Wouldn't Irene come on home while her mama was still living? Her mother, who was deeply sorry, was dying of regret as much as diabetes. *Sleep with this paper under your pillow for three nights before you say yes or no.*

It didn't take but two nights. Without the protection of any talisman or charm, Aunt Irene returned to Honeysuckle. No matter who your mama is, or how long she's been gone, you can't help but miss her. When you are born, she marks you with her milk, even if you never tasted her breast. That's not hoodoo, it's just the way the body and the spirit come together to make you a person.

Despite Aunt Irene's man already having himself a wife, he kept her content in a yellow-shuttered house. When she told him she needed to go home for one last moment with her mother, he paid her round-trip bus fare and kissed her like he would never see her again.

. . .

Whether it was the letter or the crop dirt that brought her back, it was me that kept her there. Six weeks before she buried her mama, she ended up burying her sister—my mother. I was just six months old, so new that I had lived inside the womb longer than I had been breathing air. I took a bottle at night, but in the morning, Arletha opened her pink-checked duster and fed me from her body. I looked just like her with my thick dark hair and flat nose. "See my sweet baby?" she said to anybody that caught her eye. I remember. This is not an orphan's fantasy or me making Aunt Irene's memories my own. If you have ever experienced motherlove, you can never forget the fragrance of it.

On the day that turned out to be the Day, Aunt Irene pranced around town, enjoying herself in the way a person does when she knows she's not here to stay. She was a little too dressed up in a seersucker sundress and nylon panties with a bra to match. Yes, her mother was dying, but she was passing softly, her spirits buoyed because her oldest girl didn't hate her. By the same token, Aunt Irene was lifted, letting go of the anger holding her down like the sandbags tethering hot air balloons. She had come to understand that despite it all, she had a perfectly fine life. No, she wasn't a wife, but she wasn't a whore and there were no out-of-wedlock kids desperate for a last name. A relationship that kept you dressed like a lady, even if maybe you weren't really one, was worth it for the dignity alone.

I was with my aunt, buttoned into a little romper made of the same pink piped fabric as her cross-back frock. Aunt Irene toted me on her hip over to Mrs. Ola Mae's place. The midwife liked to love on the babies she ushered into the world. "Look at this little wonder!" I gummed on a sugar tit while Aunt Irene talked about Dayton and her man. His given name was Josiah, but everyone called him Van.

The Day had been lovely. War raged overseas, but those storm clouds were not visible from Honeysuckle, where the afternoon was as peaceful as a field of buttercups. No bad mojo stirred the air. Nothing odd happened in threes. The blind boy who sold pencils in front of the post office didn't make any eerie pronouncements. But now Aunt Irene thinks that the thing that should have let us know that something was wrong was that nothing was wrong. This was Louisiana in 1941. We were colored. Something was always wrong.

That night, Aunt Irene planned to wear a red dress and dip into The Den, letting the men fill her glass. Prideful, prideful. Smoking a cigarette with the midwife, she said, "The best part about being an auntie is that you can take the baby back home when it's time to go cut a rug." Everyone laughed, and agreed. With a smile lingering on her lips, Aunt Irene climbed the front steps of my mother's house. Her arm was raised to knock when she smelled the burnt-copper scent of gunpowder.

On the other side of the door, there was my mama, dead as Jesus, and my daddy lay on the carpet, moaning. What kind of idiot can't even figure out how to kill his own fool self? Aunt Irene swung her leg, driving her shoe into his face as he groaned and wept.

Preparing to lay my mother in the plot she had bought for her own mother, Aunt Irene wrote to her man, asking him to pray for her and telling him that she wouldn't be returning to Dayton for a month, maybe two. Certainly, there was a family in town willing to take in a motherless infant. When I was clean and dressed up, I was pretty cute. Even my aunt, who didn't cotton to children, found herself kissing my plump face.

Aunt Irene's first choice for me would have been Mrs. Ola Mae, who lived by herself with Miss Jemison the schoolteacher. People whispered about the two of them, but Aunt Irene didn't give that no never mind. She liked Mrs. Ola Mae and her lady friend, too. They'd be excellent mothers. But this is how life works—the women who would be capable mothers too often don't want kids. And too many of those with children probably should have just sat that one out. Luckily, most were in between. Maybe not baby-crazy, but willing. And while they were not the sorts of matriarchs who would raise up a race of heroes, they could get the job done.

What Irene hadn't counted on was that the women of Honeysuckle wanted to see her tamed. As folks came to the house to pay their respects, no one asked Aunt Irene when she would be heading back to Dayton. Even though they coochie-cooed in my face, nobody even joked about adding this precious little girl to their own families.

The day before my mother's homegoing, Aunt Irene walked about a mile to the east to visit Annie's granny. "I don't have a husband. I don't have work down here. My situation in Ohio can't accommodate children."

Annie's granny acted like she thought my aunt was seeking advice, rather than relief. She said, "Irene, nobody knows anything about raising children. Each one is different and you just have to do the best you can to make sure that Jesus will accept them when they get to heaven. And you can find work. You got two hands, don't you? I raised every child that Jesus has seen fit to give me. And I will continue. But only the ones *the Lord* gives."

Just then, Annie woke up from one of the back rooms and gave a little bleat. Her granny disappeared into the back of the house and returned with Annie hooked on her hip. With one hand, Annie's granny prepared a glass of sweet tea and a slice of buttered toast that she offered to my aunt on a chipped plate. "Our girls can be friends," she said.

---

For an entire season, Irene dragged through her childhood home like a ghost herself—baby strapped to her chest and coon circles darkening her eyes. The toll of losing her mother was layered on top of the weight of learning to be one. Hers became a life of diapering and spoon-feeding. Finally, on Pearl Harbor day, my grandmother breathed her last, with a smile on her chapped lips, secure in her belief that everything happens for a reason.

Facing facts, my aunt wrote to the Ohio Man, who pined for his time with her in the yellow-shuttered house. She asked that he send her clothes and put everything else up for sale. A brass-buckled trunk arrived at the bus station in Baton Rouge three months later and a money order came to her via post. The Ohio Man may have been married, but he was true to his word.

At least one Sunday each year, the weather was cold enough for Aunt Irene to wear her beaver coat and pretend to be up north. For many years, it was as sleek as the animal that God gave the pelt to in the first place.

---

I never did without. I was always tidy and well lotioned. Aunt Irene informed me that Jesus loved me, as had my mother. One of the many gifts she gave me was telling me that the Lord was more flexible than most folks knew. She adored that Ohio schoolmaster without ceasing. "God will never fault you for loving someone." When I outgrew my first shoes, Aunt Irene sent them to be cast in bronze, which wasn't cheap. Around the time of my first sins, I was baptized in the name of the Father, the Son, and the Holy Spirit. Each night, I laid my head on a clean pillow slip and looked forward to a hearty breakfast in the morning. I am forever grateful for her sacrifice.

While I was tended to, I was never mothered. Many people suffered far more, even people raised at the knees of their actual mamas. Still, the hole in my spirit made me into the girl I was and then the woman that I am. One day, I will grow a person within myself and love that little person so hard that it would bind her to me like rich dirt in the corner of a canvas satchel.

This is not a play for pity. I wasn't the only bottle-nursed child in Honeysuckle. Being raised by relatives wasn't nothing but a thing, as people say.

My best friend, Annie, raised by her granny, had some thoughts on the matter. "We are not orphans," she said when we were five or six.

"I am," I said. "My mama is deceased, and my daddy is dead." (This was language that I got from Aunt Irene. "Dogs die," she said, "but my sister is *deceased.*")

"But we never lived in an orphanage," Annie said.

"I don't think that orphanages are real."

"Maybe they just have them for white folks," Annie wondered. "So colored children that's orphans must live outside. And neither one of us is outside."

Annie's mama was doing GodKnowsWhat, out in GodKnowsWhere. Nobody had seen hide nor hair of her since before Annie was old enough to sit up by herself. One Sunday, Annie had the idea to ask the pastor where her mama was.

It must have been before 1948, when Calvary split from First Iconium. In those days, we all went to the same church and listened to the same man of God. I liked Pastor Robinson's gold-toothed smile and the way he sang at the same time he was giving the sermon. To this day, I am a sucker for a melodious man of the cloth. Annie never was.

We went together to his little office in the basement. We knocked on the door and he answered, "Come on in."

The room was tight due to the oak desk, handmade by one of the deacons right after the Civil War. In slavery times, the man had been a woodworker, and the first thing he did when he got free was to make a piece of furniture for the Lord. It was magnificent, with legs and feet like the flanks of lions. Pastor looked surprised to see us standing there, two little girls wearing blue-sashed dresses.

"Pastor, could we ask you something?"

"But of course," he said with that sparkling grin.

I nudged Annie forward.

"Granny says GodKnowsWhere my mother is," Annie said.

"Well," said Pastor Robinson, "God knows all. Sees all."

I piped up. "And she is doing GodKnowsWhat. So could you ask him where she is and what she's doing?"

And then Pastor Robinson smiled that smile that people do when kids are cute. Then he straightened his face, pretending to take us seriously. As he flattened his lips, I knew whatever we were about to hear wasn't the truth. He motioned for us to sit like we were two tiny deaconesses with a concern.

"Annie," he said, "Hattie is in God's hands."

"No, she's not," I said, because I knew that my mother was

supposed to be in God's hands and that was someplace you couldn't come back from. "Annie's mama is living."

Annie raised her voice, too. "My mama is GodKnowsWhere, dancing too much. That's what my granny says. She just danced all night. And drinks too much wine. But she is not deceased with Niecy's mama."

"Or dead neither," I added.

The pastor fiddled with a fountain pen. "We are all in God's hands. Some of us on this side, some on the other side."

Annie jerked on the strap of her little pocketbook, just like her granny did when she was mad. I jumped up, too, but I didn't yet carry a purse.

"We leaving," she said, and flounced out.

I followed her, but before we left, I told Pastor to have a nice day because Aunt Irene didn't like me acting like I was born in a barn.

---

Time kept on going, the way that it does. Five or six years after we so amused the singing preacher, on the twenty-eighth of March, Aunt Irene took me to lay a clutch of paperwhites on my mother's grave to celebrate her birthday in heaven. Her name, Arletha Irene, was dug into the granite. She had been a Davis when she died, but Aunt Irene refused to lay her under a stone etched with a killer's name. But to call her Merriweather was a lie. She had readily given up her daddy's name when she said I do. In the five years she was married, she had ample opportunity to move back home, but she never did, even though her daddy was tucked in his own grave, unable to harm anyone, and even when her husband had her spitting out her teeth in bloody shards. In death she was a Davis, and I was one in life—although nobody with that name was allowed to look at me, let alone claim kinship.

I knelt to say the Lord's Prayer as my aunt said her own private words to her sister in a low humming like bees when they are creating honey. I raised my bowed head and observed the daffodils with their orange trumpets and yellow petals; I wondered how they were so beautiful but they smelled like water. Desperate to feel, I caught the fatty flesh of my cheek between my teeth and pressed until it hurt and I tasted iron.

Aunt Irene finished whatever sister communication she had come here to deliver, rose, and extended her hand.

"Don't ever let no man murder you," she said. "If you let a man kill you, I will not bring you flower the first."

Later that evening, Annie was invited over to our house for dinner because her granny had to work overnight. Standing on a stool to help cook, I asked Aunt Irene when Annie's mama would just come on home.

"Don't be jealous of Annie," she said, straining the water off of a steaming mass of spaghetti. Her apron was faded and stained.

"I'm not jealous," I said, marveling at her ability to see into my little heart.

"Yes, you are," Aunt Irene said. "And that's the one thing the Lord can't abide—covetousness. You got to pray that off your spirit. Money ain't the root of evil—it's envy."

I dropped my shoulders and tucked my head, hoping she would see my shame and pet me. "I'm sorry."

"You don't have to apologize to me. Give your sorry to the Lord."

When I was a child, I was tender as a bruise. I knew my aunt didn't like crybabies, so I taught myself how to cry without water, but I couldn't control my trembly bottom lip.

Aunt Irene spread the spaghetti and sauce in a pan and slipped it into the oven while I melted into a pool of voiceless contrition.

Finally, she turned, squatting so we were the same height.

"Listen here, Vernice. You think Annie is the lucky one because her mama might come walking in her front door one day. She got that hope. But she goes to bed every night shot down. She's a little girl now, so she can handle it. But trust me. Over time, the daily discouragement will wear her down, like the heel on a loafer. You are the fortunate one. You know you won't see your mama's face 'til Gabriel blows his horn."

I know now that her words were meant to comfort, but they lashed me sharp as any switch. I erupted in sadness so profound that I choked and gagged.

"Oh shit," Aunt Irene said, patting my arm. "I'm no good with children."

By the time the spaghetti bake was done, Aunt Irene had washed my cheeks with hard swipes of a warm cloth.

"Now get yourself together before Annie gets here. You don't want her asking you what's wrong."

I did my best to fix my face. Aunt Irene gave us heaping plates of pasta covered in melted cheese; we washed it down with lemonade, even though it was the middle of the week. I knew the sweet drink was Aunt Irene's way of saying that she was sorry for all the straight talk.

Annie ate her food but her eyes were busy checking my face and my aunt's. Annie has looked thirty-five years old for her entire life. It wasn't that she was one of those girls that developed early, ripening like a teenager way too soon. We were both built straight up and down, but Annie's old soul showed in her face. The set of her mouth gave the impression that she had seen some things.

After she drained her glass, and started in on a hunk of angel food cake, she looked not at me, but at my aunt.

"What is it?" Annie said.

"You are not supposed to talk with food in your mouth," I said, hoping to somehow shift the mood.

Aunt Irene pressed a paper napkin to each corner of her mouth and spoke directly to Annie.

"Baby, let's make us an agreement. If your mama doesn't come back by the time you reach your majority, let her go. Don't waste your life waiting on that heifer."

Annie's raised fork fell, landing with an ugly metal clank.

"My mama ain't no heifer."

Aunt Irene said, "I know Hattie. You don't."

Old soul or not, Annie balled up her face and cried like the ten-year-old she was.

"Oh Lord in heaven," said Aunt Irene. "I just don't know how to talk to children."

Annie slept over that night so as not to be home alone. We lay in bed, dressed in stiff white nightgowns, just unpinned from the clothesline. Aunt Irene had supervised our prayers and left us alone once she was convinced that our souls were safe at least until morning. We were so young that we went to bed with uncovered heads.

"Niecy," Annie said. "You sleep yet?"

"No. I'm just laying here."

"What is majority?"

"It's when you get to be a lady. When you get bosoms and everything."

"That's all?"

"And when you get your cycle, because that is when you can make a baby."

"Oh no," Annie said.

"What?" I said, propping up on my elbow, squinting at her old-eyed face in the dark. "You don't want to have a baby? You don't have to get one today."

Annie took my hand and pressed it to her chest. I moved my thumb over the nipples, puffy and raised.

"Granny says my titties will be here soon," she said.

I lifted my gown. "Pancake City over here."

"If my titties are on their way, then my majority is not far behind. My mama is running out of time."

Annie is the only person I have ever met who could cry hard yet quiet. Her folded face and heaving shoulders brought out the mama in me. I extended my skinny arms to pull her to my flat chest and stroked the hair at her temples.

"Wherever she is, she's loving you," I promised.

"What if I run into her one day, but I don't know her?"

"She will be the one to know you," I said. "You might be her spitting image. When she sees you, she will think she is looking at her own baby picture."

Annie pulled away. My gown, damp from her unhappiness, was cold against my skin.

"Do you miss your mama?"

I took my time with the question. I knew what it meant. Aunt Irene certainly missed her Ohio Man. She sometimes stared at his bow-tied photo while listening to the noise of her own breath. I had pictures of Arletha, but I studied them with a curious mind, not a remembering one. And there were times that I was every bit as downhearted as my aunt, but I wasn't sure if what ailed me was missing her.

"I don't know," I said.

"I miss mine," she said. "I just don't understand how she could walk away and leave me."

"I wish I could miss mine," I said.

"Niecy, you don't know how lucky you are."

"God don't like it when people get jealous," I said.

"Ain't no God," Annie said.

I fell back on my pillow in bewilderment. To say that there was no God was like saying that there was no such thing as air or sky.

"Annie, you gone crazy," I said. "There is for sure a God. How do you think it is that you and me ended up in the same cradle?"

That question played a song of gratitude within me. Next week, instead of buying candy, I would put an extra five cents into the collection plate. I had Annie and as long as I had her, I didn't know what it felt like to miss somebody.

*Chapter 2*

# ANNIE

Niecy and me have been friends since we smiled with our milk teeth. We were two motherless girls that everyone felt sorry for, but Niecy was especially cooed over because of her sweet face, which reminded folks of her mother, who was gone from this world and it was a crying shame. My situation also called for pity, but no one ever remembered my mother as a "poor thing." If there was one word on every lip, it was "trifling."

It's one of those words that Webster's doesn't know anything about. I looked it up one time and saw something about a cake. In Honeysuckle, we know that it can be one of the harshest words ever spoken. I say "can be" since you can soften it up with a little bit of a laugh. When you chase it with a chuckle, it just means you didn't do your best—like only rubbing lotion on the parts of your body that show, leaving the rest ashy. But when the word is sneered in disgust, there is no damnation more vicious.

It's not vulgar like when you say someone is a motherfucker—letting everyone know you are angry, but hurt, too. And one thing we know about hurt feelings is a man called a "motherfucker" one day could be "baby" again tomorrow. It's more than dismissing somebody as "ain't shit," because again, bad language holds too much fire, and where there's fire, there's caring. You can put "no-count" on the same page.

"Trifling" is its own thing entirely. Nine out of ten times, maybe more, it's used against a man, for obvious wrongdoings like cheating and refusing to work. When you throw it at them, it hurts them, but they take it in stride. By the time you get to calling a man trifling in this way, he has likely heard it before. (Although the first time he heard it from his grandmother, it probably sent him to his bed with shame.)

When a woman is said to be trifling in the tone of voice reserved for a man, there's no coming back from it.

Hattie Lee left me with my granny when I was womb-wet, having suckled just one time. (Mrs. Ola Mae insists that every baby nurse at least once.) They say Hattie Lee used peppermint oil to drive me away, the same way you do to run mice out of your attic. Three days after the cord was cut, she was gone to GodKnowsWhere. Trifling.

Maybe Granny agreed with everyone about my mother's character, but she wasn't going to say so. "'Not yet' don't mean 'not ever,'" she would say to the other ushers. "Hattie Lee will be back, by and by."

If I was near, I nodded hard, giving my two cents without being accused of adding my voice to grown people's conversation. But sometimes, this made matters worse: If the person found my loyalty sweet, they placed a damp kiss to my forehead, out-loud wondering who could be so trifling as to leave a helpless daughter behind. If the person decided that my nodding was a sign of misbehaving, there would be a tsking, chalking this up to Granny being too old to handle a child. If the person had been away to the city, they may have laid down a book-word like "indefensible." Maybe that's the best definition of the word "trifling." A person who is impossible to defend, but if you loved her, you had to try.

Maybe one day Granny would tell me more about Hattie Lee—how lovely she was, how affectionate, how tragic. Maybe she could explain what made her declare that Hattie would be back. Certainly, there were words that could be spoken about Hattie with the same soft eyes people used when talking about Niecy's poor mother, that sweet angel in heaven.

Up in the clouds, God can heal everything, even a bullet to the brain; after death, a person got a little bit more beautiful each day. By the time Gabriel blows his horn, the angels will have gotten so glorious that it would burn your eyes right out of your head if you tried to look at them. Life on this earth, on the other hand, is the thief of beauty.

I have one photo of Hattie Lee. It's a school-days photograph, sized to fit in a man's wallet. The picture is creased by a diagonal line cutting across her chin and upsetting the pleats on her blouse. I've memorized every detail, from the roller-dent in her bangs to the burnt broom straws taking the place of earrings. At her throat, a striped scarf makes a perfect square knot. Although she is only fifteen years old, puppet lines frame her skeptical mouth. She seems to know already that nothing good is coming her way.

Niecy has a whole album of photos of her mother. Our favorite is the wedding portrait where she stands in front of a mirror, arranging her pearls. She is soft as the underside of a puppy. There is no hint that the man who will undo the clasp on the necklace will eventually kill her. The fact that she is so happy and so pretty and so trusting is what makes the photo moody and perfect. My mother, rough as an emery board, seems like she was born to die.

"Maybe your granny has more," Niecy bright-sided. "Maybe Hattie Lee was having a hard time on picture day?"

After dinner, I asked Granny if there were other mementos. "Niecy has nineteen pictures. There is even one when her mother is just a baby, chewing on her fist."

Granny sawed her pork chop into tiny bites that she sucked until soft. "Each child I birthed pulled a tooth out of my head."

Her tone stopped my prattling.

She lifted her shirt to reveal a torso ribbed and puckered. "These lines are from how they stretched me. There's more, but you don't need to see it." She smoothed her shirt down and placed a tiny piece of meat on her tongue. After a while, her jaw rested and she swallowed.

"Yes, ma'am," I said. "It's just that Niecy got—"

"I had six children and it is only by grace that I have one picture of each of them. And those pictures are for the sake of history because I have proof of every one of them on my body. But the body goes the way of all flesh. Ashes go to ashes."

"So, this is all you have to show me?"

She nodded.

"But Niecy—" I started, determined to give it another try.

"Listen here," she said. "And don't get yourself confused. The road Vernice is walking is paved different from yours. It ain't fair, but that's the way life takes us. But remember always that every path leads to the cemetery and it's up to you to be ready to see the Lord."

No wonder Hattie Lee escaped on the first thing smoking. She wanted to live, while Granny looked forward to climbing in the grave and pulling the dirt over her like a blanket. I was only eleven years old, but I could feel what my mother felt sitting at this selfsame table, eating from these same mismatched plates. I let the bent tines of the fork rest on my lip, wondering if Hattie had ever eaten from it.

"She's not trifling," I said.

Granny didn't answer me until she had pushed that little piece of meat down her throat. "You have never heard me speak against my child."

"But it's what people say."

"He that utters slander is a fool."

"Yes, ma'am," I said, knowing better than to argue with an old person quoting scripture. "But they say that she left me."

Granny worked her food some more before washing it down with a gulp of water. "Don't pay them talebearers no mind. Don't give the fire a log and it goes out."

"Yes'm," I said, offering another surrender. I didn't want to fight Granny. Like my mother, I just wanted to get away from her.

Some truths are too bitter to let sit on your tongue, so I don't speak of this much. But Hattie Lee came back to Honeysuckle when I was in the tenth grade. It wasn't only that she was in town, she was in our neighborhood, the Hardwood. She didn't call on Granny. She didn't even sneak over to the schoolyard to get a look at me, hiding herself behind a pine tree and peeking around, like somebody in a movie. She loitered through town for maybe three or four hours. From what I came to know, she stopped by to see Mrs. Ola Mae. Then she ducked into The Den, a little place where people who drink in the middle of the day go to have a nip. She asked Mr. Daniel, the owner, to give her four dollars and seventy-five cents. In return he asked for her address, copying it onto a lined sheet of his receipt book.

A week later, Mr. Daniel handed it to Granny, who attempted to repay the money with the quarters she collected in an empty coffee can, but he wouldn't take it.

"Memphis?" Granny said.

"She says she likes the music," he reported back.

"How she look?"

"Tired," he said.

Then Granny got quiet before raising her voice. "Annie Kay!"

I didn't answer, pretending like I couldn't hear. But when she hollered my name again, I decided that it would be suspicious for me to play full deaf.

"Ma'am?"

"This is not your business," she said in her regular voice to let me know that she was aware what I could and could not hear. "Go outside."

And so, I went out into the yard and sat at the base of a sweet gum tree. Spiky cuckabugs covered the yard. Soon, the pecans would drop. When I was little, I hired myself out to neighbors, picking up nuts. For a couple of quarters, Niecy and I shelled them, too.

But all that was behind me. At sixteen, I was full into my majority. I had breasts for days, hips, too, but no rump. I felt like a dump truck, chunky and sturdy. While I sat under the tree, boys walking by hooted and hollered at me until I gave them my middle finger.

Carrying a napkin stuffed with pecan candy, Mr. Daniel left with a wave in my direction. I didn't go back inside until the air took on a chill, forcing me into the house.

By then, Granny had eaten her own dinner and covered my plate with a clean dish towel. I unwrapped the dish and picked up a spoon to separate the tomato sauce from the meat loaf.

"You ain't going to wash up?" Granny said.

Feeling uncouth, I lathered up in the kitchen sink. The homemade soap smelled like pine needles.

Once I was clean, my appetite left me. I made no move toward the plate. "Didn't she even want to see how I turned out?"

Granny handed me a checked napkin. "I can't say what's a harder cross to bear. Me having Hattie Lee for a daughter or you trying to *be* her daughter. She was my youngest. Number six. And how she did me when she was being born, she made sure no other baby could come behind her. She's been like that all her life, salting the fields on her way out."

"You can't blame her for how she was born," I said.

Granny shrugged. "Satan prowls like a lion."

I wiped my hands dry, then squeezed the napkin like I was trying to strangle it. "Somebody did something to her," I said.

"Somebody done did something to everybody. That ain't no excuse."

I just stood there in the center of that clean, raggedy kitchen sobbing 'til the front of my blouse was spotted with my water. I threw that scratchy towel to the floor and used the back of my hand to smear my face. "Why she didn't even come and say hello?"

Granny reached deep into her bosom, fishing out a scrap of damp paper. "This here is her address. She wouldn't have gave it to Daniel if she didn't want to hear from nobody."

A week or so later, while Niecy was at choir rehearsal, I went to see Mr. Daniel. The Den was not exactly what they used to call a "juke joint" because he didn't have a band to play on the weekends. He claimed to be saving for a jukebox, but that was just his way of acknowledging that he understood that most drinking people need something to listen to besides the sound of their own slurping. It wasn't a dreary place, just stripped down. If you had the coins, he had the booze. If you needed to take a load off, there was a stool for you to sit on. And sometimes, there were cold-cut sandwiches you could buy and even mustard in a glass jar to help it slide down.

Before it was a not-juke joint, it had been a normal house. Mr. Daniel was born in the back bedroom, delivered by Mrs. Ola Mae's aunt. His father had been a hellfire preacher and beat the sin out of everyone in the family. When the reverend finally had the decency to die, Mr. Daniel knocked out a few walls before announcing that 319 Edwards Street was now The Den. It must have been a true pleasure to smite his daddy's ghost like that. The old man had built this house with the same hands he used to terrorize his family. And now it was a dwelling where sin was not only tolerated but encouraged.

When I pushed open the door, a little light hitched a ride. The Den was very much like my house, Niecy's house, and every other house in the Hardwood. But you know what they say—every house ain't a home. With the missing walls, it was hard to say what space had been intended for which purpose. If I used my own home for a guide, the bar stretched from the room where we ate breakfast to where Granny put the radio. A half-dozen wooden stools scooted up the side of it. Greasy halos marked the wallpaper where drunk people leaned their heads.

That afternoon, there were two men posted up, each nursing a short glass holding about an inch or so of liquor the color of sunset. The man on the left smiled at me and scrunched his brow like he was trying to remember whose daughter I was. The other one squinted like he wanted to make sure I wasn't his wife before he returned his attention to his drink. They both wore the green shirts from the paper mill, and I could smell the sharp chemicals they used to thin the pulp.

"Well, if it ain't my effort to be an honorable person, come back to bite me in the ass."

"Hi, Mr. Daniel," I said.

"Just call me Daniel."

"Yes, sir," I said.

"If we ain't got no misters, you know we ain't got no sirs."

"My mama was here, you said?"

"You like my bar?" he asked.

"It's a nice place," I said.

"Not the whole place. I'm asking about the bar." He smacked the wood. "This majesty right here!"

"Nice," I said. "I heard about it, but this is my first time seeing it."

"You know why it's your first time seeing it? It's because you are a little girl and I don't allow little girls in my place." As he rolled himself a cigarette, he nodded at the two men nursing their drinks. "Although I know it's some around here that would like some sweet blood in the place."

"I'm not here to have no booze," I said. "I just wanted to ask you—"

"Barging in here asking questions is disrespectful to the fine work of art." He cut me off with a cluck of his tongue. Then he dabbed linseed oil on what looked like a bleached cloth diaper.

I turned my eyes to the walls in search of art but found only yellowing wallpaper and a sign stating the house rules, number one being USE A COASTER.

"The bar!" he roared. "This right here is the art."

I watched him, wondering how you were supposed to go about paying your respects for a hunk of wood. He shook the rag like a pom-pom until I took it and gave a few oily wipes.

He exhaled. "The proper term is 'intricate.' "

"Yes," I agreed. "It is very intricate."

He sighed. "What can I do for you in eight minutes before the mill blows the whistle? Like I said before, no little girls in here, especially when the men get off from work."

"I'm not a little girl," I said.

"The only folks that got to tell you that they ain't little girls, is little girls." He held out his palm for the return of his rag so he could baby his masterpiece for himself.

"You know Hattie Lee Henderson's my mother, right?" I said.

"Well, I can't help you with that. Anything else?"

The question seemed sincere and I knew an opportunity when one was staring me in the face. If I had a question, he had an answer. He raised his eyes like this was a game show and the clock was running out.

"Why did she come here?"

Mr. Daniel shrugged. "For a drink, I assume. Like everybody else."

"You don't have the only liquor in town," I said. "It's other places she could drink cheaper."

"But where else has such ambiance?" he asked.

I looked at his fingers, long but thick. His skin was two or three shades lighter than my own, but there was a sameness there.

"Did she come to see you?" My eyes were narrow now. "Of everybody in Honeysuckle?"

"She came calling on a different Daniel. A fellow named Jack," he said.

When I looked bewildered he said, "That's a joke. Jack Daniel's?"

When I still didn't laugh, he said, "Never mind. The point is that she came here to wet her whistle. She went to see Ola Mae, as well. So, if you are going on a confrontation spree, make sure you stop over there before you go home."

Just then, the door inched open, and who was standing there but Niecy, innocent as a hymnal.

"Hello, Mr. Daniel," she said, and for some reason, he didn't correct her.

"Little Miss Vernice. Tell me, how is that gorgeous Irene these days?"

"She's doing good," Niecy said.

"'Well,'" Mr. Daniel said, correcting her and handing over the diaper.

I didn't know if I was caught or if I was the one doing the

catching. Here I was sneaking over here so as not to get her morals dirty, but here she was tipping in here like it was her home away from home.

"Niecy," I said, but I didn't know what the next words should be.

Mr. Daniel, satisfied with the swipes Niecy had taken at the bar, pulled the cloth from her hands. To me he said, "Here's a life lesson. Put it in your back pocket. Ready?"

I nodded.

"You can never know another person."

Then he went down below and hauled up a jar of dill pickles. With a long-handled fork, he pulled one up, wrapped it in wax paper before using his fingernail to pry off the stem, and forced a lemon drop into the sour heart of the pickle. He handed it to Niecy before preparing one for me.

"Now run on, you two. Niecy knows I don't allow sweet things in here."

"But you didn't tell me," I said. "You didn't tell me why my mama came here."

"Little girl," he said, "don't try to make this into the whole mystery of the Lindbergh baby. I bet even Little Miss Vernice could tell you. And if not her, ask Irene. She will set that straight in two seconds flat."

When we left The Den, the air outside tasted sweet. Niecy munched on her pickle, but I threw mine into the ditch that ran up the side of the road.

"You didn't want it?" Niecy said.

I looked at my best friend, who was suddenly mysterious.

"You been in there before?"

She shrugged. "Just to get a pickle."

"And you didn't tell me?"

"You don't even care for sour pickles. Besides, you the one who sneaked over here while I was gone to choir rehearsal."

With the door closed and shades drawn, The Den seemed like any other house on the street. Yet people just knew.

"I didn't tell you because I didn't know what Mr. Daniel was going to say."

"About what?"

"About my mama," I said.

Niecy looped her arm through mine and nudged me in the direction of home. I could smell lemon and pickle on her breath. "Whatever they say about your mama is lies."

I know she was meaning to comfort, but it hurt. My mama was the kind of person that whatever was said about her was bound to be ugly. Without even knowing the situation, Niecy wanted to smother it with a pillow of sympathy.

"She was here," I told Niecy. "She didn't come by my house, but she came to see Mr. Daniel. Why do you think that was?"

Niecy covered her mouth and spoke through her fingers. "Are you thinking that Mr. Daniel is your daddy?"

"Maybe. She came all this way from Memphis, and that's who she pops in on. Maybe they were in love?"

I liked the idea of an educated father who lived just on the edges of scandal. Everybody knew Mr. Daniel had a wife he'd brought back from Tuskegee, which explained why he and my mama couldn't properly be together. There are a lot of men that are drawn to sad-eyed women. That's what half the songs in the jukebox are about. The way Hattie wore her disappointment like a brooch, Mr. Daniel was tempted, and who could blame a man for being a man? And who couldn't respect a gentleman who refused to leave his wife? Still, Hattie Lee couldn't bear to live in Honeysuckle and see her True Love sitting up in church with another woman. Sunday after Sunday she suffered in silence until she couldn't take it anymore.

"Or maybe," Niecy said, warming up, "she confronted him about his wife. Not on Sunday, though." Niecy sucked on the sour pickle until the next thought came to her. "Maybe it was at the butcher shop. Right after you were born. Maybe you were even strapped to her with swaddling cloth. The wife was choosing some fresh chicken legs and Hattie Lee pulled back the blanket. After that, Mr. Daniel hurt her feelings so bad that she didn't have no choice but to leave town." Niecy shook her head like she was watching it unfold at the picture show.

"You're right," I said. "Granny was likely telling her all the ways that God was mad with her."

"So, it all adds up. Hattie left town because she was shamed. She didn't want people to know who your daddy was and treat you like an outside child."

"But everybody knows I'm out of wedlock."

"That's not the same as being outside."

"To me, it's better to be outside and know exactly what you are outside of than to have some mystery daddy out there."

"Oooh," Niecy squeaked. "And what if you accidentally fell in love with one of Mr. Daniel's sons, and then you had to call off the wedding the day of—and you were already wearing your dress." Niecy was excited; her hands marked every little plot turn, and I caught the thrill with every tinkle of her laughter.

"Him and his wife don't have kids."

"Who said anything about his wife? If there's a you, there could be others."

"You think he's been slipping money to Granny under the table?"

Niecy giggled. "You did have a mighty nice Christmas last year."

Mr. Daniel was rich for a colored man in this town who wasn't a funeral director or a criminal. He was charming and talked almost like a schoolteacher. I could see how my mother could fall in love with him. And maybe if I kept coming around, he would fall in love with me.

How long did I walk around imagining myself to be the secret heiress to the Honeysuckle not-juke-joint fortune? I didn't mark my calendar, but it was more than a month or two. When I first walked into The Den, it was the middle of autumn. Leaves burned in metal cans all over town. When he burst my bubble, it was just two weeks before Christmas and he was busy adding discs of peppermint candy to his homemade hooch to make it taste a little bit more festive.

I'd taken to dropping by, just to give him a chance to see in me what I had seen in him that very first day.

"Oh, it's you again," he said as though I weren't so regular that you could set your watch by it. "I don't have pickles no more. You have cleaned me out."

"I was hoping that maybe you could give me a job."

"A job doing what, and for what?"

"I could wash glasses. Mop the floor?"

He shook his head. "Those are both late-night jobs and I don't have little girls around my place at night. Besides, you have school."

"But I need the money," I said, trying to be pitiful and scrappy at the same time.

"What for? I know your granny covers all your needs. I see you're not missing meals."

This one hurt a little bit. Couldn't he see my stocky build was just a repeat of his own body, just the female version?

"My mama is so skinny," I said. "Or so they say. You know, I never seen her when I was old enough to take notice. I don't know where I got these thick legs from."

I pulled my dress up a couple of inches to show my dimpled knees. Mr. Daniel covered his eyes.

"I don't want to see none of that! This is why I don't like young girls in my place!"

I put my skirt down, embarrassed as a naked nun. "No, sir, I sure didn't mean it that way. I just wanted you to see that I'm built like your family. That's why Hattie came here, right? To see you?"

Now he pulled his hand down from his face.

"You think—? Naw. You don't think—? Did somebody tell you—? Naw."

I stood there with my arms held out so he could take a look at me, from feet to head. I turned myself around slowly.

"Annie," he said. "I never once in my life touched your mother. I have done a great many things in this world that might bruise my chances of seeing Jesus, but I never in my life took advantage of a woman."

"I wasn't saying you took liberties," I said. "Maybe she agreed to it."

"Aww, honey," he said. "You're just saying this because you never knew Hattie. She isn't the kind of woman who is qualified to say yes or no. That girl is sadness in a skirt. You say anything to her besides 'How you doing' and you are taking advantage. My own mother was like that. So, I can see that cry-easy from way across the street. A better man might try to save her, but I'm the type to credit myself with the decency to stay away."

"So why did she come here then?"

"It's elementary, dear Watson," he said, raising his shoulders. "I let her drink for free."

"You're not my daddy? You didn't love her?"

He shook his head. "No, ma'am."

"You know who could be?"

"Could be anybody," he said. "Lot of Negroes around here got no scruples."

"I'ma go and find her," I said. "I'm going to get myself up to Memphis and bring her home."

"You get yourself way to Memphis, you will likely want to stay there," he said. "No women leave Honeysuckle and try to get back, except Raynelle Jemison, and you and I both know that is a strange case."

"You sure you can't give me a job?" I said. "I'll take a daytime job. I can get the commodes ready for the night shift. I could shine the windows. Oil the bar?"

"You know," he said, "your mother one time asked me for a job, but I sent her away. I know she needed money, but she would have gotten more than dollar bills over here with these hardlegs. I told her go to beauty school." He shook his head. "Last thing she needed was to be around liquor every day."

I felt my lip flapping again.

"Are you like that?" he said. "You got a taste for booze already?"

"No, sir," I said. "I never had more than communion wine."

"And this money you are trying to make is to get you to Memphis?"

I nodded.

"To try and rescue Hattie?"

I nodded again.

"That's stupid. The rescue part. But the Memphis isn't a bad idea. They have opportunities up there. LeMoyne-Owens College, for one."

"Yes, sir," I said, not sure if my luck was turning up or down.

"Let me think about it," he said. "And you know I will need to talk to your granny. Last thing I need is her clubbing me with a Bible."

"Granny don't know everything I do."

"One—she probably does. Never underestimate colored grandmothers. And secondly, and most practically, I don't need a helper. My sister sent her sorry son over here to get some discipline."

I frowned because it didn't make sense to send somebody to an almost–juke joint to steer him onto the straight and narrow.

"My point exactly," Mr. Daniel said. "So why do you think she sent him?"

"He don't have a daddy?" I asked.

"Winner, winner, chicken dinner," Mr. Daniel said. "And I don't have a son. So, it's a match made in her imagination. No offspring. Why doesn't it occur to anyone that that's how me and my wife like it?"

"I don't have a daddy," I said. "It don't keep me up at night."

"Then why did you come here sniffing around me? This is why I don't like little girls. Too confusing. You know my wife is eleven years older than me? I don't like nothing that is young and female at the same time."

"I just want some answers," I said.

"I thought you wanted a job."

A voice from behind me stirred me in only the way teenagers can communicate, just under the skin.

"Uncle Daniel, when I asked you about hiring Bobo, you said you didn't need no more help."

I pivoted to meet my destiny—Clyde, the nephew we had been talking about. He was raised two towns over in Ville Platte, but he wasn't creole or redbone. He was a regular-looking person, complexion straight up the middle, height just under the six-foot line. What got your attention about him was his smile, and not really in a good way. It was like he opened up his mouth and God tossed in a handful of teeth, not caring what went where. But he grinned like he didn't have one thing to be ashamed of. And in that way that men have of getting you to see them the way that they see themselves, I found myself grinning back.

"Oh Lord," Mr. Daniel said.

Then the two of us watched Clyde as he maneuvered around the space with his mop, occasionally lowering it at an angle and singing. Maybe he was cute, in a Jackie Wilson kind of way.

He turned out to be almost satisfactory, if you could get around his ignoring the details. And he turned out to be mostly reliable, if you could get over the tardiness. He almost always showed up, eventually. And when he couldn't, he sent his steady cousin Bobo to take his place. There was a lightness about Clyde that made you want to smile. The customers always left an extra nickel or a dime to thank him for filling up a bowl of peanuts or swapping out the soggy napkin up under their drinks.

But apparently, having a half-assed employee made Mr. Daniel realize that he needed an actual worker. Of course, he had to go to Granny and ask for her permission like he was seeking my hand in marriage. All three of us sat up in the living room dressed like it was Sunday. Mr. Daniel held his stingy-brim hat in his hand. I crossed my legs at the ankle, despite my ruffled socks sliding down off my heel. Granny, sitting on her gray upholstered chair, mulled it over like it was more than just a way for me to earn some pocket money.

"How do you plan to keep her away from the mens?" Granny's speech was different when she had her teeth in. It was like listening to someone try to talk left-handed.

Mr. Daniel assured her six ways to Sunday that I wouldn't be in any danger of corruption. "Ms. Irvina, you have known me forty years," Mr. Daniel insisted. "I won't let no harm come to your grandbaby."

"Me too," I piped up. "My whole life I never got in no kind of trouble."

The two of them turned to me, rattled, like a goldfish had jumped out of the bowl and started playing the violin. I turned my face to the floor to prove that I was sorry, humble, and innocent.

"Summertime." Granny twisted her face to let the words out from around those bulky teeth. "When I was little, they used to pull us out the schoolhouse to pick tobacco. I was good with my lesson, but I never got to go past fourth grade. I was smart, you know that?"

"Yes, ma'am," I said.

"You got to be the one to pay her," she said to Mr. Daniel. "She can't be working for tips."

"Fair enough," said Mr. Daniel.

"And you got to bring her wage to me. I'll keep it safe for her."

I let out a noise then that wasn't quite a cry and it wasn't exactly speech.

"Now, Ms. Irvina," Mr. Daniel began.

Granny shrugged. "When my husband was living, he brought his envelope home every Friday. That way he didn't accidentally drink it up."

"I want my money," I said.

"For what?" Granny said. "What are you planning behind my back?"

"Nothing," I said. "I'm just trying to grow up. Won't you let me?"

With her tongue, she stretched her mouth around her dentures. I found myself rocking at the same rhythm. Mr. Daniel waited to see which way the wind would blow. Finally, Granny set the teeth where she wanted them and spoke.

"I reckon you can keep half of it. You are not like Hattie Lee. Her, I wouldn't trust with a wooden nickel on Easter Sunday."

To Mr. Daniel she said, "You remember that time she robbed the poor box?"

"Indeed I do." He shook his head at the memory. "Your husband got after her. We heard her hollering up and down the block."

"We didn't spare the rod," Granny said. "But it didn't help at all."

Every blessing has a backside. The money was the gift, but the cost was learning another one of the many ways that my mother was trifling. Grateful tears and painful tears both wet the same way. At the end of the day, Hattie Lee pulled the skin off of me every single time.

*Chapter 3*

# VERNICE

When we were on the brink of finishing high school, Annie and I wore circle skirts over stiff crinoline. We used double-sided razor blades to skim the hair from our legs, then we slathered our shins with Vaseline so they gleamed over our bobby socks. We took care of our clothes, darning any holes and rinsing any stains with cold water. My aunt and her grandmother had sweated rivers in white ladies' kitchens to buy the lengths of cloth that we snipped around patterns traced on butcher paper. Every garment was a triumph and we knew it.

Of course, we both stitched together simple white dresses for graduation, but we also needed special clothes for Easter. I had sewn a butter-yellow pinafore and Annie made herself a sheath the stunning blue of South Carolina crabs. She added darts so it accentuated the nip of her waist and the flare of her hips. Closed up in her bedroom, she twirled to show off her handiwork.

"Can't you see me wearing this in Memphis? They are music people up there. Honeysuckle is too saved for people to dance and let loose. That's why folks here have no imagination."

"I imagine things," I said.

"Not you," she said, "I mean all the others. If I wasn't going to Memphis after graduation, I would move to Savannah. If you can't get a music man, you want one raised on the water. Clyde was raised nearby to a river, you know."

It was strange to hear her use the word "man" to describe anything that had to do with us. I still called the boys we went to school with "fellows." Men were dangerous; I knew little else about them.

"Come with me," she said.

"Why don't *you* come to Spelman College with *me*," I said.

"Vernice," she said, "stop acting like me and you knit with the same needles."

"Why do you say things like that?"

"Nobody is saying that we are not girlfriends. I am just saying that we got different circumstances. Miss Irene been training you to be a young lady since the day they told her that she had to raise you. My granny just wants me to be able to put food on my plate without laying on my back for it."

"But what do you want, Annie?"

She gave me my words back in my own high-pitched voice. "What do you want, Vernice?"

"Don't you think I will be a good mama? Can't you see me with two or three kids? Me and the girls will wear dresses from the same bolt and maybe a vest for my son." I knew this kind of talk irritated her, and I made my voice light so that she would think that maybe I was playing, but also hoping she could hear the pleading behind my chuckle.

"Chile," Annie said, "you have spent too much time with the deaconesses! Come with me to Memphis. See the world before you decide what you want to do with your life." Her voice was jagged at the edge to let me know she wasn't the least bit fooled by my breezy tone.

"I'm going to see Atlanta," I said.

"Doesn't count," she said. "You can't figure out who you really are in a classroom. And besides, these matchy-matchy kids you want are going to be attached to a husband and you haven't even tried to find a boyfriend."

"I don't want a husband from the country," I said. "Send me to Atlanta and I will find somebody like Adam Clayton Powell Jr.

I could get seasick looking at his wavy hair." I flopped on her bed like I had fainted.

"Save that lie for the white folks," she said.

She knelt and reached under her bed and slid out an Oshkosh suitcase. It was gray and showed black where it had been dinged up when her grandmother's employers had taken it on vacation somewhere. Luggage was one of the few hand-me-down items that became a little more dignified due to its wear and tear. This valise had been GodKnowsWhere and whoever carried it seemed worldly, even a poor landlocked girl from Honeysuckle.

"Come with me, Niecy," she said again. She twisted to undo the zipper along her back, then raised her arms, wiggling, as she pulled the blue dress over her head. Her plump body rippled and I envisioned my own body, all lines and angles. Annie was built like a woman, making fellows and men alike bear down on their bottom lips. Unaware of her heavy beauty, Annie hung the dress on a wire hanger and covered herself with a worn duster.

The gray suitcase was already full, but she added two more blouses and removed a half slip and a girdle.

"Bobo says that I can't have but one suitcase." She laughed. "Why would he think I own more than one suitcase?"

When I went away to college in August, I would have three brand-new cases that Aunt Irene put on layaway downtown. They were the pale green of pistachio meat. The smallest was a hatbox, round with a silver handle. I had admired them for the year we had been paying them off, but I had never mentioned them to Annie.

"Bobo? I thought Clyde was the one for you."

"They cousins. They both going. See, you should go and be with Bobo."

"My auntie didn't spend all these years cleaning white folks' commodes for me to wind up with some Negro named Bobo!" I laughed, but my friend didn't join me.

"He's nice. Don't be so siddity."

"Aw, Annie," I said. "Stop being so tender. I see you didn't pick Bobo. You take Clyde for yourself and put me off on his raggedy cousin."

To formally change the subject, Annie removed her duster to stand nearly naked. I was struck again by her loveliness, like an overripe plum that was about to split. In the tiny mirror over her chest of drawers, I caught a glimpse of myself—cotton blouse, pleated skirt. Underneath I was bound in a girdle, brassiere, panties, and even pads under my arms to catch any perspiration.

"Not to be in your business, but packing your stuff so early is going to get you caught."

I didn't want her to think I was being contrary, but I would have hated to see her brave adventure derailed because she was overly eager. I was the only one who knew that Clyde had access to a car and that Annie had her money from working all last summer. Annie would take her diploma and run—like life was some kind of relay race.

"Are y'all eloping?"

She giggled, explaining that they were just going-together and they were going together to Memphis.

Annie rested her fists on her dimpled hips and said, "I just don't know what to carry with me and what to leave behind."

"Are you sure-sure that you are not in love?"

"Don't you think I'd tell you if I was in love? Me and Clyde are in like," she said. "Don't be so sad. Give me a hug."

My legs lifted me out of the chair by themselves.

Annie spun and pulled me close. "Don't make me go by myself."

In that moment, I would have left everything in the entire state of Louisiana behind me—the two suitcases and matching hatbox, the white dresses that Spelman girls had to wear to chapel, and the guilt I felt whenever my aunt, who never wanted children, put away coins for my schooling. I would do like Annie was about to do, and how my aunt had done so many years ago—just go where the road took me. Annie was running behind Clyde and I would run behind Annie.

I stood beside my friend, drunk on the smell of Blue Nile pomade.

Hearing a sound that hadn't yet reached my ears, Annie twisted away.

Stung, I flinched.

"Damn," she said. "Granny's back."

I scurried back to my chair and picked up a hardcover book. Annie fastened the Oshkosh and shoved it back under the bed. She snatched the duster over her head just as her granny entered the room.

"Why you got the door closed?" Annie's granny had the attitude women get when they are tired of children.

"I was changing my clothes," Annie said.

"No need to close the door. We all got the same things. You know I don't believe in children shutting doors."

"Yes'm," Annie said.

"Yes, ma'am," I added for emphasis.

To me, her granny said, "Irene needs you, so run on home, hear?"

I didn't know if my aunt was seeking me or not. Annie's granny said that type of thing if she wanted you out of her house. What had she seen that she couldn't abide? What had she felt that her spirit couldn't accommodate? I went on home, I worried that she had noticed the corner of Annie's suitcase protruding through the bed ruffle.

---

That night, settled in my own bed, my body snugged into the dent it had made for itself in the familiar mattress. For some reason it made me think of my mother sunk into her grave all these years. She was just twenty-two when my father did what he did, just five years ahead of where I was now. Had she finished high school, maybe she, too, would have had a set of suitcases waiting on her. Instead, her days were filled with folding laundry, her lungs singed by the fumes of boiling bleach. My father wasn't from Honeysuckle, but he was familiar, as his cousins lived here in town and he popped in from time to time, especially in the summer when farmers needed extra help. He was tall and knobby. In the summer, his arms were burnt from fig milk. His cheeks were plump like baking bread, but his eyes were mean like a snake's.

My mother had been walking down Russell Street with a basket of clean laundry against her narrow hip when a Rambler came barreling down. She didn't have a choice but to step to the very edge of the road. The heavy-bellied laundry basket tipped her to the east and the clean sheets tumbled into the ditch. My mother didn't cry out. She just sat there waving in tongue-tied despair. And then a bun-cheeked man, who eventually put a baby in her belly and a bullet in her head, came around to see about her.

I hope she was in love, that she got to feel the thrill of desire and spirit aligning. And as I lay there, the bed seemed to want to swallow me. I was dreaming, but I was awake. I was breathing and at the same time I was choking to death.

When this happens, old folks say that a witch is riding your back. I don't believe in witches in the godly light of morning. But at 2 a.m. we believe whatever the night tells us. When I was finally able to draw breath, filling my body with the invisible thing we all desire, I called for her. "Mother!"

Aunt Irene, on the other side of the thin wall of this house her own daddy built, must have heard me. But she didn't come because it wasn't her that I called. The night was warm for April, yet the air was cold. Although I was alone in my bedroom, I didn't feel unaccompanied. Only I had ever lain upon this mattress, but the nine-patch quilt had been pieced by my mother, pinned by my aunt, and quilted by my grandmother. I slept each night, warmed and weighted by my family's beckoning memories.

No longer straddling the line between sleep and woke, here and there, I called her Christian name. "Arletha?"

And whatever was in the room with me departed. I wanted to welcome her, but I banished her. What child calls her mother by her given name? Not even a spirit could bear such disrespect.

Aunt Irene finally rose. Tugging the chain to light me, she found me slapping my own face.

"She was here," I said.

"Who?"

"My mother."

Aunt Irene belted her robe and jutted her bottom lip the way she did when she was interested. "What Arletha have to say?"

"Nothing," I wailed.

"She came all the way out here from the graveyard and didn't bring a message?"

"I think I hurt her feelings."

"You hurt *her* feelings? She's the one who didn't get you nothing better but a murderer for a daddy. She had herself a job, and I was working out a plan to get her up to Ohio. For every penny she put away, I was ready to give a nickel. But she went and laid down with that fool. As you know, ain't no woman in this family *have* to get married. None of us ever got knocked up by just laying down. For us to get a baby, we need loving, prayer, roots, and luck. For her to end up where she did, how she did, she had to work at ruining her life. And then have the nerve to become some half-ass haint. These women never cease to amaze me."

When she noticed my whimpers, she said it again. "Lord. I never know what to say to children."

I woke the next day to find the weather playing games. We were just into spring, but it was hot like summer. I wondered if it was a sign and wanted to talk to Annie about it on our walk to school—which she called our talk to school. St. Patrick's Day was nearly a month behind us, but I wore a green ribbon at my hairline, to avoid being pinched by the boys who refused to let it go. But even before I rounded the corner onto her block, I heard her grandmother squalling. I picked up my pace, scuffing my loafers.

Adding my voice to that terrified chorus, I asked, "Is it Annie? What happened to Annie?"

I recalled the offended spirit in my bedroom last night.

"She's not dead, is she? Please tell me she's not dead."

Her grandmother sat on the porch and let her feet hang down.

"I can't take no more," she said. "I birthed six children. Three are in the churchyard. Two of my others, I don't know where they are at. They could be anywhere. Somebody said they saw Hattie up in Newark, New Jersey. Somebody else said she was in Memphis with a soldier. When I finally get to take my rest, won't even be a space for me in the cemetery. Why God give you these children just to snatch them? Why give you these husbands just to run them off? The Lord is my shepherd, but I am wanting."

By now, other neighbors were in the yard, whispering about what might have happened and how they had just seen Annie yesterday. Miss Jemison entered the yard, breathless. Mrs. Ola Mae, the midwife, met her at the center of the small yard and they exchanged words behind their cupped hands. No one could imagine one without the other. Miss Jemison went off to Atlanta for her education and came back to Honeysuckle—for the children, she said. Mrs. Ola Mae was married for a hot minute, after an old man gave her daddy a goat plus an acre and a fourth. But the Lord is crafty. The groom barely survived the wedding night. Before her first Christmas as a wife, Mrs. Ola Mae was a widow, and not even seventeen. They say the old man put a baby in her on his way out, but all Mrs. Ola Mae's people know midwifery and they never birthed a baby they didn't want. Even her grandmother, born under the yoke, had only three children. Two girls and then a boy to satisfy her husband, who, by most accounts, was a nice person.

Once Mrs. Ola Mae put her husband in the ground, she planted all the herbs and roots she needed to do the work her mother had done and her grandmother before her. No gentleman ever came calling and she never went looking. When Miss Jemison came home with her teaching certificate, Mrs. Ola Mae took her in and called her a boarder.

After conferring with Mrs. Ola Mae, Miss Jemison took me by the hand.

All the other women were gathered around Annie's grandmother, petting her and circling her in hymns. Mrs. Ola Mae encouraged her to drink from a thick clay mug. Miss Jemison joined the huddle, murmuring an "amen." I spoke to Annie's ghost, apologizing for not recognizing her. "I thought you were my mama."

Miss Jemison heard me and glanced up with worried eyes. "I knew Arletha," she said. "Used to call her Tulip."

Mrs. Ola Mae joined us. "You go in yet?"

Miss Jemison said, "Vernice and I are on our way."

Mrs. Ola Mae touched Miss Jemison's face. Her movement was quick and soft like the brush of a feather floating to the earth. I saw it, then I thought maybe I didn't. "I would go in with you," she said, "but there will be a baby this evening." And Miss Jemison and I nodded, understanding that it wasn't wise to tend to the dead and the newly born in the same day. Spirits get discombobulated and nothing good can come of that.

"The last gift you can give Annie is to ensure that she is fit for people to see her," Miss Jemison said. "After that, you will be a grown woman."

When we approached her bedroom, I steeled myself and thought of Aunt Irene. Was this how she discovered my dead mother, my dying father? Someone has to find the body. If I was the one lying lifeless, I would want Annie to be the one to do it for me. I pushed past Miss Jemison to be the one to see her first, to shut her eyes with my right hand.

But the room was empty. No dead Annie on the bed. No suitcase disturbed the dust ruffle. Tacked to the mirror was a note.

Me and Miss Jemison figured it out at the same time.

"She ran away," I said.

"With a fellow, most likely."

"Clyde, I believe."

"She expecting?"

"She wasn't yesterday."

We sat on the bed and laughed with an intensity and pleasure that I had never experienced before, or since. Miss Jemison wrapped her strong-wire arms around me and pelted my face with kisses, the way you do with a fat-cheeked baby. I closed my eyes to accept her sweet relief.

"I think she's gone to find her mother," I said to Miss Jemison.

The teacher let herself fall back to Annie's carefully made bed. "I thought she gave that up years ago."

I wanted to tell Miss Jemison about the time when Annie and I had gone to the picture show in Alexandria. We were about nine or ten years old. Aunt Irene was down below with her charges, wearing her full maid's uniform so everyone knew that she was down there for work, not trying to make history. Waiting for the picture to roll, Annie and I nibbled on the jelly beans stashed in our pockets, biting them into fourths to make them last.

Before the main event, we watched a newsreel of African boys and girls who were starving to death. People around us tittered, embarrassed at seeing colored folks in that condition. I wondered how Aunt Irene felt down there with the white folks. I didn't laugh even a little bit because I felt so sorry for the children with their arm bones covered over with just a stretch of skin and their faces bothered by flies.

"Annie," I asked, "why do you think their stomachs are all pooched out like that when they haven't had anything to eat?"

Annie bit off a sliver of jelly bean and let it melt on her tongue. Then she said, "Their bellies are pretending because they don't want anyone to know how empty they is."

This sent tears pouring behind my eyes, filling up my own stomach. So many layers of sadness. To be starving to death. Then to be ashamed so much that your body malformed itself to save you from being embarrassed. But everyone could tell anyway.

"I wonder if they know we see them all the way in America."

Annie sounded as sad as I felt. "I hope don't nobody never tell them."

"Maybe she didn't go searching for her mother. Maybe she was just running off with Clyde for the regular reasons," I said.

Miss Jemison sat up from the bed. "You're not a good liar, Vernice."

I wasn't sure if I should protest or not, but then she said, "That's a compliment."

. . .

If anyone had asked me, I would have said that Annie wasn't much of a liar herself. In all these years, she had never said a word that would dirty the wash water. But secrets, apparently, she was good at. There with Miss Jemison, I struggled to decide if secrets and lies were twins, regular sisters, or just cousins.

*Chapter 4*

# ANNIE

It was the middle of the night. I had just eased shut the window I'd just finished climbing out of. My suitcase was tight as a tomato ready to bust. If you can imagine a car stepping on tippytoe, that's how the old Packard inched up to the house. Part of it was that we were running away from home, so there was a general need for hush, but also the car was stolen from Clyde's mama's boyfriend. Since Clyde was already named Clyde, I just had to be his Bonnie. And Bobo was just in it for the ride. At least this is how it was explained to me. So, there I was, pulling open the front door ready to slide in next to my boyfriend, and I see this pretty girl scootched up so close to him that her titties seemed to grow out of the arm he wasn't using to drive.

"This Babydoll," he said.

"My real name is Ruth," she said. "People just call me Babydoll."

This was well after the witching hour and I was fixed in the road with that heavy suitcase hefted with both hands. The wide moon shone orange, scuffed with courthouse red.

"You coming?" Clyde said, like he was just wondering.

I peered in the car again. Babydoll smiled at me, showing her dogteeth on the sides, and I knew exactly what had happened. This girl had gone and gave him some. I had considered it myself, once we locked our plans to run away. My cherry would seal the deal, like a slick pinky promise. However, I decided that he might be more motivated to follow through if he knew something wet and funky awaited him at our destination.

While I kicked myself for carrying on like I had the only you-know-what in Allen Parish, the back door swung open and Bobo popped out.

"Hey, Annie," he said.

"Don't 'hey' me."

"Now, Annie," Bobo said, "may I load your suitcase in the car? We can manage the details, negotiate truces, and clarify relationships once we get on the highway."

"But Clyde—"

"Clyde is my cousin, so you know I can say no word against him," Bobo said. "But I imagine that this arrives as a shock. Nevertheless, we are traveling to Memphis and it would be my honor for you to join us."

"Why do you have to talk like that?" I said, but I didn't fight him as he removed my fingers from the handle of the worn suitcase and fit it in the trunk beside three others that were just as beat up, if not more.

"Y'all got your suitcases from your mamas' white folks, too?" I asked.

"Babydoll and Clyde did. Mine was a gift from a lady friend."

I frowned. What lady friend helps a man leave? And what lady—friend or no—carries a burgundy leather valise?

"Where she get it from?"

"Her husband," he said with a chuckle. "That girl was something else."

From the front seat Clyde barked, "Bobo, stop lying and get in this car."

On the bumpy dark route, we could only see as far as the one headlight allowed. For a few miles, we enjoyed music from the radio, but mostly there was only static and the tap of my beaten heart. According to the *Green Book*, we would have at least another two hours to go before there would be a safe room for us to lay our heads. The problem was that we all had to pee.

. . .

To everyone's relief, Clyde pulled the Packard by the side of the highway. The fellows bounced from the car like springs, walked a few paces away for modesty's sake, and turned their backs.

"Follow me," Babydoll said.

I didn't want to, but I was frightened to go off in the bushes by myself.

Guided by instinct, Babydoll divided waist-high shrubbery and bent back thin saplings until she found a clearing. She stomped her feet a couple of times, running off small red-eyed critters. Chuckling, she reached into her cleavage, producing a few squares of limp paper. She gave a sniff before dividing it and offering me three squares.

When I didn't uncross my arms, she raised her voice up high like when you try and reason with an infant. "You sure you don't want the other half of this tissue?" She waved it like a white flag, but when I didn't reach for it, she returned her voice to its usual pitch, low with flecks of glass in it. "You can't wipe yourself with pride. Besides, nobody wants to be cooped up in the car with somebody pissy and pissy both."

"I don't want nothing from you."

"Stop being such a baby," she said. "He was mine way before you even met him. Why do you think his mama tried so hard to get him work in Honeysuckle? If anybody got a right to feel robbed, it should be *me* what's mad at *you*." She shook the scrap of tissue like a pom-pom.

As I chewed on this information, she hiked up her dress and squatted. She had let loose a long, strong stream before it occurred to me that she wasn't even wearing panties. Like she was reading my mind, she flashed her teeth and cleaned herself with the paper.

Listening to her pee made my bladder so jealous that I had to press my thighs together to keep from humiliating myself.

"Take the tissue," she said with a very adult sigh.

Mad, but reasonable, I snatched the scrap before tugging my panties down. I prayed I was sticking my booty out far enough so as not to soak my socks.

"He was going to ditch you," Babydoll said. "But Bobo said it wasn't right to leave you high and dry."

"What did he tell you about me?" I was done with my toilet but I didn't want to give her the satisfaction of seeing me wipe. Still squatting, I bounced a little bit to aid with the drying.

With an exasperated snicker, she finally turned her back to give me a little privacy.

"You must be your mother's only child. That's why you are so shy."

"Shy?" I said, wiping myself as quickly as I could. "Nobody ever said that about me."

"I can tell you were raised like a princess," she said. "Just you and your mama. You too soft to have been brought up with men."

"Whoever sold you that crystal ball need to give you your money back," I said. "Truth of the matter is that my mama ran off before I was even weaned so I don't know who my daddy is or what brothers and sisters I might have."

I told her this for the same reason that I fixed my dress into place with a sassy jerk. I wanted her to know that I wasn't the feather pillow she had mistaken me for. In the powerful blackness of the night, I longed for Niecy, someone I never had to explain myself to.

Nobody would for one second think to call me shy if I stood next to Niecy—who has been a Junior Miss since the day she was born. And with me around, nobody would ever call Niecy poor or homely. In that way, we kept each other from being the thing we most didn't want to be. Leaving Niecy behind, I would be compared to girls like this Babydoll person and come up short.

"What's in Memphis for you?" she asked me.

"My mama, folks say."

"I see!" Babydoll laughed up at the stars and clapped three times. "You didn't want Clyde. All you wanted was a ride!"

I fixed my mouth to protest. It sounded ugly to hear it the way she saw it, like I faked affection just to earn my passage. Somehow, she had crisscrossed the nature of things where she got to be the virtuous woman and I was the jezebel.

"No," I said. "I like Clyde."

"No, you don't," she said. "And it's better that way."

I was wise enough to know to leave this thread of conversation swinging in the wind. "Well, what about you? Why are you going to Memphis?"

"Oh, I want Clyde. I want to be wherever he's at."

A voice from a shrub said, "Somebody call my name?"

"Now, baby," she cooed. "You know the difference between us talking about you and us talking to you?"

Clyde reached for her waist like they were all alone. "Good things, I hope."

"Girl things," she said.

Now Bobo was there with us. "While all this is fascinating and perhaps even confounding, I would prefer not to get lynched, so could we get back in the car and get the hell out of here?"

"Do you have to talk like that all the time?" Clyde said.

We piled back in the Packard and Clyde gave it a crank. As the engine caught, he said, "Thank you, Jesus," like our Lord and Savior was out there tinkering under the hood.

Beside me, Bobo said, "Giddyap."

Babydoll said, "Here we go."

I didn't say anything at all. My mind was on Niecy. The next day she was going to show up at my granny's ready for our "talk" to school. She would be all starched and pressed like excitement waited right around the corner. She might even want to stop past the post office to see if there was a card in her box, although she hadn't sent any letters out.

Maybe that could be a bright side of me being gone. She will have somebody to get mail from.

Granny would likely whoop and holler about my empty bed and chifforobe, but her heart would hum like two legs on a cricket. She never said it, but she was sick of kids, girls especially, sleeping in her house, then hatching more butts for her to wipe. Who can blame her? I can't picture what I would be like if babies kept showing up at my step whether I kept my legs together or no.

I rode the next three bumpy hours apologizing to Niecy for not saying goodbye. And apologizing to Granny for never saying thank you.

---

It took the rest of spring and half of the summer to get to Memphis. All of it, except two days, we spent posted up just west of Bogue Chitto, Mississippi. Before day broke on the first day of our travels, the Packard overheated. We had to stop every hour or so to pour water into the radiator. Thinking ahead, Clyde had two gallon jugs at the ready. On the one hand, we were grateful for his foresight because this was the deepest of the deep South and nobody wanted to be stranded. But him being so prepared was proof that he had sold every one of us a pocketful of wolf tickets. By daybreak, all the water was used. We were glazed and sticky, not to mention tired and irritated. The car wasn't the only thing on its last legs when we pulled up to a cheery rooming house that had been vouched for by the *Green Book*.

Clyde had barely cut off the engine when a plump lady emerged from the front door tied into a dark blue apron embroidered with grapes on a vine. Underneath, she wore a green duster ironed so stiff that you could snap it in two.

"Lurelia Dubose." She spoke her name like it was an accusation.

"Annie Kay Henderson," I said like it was a confession, but she had her eyes on the fellows.

"What y'all want around here?"

"Place to sleep for a night or two while we find someone to fix our car," Clyde explained.

"You got mechanic money?" said Lurelia. "You got head-laying money?"

Babydoll jumped in with attitude for days. "Dollar bills don't have no use wrote on it. We got money to pay you for a room. That's the only part that's your business."

Lurelia whipped her head so hard that her wig almost came loose. "Young lady."

Babydoll wasn't cowed. "We grown. Not one of us is your child."

"But are you married?" Lurelia said. "Because this ain't a place for grown people to lay up."

We fell silent and Lurelia chuckled victoriously. "Y'all will have to rent two rooms. A separate place for the girls. And," she said, stretching the word out. "And, you have to stay at least two weeks. This is a place for people to live. Not no hot-sheet establishment."

I would have wrestled an alligator for a shower, but there was no way we could afford to pay rent for two weeks, let alone double. The landlady, counting our money through our clothes, probably came up with that rule on the spot.

Granted, the four of us looked like escapees from the Country. I had sweated so much in that car that my hair was balled up like a bird's nest. Babydoll and Clyde hadn't had any time alone since we headed out, but hoochie-coochie wafted off them in waves. But who ever heard of somebody in Mississippi turning their nose up at anybody? I felt myself getting as mad as Babydoll.

When Bobo opened his mouth to talk, it made everything seem like a better idea than it was. "Madame," he said, "we have no intention of offending your values. Perhaps you can recommend another venue?"

"No decent place around here will take colored," she said. "Why don't you just head on 'til Jackson."

Bobo spread his hands. "We would like nothing more, but we are having some trouble with our motor vehicle. It will take a mechanic to get it road-worthy, you see." He smiled. "Should you allow us to shelter here, I give my word that the girls will sleep on the bed, and Clyde and myself will take the floor."

"Can't help you," she said. "I am a Christian woman and nobody shacks up at my place."

"No room at the inn?" Bobo said, with his smile unchanged.

"It's Easter time, not Christmas," she said. "Don't try and be flip over here. But I am about to give you some Christian charity. Head on down the road two miles, then when you get to a crossroads go to the left. Lulabelle might put you up."

Bobo fetched a little notepad from the glove box and jotted down the instructions.

"One more thing," said Lurelia. "You can't call on Lulabelle before lunchtime."

"What we supposed to do in the meantime?" Babydoll shot back, which made Bobo throw up his hands, as her attitude undid all he had accomplished with his vocabulary.

"Not my business," Lurelia said.

"Madame . . . ," Bobo began, hoping not to be at square one.

He was able to get us four sandwiches of butter and sugar, water for the radiator, and directions to a live oak tree that would provide some cover from the cruel sun until 1 p.m. or so, when it would be okay to call on Lulabelle.

They call them live oaks because they don't drop their leaves in the fall. They are sometimes as wide as they are tall, shading whole fields. Bobo said that in South Carolina, the people give the trees names like they are cities unto themselves. "You ever hear of Secession Oak?"

Obviously, we hadn't. So, he explained that this was the tree under which the South decided to declare war. "Angel Oak, in contrast . . . ," he said, warming up.

"Negro," Clyde said, "could you just shut the hell up? Just for five minutes. I didn't drop out of school to listen to you play teacher all damn day."

Bobo pulled back like Clyde was spraying spit in his face. "I was just trying to make our time a little more interesting."

"It's interesting to me," I said.

We headed out at one, on the nose. We had barely gotten beyond the crossroads before the knocking engine added growling and screeching to its range; before Clyde could even shift gears one last time the Packard just stopped. It quit the way a woman does when she can't stand a cheating man for one more second. The car shut down like it was on strike. It didn't care about Clyde hard-twisting the key or the cooing noises Bobo made as he rummaged under the hood. This car rejected us. Sick of this journey, it refused to ferry us another inch.

The fellows cranked the windows down and pressed their shoulders to the frame and pushed the Packard with whatever strength they had. The tires popped against the dirt and gravel road. Babydoll roosted in the driver's seat, in charge of the steering wheel. I was too much of a lady to help them push, but I was too nice of a person to add my weight to the load. To compromise, I trotted beside, wondering what I had gotten myself into.

Bobo sang Hambone songs he learned from his daddy, who had fought in the war. "Ain't no use in going back/Jody's got your Cadillac."

Clyde had nearly sweat his shirt see-through when I decided that being ladylike isn't all it's cracked up to be and lent my strength to the effort. Attaching both my hands to the bumper, I strained through my legs. The car felt like an extension of my body, weighty and able.

"All right, Rosie," said Bobo.

"Who?" Clyde said.

"Rosie the Riveter," I said. "He's being cute."

"Encouraging," Bobo said.

This went on for nearly an hour, us moving west as slow as the sun.

---

We pushed the car through a gate gooey with too many layers of paint. Were it not for the wood sign painted LULABELLE's in loopy letters, I'd have pegged this place as an abandoned farm. No crops grew in the dusty fields, and the barns and silos were near falling down, and there wasn't nary sheep, goat, cow, nor chicken. Nearly a dozen cabins dotted the property, made with warped planks, up vertical. The unvarnished wood was gray like meat gone bad. Each one sported a little porch, but no rocking chair to make it homey and no lip of roof for shade.

Babydoll said, "This looks like slavery times."

"Sharecropping," I said.

"Potato, potahto," Bobo said.

"Can't you just be normal?" Clyde said to his cousin.

"Hello?" Bobo said to the air.

Now that we were on the property, we could tell that the shacks were occupied. Ladies' clothes hung from short clotheslines out back. The odor of frying food wafted from somewhere, reminding us that we hadn't eaten. Despite these sounds of life, I didn't hear any voices other than ours.

To the north, a good distance from the shacks, was an impressive Jim Walter home, gray with black shutters. Five or six plaster posts propped up the roof. I knew this house from a catalog that used to come for Mr. Daniel. Let's say you had a piece of land but no house to live in. You could just order one up and voilà. Every board, joist, and shingle would be delivered. Then you got your sons together and built yourself a modern house. I had never seen such a structure in person. In Honeysuckle, colored people couldn't even get mail brought to our doors—that's why we had PO boxes. So, you know that you couldn't expect somebody to drop off a whole house. Besides, such pretty homes cost pretty pennies, shiny quarters, and beautiful dollars, too.

We stood there gawking when a woman dressed in black trousers and a white collared shirt opened the door. She looked a little familiar, but I couldn't place her.

"I'm Lulabelle," she said.

"Ms. Lurelia sent us here. We don't have any place to stay," I said.

"Just for a little while," Babydoll added.

Lulabelle considered us for a long minute, aiming to figure out what our hustle was. Then she made a statement that was more like a question. "You must have rubbed my sister the wrong way if she sent you to me."

"No," I said. "We didn't do anything rude. We just couldn't afford to get more than one room and we are not none of us married and she said—"

Lulabelle pitched her head back and laughed. "She said you were not going to be shacking up in her place."

“That’s the thrust of it,” said Bobo.

“A little schoolteacher,” she said to Bobo. “Are y’all four Christians?”

We looked at each other, not sure of the best answer.

“We are all of us baptized,” Clyde offered.

“Clyde was raised up sanctified, but I’m Catholic,” Babydoll said like this made a hill of beans’ difference to anybody but her.

Lulabelle waited a beat, giving anybody else a chance to profess their faith. When we didn’t, she spread her mouth into a welcoming smile. “This here is a whorehouse.”

*Chapter 5*

# VERNICE

For me, Annie left her paste-pearl earrings and the crab-blue dress. Pinned to the bodice was a note letting me know that she had chalked it to fit me. "Alter and carry it to Spelman." I hung it in my closet, never intending to rip the seams. This was Annie's dress and no alterations could change that. And by the same token, she had deserted me. No dress, I didn't care how lovely, could change that, either.

"What you mad about?" Aunt Irene asked. "You moping around here like your little boyfriend dropped you."

She asked me this as I stood at the sink, washing a half bushel of greens. It was Easter Saturday, and Annie good and gone. I agitated the water to flush the grit from the curly leaves. Aunt Irene wasn't particular about much, but she could not abide sand between her teeth. She taught me to wash the greens until there was no dirt in the bottom of the sink, and then rinse it once more. Whenever you ruin food, you disrespect the hands that grew it, and the Almighty hand that created it.

I kept my fingers occupied, pretending that I couldn't hear and inspecting the greens at the same time. When I detected an orange caterpillar, I squinted as it inched up my finger. Annie would have set the bug on the front step and even torn a corner off a leaf so it would have something to eat. "She's a future butterfly," she would have said. If we were together, I treated creatures gently, too. But we were not together and I didn't care about the fact that one day this worm would fly.

"You know you hear me," Aunt Irene said.

"I'm just thinking about graduation," I said.

"You just lying, you mean."

"Can't I just have my own private thoughts?" I asked, driving the greens under the water so hard that water overflowed the basin and wet my legs. "You want to know how I feel, but you never care how I feel."

Aunt Irene looked at me like one of the caterpillars had stood up and taken the Lord's name in vain.

"It's me you're talking to like that?" she said, like all she wanted was clarity.

"No, ma'am," I said. "I'm trying *not* to talk."

If I wanted to have silence, Aunt Irene was going to give it to me. We ate our dinner without a syllable passed between us. The burst and bulge of chewing filled the room, but not one word in the English language. I splashed pickled pepper sauce on my greens, too much. My mouth was on fire, but I didn't soothe myself with water because I didn't want Irene to have the satisfaction of knowing that my tongue was throbbing. The scrape of a tin spoon against a porcelain platter caused my scalp to contract, but I was determined to outlast my aunt.

When we had eaten every morsel, I rose from the table and gathered my silverware.

"That's rude," Aunt Irene said.

I sputtered, not sure of the rules of this standoff.

"You can't just stuff your face and walk off."

I fell back into my seat and flailed my arms like a bug. Aunt Irene laughed, deep and throaty. She helped herself to another scoop of chicken and noodles. She talked as she ate, mimicking me. "Thank you, Auntie, for putting food on the table. How was your day, Auntie? I hope your white folks weren't cutting up too bad. How are *you* feeling, Auntie? Your feet bothering you?" To punctuate this last detail, she extended her left leg, to display her ankle, which was puffy and mottled.

Guilt is my oldest friend, even older than Annie. "I'm sorry," I mumbled.

"Sorry for what?" she prompted.

The question was likely bigger than my aunt intended.

"Why did Annie treat me so poorly? She just climbed in that car and slammed the door. My whole life people been up and leaving, and she knows that. But she still just . . ." I didn't have the word for this feeling. "Abandoned" was a school word, borrowed from Miss Jemison's list. I wanted a word I had used before, some sound hatched from an egg of my own. "No good-bye, no nothing."

Where the hair shone gray at the roots, the veins at Aunt Irene's temples bulged. "I have been here every day for the last seventeen years. Let's be clear; *everybody* didn't leave poor little you."

"Arletha did." Even before the words launched from my tongue, I knew how ridiculous it sounded. My mother didn't murder herself. But there was part of me that believed that if she had loved me more, she would have figured out how not to die that day. But that part of me was buried under so many layers of sadness that I couldn't make out its shape or edges.

I let my eyes travel the room and lighted on the picture of Arletha and Irene together, grinning behind their cat-eye glasses. The photo must have been taken just before Aunt Irene ran away with the singing preacher. A pixie cut ended at ears decorated with shiny gold buttons. At the base of her turtleneck collar hung a small gold cross. Arletha's hair was longer, flipped up below her chin. Her face was plump and ripe, like an August peach. My grandparents had paid hard-earned money to have that photo made. They had been proud of their lovely daughters, six years apart but close anyway. The tilt of my aunt's head gave her away as one you had to watch. Arletha's eager posture marked her as a sitting duck.

"If you hadn't run off to Ohio, she might not have gotten killed," I said.

Aunt Irene took a breath. "You can't put that one on me. My mama tried that same mess before she passed. That's why she was so intent on me raising you, to glue back together what she told herself I had broken."

"Was it so terrible?" I asked Aunt Irene. "All my life I lived so as not to bother you. I can't help that I was a child. If I could have raised myself, I would have. Some people may say that I did. Nobody ever hugged me or told me I was adorable. No birthday cake with candles. I feel like I grew up in a rooming house. And I had one friend, Annie. And then she just grabbed her suitcase and got the hell out of Dodge and you can't even figure out why I'm devastated."

"I have told you a thousand times that I don't know what to say to children. But you are one summer away from leaving this house, so I can talk to you like a grown woman," she said. "Finally."

Aunt Irene went to the kitchen and returned with a pint bottle of whiskey. She poured herself a slug and gave me a splash. She swallowed hers, finishing with a little cough, and motioned for me to do the same. "I'll be back to talk to you in a few minutes. Let it marinate."

A quarter hour later, Aunt Irene had taken off her work clothes and put on a shirtdress with a large collar. Her feet were bare; a coat of red lacquer gleamed on her toenails, even though bunions warped her feet. She studied the table and decided to sit across from me, as though we were ready to play a round of spades.

"Here go a little more," she said, tipping the bottle over my glass.

The whiskey in my mouth was hot but welcome. "Thank you."

"Vernice Irene Davis." She said my name like she was invoking it for some record. "You know my Christian name is Viola Irene. Your mother was Arletha Irene. Our mother was Vertena

Irene. I know you think you are all alone in this world, despite the fact that you never wanted for anything. Niecy, you may be lonely, powerfully lonely, but you are one spoiled little girl. Do you know that? Has it crossed your mind that you are not all that people have to think about?" she said. "You are not the only person in this town—hell, at *this table*—with feelings. Lord knows, you are not the only one that ever got left."

"But I am the only one that never got to do the leaving."

Aunt Irene said, "I am past forty. There are more years behind me than out front."

"Yes, ma'am," I said.

"Don't 'ma'am' me. You want to talk like a grown woman, nobody here is a ma'am."

"Okay," I said. "I'm seventeen."

"You don't have to tell me how old you are. I'm the one who made a special breakfast every year for your birthday. I did it seventeen times. And I didn't mind it. You were a sweet child and you have grown into a nice young lady. I am proud of you. But there are many things you don't understand. And you are blessed to be so stupid."

"I'm not stupid," I said.

"You're not. I shouldn't have said that. But you are ignorant about life, and this is something that you should give me some credit for. You don't see why Annie had to leave Honeysuckle? And you really don't see why you don't have those new suitcases packed yet?" She shook her head like she was genuinely befuddled.

"That Clyde boy wasn't anybody to run away from home over." I waved my glass, having taken to drinking like a duck. "He wasn't like your Ohio Man," I said. "Clyde has buckteeth. He puts on cologne when a bath would do better—"

Aunt Irene cut me off. "Clyde could get her to Memphis."

"But you are the one who told her not to go chasing her mama."

"I never told her not to get out of town."

"But—"

"All this butting! You are about to burn rubber and leave me here in Honeysuckle, where they will end up burying me in this black dirt next to your mama. Next to my mama. Three Irenes in a cold row. You are going to, one day, lay dead in entirely different soil, feeding a whole different breed of worm, growing flowers with different petals, maybe even fertilizing redwood trees. And I don't begrudge you that. But you can't be ready to fight Annie for trying to find herself a new life."

"But she could have at least told me."

She smiled a slow smile. "If you are not Arletha come back," she said. "Your mama never did forgive me. But if she had lived longer, she would have let me back into her heart. If she had just survived five minutes more, she would have understood." Tapping her empty glass against the table, she blew a sharp breeze. "Staying here only got her a closed casket."

"I wish I got to know her," I said. "I hate that I ran her away when she sent her spirit to me."

"Girl, you don't know who that was. It might have been your sorry-ass murdering daddy."

"You ever seen a ghost?"

"Of course," she said. "But never your mama. Not once. She's gone from here forever, and I am glad for her."

"It's sad to never have a mother."

"That's what you and Annie have together, this silly sadness. I'm sorry you didn't get to know Arletha, although she couldn't have lived up to your imaginary mother adoring you from heaven. Hattie Lee was trifling from the day she was born, but I guess Annie will figure that out in her own time. But listen: y'all both are so devoted to your mothers, but you have been more to each other than what either of your mammies ever gave. So, give Annie some of that devotion that you have been wasting on a daydream. Write to her. Don't wait 'til one of you is dying to try and understand."

"I don't have an address for her."

"You will. Get the letter written now, so when you hear from her, you can just drop it in the mail."

. . .

A day or two later, shamefaced, I bought a stamped envelope from the post office and dashed off a stingy little note. I gave her the update on everybody we knew, but after I signed my name, I added a PS, hoping to be casual. *I am very relieved to know that you are not dead.* Then a PPS: *Did you ever get ahold of Hattie Lee?*

*Chapter 6*

# ANNIE

I don't know why I was surprised to discover that this place that used to be a farm was now a brothel. In those days, nearly everything that was for colored folks was molded into whatever we needed it to be—except churches. Those, we built from the ground up with only the Lord in mind. But on occasion, when there was no hallowed temple available, we blessed a clearing in the woods, purified a storefront, or even sprinkled holy water on a street corner—and then bent our knees and got to worshipping. If there was a Negro motto in those times, it would be "We Make Do."

As we returned to the car, we whispered among ourselves about the strangeness of this particular misfitting of purpose.

Clyde said, "Whoever is screwing in these shacks will walk away with an ass full of splinters."

Babydoll puckered her lips like a kiss to the wind. "What these girls got must be so juicy, don't nobody care."

Bobo opened his leather bag and retrieved his hairbrush and worked on his head. "This is interesting."

I fisted my hands on my hips. "I know what I am *not* about to do."

Lulabelle, way on her front porch, had that same supernatural hearing as Granny, because she threw her head back and laughed, flashing a front tooth trimmed in gold, like a picture frame.

"Don't you worry. I don't allow virgins to work at my place."

My so-called friends joined her in the mocking, as they had "tasted the fruits of the garden," like people used to say. Clyde and Babydoll with at least each other, and Bobo had some strange short-dude magic that earned him panties for days.

As they were all but slapping their thighs, Lulabelle crossed the distance, cutting them off with a twist of her wrist and a jangle of gold tapping gold.

"I'm the only one that gets to tease Little Missy. The rest of y'all listen here and take notes." She lowered her voice to a pitch that sounded almost like a man's. "More lives have been ruined due to fucking than to not-fucking. I bet every one of your mamas could tell you about that."

They turned their eyes to their scuffed shoes, like caught schoolchildren.

"From the looks of that car, y'all need more than just one night."

"Yes, ma'am," Bobo said. "We'd be much obliged."

"How long?"

Now Clyde took center stage, asking if maybe she had some work the fellows could do, to earn some money for a mechanic. "Surely you got jobs that need doing on a place like this."

He said "a place like this" in such a way that everyone knew he meant "a raggedy-ass place like this." We took in the shacks with their warped roofs and front steps missing vital planks of wood. A woman dressed in a sleeveless smock poured a pan of water onto a cluster of dandelions. With her free hand, she waved in our direction, and Clyde returned the greeting, prompting Babydoll to swat his shoulder.

Lulabelle smiled with just one half of her face. "When men do work around here, I don't generally pay them with cash money."

We stood there with our heads cocked like dogs do when they are confused. Lulabelle continued that one-sided grin while she waited on her words to kick in. Bobo tapped his foot, working to solve the riddle. Clyde was twisted up, too, but he didn't have the patience to figure it all out.

"What you going to pay us with, then?"

"We barter," said Lulabelle.

It was a word that I didn't know, but Babydoll untied the knot, matching Lulabelle's leaning face, twitch for twitch. "You pay them with screwing?"

"Whatever a man will do for money, he will do for snatch. After all, half the money they spend in life is to get into people's drawers."

Bobo nodded like this made sense. Clyde grinned like somebody had just offered him a T-bone steak with a side of candy yams.

Babydoll was all business. "What if Clyde and Bobo do all the handyman stuff, and then you give the pussy payment to the mechanic."

All this talk about pussy and snatches made my face burn so hot that blushed through my dark complexion. Couldn't she say something a little more civilized, like "loving" or even "nookie"?

Lulabelle never changed her facial expression. "Not a bad idea. But let me make it clear that I won't be the one providing the service. It would be one of my ladies, of course."

Clyde raised his hand. "Do we have to work more depending on which girl it is? Because I think a medium-pretty girl would be enough. The car ain't all that broke down."

Lulabelle full-on laughed at this one. "I'll pay you by the hour—in my ledger of course. Like I said, I will be dead in my grave before I ever lay one Yankee dollar in a man's palm. And then I will deduct your expenses—room, board, miscellaneous. And with what remains, you will have a credit to hire one of the ladies to befriend the mechanic. His name is Shadrack."

We nodded, dizzy from so much information.

Lulabelle turned her attention to me and Babydoll. "And, little girls, how do you propose earning your piece of keep?"

"I can cook," Babydoll said. "Your girls need to eat, right? And you yourself want a nice meal?"

"And I can fix cocktails. Back home I used to work in my uncle's juke joint. I know how to make a gimlet, a whiskey sour, a screwdriver . . ."

"Laundry," Lulabelle said. "We go through a lot of sheets around here."

And there I was blushing once again, but everybody, by now, knew to let Lulabelle laugh at me all by herself.

---

Every colored girl south of the Mason-Dixon knew how to wash. Some white girls, too, as everybody needed clean drawers to wear on Sundays. White folks hired my granny to launder their clothes, leaving her no energy left to do her own. As soon as I was old enough to reach the clothesline, it became my chore. Granny's lye soap wasn't harsh the way some other women made theirs and she occasionally grated a little lemon peel for scent. Also, I appreciated the time by myself in the backyard on Tuesday and Saturday mornings. I found a rhythm on the washboard, then I rinsed until the water ran clean. If the clothes looked right and smelled fresh, Granny was pleased.

Lulabelle, oddly enough, had a thing about clean sheets. She didn't pay the towels no never mind, but when it came to bed linens, she was near about religious.

I couldn't make hide nor hair of it. The mattresses that lay on the floor of the shacks were thin—stuffed with straw, horsehair, and chicken feathers. After all, Lulabelle didn't want the men to be so comfortable that they wanted to just lie there and chat, falling in love or some foolishness. "Geechee madams put Spanish moss into their bed pads, so the chiggers let them know when it's time to leave. But I would never put my ladies through all that itching."

Babydoll nodded. "Besides, nobody wants to see a whore scratching. People will think that they got something."

Lulabelle aimed her pinky at Babydoll, which was her way

of offering a gold star. "Point is, this a come-and-go business," Lulabelle said, and Babydoll joined her chuckle. Apparently, there was a joke in there somewhere.

But despite the fact that the beds themselves smelled like old sheep, Lulabelle insisted on sheets boiled 'til they were nearly blue and ironed crispy—changed behind every john, which she insisted that we called "sirs," even when they weren't around.

All this me and Babydoll learned on day one.

We got up before the sun and were busy boiling water, bleaching, and scrubbing. At 9 a.m., I was hungry and a little bit woozy since there was nothing on our stomachs but black coffee, toast, and pear preserves. Even with the shakes, we had gotten two or three loads of sheets up on the line, billowing with the breeze, smelling like the satisfaction of hard work.

Lulabelle was foxy that day in a snug black skirt that showed off the shelf of her behind and tight little waist. She didn't have much by way of bust, but with ass like that, who needs titties—or face either, truth be told.

Anyway, she was out back strutting like *Jet* magazine come to life, leather shoes sinking into the mud. She inspected our clean sheets with her face crinkled like she smelled something funky.

"Ma'am?" I said, hoping that I didn't sound challenging, but also not like some pushover.

"Miss?" she said back, reminding us of our rank. Then with a bracelet-jangling jerk, she sent the sheets from the line to the dirt. It was like a magician's trick. The sheets were on the ground and the clothespins remained clipped tight.

"This ain't a nasty-bed kind of business," she said.

"Like hell it ain't," Babydoll said. "You didn't see those sheets before we scrubbed them."

Lulabelle turned. "You talking to me, little heifer?"

Babydoll said, "All I am saying is—"

Lulabelle stepped on the sheets, like they were doormats. Twisting on the balls of her sassy two-tone oxfords, she ground them into the wet earth. "Little girl," she said to Babydoll, "I am not your mama or your auntie. I don't like you and I am not a nice person. The only reason you are not stripped and up under a sir is that I promised my sister I wouldn't. So, it is a gift that I let you wash these sheets. It is an honor. You hear me?"

"Yes," Babydoll said. "I hear you."

"So, what is it you say when someone gives you a gift?"

"Thank you."

Lulabelle tapped her foot, making a squishy rhythm.

"Thank you, ma'am." Babydoll hung her head to match her tone, but her eyes, under the fringe of her bangs, were furious.

---

At night, we slept all four of us in one of the cabins on the west side of the property. This was a rainy night and we were all a little bit hungry, but not hungry enough to trudge to the main house, where there were beans and rice sitting on the stove—not free for the taking, but included in our room and board. Furthermore, we got charged whether we ate it or not. The red beans were tasty cooked down with sausage, and all the magic women from the Delta know how to sprinkle in a pot. But on the sixth night in a row, I hankered for a meal I could chew.

We were situated on two pallets on the floor. This doubling up had been the fellows' idea, of course, but they were right that sharing two thicknesses of sheets and blankets was better than damn near sleeping on the floor.

"I won't lay a finger on you, unless you want me to," Bobo swore.

Clyde made no such promises to Babydoll, but they had a different kind of relationship. For the moment, they had fallen out of love, which was a blessing because I didn't want to be three feet away from their bump and grind. I had heard enough moaning and groaning as it was.

This was a Wednesday night. We had worked hard all day. Me and Babydoll at the washtub, and Bobo and Clyde had been hauling hay, as Lulabelle had hired them out to the farmers down the road. Bone-tired, we just lay on our pallets, listening to the rain dance on the tin roof.

Beside me, Bobo said, "I bet you ladies are glad me and Clyde patched the ceiling." He murmured the words into my neck, just below my ear. My hip, turned toward the wall, tingled. Before I could decide how to respond, Babydoll piped up. After all, she and Clyde were barely an arm's length away.

Babydoll said, "Y'all should be grateful for the clean sheets."

Clyde snorted. "We would be more grateful if they didn't stay so clean."

"You so nasty," she said with a giggle that let me know that they'd be back together real soon. I just hoped it would be after we were done sharing such tight quarters.

"We get paid tomorrow," I pointed out. "At least me and Babydoll do. Likely it will be enough for us to get the car fixed and head out."

"Well," Clyde said.

"Well, what?" Babydoll sat straight up. Moonlight from the window gave her an eerie glow.

"A man has urges and, Babydoll, you been so mean here lately."

"So, you did what?"

He didn't reply but the understanding settled around the room. Although I was the last to figure it out, I was the first to speak.

"Clyde," I said real slow. "Clyde Robinson, are you here telling us that you been getting the you-know-what that was meant for the mechanic?"

"Not all of it," Clyde said. "Shadrack says this job ain't no get-it-and-go repair. It's going to take several, ummm . . ."

"Sessions," Bobo said. "That's the word you want."

Babydoll stood up, wearing only panties, brazen as I don't know what. "Who was it?"

I was mad, too, but for different reasons. I got to my feet, feeling like Granny in my cotton gown. "How many sessions?"

"Just two," Clyde said. "I thought it was just a tip because I fixed the leg on her chifforobe. She acted like she liked me." He paused. "Maybe she did. You know people like me."

"Clyde," Babydoll hissed.

Clyde held his pleading hands out in front of him. "I didn't mean anybody any harm. But Lulabelle said it was going on our account."

"Jesus, Clyde," said Bobo. "What part of sharecropping do you not understand?"

*Chapter 7*

# VERNICE

Come summertime, I wasn't the only one who left town. Aunt Irene went out to the shed and retrieved the brass-buckled trunk the Ohio Man sent all those years ago, when she had accepted that her visit to Honeysuckle had turned into a relocation. The brown leather was supple, like she had tipped out to the shed from time to time, rubbing it down with saddle soap.

"Dayton," she said. "It was so nice up there. I miss the autumn leaves."

"I think you mean you miss the man," I said. Ever since we'd had our woman-to-woman, we'd never gone back.

"I do miss him," she said. "But he passed three years ago. His wife sent me a funeral program and one of his silk ties. I don't know what message intended to send, but I appreciate that she did it. I plan to lay some flowers at his stone, and then I will spend some time just staring at some different sky."

"Will you pass through Memphis?"

"No," she said. "Nashville. But when you talk to Annie, tell her she kicked off a jailbreak. She left. You leaving. I'm leaving. I wouldn't be surprised if Raynelle Jemison didn't try to make a run for it. She would, if she could pull Ola Mae out that house."

She laughed but nodded at me in a meaningful way. "If you got something to say, this is the time to say it."

I thought it over, this generous offer. I knew she was asking me about Annie, for an additional explanation for my tears, far more biting than the situation called for. But I didn't have anything else that needed saying. Whatever I yearned to share with my aunt had been expressed at the kitchen table. "My condolences," I said. "I know you cared for the Ohio Man."

Aunt Irene pulled me close for the only hug I could ever remember from her. Her skin smelled like cloves and hard work. "Oh, baby, you don't know how hard I loved that man. And now there's no more Van. Not one moment more. Not one more word from his delicious lips. These are the saddest words in the dictionary. 'No more.' The world has got all the Van that it's going to get."

"There no more of my mama either."

Aunt Irene said, "No more. But there is so much more ahead for you. And maybe a little bit out there for me."

---

Aunt Irene returned to the great state of Ohio on the Trailways bus. There was a line that came through Itta Bena, changing buses in Mobile, and after that, a straight shot to the promised land. The journey would be shorter and a few dollars cheaper. But Aunt Irene bought herself a ticket that left out of Baton Rouge, two hours' driving, and this involved bowing west, although Ohio was north, like a star.

"It's the waiting room," she said. "Buses are late half the time. I want to leave out from a station where I can wait in some peace."

By "peace" she meant "dignity." In Baton Rouge, there was a proper colored waiting area with plastic chairs and a restroom. In Itta Bena, you had to sit outdoors. By the time you got to your seat, your clothes would be spoiled by the gray highway dust. In Baton Rouge, she was sure a gentleman would give up his seat for her, hoping to share her shoebox filled with fried chicken and pound cake. She packed extra in case there was a child traveling alone.

Mrs. Ola Mae and Miss Jemison arrived in their burgundy Thunderbird with T-top roof. My aunt was fashionable in a baby-pink suit and netted pillbox hat. Her hair was pressed so hard that her wake was marked by the distinctly feminine odor of singed curls. Mrs. Ola Mae opened the front-seat door and bowed from the waist like a butler as Miss Jemison loaded the brass-buckled case into the cluttered trunk of the car.

Before she took her seat, my aunt opened her arms and I opened mine in return.

"Thank you," I said. "For taking me in."

"Your mother was my baby sister," she said. "My heart."

And I understood that this borderline affection was all there was. For once I was satisfied with what she had to offer.

Miss Jemison waited in the driver's seat, allowing us our moment. But Mrs. Ola Mae stayed within earshot.

"Tell that child you love her," she said. "You fed and clothed her all these years for a reason. Irene, you as bad as a man."

Aunt Irene said, "Ola Mae, get out my business."

Mrs. Ola Mae said to me, "She loves you. I don't know why she is being all tongue-tied."

Aunt Irene said, "I do." Then she disappeared into the car.

Miss Jemison and Mrs. Ola Mae returned three days later to carry me the forty-three miles to Kinder to catch the bus to Atlanta. Like my aunt, I had chosen my route with dignity top of mind. At my age, I didn't need the full comfort of a dedicated colored waiting room, but the driver who owned the route that passed through Itta Bena was known to be a nasty cracker. Once, he left a little boy behind in Little Rock because he took too long getting back after relieving himself in the bushes behind the diner where the white folks got to eat inside. Imagine being just nine years old and all alone. It took his parents nearly a week of time, and a month of savings, to get him back. The Trailways stopped in Kinder; I could get on there, wait half a day in Jackson, and then cruise into Atlanta on the same bus.

On August 17, at 11 a.m. sharp, the ladies pulled up in front of the only home I had ever known. I was ready, wearing my best blouse. My luggage was stuffed with coed outfits, our best imitation of what we had seen in *Mademoiselle* magazine. My clothes may not have had tags saying Bobbie Brooks, but the shirtwaist dresses looked snappy on me. Then there was every toilet item you could think of and even a little caddy to keep it all organized. Every member of the usher board had donated books of S & H stamps so that I could live in Atlanta with style. The three Samsonites were so full that I had to reinforce the buckles by tying jute cords around each suitcase to make sure they didn't pop open like cans of biscuits.

I locked the door behind me and handed Mrs. Ola Mae the key.

"I'll get Irene a civilized tenant," she promised.

I descended the three chunky stone stairs and took a look at this house my granddaddy built. The morning sun sparkled the clean window glass.

"I'm fixing to go," I whispered. "In case you want to give me a sign."

The house didn't as much as creak in response.

From the trellis edging the porch, I harvested a handful of pole beans and tucked them into my purse.

Miss Jemison said, "You look nice."

Mrs. Ola Mae agreed. "Classy. Because how you *get* there is how you'll *be* there."

---

I swear to God that I didn't wake up that morning rooting around for trouble. Of course, any time you mix with white folks, things could get dangerous, like when you spring-clean your house. The job calls for both ammonia and bleach. But you have to be careful not to let one splash to the other because that's how people get killed just scrubbing their bathtubs. I had taken precautions. I didn't drink more than one small cup of coffee with my breakfast. And my hatbox was filled with enough food for myself and maybe one more colored person who might be hungry. From my thermos, I would sip gingerly so as not to need a commode. I would have to find a seat toward the rear, in the colored section, but I enjoyed the company of my people. Nobody wanted to ride across-country next to somebody that was scared to touch your shoulder.

This is not to say that I didn't mind segregation. Who didn't admire Mrs. Parks down in Montgomery? And what about Barbara Posey and the lunch-counter kids in Oklahoma City? Don't forget the young folks in Little Rock, dressed to kill, determined to bust up that white high school—what courage. But all of that was city life. In the country, we didn't take buses. I supposed we could try and force our way into Honeysuckle High and demanding new books and stable desk chairs. I will admit that these were thoughts that danced in my mind as we traveled up Highway 165. And maybe I did imagine myself in Atlanta joining some Movement. Who doesn't dream of city things when moving to a city?

When I boarded that Trailways in Kinder, I called myself sitting in the first row of the colored section—the front of the back, the top of the bottom. This bus would travel all the way to Syracuse, New York. I wondered if the folks in the back would be allowed to relocate once they had crossed the Mason-Dixon. With a little sigh, I settled myself by the window, waved to Miss Jemison and Mrs. Ola Mae, and waited for my life to begin.

When the driver approached me, I thought he was asking for my ticket.

"You punched it already," I said.

As soon as the words bounced from my lips, I knew that I sounded a little too flippant, so I added. "When I boarded, sir."

"What are you trying to prove?" he asked.

"My ticket is valid," I said. "Sir. You punched it when I got on."

The bus was just about full, smelling like summertime, salty and steaming. Some folks had been aboard a couple days already and were cranky, the driver included, or maybe especially.

He tapped the placard to my left with an angry knuckle. "Can you read?" Except he attached another word in front of it.

All the white folks stared at me with hot eyes and all the colored folks made a point not to look at me, except for a little boy gnawing on a teething biscuit.

The sign the driver was rapping on said COLORED SECTION, and I realized my error. The notice was on the left and I sat on the right—one seat ahead of where I was allowed. Instead of the front of the back, I had found my place in the back of the front.

"Can you read?" he asked again, with the ugly word pinned to the end, this time.

Having been colored my whole life, I knew what I was supposed to do. I was to cast my eyes down, clamp my chin to my chest, gather my belongings, and take my place behind the barrier that kept white from colored.

I looked over my shoulder. The six or so seats were occupied by adults who didn't meet my eyes and two children. The boy was frightened and the girl, curious.

"It's no more seats back there," I said, hoping to seem pleasant and reasonable. "So, I'm as far back as I can get."

"But were there nigger seats when you got on my bus?" he asked. "Yes, or no?"

This was what Aunt Irene called a Tar Baby question.

"It's too far to ride standing up," I said. He was talking *at* me, but talking *to* the white folks posted up in what counted as the front, even when it was the middle, even when it was just inches from what was considered the back.

"Were there nigger seats when you got on?"

The truth of the matter is that I selected this seat with the humility required of those of us tucked under the smelly wing of Jim Crow. Choosing this row, I believed it to be the best seat among the worst. But by accident, I situated myself in the worst among the best. The distance between the seats was shorter than my arm.

The driver dug deep for his words, mining the center of his chest and hauling them out like he was saying his Easter speech. Did I see any nigger seats before I chose this non-nigger seat? In other words, was I suggesting that I was not a nigger? Sticky, sticky, sticky.

But at the time that I was facing these tacky questions, I was seventeen years old and had lived in central Louisiana my whole entire life. And even though I had heard the word before, I was shocked by its aggressive unkindness.

"You are not a nice person," I said.

The driver paused, as though I had spoken in tongues. "What was it you said?"

"You are not a gentleman."

He took off his hat, revealing an angry red line above his brows. With his open hand, he swiped at his forehead.

"So now you're supposed to be a lady? Get your black ass off my goddamn bus." He replaced his cap and then snatched my light green hatbox and stomped toward the front.

I followed without protest, or maybe lack of protest was a protest in itself. I didn't look at the people in the colored section because I didn't want to shame them for staying seated and I didn't look at the white folks because I didn't want to shame myself.

Is my memory playing tricks on me? The inside of the bus was gray and choppy like a newsreel. Mrs. Ola Mae's voice was in my head with the authority of Harry Truman. "How you get there is how you'll be there." The spirit on that bus wasn't anything I wanted to take with me into the rest of my life.

When I took the two steps down from the bus to the filling station that served as a depot, the sun was white-hot and the air was thick with August. A Negro man wearing khaki coveralls pumped gas into a beige Studebaker. Watching the driver toss my hatbox to the ground, spilling the travel feast on the pavement, his face bent with worry.

The town of Kinder was an hour's drive from Honeysuckle. This was close enough that they got rain when we got rain, but too far for him to know my name or my people. Still, his concern seemed personal.

"Everything okay with the bus, Mr. Isaac?"

"My bus ain't the problem," the driver groused.

"I'll take my ticket back," I said. "That's all I want."

The bus driver turned to the gasman. "You know this gal?"

"She's my sister's girl," he said. "She don't mean no harm."

"I just need my ticket back," I explained to the gasman, since he was on name-basis with the driver.

"Your sister know what this gal was planning to do?" The driver shook his head. "Like I would let a nigger disrupt my whole route."

"Mr. Isaac," the gasman said, "this girl has always been a little feeble in the head. One morning she woke up and told everybody to call her Mrs. Roosevelt."

I opened my mouth to protest, but I shut it when I heard the bus driver laugh.

"I'm serious, sir." The gasman bugged his eyes. "Whatever she did, it wasn't the first time, but I will take my belt to her and see to it that it will be the last." He clamped my arm with a grip that I knew would leave a mark. "Who she tell you she was? Elizabeth Taylor?"

"You funning me, Larry?"

"Naw," he said. "Ain't nothing funny here. And when I get done with my strap, she will know there ain't nothing silly about all this confusion she's causing." He shook me a little. "A colored girl thinking she's somebody important."

The bus driver kicked the hatbox. "I can't return that ticket. One, it's already punched. And secondly, it ain't safe to have somebody like that on the route."

I tried to twist away from the gasman. "I got to get to Atlanta. I saved for that ticket."

Larry clucked his tongue and jerked me hard. "Don't pay her no mind. I'll see to it she don't try that mess ever again."

The bus driver softened. "Don't whip her too bad. But you should think about maybe keeping her locked up."

"I ain't going to beat her bad," he said. "But we'll beat her good."

Satisfied, the driver got back on board and settled himself in the driver's seat. The gasman gave me a hard shake.

"Stop touching me." I swatted, catching him on the head, just above his ear. I felt all of the eyes upon us, colored and white, young and old. I swung my arm again, but this time the gasman struck me so hard my jaw snapped together, catching my tongue between my teeth.

"What the hell is your problem?" He didn't just speak it, he asked it like a legitimate question.

I stumbled a couple of paces back, dizzy from the blow, the heat, and the world I had been born into. And in this state, I pondered his question. What the hell was my problem? The list was long and various, probably starting with the fact that my daddy murdered my mother and the heifer didn't even have the decency to visit me in my dreams. Then there was Annie, precious Annie, God knew where, God knew what, and I missed her so much it made my eyes burn at night. There was the lost ticket. Now how was I going to get to Atlanta? And there was my luggage.

"My suitcases," I called out, and ran behind the bus as it merged with the highway traffic. "He's driving off with all of my stuff. Wait!" I called. "Wait. Wait. Wait." I chased that Trailways like how a dog chases a turnip truck. And like a dog, I didn't get far before I gave up. I sat down on the side of the road and hid my face in the nest of my hands. In my mouth, my bit tongue swelled and bled.

Disastrous, catastrophic, calamitous. All words Miss Jemison drilled into our heads in her classroom. So many ways to talk about what was happening to me. Annie gone one way to Memphis. My suitcases with all my clothes, notebooks, and bedding locked in the belly of a Trailways bus heading to Syracuse, New York. I thought about Aunt Irene, snatching her bit of grace in the colored waiting area in Baton Rouge. I imagined a sophisticated man setting beside her. I could see her delicately dividing a chicken wing in two, offering him the half that looked like a tiny drumstick. I turned to the filling station, where my pistachio-green hatbox lay spoiled on the pavement, and the food I packed for myself and a stranger spoiled in the dust.

Unjust. Unkind. Unfair. Inequitable. And just unlucky and stupid. The back of the front or the front of the back. I didn't want trouble. I had been willing to sit in the back, to pretend to be what they called me, until I got to Atlanta.

As pitiful as a cast-out puppy, I sat close enough to the road that someone could hit me by accident if they wanted to. The air tasted flammable with exhaust. The powerful breeze lifted my hair; it was nappy again, like I had been swimming in the polluted stream that ran behind the papermill.

The gasman snatched me back a few inches. "You might be for-real crazy," he said. "Why did you make me hit you like that?"

"Nobody made you do anything," I said. "I was supposed to be going to school."

"I guess now you don't have no choice but to stay here in Kinder and marry me." He grinned.

Until then, I had never thought that rage could live in a body without a person knowing. It was like the idea of having a tiger camped out in your living room, so quiet and docile that maybe you mistook it for an easy chair. Maybe you even sat on it. Rested your cup on its paw.

"Don't nobody want you," I said. "I'll walk all the way to Atlanta before you lay one nasty finger on me."

"Oh," he said. "My fingers nasty now." And with that selfsame finger, he reached out and traced my bottom lip.

I had been to the picture show and watched white men and women fall in love like this. She says no and he thinks it's charming, or what have you. I knew what I was supposed to do. But on the screen you can't smell his lunch on his breath. You can't see all the people gawking from inside the filling station.

There are angels in this world, but this man wasn't one of them, no matter what Hollywood might have you believe. When he smacked me across the face, he didn't hate to do it. When I was about seven or eight years old, Aunt Irene hit me in the same way, for being a leg in almost the same triangle. We had gone to town and I didn't cede the sidewalk for a white lady wearing a half-moon hat with a little silk flower perched over her ear. It was Easter and I didn't want to ruin my frilly socks, so I didn't step over into the mud over by the side of the road. The white lady gave an amused smile and stepped around me and went on to wherever she went to praise the Lord. To Aunt Irene she said, "He is risen." And Aunt Irene said back, "Indeed," the way everyone did. But as soon as we got around the corner, she near about slapped my lips off my face. I was so shocked I stumbled two steps back and ruined my socks. But I could tell that she hated to do it.

This man in these cheap coveralls didn't hate anything he did that day. And he didn't hate whatever it was that he planned to do next.

But like I said, I believe that angels visit this world. Not often, but they do come around. Picture me, marooned in Kinder. All my stuff was speeding down the highway in the other direction and this man was over here acting like I owed him something in exchange for the smack he gave me to save me from whatever the bus driver believed himself to be entitled to do. In my brassiere, I hid a tight roll of money bound with rubber bands, but I wasn't about to give it to him. Besides, I was old enough to know that money wasn't all he wanted.

When people talk about *the devil and the deep blue sea*, it has to do with a boat. But it puts you in mind of the Old Testament. So that's how it was for me on the side of the highway, cars zipping by on the left side, this ashy man on my right, and this thick August air all around me. As the sun climbed up to the noon position, there was nothing left for me to do but pray. I did the Lord's Prayer because you could do it just by humming a tune.

And there she was, like I had summoned her. A five-foot angel hailing from Breaux Bridge, not too far from Lafayette. She was light skinned with curly black hair cropped over her ears. She was dressed mannish, in coveralls stained with oil and other dirt, demonstrating that she was a person who worked for her money.

"Larry," she said, "what the fresh hell is going on out here?"

"Nothing, Carmen," he said. "I'm just trying to help this young lady."

She regarded me. "You the one tried to ride in the front of the bus?"

I considered explaining to her about the back of the front and the front of the back, but she seemed a little impressed, so I nodded. "Yes, ma'am."

"And you thought they was going to just let you ride up there?"

"I'm supposed to start college in Atlanta."

She shook her head and wiped her face with a red bandana she fished from her pockets. "I admire you young people. I'm too old to change the world. But, baby, you should have gone to school up north. You are going to mess around and get yourself killed down here in Louisiana."

Larry said, "That's all I was trying to tell her."

Carmen said, "That's why you smacked her?"

Larry looked hangdog now. "Naw. That was just to get the white man off her back."

"Uh-huh," she said. "That's all it was.

"Where you from, cher?" She said her words in the way of people from the southern parishes. They get their talking the same place they got all that hair.

"Honeysuckle," I said.

"Oh," she said with teeth marked by cigarettes. "I know folks down there. Ola Mae Simmons?"

"She delivered me," I said.

Pointing at Larry, she said, "I was married to his father's brother, and big pregnant when I heard he had posted up in Honeysuckle. He was planning on making a run for it and begin a whole new life in Port Arthur."

Larry said, "So that makes her my auntie. But ain't no blood between us." This, he said with a greasy grin.

She waved him away like he was a biting horsefly. "I went down there to find Othaniel, and my boys decided they wanted to be born in Allen Parish, instead of Evangeline like everyone in our family since slavery times. That's how they are, to this day—steady wanting to be different. I hadn't been in Honeysuckle for a day before they got to kicking and next thing you know, my water broke, ruining my good shoes. Baby, it was life and death! One of my sons tried to come through backside-first. But Ola Mae reached in my holiest of holies and turned him."

"She didn't ask all of that," Larry said. "Now you got me feeling queasy. I better go pump some gas."

As he ambled off, she said, "That's how men are. All they think about is pussy, pussy, pussy, but when you really talk about pussy, they have to leave." She laughed a hearty laugh. "I can't carry you all the way to Atlanta, but if you want, I can return you to Honeysuckle. Be good to see Ola Mae. You sure your mama didn't put no dirt in your suitcase? You know that hometown dirt will keep pulling you back. Not usually this fast, but hoodoo do what hoodoo do."

"No'm. My mama passed when I was just a baby."

"Oh, cher." The sympathy in her voice was thick and sticky like PET milk. I opened my lips like a baby bird, starving in a forsaken nest. She shook her head and shut her eyes like just the sight of my sadness could give her cataracts.

All this mama talk pulled up all my memories of Annie. Despite Aunt Irene's scolding, I envied my best friend so hard that I knew it was just a matter of time before God punished me. Every morning, Annie woke up knowing that there was a living, breathing, dancing mother in the world for her. I know she felt ashamed of the way that everyone clucked out that word, "trifling"—but triflingness was a condition that could be cured or endured, like measles or whooping cough. How many preachers had been delivered from being sorry? It took a little more for a mother to find her way back, but it was possible, and didn't take a miracle.

Carmen cupped her hand around my cheek. Her palm was dainty, in line with her size, but her work left it tough like a man's. I was embarrassed at my neediness, but I pressed my face to her touch, soothed by the warm pressure of the calluses.

Did Annie do this, fall into the arms of anybody with a soft bosom and open spirit? Or was she saving herself for Hattie Lee? This might be the real difference between us. It wasn't that some people mistook me for a pretty girl and these same folks missed Annie's beauty entirely. It wasn't that I was destined for more education and a husband who made his living sitting in a chair, and she was hoping for factory work and a man who didn't drink up his pay. These were details that made it easy to tell us apart, but the thing that made us different is that Annie could possibly be straightened where she was bent, while I knew I could never be upright.

I allowed myself the comfort of Carmen's touch until the shame of it was greater than the salve.

"I'm fine," I said. "It was all a long time ago."

But Carmen didn't give that lie even the courtesy of a nod. "When you lose your mama, there's no such thing as a long time ago." Then she fanned the air around my face like she was chasing away a cloud of gnats. "She hated to leave you," Carmen said. "Even heaven ain't heaven without your baby."

I knew she was speaking about mothers in a general way, but it felt like her words were about me and Arletha alone.

*Chapter 8*

# ANNIE

Lulabelle's was the only whorehouse I had ever seen, let alone lived at, but I assume that each proprietress has her own house rules. It only follows that Lulabelle wanted to master her own dominion, the way that Mr. Daniel made it clear that he was the one in charge at The Den. And like at the bar, the rules were mostly common sense—set down to keep profits up and chaos down. But just like how Mr. Daniel surprised you with his insistence that you admire the carving on his bar, I was feather-shocked that Lulabelle made everybody attend worship service behind her house on Sundays, rain, shine, boiling heat, or not. She didn't make you dress up, which everyone appreciated. The biggest stunner was that Lulabelle herself delivered the Word from behind a podium so handsome I had to wonder if Mr. Daniel's bar maker had himself a little barter agreement in Mississippi.

I had been there for ten days when one of the women came out back and told me that Ms. Lulabelle needed me to come to her house to help her prepare her sermon. It was hot as Hades as Babydoll struggled with a massive wad of sheets. The working woman said, "I'll help you with the wringer."

---

The Jim Walter at the end of the dirt road looked even better than it had when we arrived. The fellows had been tasked with freshening up the trim with a coat of paint, the color of Christmas trees. The porch was wide enough to accommodate a pair of rocking chairs and a little table perfect for a jar of sun tea and a couple of glasses. But the whole time I was there, I never witnessed anyone lounging, rocking, or swigging.

I climbed the three stairs and used the knocker fashioned in the shape of a lion's head. After tapping, I busied myself watching the bees molest the cluster of tea roses. Lulabelle clearly had a thing for flowers. Across the field, kitty-corner to the most run-down shack, was a picket-fenced garden, wild with roses in colors you didn't even know existed, blooming every whichaway. Babydoll named it the bumble-briar because of the bees winding through all the thorns. The porch flowers were deep but not blood red. Not apple red either. They were just their own shade. Lulabelle red, I would call it, if I were to ever see it again.

After a few minutes, the door opened and I found myself face-to-face with a girl about my age. She reminded me of Niecy with her slim figure and Gibson girl wardrobe. I could tell from the way the sash cinched her waist that under that pinafore dress were three or four layers of complicated underwear.

"Ms. Lulabelle sent for me," I said.

The girl gave a quick nod. Without a word, she moved three steps away from the door, and I took this as permission to go inside. I followed her to a sitting room, proper as anything. A purple-cushioned divan resting on sweetly bowed legs faced a chair that put me in mind of a throne, upholstered in a floral fabric, heavy with sea green and pink. A creamy marble coffee table was the centerpiece of the room, and atop that was a Bible cased in bright blue leather.

"Mama will be here in a minute," the Gibson girl said, and vanished.

Mama? I was choking on the word when Lulabelle joined me in the sitting room. She was, as always, sharp as a tack, but her bare feet exposed toes lumpy with corns, pink as burns but gleaming with oil.

"She's not my child," Lulabelle said. "She just calls me that because she don't have nobody else to give that name to."

I gave a silent nod, no less puzzled. I had never thought to lay that title on any woman of my choosing.

"She has been with me since she was about ten years old. Her daddy sold her for five dollars, can you believe that? Far as he knows, I put her to work. You know I don't believe in putting money in men's pockets, but for this situation, I made an exception. So, I let her be my maid."

I bounced my chin like a bird in a cage.

"So, count your blessings," she said. "I heard from your little boyfriend that you are on the hunt for your mama. When you find her—*if* you find her—and you are let down because she ain't nothing but a woman and not some goddess, just remember that she didn't try to sell you for five bucks and a drink of cold water."

There was much to be said about this, but all I could croak out was, "I don't have no boyfriend."

"You do," she said. "You just don't know it yet. Bobo is the one with your name on his forehead. I give it another week to seal the deal."

"We'll be gone by then."

She laughed, rotating her back until her spine clapped like a slamming door. "You obviously haven't checked the ledger. Clyde is humping away all your profits. But that is not what we talk about on Bible Wednesdays. I want to noodle on Sarah and Hagar."

I thought about my own Bible, left behind in my top-right dresser drawer. The book was in the same unbent condition as when Granny purchased it from a traveling salesman, who also sold her a pencil sharpener. It wasn't that I didn't have a use for the good book. Everybody should consult with the Lord from time to time; I don't care who you are. But when I wanted the Word, I looked to Granny's—weathered pages that had been turned by generations of licked fingers. On the front page was the family tree with ink dating back to before we were free. When I was little she made me memorize every name. The paper, thin as butterfly wings, was heavy with wisdom. The salesman's Bible was like *Seventeen* magazine. Cute as can be, but empty as a hole in the ground.

Lulabelle's Bible was too nice to have been passed down through the generations. If her family had a Bible, it was likely with her churchy sister, Lurelia. But Lulabelle's had substance to it in its own right. The leather binding was flashy, but soft from seeking. I was honored to hold it on my lap.

Lulabelle snapped, bringing me to attention. When I opened the cover, the book opened up to Genesis, all by itself.

"You know I can read," Lulabelle said. "But the word of the Lord is best heard. Let it enter the mind through the ear, not through the eye."

I nodded like I believed her. But my granny couldn't much read, so I know the ways of folks who have trouble deciphering letters. If you are a believing person, you wouldn't want to misread the word and end up in hell over a miscommunication.

Lulabelle told me to read Genesis 16, about Hagar, Sarah, and Abraham. Sometimes she asked me to read it from beginning to end, tapping her toes so I would pick up the pace. Other times, she wanted it slow, twirling her index finger to let me know to repeat whatever I had just read. Like everyone, I knew the story, but these hours-long dives made me think about it differently. This was like Bible study back home, except that there was no one present with standing to settle any confusion.

I read the words to her just how they lay on the page, with all the sayeths and doeths. Usually that was how she liked it, and other times, she cut me off, ordering, "Tell it to me colored." In that case, I did do my best to make the word of God hit like Granny and Miss Irene gossiping about the rich folks they worked for.

"So, after Hagar was pregnant for Abraham, she got a real attitude with Sarah. It don't say exactly what she did, but Sarah complained. My guess is that she didn't feel right being a maid since she was carrying this man's baby."

Lulabelle said, "But we both know that people get stuck

with Massa's baby all the time." To illustrate, she touched her keen nose and smooth edges of hair, as proof of the race mixing. "Even you," she said to me.

"Me? Black as I am?"

"Yeah, but you got an ironing board for a behind. It ain't always fair," she said. "Look at your little friend Babydoll. They stole her lips."

"Can we get back to the Good Book?" I said, stung by her comments on my figure.

"You are a cute girl," Lulabelle said. "No harm intended."

I continued my colored commentary. "Seems that Hagar's pregnancy was cause for celebration. That's different than what happened to our great-great-grandmothers—"

"My grandmama," Lulabelle said. "It wasn't that far back on the tree."

"Well," I pointed out, "you are older than me."

"Not by much."

"But what I am saying is that what happened with Hagar was out in the open."

"How that's different?" Lulabelle had that way of putting a question mark on something she was telling, rather than asking.

"Because they wanted the baby for themselves."

"How that's different from wanting the baby for themselves *to sell*?"

"They wanted it for their family," I said. "You know that's a horse of a different color."

"I can agree with the 'different color' part. But to my mind, a stolen baby is a stolen baby."

She leaned forward to the marble table and picked up a comb shaped like an alligator with its long handle and triangular teeth. She plucked the tines and made a sort of music. "I would think that you'd be more concerned about babies being taken from their mothers."

"No," I said. "Ain't nobody take me from Hattie Lee."

"Maybe not directly," said Lulabelle. "Our mama didn't leave me and Lurelia, but she couldn't love none of us. She was born not even ten years after the Civil War. The ground was too dry for love to grow."

"That's what your sermon is going to be about on Sunday? Stolen babies? Stolen love?"

She shook her head. "Oh no, no, no. I think about the Old Testament all the time, but I don't care to preach about the world before Jesus. Having a son mellowed God, you know."

I hadn't thought of it in that way, but I could see her logic.

"That's why I hate what happened to our mama. God so loved the world that He gave His only son. It wasn't just *being* a father that made him a better God, it was the *loving*. Me and Lurelia missed out on being loved but also she missed out on loving us. That's why I put these roses all over the place. They were her favorite, and I want something here for her to love."

The only thing I had ever heard of Hattie Lee loving was liquor, but after working at The Den, I knew that nobody loved booze. They might at first, but then they just keep doing it because they have to.

"Scratch my head," Lulabelle said, closing her eyes. "Tell that girl to get something to put over my shoulders."

I turned, ready to yell for the girl, but I didn't know what to call her. But as if sensing the need, she appeared with a soft green towel that she draped over Lulabelle, like a cape. Once she was gone, Lulabelle spoke.

"I like to read about Sarah and them when Mother Nature puts her nose into my business."

I tried to make sense of it, as I used the tail of the comb to push her hair away from her scalp. I rubbed the teeth against the gleaming skin.

"Your head looks faucet fresh."

"It is," she said. "Scratching helps me think."

I scratched, and she thought.

"Annie, you have never seen your mama's face?"

"I wasn't even one month when she left."

"And went where, with who?"

"Don't know. But now she is likely in Memphis," I said. "That's why I have to go there."

"That's a fool's errand," she said. "But if there is one thing I have learned in my line of work, it is that girls are stupid. And virgins like you are the worst of all."

My hands were on my hips when she snapped, "Scratch!"

And I did because she is the kind of woman that you can't help but obey.

"There should be a rule that you can't go hunting for no lost mamas until you have kids yourself. Or at least until you have missed your period and said that prayer that wasn't nothing up in your stomach but what you ate for lunch." She clucked her tongue. "Once Mother Nature gets up in your business, it changes the way you think about things, I'll tell you that much for free."

I pulled in a chestful of air. "Are you pregnant?"

Lulabelle laughed and snorted. "Me? Lord, no. I don't let men anywhere near me. Mother Nature has been chasing me since I was eleven years old and that bitch ain't finna catch me. She is in my business, and by that, I mean she is in my money. All the screwing that happens on this property, things happen."

I massaged her temples as she did her figuring.

"You know how to cornrow?"

"Don't everybody?" I asked.

Her soft hair put me in mind of Jesus and his lamb's wool as I drove my fingers through the crinkles.

"That's good," she said. "Very nice."

I felt myself blooming with her praise and contented sighs. Pretending to stifle a sneeze, I put my hand to my face and inhaled. The fragrance wasn't bracing like Ivory soap. It was more like rosewater crossed with sweat in the crease of a neck.

It took me about three hours to transform her coiling crop into a weave resembling the basket Granny used to hold blackberries harvested near the creek. For the first time since I'd been gone, I was blue to remember my grandmother.

"Could I get two postcards?" I asked the question as I pulled, tucked, and twisted. "Just out the drawer."

"You don't need stamps?"

"I guess so," I said.

She stood and looked at herself in the mirror and smiled. "I won't charge you but for one stamp. You got gifted hands."

I felt flushed with her compliment as she admired her reflection this way and that. Then she sat herself between my knees again.

"Now take it all down. I can't run no whorehouse looking like some kind of pickaninny."

Stupid tears stung my face as I used the tail of the comb to unravel my work.

"When somebody gets pregnant we got three roads to take. The first is the obvious one. We just let her work here until she starts showing, cash her out, and send her on her way. That happens a couple-three times a year. She goes back to whatever life she came from, but with a mouth to feed. Frying pan, fire." Lulabelle shook her head and turned her eyes to the ceiling. "Another way is that she could have the baby on the property and I find somebody that wants it, but that's too much like slavery for my taste. Anyhow, pregnant girls ruin the fun at a whorehouse. It's like eating right next to a latrine. And second, everybody gets shook up watching a girl carry, then give the baby up." She snapped and the Gibson girl appeared with a glass of water. Lulabelle took a couple of gulps before she continued. "I'll never forget it. The girl didn't have any idea who the daddy was—I mean, she fucks for a living. But in the three days after she had the baby, she gets to feeling motherly. Of course, the schoolmaster and his wife pulled up, ready to get what they paid for. The wife had on a maternity dress and padding. Anyway, that girl hollered and cried for a day and a half. It was a sight. It was a ruckus."

She finished the water and handled the glass like it had insulted her. "So mostly, I use the white doctor from Meridian. You have no idea how hard it is to find a doctor willing to help colored."

"So, what are you going to do this time?"

"What do you think?"

She rested her cool face on the inside of my thigh as I wiggled the comb's tail to loosen the weave of each cornrow. After that, I used the alligator teeth to coax each narrow section into waves. As I pulled and smoothed, I thought about Abraham and Hagar and wondered if her baby had pretty hair.

By the time I had unraveled the last tight plait she said, "Let me get this white man on the horn. Tell that girl I need to go down to Lurelia's to use the phone."

From nowhere, the Gibson girl appeared. "I'll get you a ride set up."

Lulabelle stood with her hair standing out in crinkles like the rays of the sun.

"You leaving like that?" I asked her. "Let me pin it down."

"I ain't going nowhere but to my sister's house. We twins at that. What I got, she got."

I left the Jim Walter house with one postcard, two sheets of letter paper, an envelope, and a pair of two-cent stamps. Me and Niecy weren't sisters, and nowhere near twins. I didn't have what she got nor the other way around. What you *have* the same isn't what binds you. Hearts grow strings because of what you *know* that's the same, what happened to you that's the same. And when what you want is the same.

I was halfway back to the shack when I realized that I had envelopes and paper, but no pencil to write with. It was all I could do not to cry at the story of my life.

*Chapter 9*

# VERNICE

Mrs. Ola Mae and Miss Jemison ended up driving me to Atlanta, my first road trip. Beside me on the back seat was a carpetbag stuffed with clothes that were approximately my size, donated by the congregation of First Iconium. I was ashamed to accept their gifts after they had just passed the plate the month before to help with my tuition and the saints had given up a year's worth of S & H stamps.

"No weapons formed against you shall prosper," said the First Lady as I hung my head.

"Thank you," I said. "I never intended—"

"You are not the only one this happened to. After they cut Christ down from the cross, the soldiers cast lots for his clothes. Don't you remember that? Young lady, you are walking a path trod by the King of Kings."

---

All that endured of my original plan was my round hatbox, bound by masking tape the color of the ugly bus driver's face. What had just been so elegant now looked like the entire history of the Negro race—battered but held together somehow. My own face was in similar condition, marked with the print of Larry's hand. Don't ask me how or why, but my spirit was fortified by the experience. I felt a little more like Annie and Aunt Irene, eager to get away from Honeysuckle, not caring if I never saw the state of Louisiana ever again.

From the back seat, I studied their heads. Mrs. Ola Mae covered her pin curls with a floral scarf. Her skin, inky black, shone with a coating of what smelled like evergreen needles. Miss Jemison wore her thick hair split in two, braided down the sides, pulled up, and pinned tight. As soon as we passed the sign that said SUNNY SIDE, meaning we were officially out of town, Mrs. Ola Mae said, "Call her Raynelle, and call me Mae." Then they released whooping laughs.

"Congratulations," said Miss Jemison. "You have officially broken free."

Mrs. Ola Mae clapped, but her hands were so soft, they hardly made a sound at all. Then she reached up and tucked Miss Jemison's braid back into the teeth of a tortoiseshell comb. As her hand retreated, Miss Jemison twisted her head to graze Mrs. Ola Mae's palm with her lips, confirming the rumors with pleasure. My teacher watched me in the rearview mirror and I felt myself smile. She nudged her wife with the hand not guiding the wheel.

It tickled me a little to think that word, "wife." I was glad that I had only pronounced it in my mind. Ladies couldn't marry ladies, but it was exciting to think that maybe they could. Or maybe it was thrilling just to see that ladies can be that way to each other. My mind went to darling Annie, run off to Memphis. And while I knew that it would have been a disaster to follow her, I couldn't help imagining what would have happened if I had.

"At Spelman College," Miss Jemison said, "there is much to be navigated. I am class of 'twenty-seven."

"The year of the flood," I said.

Mrs. Ola Mae said, "Raynelle, she's saying you are old as Noah!"

"Not that flood," I said. "The Mississippi flood."

Miss Jemison said, "Ola Mae, the girl is just only giving some context. In return, I will provide her with the same."

In the voice I recognized from the classroom, she gave me a condensed history of my new home. Spelman College was founded in 1881. "So how long was that after Emancipation?" While I scrambled to do the math, she said, "Eighteen. Unless you lived in Texas. So, these two white ladies decided to make a school for colored women. They just had eleven girls and one hundred dollars. This is why I don't divide the world by color. These two missionaries from up north came down to Georgia to truly do the Lord's work."

Mrs. Ola Mae wasn't as convinced. "You know they don't do nothing unless they have their own reasons."

"Man has his reasons; God has His reasons."

"Maybe they were each other's reason." Mrs. Ola Mae let out a zesty laugh.

"And I got my reasons," I piped up from my place behind them.

"She can talk," said Mrs. Ola Mae. "You know, I was there when you barked out your first word. You shook the whole house. MOTHER! I thought Irene was going to stroke out."

Miss Jemison said, "Mae, stop talking over her."

Mrs. Ola Mae said, "Forgive me, Raynelle."

Miss Jemison said, "Forgiven."

From the back seat I said it, too, "Forgiven," because it felt like the way everything in church was punctuated with "Amen."

"So where were we?" Mrs. Ola Mae asked.

"Vernice was giving us her raison d'être."

With a wink, Mrs. Ola Mae said, "See? I got me a schoolteacher."

"And I'm going to *be* a schoolteacher!" I said.

"For somebody to get?" said Mrs. Ola Mae.

"Mae," said Miss Jemison. "Be serious for a minute."

"Okay, okay. I'll behave." To me, she said, "What's your reason, baby? Why are you heading off for Atlanta like one of the three little pigs? Seeking your fortune?"

"Just to see what's out there, I guess." I looked out the window. "And I suppose I should be thinking about finding a husband?"

"Well," said Mrs. Ola Mae, "they got Morehouse College, the boys' school, right across the street. It's a husband factory."

Miss Jemison said, "I'll say this. If your aspiration is to be a wife, one you shall be." Her voice was flat, like she was reading from the hymnal without the benefit of her reading glasses. Then her voice regained its sass and humor. "But do you want a husband?"

Mrs. Ola Mae turned completely in her seat, peering at me over the seat, watching me like I was a movie.

"Speak up," she said, laughing. "You can tell us anything, especially me. You know how come me and Raynelle know everybody's business in town? Because they know ours. And more than that, I know every Negro in Honeysuckle on a spirit level. Me, my mama, my grandmother before that—one of us has put our hand up inside them, or their mothers. No matter who you are in life, you get here the same way—through screwing, and after that, your mother pushed you out of her body. When a lady comes to me with her womb buckling, don't nothing else matter. She don't care who Raynelle is to me. You know, I was the one who caught you when you were born." She pointed at me with her chin. "This black face was the first thing you ever saw on this earth. I held you even before Arletha."

I felt my insides collapse. "I can't remember her at all. You say her name so easily, but it hurts me to hear. I was so cheerful five seconds ago, but it's like my mama is waiting for me, dead, around every corner."

Mrs. Ola Mae said, "That's because she is."

We bumped along that road with only the radio to chop up the air. Sam Cooke swore, *Darling, you send me.*

In my lost suitcases, wrapped in tissue, was a framed picture of my mother on her wedding day, pretty like the angel she would soon become.

"I would die tomorrow if I knew I could see her."

Mrs. Ola Mae snapped her head toward the back seat. "What did you say?"

The only person who didn't feel the crackling in the air was Miss Jemison, who trilled, "*Honest you do. Honest you do. Honest you do.*"

"Raynelle, how long before we can stop for lunch?" Mrs. Ola Mae asked with a steady voice.

Miss Jemison said, "Twenty minutes, more or less."

As I shivered in the back seat like some desperate person on a newsreel, Miss Jemison kept us on the road, between the two white lines. Mrs. Ola Mae climbed over the seat and joined me in the back of the car. She smelled like hickory trees and cloves.

I have been tall all my life and narrow like a needle. If I turned to the side, people said I disappeared. Mrs. Ola Mae was my opposite. The same people snickered she was two feet tall, two feet wide. Somehow, she climbed over the bench seat with enchanted grace.

Sitting on the far side of the car, against the door, she patted her thighs, and out of some buried instinct, I contorted myself to lay my head on her soft lap.

"Oh, sweetheart," she said. "Just let it all out."

My shoulders heaved, but I only knew the mute cry I had taught myself as a child.

"Uh-uh, baby," clucked Mrs. Ola Mae, "you can't get nothing done grieving like that."

We bumped along the highway for many minutes more. The car was quiet except for road sounds, the bump of a not-new car, on a not-new highway. The motion troubled my stomach, but I knew it wasn't wise for us to stop. You didn't want to detour through a small town, unless you knew people there, who told you where it was safe to go.

"Irene ever carry you to Lookout Mountain in Tennessee?" Mrs. Ola Mae asked me, out of nowhere.

"No, ma'am," I said.

"You need to go there and see Ruby Falls, a whole entire waterfall underground. Raynelle took me there, many years ago. God's whole creation is purposeful, and there is beauty in that. But that waterfall up under the ground disturbed my spirit. Standing in that dark cave feeling the spray on my face, I felt like the Lord was teaching me a hard lesson. Midwives, we listen when God is talking. It was cold down there, and I took Raynelle by the hand. I didn't care who was watching. But that's what I feel right now, baby. You got a whole river running off a cliff inside you. You need to cry the regular way to get you some relief. Tears are meant to flow outward."

"Show me how to let it out, please, Mrs. Ola Mae."

"I can't do that, any more than I can teach you how to breathe, or how to love."

"I can learn," I said.

"You have to," she said. "I have seen colored women die from the tears in the blood. The salt doesn't agree with the organs and wreaks all kind of havoc. That's what I feel inside you. Havoc."

"I need Annie. I need my mama. I need things I've never ever seen before."

"That ain't havoc," said Mrs. Ola Mae. "That's the sadness. The rage that's in you—that's the havoc."

I nodded and wept with a dry face.

Mrs. Ola Mae palpitated my throat with a firm touch. "This right here is the only real harm Irene did you. Teaching you to block off your love." She clucked her tongue. "Goiter will be here afterwhile, unlessing you let flow what all needs to come out. You better go the opposite of the angel advice. You best weep and moan."

I wanted to. I made a humming sound the way people do when they are dying but they still have something to say.

"Bear down," Mrs. Ola Mae said.

"I don't know how."

"You will," she said. "For now, just close your eyes."

I did as I was told, enjoying the feel of her fingers on my face, the same fingers that had guided me from my mother's body into the world.

"Raynelle," she said, barely above a whisper.

"Yeah, honey?"

"We got gas enough for a while?"

"I believe so," Miss Jemison said.

"Then let's just keep going. Let this child rest."

---

College was a different world.

At Spelman College, you could taste the femininity. I was

assigned to Abby Aldrich Rockefeller Hall. The front door was flanked by a pair of pillars supporting a little roof that Miss Jemison called a "portico." Cheery blue shutters framed the first-floor windows, but my room was all the way up on the third floor. I didn't have a father to help and Mrs. Ola Mae and Miss Jemison didn't have husbands. And while I was listing my didn'ts, I didn't have any luggage to carry, so why did it feel so bad that we didn't have a man accompanying us? My curiosity flashed on my father. This may have been the only time in my life that I missed him. I felt like a bride ambling down the aisle alone.

The winding stairwell was thick with families. Well-dressed mothers snapped directions at fathers who sweated dark rings through their shirts. The girls in this building weren't freshmen like me. They squealed and hugged each other as they passed in narrow hallways. I tried to seem relaxed but I shivered under my skin.

When we finally reached my room at the end of the hallway, I fitted the silver key in the lock, but the latch wasn't engaged. I found my roommate moved in, mostly. She had taken for herself the bed beside the large window and covered it with a purple eyelet bedspread that matched a pair of lavender tie-back curtains. A woman, who I assumed was her mother, organized dresses in the chifforobe as my new roommate filed her nails into ovals.

"Hi," I said. "I'm Vernice, but people call me Niecy. These are my aunts, Miss Jemison and Mrs. Ola Mae." I held out my hand like I was at a job interview.

The older lady smiled awkwardly and said, "I'm Fanny."

The girl rose and said, "My name is Joette. Joette Cunningham." She didn't hold out her hand, so I put mine down.

Miss Jemison set my worn carpetbag on the bed. "Raynelle Jemison. Class of 1927."

Mrs. Ola Mae said, "Mae Simmons. No class, no class at all." She nudged me as she cackled and I somehow produced a weak chuckle. I suppose my response wasn't robust enough because she made her own laugh loud enough for us both.

I wouldn't say that I was embarrassed by Mrs. Ola Mae, but I wanted to explain to anyone who may have cared that this country, eccentric woman was not my mother. For the first time in nearly two weeks, I missed my aunt Irene. She may not have been maternal, but she knew how to behave in public. And then I felt washed over with guilt. Hadn't Mrs. Ola Mae soothed my dry tears just a few hours earlier, and was I not grateful? And now here I was, acting too good, and I hadn't even begun my college education.

I wasn't the only one cycling through conflicting emotions. The purple-spread girl seemed a little bit at loose ends herself. "I'm sorry. I hope I didn't sound . . ." She paused and turned to the ceiling, sorting out what impression she was trying hard not to make. With a wave of her oval nails, she fanned the incomplete sentence away. If there was one thing I would come to learn about Joette Cunningham, it was that she would rather say nothing than speak words that she didn't precisely mean.

"I was told you wouldn't get here until tomorrow," she said finally. "I was just off guard. Do you want to coordinate? My mother sent a second bedspread."

I looked to Miss Jemison, since she was the one who knew how things operated here. Even if I hadn't lost my luggage, I wouldn't have had a bedspread. I had only packed two sets of sheets and a wool blanket. Judging from the way the other side of the room was arranged, I realized that I had prepared for school like I was getting ready to go to the army.

"That would be lovely," Miss Jemison said. "Symmetry is always a plus."

I smiled in grateful relief. "Yes. It will be nice to match."

"Fanny," Joette said to the woman who wasn't her mother.

"Yes, Miss Joette," said Fanny.

And this is when you could have knocked me dead with a peppermint. Out of all the women we knew who cleaned houses, took in laundry, or looked after babies, not one called a colored child "miss," and not once ever had I heard a colored girl call a woman older than her mother by her first name.

Me and Mrs. Ola Mae both swung our heads to Miss Jemison. Then we stared gape-mouthed at each other. This girl had come to college with a maid? It wasn't that we had never seen colored folks with more pocket change than others. Honeysuckle didn't have a Meharry doctor, but one kept an office the next parish over. Mr. Daniel was said to have a brother in Jacksonville making money hand over fist from insurance. But never, not once, had we ever heard tell of any Negro hiring an actual maid.

Miss Jemison, apparently, had seen it all. She helped smooth the bedspread onto my bed without even glancing up. "Who is your mother? What's her year?"

"Albertina Cunningham. Her maiden name was Robinson. Class of 'thirty-eight, I believe."

"'Thirty-seven," Miss Jemison said, correcting her. "I've met her. Tina is an Eastern Star. Give her my regards."

"Okay," Joette said.

Miss Jemison crooked an eyebrow in a way I remembered from when she was my teacher.

"Yes, ma'am," Joette said.

Fanny, the maid, fought a smile. Mrs. Ola Mae didn't bother hiding her delight. I found myself confused as to whether this was a generational showdown, in which case I should side with this mysterious girl with the oval nails. Or maybe this room was split between those who had maids and those who did not. In which case, it was clear what colors I wore. But the part of me that wore nothing at all liked this saucy girl very very much.

Not the least bit humbled, Joette said, "I'm a junior."

"Excellent," said Miss Jemison. "You can show Vernice around. She's a country girl, you know."

"Did she get kicked in the face by a mule?"

My cheek now burned in the shape of a man's hand.

Mrs. Ola Mae volunteered an explanation. "She had a run-in with some crackers on her way here. Things got out of hand on a Trailways bus."

Now Joette looked interested. "My cousin Marylinda, a Movement girl, went to jail in Birmingham for two days. She's down on the ground floor. Are you a sit-inner?"

"Not exactly," I said.

"Tell that to the white man that threw her off the bus. She

was standing up for her rights and next thing you know . . ." Mrs. Ola Mae wagged her hands like she was starring in a play.

"Mae," Miss Jemison said with a note of warning in her voice.

Mrs. Ola Mae shrugged. "You know Niecy is not the type to toot her own saxophone. I just want people to know how she ended up looking like she went three rounds with Jack Johnson."

Gently opening the taped-up hatbox, I set my toiletries on a small shelf underneath a mirror. "I wonder where all my stuff is at."

Miss Jemison flinched a little bit at the preposition hanging at the end of the sentence, but she didn't correct me.

"There was no cause for anybody to hit me across my face."

"She speaks," said Joette, sounding almost like Mrs. Ola Mae.

Everyone laughed, even the maid.

"I have a lot to say," I said.

Joette turned a straight-backed chair away from the desk and sat on it backward, gap legged. She made a cushion for her chin by crossing her arms, revealing two shocks of dark underarm hair.

"Tell us," she said.

Under her gaze, my defiance became less of an accident. When Joette looked at me, I felt brazen and admired. And more than that, I felt worthy of it all—having paid the same price that would have been levied against a braver person.

"I just wanted to ride with my head up."

Joette nodded. "That's all we want. You know, you could maybe sue the bus company. There's a family at our church—the husband and son are both attorneys. I could arrange a meeting. Would you like that?"

"Little lady," said Mrs. Ola Mae, with respect. "You know, you something else."

"The Cunninghams are very well regarded. Her father is the most—" Fanny said to Mrs. Ola Mae, but she shut up, feeling Joette's hot glare.

"I'm not a debutante," she said.

All of our eyes pinballed around the room, as we were none

of us debutantes, but only she was the sort that had to make a declaration about it.

Aunt Irene had a name for girls like Joette: "soft-foot." These were women whose life unfolded in such a way that their feet stayed as soft as their hands, and their hands stayed as soft as their feet. They never walked barefoot or scarred their knuckles on a washboard with lye soap. It would be many years before I learned that soft feet were often mangled by pretty shoes, but that was information that I had no use for as I got to know Joette Cunningham. From her voice alone, I could tell that her feet and hands both were plush like Aunt Irene's Ohio fur coat.

I hung my few clothes on three wire hangers. Miss Fanny eyed the empty space as she crammed Joette's clothes into her own closet so tight that everything would need to be ironed. I opened my mouth to offer up my closet but Mrs. Ola Mae said, "No, you don't."

Just then, there was a timid knock at the door.

"Come on in," said Mrs. Ola Mae like this was her house back in Honeysuckle.

The person at the door was a stocky girl holding a tan envelope.

"I'm here for Vernice?" She looked around the room. "Oh, hey, Joette," she said.

"Hi." Joette had a way of speaking to people without really talking to them.

The girl moved her weight from leg to leg like she was in a hurry. "This must be for you," she said, pushing the envelope in my direction.

"That's a bill," Mrs. Ola Mae said. "I don't know what it is about bill envelopes but they just look different, like sponges sopping up all your pennies."

"Aunt Irene handled my fees already," I said, embarrassed to have words like "bill" and "fees" floating in the air in front of Joette. "We used a money order."

"How much they say you owe?" asked Mrs. Ola Mae. "You got enough? Because I got a little extra over here in 'Titty Savings and Loan.'" She patted her bosom, where she had apparently stashed a few dollars. "I was going to give it to you when it was time to go, but if you need it now—"

"No," I snapped. "We paid it already."

Aunt Irene saved for two years, and then there was the money raised by the congregation. The whole point of paying in advance was so I didn't have to feel poor, but all this talk of money made me feel like I was shaking a tin cup by the side of the road. Across the room, Joette made like the trees on the opposite side of the window were so fascinating that she couldn't bear to look away.

"Let's go to the bursar's office," said Miss Jemison. "Let's get you all squared away." She paused, deciding if it was wise to leave Mrs. Ola Mae in the dorm room, where she might say who knew what to my new roommate, or if we should take her with us to the administration building, where she might say who knew what to somebody in charge.

"I'ma stay here," Mrs. Ola Mae said. "I'm tired."

After tromping down the three flights of stairs, we were in the center of the campus, on the north side of an oval lawn cut across with paved walkways. I set my clean saddle shoe on the thick grass, but Miss Jemison clucked her tongue like she was disciplining a horse. "We don't disturb the landscaping."

Then she strode along the pavement and I followed, embarrassed again.

The bursar's office was located inside a large brick building, just across from the president's cottage. The words ROCKEFELLER HALL were dug deep into the arched doorway. Flecks of stained glass decorated the curve over each window. The effect was elegant but not fussy. Seated at the front desk was a girl about my age; her name tag said MISS LAJUNE MCDONALD. "May I help you?" she asked. And it seemed like a real question, not like a line that she was being paid to say. Seeing the envelope, she sent me to the third floor.

At the bursar's office, I was in line behind several girls, all of whom held bundles shielded by their bodies. The girl in front of me smelled like camphor. Her wallet was a sock, stretched and heavy with coins. The clerk emptied the contents into a drawer, folded the sock, and then returned it.

"They say I have a balance?" I said when it was time for me to talk to the man seated behind a gated window.

"Seventeen thirty-seven."

What money I had, folded over and rubber banded, was zipped inside my handbag. Thirty-eight dollars, all the money I had to my name. Seven fives, a two, and a single. Most of the bills were limp like they had been passed from hand to hand to hand to hand. As I counted it out, the man who received it wrote me a receipt. Ripping it from a pad, he said, "To God be the glory."

"How do you feel?" Miss Jemison said once we were back out into the summer air.

"Locked in," I said.

"Because you are. Does it feel good?"

And strangely enough, it did.

"But I'm not like these girls."

"Which girls?" she said with her schoolteacher authority. "You have seen ten kinds of girls just today alone."

"I'm not like the girl they gave me to live with, Joette."

Miss Jemison led me to an iron bench. "Spelman is an opportunity for you. For Joette, college was an inevitability."

"She has a maid and I barely have clean panties to put on."

"Do not squander this chance."

"I look poor," I said.

She spoke with shades of a disciplinarian. "Just be grateful that you have a nice library job lined up. You are so blessed not to worry about anything but fashion."

"Where do you reckon my suitcases are?"

"Put those material things out of your head," she said. "Clothes are merely garments."

"Yes, ma'am," I said, struggling to feel lucky.

Finally, it was time for all of the parents, relatives, play-aunties, maids, and anyone else to leave. The last day of my old life had been a long one. Miss Jemison led me to the corner of the room and spoke in a voice so low that it bypassed my ear and traveled from her heart to mine.

"Now, listen," she said. "If you repeat this, I will deny it."

"Yes, ma'am," I said.

"Ola Mae is the light of my life. Teaching is my calling. I do not regret any decisions that I have made. But your aunt didn't sacrifice her whole life for you to come back to Honeysuckle—whether it is our town or any other. There are Honeysuckles everywhere and if you end up in one of them, then you may as well reclaim that little roll of money and come on home. You hear me?"

Then she kissed my face and her voice returned to normal. "I hope I didn't hurt you."

---

That night, I lay pinned under the thick, unfamiliar bedspread. In the dark my eyes adjusted and I studied the steep slant of the eaved ceiling. The mattress beneath me was thin, firm, but comfortable, I decided after rearranging my body several times.

"You okay over there, little country mouse?" Joette asked me.

"Yeah," I said, and I wondered why the nickname didn't bother me.

"'Unwelcoming,'" Joette said. "That's the word I wanted when you first came in. I didn't want to seem unwelcoming."

"Well," I said, "I didn't want to seem . . ." There were so many words that I could have used to complete that sentence, as there was so much for me to be ashamed of. I didn't want to seem like an orphan. I didn't want to seem poor. I didn't want to seem like whatever Raynelle and Ola Mae were. But because I couldn't bring myself to utter any of these truths, I told a lie. "I don't want to seem ordinary."

"Girl," Joette said into the thick dark, "you are anything but."

I could tell from her tone that she intended this as a compliment, but I wondered what it was about me that she could see, even without light.

"Mortuary," she said. "That's where the money comes from. I know you want to know."

"That many people are dying up here in Atlanta?" I said, hoping to sound nonchalant. “Maybe I need to go on back home, if y’all are getting that rich off of funerals.”

“People die every day,” she said, with a faintly defensive rasp. “My father helps colored folk go on to glory with dignity. In my granddaddy’s time, they just chunked us in the ground with nothing but our mama’s tears. You might not even get a hole to yourself. I don’t see eye to eye with my parents, but I can respect their work. When you mistreat the dead, you torment the living.”

“My mother is dead. My father, too,” I said.

“Did they have a good death? Likely not, being young. Did they have a nice service at least?”

“I don’t know,” I said. “I was a baby.”

“He killed her?” Joette asked.

“How did you know?”

“Happens more than you think,” she said.

*Chapter 10*

# ANNIE

Six weeks is either a long time or no time, depending on how much you are enjoying yourself. For Babydoll, every instant in Mississippi was a second too many. Sundays we gathered with every soul on the property behind the Jack Walter house and listened to Lulabelle preach. It was beautiful, like Jesus making friends with Mary Magdalene and whatnot. Clyde was bored the way men are whenever women drag them anywhere. Bobo took notes in a little bound book that Lulabelle sold him, along with a ballpoint pen—that wasn't free either. Babydoll used each worship day to remind everybody how long we had been there.

"First off," she said, "I am Catholic. We don't believe in anybody-can-speak-for-God business. And even if we did, it wouldn't be her." She capped it off by saying, "I haven't been to confession in three weeks . . ." Then "Four weeks . . ."

Finally, Lulabelle said, "You want me to get you a priest? We got one that comes on Thursdays . . ."

Everybody busted out laughing, especially the girl who was the father's favorite. I didn't laugh because Babydoll and I were friends by that time.

After seven Sundays, Babydoll had harassed me into asking Lulabelle if I could have a peek at the ledger to see where we were, debt-wise. Lulabelle unlocked a kitchen drawer and fetched a notebook. With a licked finger, she flipped a blue-lined page. Like they say, "The doctor was smiling, but the news wasn't good." I can't recall the exact dollars and cents but after we had slept, eaten, and bought supplies to clean ourselves with, Babydoll and I didn't earn a dollar a week. As for the fellows, I couldn't even decipher the way the wages were doled out. Their work was recorded in a system of little stars, dashes, and swirlies. By Clyde's name was a little cluster of exclamation marks, which I figured was French for doing "the do." There were one or two beside Bobo's name as well.

"That's not how he writes his name," I said. "It's Bobo, all one word. Not Bo-dash-Bo."

"Jealousy is ugly," said the Gibson girl.

"You are one to talk," said Lulabelle.

---

I didn't question the math, because I didn't mind the time we stayed there. For the first time I could remember, I didn't miss Hattie Lee. Yet, I knew I couldn't live the rest of my life scrubbing sheets at a whorehouse. Even if my spirit was willing, my body couldn't take it. Nearly from day one, my hands were chapped and sore. Their condition wasn't too far from the inside of a banana peel. And you know what the old folks say: when it's time, you'll know it's time.

It was week ten and a half. Babydoll and I were out back heating up water to do our work. Babydoll was surly but I was starting to feel at home, or at least like I was having a meaningful life. On a Sunday afternoon, one of the ladies shared a slice of peach cake that her auntie brought her after church. I don't care for cooked fruit, but I appreciated the fellowship. Granny had friends like that. Sometimes they sagged, but when they were together drinking chicory coffee or plaiting hair, life was good enough to live it for another day.

Babydoll wouldn't have been so salty if she could have stopped being so stuck up and tried to make friends, but she didn't want to have anything to do with none of them. Her own mama sometimes kept company for money, mostly colored, sometimes not. Babydoll had a butter-colored brother to prove it, and this is why her real daddy hightailed it over the state line to be with a tall woman from Arizona—who was neither white nor colored, and I don't mean mixed. They also had butter babies that everybody said were so darling and all of that. As a result, Babydoll kept her distance from all the farm business. She said just the sight of them going into the shacks with the sirs made her stomach cramp like she was getting her monthlies.

Besides, she was eaten up with spite, and let me tell you, it did not look good on her.

That muggy summer day, I was late to the washtub, having lingered too long at breakfast. Babydoll was posted up by the pump, bitter as pecan bark.

"Don't you even care about Memphis no more?" she asked me. "On the ride up here, you were all Little Orphan Annie. But now you act like you are content to spend the rest of your life on this ho farm."

"We will likely only be here a few more days. Shadrack towed the car on Sunday."

Babydoll shook her head. "You do not understand this situation at all. If we stay here much longer, Clyde will get a taste for things that I am not serving."

I nodded like I understood.

"These girls," Babydoll said, fanning at the row of shacks. "You know they hope to hump their way out of here. And a fine fellow like Clyde, with a car? They'd change places with me in a minute."

"Like you changed places with me?" I said, surprised that I had a little pecan bark on my tongue, too.

She flicked wash water in my direction. "Why don't you just get with Bobo so you can stop whining about my man."

"You the one that brought him up." I dumped the pile of laundry to let her know that I was done with this conversation."

"Mary, Mother of Jesus," Babydoll said.

At my feet was a wad of sheets bloody all the way through; some parts were brown and stiff and others dark red and musty.

"Somebody died," Babydoll said.

We took the stained sheets and placed them in the washtub gently, like we were handling a shroud. The greasy lye lather went baby-girl pink. Stirring the pot with the heavy wooden paddle, I recalled my conversation with Lulabelle while I fixed and unfixed her hair. I guess she had been able to get the doctor on the phone and she sicced him on Mother Nature's business. I wondered if he got his payment even if the girl had died.

"I think she was pregnant."

"Ain't no more," Babydoll said.

"You think she's dead?"

"This is a lot of blood," Babydoll said. "But people live through all kinds of things."

We agitated the water and then filled the pot again. "Lulabelle is just going to have to throw these sheets out. I know she won't want us hanging them for everybody to see."

We finally fished the ruined sheets out of the water and left them in a pile beside the porch steps. Then we completed our daily chores in silence.

"I'm ready to leave," I said.

Just before lunchtime, Bobo showed up carrying a shovel.

"Lulabelle said for me to dig a hole? There are some sheets that need to be buried?" he asked with his head on a swivel.

I nodded and pointed my chin to the dirty mound in the corner creating its own mud puddle.

"Shit," he said. "She shanked somebody? I hope it wasn't nobody white."

"No," I said. "I think there was a baby."

"Somebody had a baby in here? That's an inauspicious way to begin your life. Born in a whorehouse." He shook his head and removed his hat.

Babydoll snapped, "It wasn't a baby yet. The doctor came and tried to take it out. But we don't know that it worked. She could be dead."

Now Bobo put his hat over his heart.

Babydoll crossed herself. "Hail Mary, full of grace, blessed are thee among women."

Bobo gave a quiet amen, as I just let the tears collect behind my eyes as I thought about Hattie Lee.

With soft grunts, Bobo opened the ground, exposing a layer of black dirt, followed by clay the same yellow as baby shit. This went on long enough for him to soak his cotton shirt and for me to pray for my mother.

Babydoll and I folded the sheets, sodden and weighty. We wedded the corners and passed the cotton between our hands. It was like a clapping game crossed with the maypole dance. When we had each of the sheets shrunk down to a tragic triangle, we lowered them into the hole Bobo had dug. He replaced the dirt, then the three of us tamped it back until not even a scar remained where the sheets were buried.

"We need to get the hell out of here." He sat on the damp ground. "This place got ghosts."

That night when he and I were settled on our pallet, we spoke in whispers, as we tended to do. Bobo's voice was quiet so I had to strain to hear him, forcing my mind to focus on the words from his lips instead of the sounds coming from Clyde and Babydoll.

"I did see a ghost," he said. "At least I think that's what it was."

"Where?"

"Lulabelle told me to reinforce all the steps in front of the shacks. The only one left was the place across from the roses. This lady, older than us and younger than my mother, came out on the porch and said she needed me to patch the wall. She was dressed like a for-real sharecropper. And she called me by my given name."

"Your name's not really Bobo?" I broke in.

"Hell no," he said. "You think Mama was a vulgarian? She gave me her maiden name, Carver. The scientist was her cousin in some distant way. So, this lady, she said, 'Carver, I need you to help me.'"

The way he copied her voice made the hair on my arms stand up and dance. "That's how she said it?"

"It was like she was maybe offering to break me off a piece for my trouble. But I don't want no more loving that's for sale. I'd rather be with my own palm, because at least I know my hand wants to be there. So anyway, I tell her I will be over there afterwhile to get the step together.

"As I walked off, she laughed, but it didn't have any joy in it."

"How did she sound?"

"Mad," he said.

"At you?"

"I mean 'mad' like 'crazy.'"

Bobo snuggled up close to me, but this time I didn't push him away. Across the room, Clyde and Babydoll tangled in the covers. They didn't care about modesty and after all this time, their soft cries and movements were like a filthy radio show in the background. Bobo held me around the waist and pressed his chest into my back and his lips near my ear.

"When I returned to the shack after lunch, I knocked and no one answered. So, I got busy repairing the step. I put some plaster to hold the stones together. Then I opened the door to see about the wall she wanted patched. Annie, I swear I knocked and nobody answered. Not a sound from the shack."

His voice was clotted and his breath on my ear was hot. "When I opened the door, she was up under a white man and he was giving it to her bad but she was still as Lot's wife. But then she opened her eyes. The man was doing what he came there for but nothing on her was alive but her eyes. Her eyes begged me to be Superman. But what was I supposed to do? I mean, this was what people paid for. So, I backed out, mumbling my apologies. But when I looked over my shoulder, there was nobody there. Stone-cold empty, except for a squirrel in the corner snickering at me."

I turned so my front was to his.

"I never been so terrified in my life," he said.

By now, Clyde and Babydoll were done. I didn't chance speaking and possibly being overheard. So, I stroked his back and tried to make sense of his spasms.

"It's over now," I whispered. "Whatever shook you so bad is gone."

"I'm not scared now. Soon as I walked back into the sunshine, the fright just dried up. But what took its place is worse."

"Shh," I said, like he was a baby, crisscrossing my hands over his quivering back.

He whispered, "When I thought she was a whore, I turned my back on her and just let the sir do what I knew she didn't want him to be doing. When I did that, I failed as a man. But, Annie, she wasn't a woman, she was a spirit. And when I left her there, I failed as a *soul.* I am going to have that with me for the rest of my life. Maybe even after."

"Naw, Bobo," I said. "Your soul is clean."

We became lovers that night, although all we did was sleep with our arms and legs entwined. The bodily aspect came later; we both knew that it would. And when it did, it sealed a deal that had been written maybe before we were even born.

"Annie," he said, "I feel so sorry for your mama. Poor, poor Hattie Lee. All these years, she has been deprived of you."

*Chapter 11*

# VERNICE

Joette's cousin Marylinda was so pale, she was nearly see-through. They were related on her mother's side, where everyone had been keeping things pale since Reconstruction—with the notable exception of Joette's mother, who married a man from South Carolina. But according to Joette, Marylinda's mother had taken it to another level by marrying a man so bright that he displayed a strawberry birthmark on the back of his bald head. "There's a story there," Joette said. "But I promised my mama I wouldn't tell it."

This was a couple of weeks into my life as a coed. I was making do with my carpetbag wardrobe. It was amazing, the breadth of alterations a person could achieve with safety pins, paper clips, and rubber bands. Some of the dresses I cinched, others let out. I ripped out hems and folded makeshift darts. I didn't have the Suzy Brooks style of Joette and her cousin, but I was acceptable. When I reported to my job at the library, nobody thought I was a charity case. And I must have looked halfway nice because my boss kept making excuses to rub himself against me.

"My guess," said Joette, "is that your suitcases are right here in Atlanta at the bus station."

"So, we could go get them? We could just go to the station?"

Joette gave out a little chuckle. "You want to ride a Jim Crow bus to get your luggage that you lost because you refused to ride a Jim Crow bus? What on earth would Mrs. Parks think about that?"

"Stop playing. I'm serious."

"I am, too. But you can't get them because you said they tore up your ticket. How will you prove that those Samsonites belong to you?"

"I thought you said you had an idea."

"I do," said Joette. "I just hate asking Marylinda for help."

Marylinda's room was on the ground floor and faced Greensferry Avenue. It was prime real estate, I would come to know later. Girls called room 104 the Underground Railroad because it was perfectly situated to climb out the window if you needed to leave campus after curfew, or if you needed to return. She didn't have a roommate because her parents paid extra.

The room was a flurry of lace and ruffles. A caramel-colored teddy bear lounged on a stack of pillows covered with seersucker shams.

Joette picked up the bear and punched it in the face. "You are fooling absolutely no one with this shit."

"The Underground Railroad can't look like an escape route. All these pillows evoke virginity."

"I need you to do us a favor," Joette said. "Country Mouse, tell her what happened to your luggage."

My story got a little bolder with each recitation. I never lied. Let the record show that. I did take a seat in the whites-only section. I was tossed off. Someone did hit me in the face. My luggage was, in fact, left aboard. A kindly colored woman did get me back home. The carpetbag did represent the love, poverty, and bad taste of my community. And I did, in fact, need help.

Marylinda listened to the story, not rapt exactly, but with an eye to detail. She had questions like "Did you retain your ticket?," "What was the reaction of the other passengers?," "What exactly was your desired outcome?"

By this last question, Joette said, "Counselor, that's enough. You are traumatizing her. Damn."

Marylinda said, "Sorry. After I escape this convent, I am going to Howard for law school to work with Dovey Roundtree."

"Who?"

"She's a warrior," Marylinda said.

Joette cleared her throat. "How much you wanna bet that her suitcases are sitting at the bus station downtown?" Joette said to her cousin, while I sat trying to be brave yet pitiful.

Marylinda pinched her eyes. "Likely."

"We need to go and claim them so she won't be walking around here looking like . . . like she's looking."

They both sized me up. I wore a plaid dress intended for someone a couple sizes larger and maybe ten years older, but two rubber bands and a paper clip had made a world of difference.

"No offense," Joette said.

Marylinda said, "I see your point. She does resemble a mothball. What's the holdup? It can't just be a matter of car fare. I can let you hold a dollar."

Joette said, "I have money."

Even I had a dollar, but since I needed it, I kept quiet.

Marylinda sat on her bed and it gave under her hips. "You must want me to go get it."

Joette said, "She doesn't have a claim slip. The bus driver ripped her ticket before he hit her across the face. You can't tell me that that's right."

Marylinda said, "I hate it when you do this to me."

Joette said, "I thought you were so into the Movement. This is race work, too."

"When are you going to do some race work, Miss Joette? You haven't come to Rich's with us, not one time. But you want to guilt-trip me about this luggage."

"Oh my God, Marylinda," said Joette. "Why are you acting like pretending to be a white girl is the hardest thing in the world? Just go, tell the people you want to collect your bags but you lost your claim slip. Bat your eyes and say you hope some colored person didn't steal them . . . And watch them scramble to find your shit."

Marylinda flopped onto her frilly bedspread. Her cheeks were marred by a series of tiny red bumps. "I'm not blushing. You know it's just my rosacea. Don't think you got under my skin."

Joette said, "You know how you can tell you are under someone's skin? They say you are not under it."

"Y'all don't know how good you have it," I said.

They both turned, like they had forgotten that I was even in the room. From their stricken faces, I knew they thought I was saying that they didn't know how lucky they were to be rich girls with closets stuffed with clothes. But really, I was thinking about how fortunate they were to be members of a family, to have the luxury of cousins.

"I have a dollar," I said. "And I can give you another if you want to have it. I just really need my things. My aunt worked so hard to buy those cases. And I sewed half the dresses in there. I'd do anything to get them back."

Marylinda tossed the teddy bear before she relented. "Fine. Give me the money."

"You can't take her money," said Joette. "She can't spare it."

"I can," I said.

Marylinda kept her hand out. To Joette she said, "Don't be so damn condescending."

Sliding my two-dollar bill into her pocket, she asked, "What color are the bags?"

"Thank you, Cousin," Joette said.

Raising her middle finger, she said, "This is the last time, Joette. The very last time."

*Chapter 12*

# ANNIE

We didn't leave Lulabelle's the next day, or even the day after. Clyde didn't get motivated until Bobo told him that the place was haunted and that whore-ghosts were known to deprive a man of his ability to get his mister to rise. And shortly thereafter, wouldn't you know it—Clyde's mister refused to get off the divan. Babydoll told me this as we wrestled with a large batch of wet towels.

"But between me and you," she said through a mouthful of bubblegum that we were being charged for, "I was glad that thing didn't get hard. You can't get a man to do squat as long as he is getting all the loving he wants. And even if I keep my legs closed, he can just get it elsewhere. I'm happy a ghost hexed his dick."

---

That Wednesday, I went to Lulabelle's house to read the Bible and find out our standing, ledger-wise. The Gibson girl answered the door, as always, but this time she didn't let me in right away. Instead, she settled herself into one of the cane rockers. She pushed herself back and forth on the balls of her burgundy-and-beige pumps.

"I'm here to see Ms. Lulabelle?"

"I know. But sit with me for a minute."

I took a place in the other rocking chair.

"I saw your man over by the roses," she said.

I sighed. "He works here."

"Did he see her? Mama doesn't have anybody use that place, but sometimes the ghost beckons people over. One girl was frightened to death. Her heart just exploded, I think. Mama paid for her to get buried in Mobile, where she's from."

I put my feet down to hold my chair still. "Who is the haint, then?"

The Gibson girl shrugged. "One time, a jackleg preacher offered to cast her out as a demon. He said she was here on account of all the sin going on. Then Mama said he could kiss her A-S-S and anyway, everything that dead-alive ain't necessarily evil. Same as how everybody living ain't always holy."

I had my face balled up in concentration. "The haint got a name?"

"She must," the Gibson girl said. "But I don't know it. One thing you don't want to do is call a spirit by their name. They don't like it. And another thing you don't want is to get a spirit mad with you. But anyhow, I am glad your man didn't drop dead."

"Me too," I said.

"Okay," the Gibson girl said. "You ready to see Mama?"

By the time I was ushered into the living room, Lulabelle was waiting, but she didn't have the leatherbound Bible on her lap. Instead, she held the schoolbook that served as the ledger.

"Ma'am," I said.

"Shadrack is over by the creek getting his due," she said.

"Who?"

"The mechanic," she said. "It's time for you to get on your way."

Although I was eager to go, Lulabelle putting us out nicked my feelings.

"We appreciate you letting us stay here," I said.

Lulabelle stretched herself like a cat. "*You* don't have to leave. The rest of them got to get the hell off my property. One of y'all is agitating haints. It's one thing to sell pussy in Bible Alley, but the Jesus folks will be out here with torches and holy water if they hear that I got spirits out here mingling with the living."

I nodded. "How long has she been here?"

"Nearly all my life. The only place anyone has ever seen her is in the shack by the roses. When I peeped that your little boyfriend freshened up the stairs, I knew she was back." Lulabelle laughed. "Even that haint knew better than to ask Clyde to work."

"Bobo said she was getting violated. By a white man."

"Did he get turned on? That happened to one of the sirs. He stumbled in there, saw what he saw, and he couldn't get his pecker to go down. I heard he was locked and loaded for three days."

"Bobo was crushed near to the point of crying," I said.

"You need to marry him."

After I read from the Book of Revelation, she gave me an envelope containing thirty-three dollars. Ten was for Babydoll. The rest for me. My ten-dollar wage, plus a love token.

"Keep the extra someplace secret. Every woman should have a private stash."

---

Our last night at Lulabelle's, Babydoll and Clyde slept in the shack near the old barn. When I entered the near-empty room, fresh from my bath, Bobo stood there, sheepish.

"Where's Babydoll?" I said. "I saved her some hot water."

"They have decided to stay in one of the other buildings."

"Lord," I said. "After all these nights, they decide they want some privacy? That money must just be burning a hole in Babydoll's pocketbook."

"No," he said, looking right in my face. "I was the one who paid for them to have a space."

"You don't have money."

"No," he said. "But I had some barter credit. I told one of the girls that she could have the night off if she let them stay over there."

"Why?" I started, but his face gave me the answer that I needed.

"You saved my soul, Annie," he said.

He took a couple of steps in my direction and I knew he was about to kiss me. I had been kissed before, but I felt that this was a mature touch that could not be undone.

We lay on the pallet with me looking up at him, propped on his elbow.

"Do you want to be my woman?" he asked me.

"What do I have to do?" I touched his collarbones. "Besides this?"

"You don't even have to do that," he said. "That's two separate questions."

He twined his leg through mine, leaving me exposed, despite my clean gown. He kissed my neck and undid a few small buttons, brushing his lips over the skin revealed.

"All I need is for you to love me. And however you love me, I will love you back twice as hard."

"I want it," I said. "The love. Everything."

"I'll give it," he said.

---

I woke up before day in the morning feeling like a woman. I washed myself with a basin of cool water in the corner of the shack that was roomy without Babydoll and Clyde. As I wet the towel, I felt Bobo's half-asleep eyes on me, but I didn't feel ashamed, not even when I soaped the hidden places before rinsing and patting the tender skin dry.

Nothing in my repacked suitcase felt right now that I had entered this new phase of my life. Even my well-worn panties seemed to belong to someone else's hips, straining as I tugged them to my waist. I made do as I could only put on what I already owned. I selected a green blouse and left a couple of the buttons undone.

Bobo, nude and gleaming like a peeled grape, eased his hand into the space above my collarbone, curling his fingers behind my neck.

"It was good?"

I nodded, failed by words.

Before I opened the door, I said, "I love you," tossing the words over my shoulder like a handful of wildflower seeds.

---

Lulabelle answered the door before I could take my hand off the lion knocker. She let her eyes pass over me from ankle to hairline, then pushed my shoulder like she was twirling a merry-go-round. From a space up under her breasts, she laughed.

"It's about time," she said. "Did Bobo do you right?"

She was probably expecting me to tuck my head but I did not. "We care about each other."

She clucked in approval. "Good, good. Take it slow. That's why you got to be careful who you give it to. They can put your love in their back pocket and never give it back. But that Bobo never struck me as a soul thief. I keep telling you to marry him."

"Well, we will cross that bridge when we come to it. And we might be crossing it pretty soon because we are leaving later this morning."

"Not just y'all two," she said. "You got to take them other ones with you. Especially that Babydoll. Get her off my property." She laughed. "She don't know how lucky she is that my sister took a shine to her."

"All of us going to Memphis," I said. "But I wanted to come to say goodbye, personal."

Lulabelle spun me around again, and then once more.

"Safe travels," she said. "I hope I never see you again."

I was a little wounded by this and I guess it showed on my face. "You won't miss me even a little bit?"

She rose and took a few steps toward me and held her hands about six inches apart. I fit my face into the cradle of her palms. She kissed me five times, on my forehead, my chin, my nose, and both my cheeks. "Oh, but I love you, little girl."

Her face was soft and serious at the same time. "But hear me good. If you get gone from here, you best pray that God lets you stay gone."

*Chapter 13*

# VERNICE

If I had to summarize my first semester at Spelman, it would be with one word—"curfew." Annie's grandmother was absolutely the type to keep us locked up like a pair of country nuns, but she didn't have the energy to make that chaste dream a reality. Aunt Irene had plenty of energy but was no hypocrite. And besides, there was only so much mischief to get into on the colored side of Honeysuckle. The only threat to a girl was boys, and Aunt Irene knew that boy-trouble could be gotten into at any time of day. She liked to point out that sons were the ones you had to watch because white folks would string them up as soon as they would say merry Christmas. But that, too, was an all-day-long worry. Curfew was irrelevant.

This was to say, I wasn't used to being on the clock. But at Spelman, young ladies needed to be accounted for by dinnertime—even in the warm months when the sun was high in the sky until nearly 8 p.m. The penalty for tardiness? Well, that depended on whose daughter you were. For somebody like me, I would be sent back to Honeysuckle with barely enough time to return my library books. Joette had missed the mark twice already and was punished by having to spend three days at home with her family, sleeping in her childhood bedroom. I pined in her absence, standing in line each evening and spending hard-earned dimes to ring her from the payphone in the hallway. When she finally answered, my voice sounded high and unsure even to my own ears.

"What are you up to, Country Mouse?" she asked me.

"I got a letter from my cradle friend, Annie. Remember I told you how she ran away? I am so glad to hear from her." My words rushed out, as I was thrilled about Annie's message and delighted to speak with Joette after two days apart. I was midway through what was probably a tangled recounting of what all Annie had written, but Joette cut me off before I could even get to the part about the Mississippi whorehouse.

"You spent a whole dime to call me and tell me about your other girlfriend?" Her laugh sounded like the lady-cigarettes she kept in the desk drawer.

"Why you got to be so womanish," I said, worried that I'd be overheard. "Me and Annie are not like that."

"Like what?" Joette said. "Say it."

"Like us," I whispered into the phone, and was rewarded with a contented sigh on the other end of the line.

"I miss you," she said.

"Then stop getting sent home."

There was no excuse for Joette to be flagged for curfew violations, again and again. For one, the conductor of the Underground Railroad was her first cousin. A double tap resulted in an open window and a helping hand. But Joette refused to ask for Marylinda's assistance. And on top of that, she enjoyed tormenting her father by pretending to be fast and running the streets. I was baffled how someone as observant as Joette could fail to understand that her cup more than runneth over. How couldn't she see that she shared a room with someone who didn't even have a cup at all?

Time at home made her look to be a different sort of person, like in the movies when Bette Davis plays two roles. The drop-waist dress with a Peter Pan collar fit her like a costume. As Joette got settled back into her room, the first thing she did was pull her brush through a crunchy roller-set. The strands crackled and popped as the dorm mother warned, "There's nothing going down after curfew but drawers."

Curfew was so early that there were all manner of things going down, including drawers, of course, but so many other appealing options. There were movies to go see, soul food to be eaten, and hairdressers to visit. Or, for Marylinda, there was a whole movement to organize. I don't know what Joette was doing in the dusk, but her parents' fear of a crooked-yoke pregnancy was unfounded. Joette didn't care for men. This she told me late one night as we snuck swallows from a silver flask of gin she had swiped from her father's cabinet.

"They just don't smell right to me," she said. "What about you?"

She handed me the flask; I let my fingers cover the monogram and fitted my lips exactly where hers had been. "I don't mind them. They're okay."

"I can't stand it," she said. "I tried it and I couldn't stand it."

---

Yet, there was a benefit to being cloistered. I felt like I had forty-seven sisters. I loved the smell of body powder and shampoo that clung to the upholstery. We let our douche bags hang from our closet doors without shame. We talked about our periods and prayed together when they were late. If I could have, I would have lived in Abby Hall for the rest of my life.

On Sunday evenings, like she had some kind of schedule, Marylinda came by, recruiting for "the struggle." Like the Jehovah's Witnesses, she knocked on every door. Everyone put up with it because we all, in general, thought the Movement was positive, whether we were in it or not. And also, nobody wanted to fall on the wrong side of the Conductor.

She always saved our room for last.

Marylinda had her long hair wrapped on hard curlers held in place with heavy clips. "We have trained our sights on Rich's," she said. "Our target is the Magnolia Room."

She directed her attention to Joette, as most people did. I was just part of the furniture to people like her. I didn't have money, a name, or any particular gifts.

"What for?" Joette said. "Why you so eager to eat down there? You know they don't use hot sauce on anything."

"You know this ain't about lunch. If I wanted a sandwich, I would go on over to the Busy Bee. This is a matter of principle."

"You want your principle sandwich toasted? You want a pickle with that?" Joette laughed.

Marylinda jutted her hip. "Joette, you know what's at stake. Negroes like you make me sick."

"Negroes like me, you say?" Joette raised up just one of her eyebrows. Then she examined her pretty hand, a couple of shades deeper than me, and a continent away from her cousin.

"Everything ain't about skin tone," Marylinda said. "You just throw that in my face so you don't have to step up. Negroes are out here dying every day."

"They aren't dying for sandwiches," Joette said.

"If you are scared," said Marylinda, "just admit it. But don't try to act like you don't comprehend."

"Oh, I understand. You will go downtown with your little sign and let them take your photo getting arrested. Then Uncle Harold will bond you out."

"You are so wrong," Marylinda said. "Desmond says we will serve whatever sentence they give us. Jail, not bail. Ruby Doris and some of the others are aiming to get King to join us. It's only right. Atlanta is his home, and he is a Morehouse man. I can't see how he could refuse."

"So now the protest is a who's who?" Joette asked.

I didn't want Joette to see me perk up at the mention of Reverend King, but he was a person that I'd have been delighted to meet. He was not well-known like, say, Jackie Robinson, but the appeal was different. King was a significant person. I would have liked to one day say that I stood with him.

Joette went to her chest of drawers and produced her comb, brush, and pink rollers. "What happens if they mistake you for a white girl and let you order a meal?" She laughed, and I had to admit that it was a little bit funny.

"Why are you so reactionary?" she asked.

Rather than respond, Joette wrapped a thick section of hair around a curler and forced a cover over it. The effect was like a judge setting down a gavel.

"What about you, Country Mouse?"

I closed the book I pretended to study. How in the world had I got into the middle of this? And how had Joette's little name for me, which had sounded sort of sweet between us, become a full-on nickname?

"I'm not a country mouse," I said.

"It's affection," said Marylinda. "Besides, you have nothing to be ashamed of. These Atlanta Negroes prance around here like their shit don't stink, but trust me, it does. Joette doesn't want to demonstrate at Rich's because they let her mother shop there after-hours. In the day, they get treated just like the rest of us, but after dark? Green is the only color that matters. It's a high-class conflict. Be glad you are a country mouse."

"Leave my mother out of this," said Joette. "And we will leave your daddy out of it."

The cousins glared at each other. Finally Marylinda twisted away.

"Mouse? What say you?"

And now the nickname had even spun off a nickname.

"Her name is not Mouse," said Joette.

"Vernice," Marylinda said, her voice kinder now, "don't you want to be part of history? Don't you want to make things better for our people? Mouse, you are from the country so you can tell how bad things are. This is why we have to say *enough*. Six fellows are going, and we want to have six girls, too. We got four. I was hoping to get Joette to step up, but she's too much of a SWAN to get her hands dirty."

"A swan?"

"'Southwest Atlanta Negress.' She's one, like her mama, like my mama."

"Kiss my ass, Marylinda," said Joette.

"Vernice, come with us. You have a powerful moral authority, being from Mississippi."

"Louisiana," I said, correcting her. "Anyway, Honeysuckle isn't the country. It's a small town. It's not like I was a sharecropper."

"She can't afford to get kicked out," Joette said.

I didn't like her speaking for me, but she was right. At the same time, her logic didn't quite add up. Was there anyone in this world too poor to be free?

"Come on, Mouse," said Marylinda. "You have your own mind."

Joette didn't say a word to sway me. She didn't have to.

"I can't," I said. "I wish I could, but I can't."

---

For high chapel days—Founders Day, Class Day, Baccalaureate, and graduation—all Spelman girls were required to wear white dresses, flesh-colored hosiery, black pumps. The dress should fall below the knee by at least two inches. The shoes must be closed-toe. Underneath, we wore sturdy brassieres, slips, and girdles. Even skinny girls were trussed. Those who were able decorated their lovely collarbones with a single strand of pearls. Joette, of course, owned pearls for her neck and ears alike, but she left her throat bare and threaded silver hoops through her ears. Screwed to my earlobes were the paste pearls given to me by Annie. I fastened them tighter than I needed to, but I had already lost so much of my life before.

The white-dress portion of the uniform was simple, as every Southern girl owned at least one. Annie and I had sewn our dresses together, planning on being friend-twins for graduation. But of course, I had ended up alone on that afternoon. The dress reminded me of the feeling of sitting beside someone who was not my best friend, when everyone else was two by two like Noah's ark. I wondered what Annie was doing over in Memphis. I wondered if she had joined a church and if she'd had a chance to wear the dress that matched mine.

I was cheerless as I gingerly slid my one good pair of hose over my legs and clipped them to the belt. They were only nylon, and the color didn't match my complexion. However, they were the same as some of the other girls wore. My skin was a middle-of-the-road brown, so "suntan," the darkest shade at Yates & Milton, didn't give the "nude" effect, yet it didn't mock me the way it did the darker girls, like Joette. Although her second dresser drawer contained several pairs of genuine silk stockings, she chose to go bare-legged, drawing a line up the back of her shin with a kohl pencil, mimicking a seam. I hadn't watched her dress but doubted that she'd hooked her strong, lean body into a long-line Maidenform.

"You are going to get in trouble," I said.

"I don't care. They are lucky I am wearing underwear at all."

"You know why you like waging war on all the rules?" I said. "Because you know you won't be expelled."

Joette said, "I wish they'd kick me out of this place."

"Don't say that," I said. "Don't pretend like you want to leave."

"I don't want to leave you, Country Mouse. I just want to get out of this hellhole."

*Chapter 14*

# ANNIE

*Dear Granny,*

*I am writing you a real letter now that I have a proper return address. Has there been talk in Honeysuckle? Well, whatever you heard must all be lies because I have not run into one single soul from our neck of the woods. Just so you know, I was staying with a nice lady who owned her own business. She hired me to read the Bible to her. It was good to be able to spend time really thinking about the Word.*

*Here are two dollars. Please use it to get you something special from the grocery. I know that you do not care for clothes and other niceties, but everyone can appreciate a nice cut of meat or even a coconut haystack. You always tried to hide it but I know that you have a sweet tooth! Spend the money right away. There will be more where this came from.*

*I know you want the answer to the $64,000 question. No, I have not yet run down Hattie Lee. I have the address that she gave Mr. Daniel, but I don't want to go over there until I can show her that I am on the right track with my life. Do you have any message for her? If you don't mind, I will tell her that you love her because you are her mother and that's what everyone wants to hear—that their mother loves them. I believe that this will be like birthday and Christmas put together for her.*

*I hope you can forgive me for two things—coming into your life without an invitation, and leaving without saying goodbye.*

*Love,*

*Annie Kay*

---

*Dear Niecy,*

*Are you still mad at how I made my great escape? I hope that by now you have taken to heart my farewell letter. We have been friends since we were two babies sleeping in side-by-side dresser drawers. And if you search yourself, you will know that I had to leave the way that I did.*

*Once you get settled in Atlanta, you have to hop yourself on a Greyhound and come to Memphis! You have to come here just to hear how people play music. Bobo carries me with him to Beale Street, where bands fill the place with sound. I swear, I lose myself from dancing. When the songs get to swinging, I feel tiny, like a piece of dandelion fluff floating on the breath of God. They say it's the Mississippi that's mighty up here, but it's the music and the people that make it.*

*Also—I, Annie Kay Henderson, am madly in love. And because the Lord works in mysterious ways, it is not Clyde that I am so taken with. No, it is Bobo, his cousin—the one that plays piano. I know you think he is too short, but there is more to life than just big and little. He treasures me and I can now see that I have never known what it is to be truly cherished. He has found a job in a hotel and has already given me some money for Granny.*

*We live together in the same room. I suspect you will catch my meaning. I wish that I could talk to you about it. If you meet somebody special when you get to Spelman College, do not be fearful to take that step. If he loves you, everything will feel perfect. It's like dancing, but rougher and softer at the same time. (Please do NOT show anyone this letter!) It's a little sad not to have anybody to talk about it with. There is another girl with me, Babydoll, but she has seen it all and done the rest. I like her a lot, but she is not someone that I want all in my business.*

*Anyway, I pray that you write to me soon.*
*Love forever,*
*Annie*

---

*Dear Mr. Daniel,*

*By now you know that I made good on my threat to run away to the Bluff City. I suspect that you are the only person that is not angry with me. And since you are not mad, I hope that you will write me a letter of introduction saying that I know how to mix cocktails and that I am a ladylike and trustworthy person. I want a job at a drinking establishment where I can make decent tips.*

*And while I am asking for favors, I would also appreciate any advice you can give me for when I finally see Hattie Lee. I look at the piece of paper with her address every day. Bobo and me are waiting until we have saved up enough money to offer her some help. So, I know what to DO, I just need to know what to SAY.*

*Respectfully,*
*Annie Kay Henderson*

---

*Dear Ms. Lulabelle,*

*This is a letter to let you know that we have arrived in Memphis—safe and sound. Thank you for the help with finding a place to stay. Our new landlady is a very nice person. When we got here, she didn't ask us any questions beyond whether or not we had the funds for the deposit. She gave us two rooms and didn't care who sleeps where. I told her you said hello, but she gave that same line about how both of us should pray that we never see you again.*

*I just want to say, for the record, that I would be glad to come and visit sometime. Maybe by Christmas, me and Bobo could be engaged and we could bring you a gift. After all, you sensed that we were made for each other. As you can probably tell, I have crossed the river of love and burnt the bridge behind me!*

*He will go with me when I finally work up the nerve to ring my mother's bell. Our plan is to do it around Thanksgiving.*

*Can't you see me strolling up to her door carrying a ham, sweet potatoes, pound cake—like a horn of plenty walking on two feet? I want her to see that I am a good thing in her life, not some crumb snatcher.*

*Once she can tell that I am not holding grudges, we can get to know each other. At first, we might be like sisters—Granny raised us both—but I am sure the mother instinct will kick in.*

*Bobo, Clyde, and Babydoll all think that my plan is a little silly. But all three of them have their mothers, so they don't know what it is to do without. Babydoll is the main naysayer because she and her mother do not see eye-to-eye. Clyde is offended because I don't care about finding my father. But you know Clyde is a little bit slow. Bobo is just worried that I will get my heart broken. He cares for me, Lulabelle.*

*Now, do not take this the wrong way. I won't start calling you "mama" like some people we know.*

*Lulabelle, you gave me the closest thing to mother-love I have ever felt. You didn't know me from Eve, but you gave me the care that people save for kin. Don't try and say that you offer your softness to everybody because you didn't treat Babydoll like that and you met us on the very same day. You saw something in me and I saw something in you, too. This is why I can ignore Clyde when he tells me that my mother will be a stranger to me, because you showed me that you can love a stranger as deep as you can love somebody you have been knowing for years, maybe easier. My granny slept me in her house my whole life but she never doted on me like a grandbaby.*

*God will make a way. I was like Moses and you plucked me out of the water. This is why I don't believe you when you say you don't never want to see me again. This is a letter to say I miss you back.*

*Love,*

*Annie Kay*

---

*Dear Annie,*

*Yes, I received word that you had flown the coop, as it were. And I knew it was no coincidence that my sister mentioned that her sorry son had simultaneously vanished. And if that wasn't proof enough, your grandmother came into The Den at 10 p.m. on a Saturday night and blessed me out before all the regulars, who cheered her on, out of sport. She holds me responsible because I provided you with fair wages, as well as Hattie Lee's address. I reminded her that it was to SHE that I gave the coordinates and she accused me of collaborating with Satan.*

*The incident reminded me how starved my patrons are for entertainment alongside their libations. Maybe I will go ahead and invest in a jukebox.*

*In your letter, you mentioned "me and Bobo." I take this to mean that my poor nephew has been cast aside in favor of his cousin? If these two were the only fellows remaining on the planet, I would applaud your choice. However, this is a large world. Why on earth did you go through all the complications of flying the coop only to perch with someone from a neighboring roost? As I have said countless times, I don't understand little girls.*

*But enough of advice you did not solicit. You asked me about Hattie Lee. My strong inclination is that you not seek her out at all. As I have made very clear—it was with your grandmother that I shared her location, not you. A mother's need and obligation is far different than that of a child. I am sure that your grandmother could provide scripture that says parents are meant to chase down wayward children, but not vice versa.*

*Fantasies very seldom come to pass. You have already tied yourself to one Louisiana refugee. That's plenty. At least Bobo is able-bodied and, to my memory, reliable. Hattie Lee, by contrast, will leave you for a pint of ten-cent hooch every time. She doesn't love you, because she doesn't know you. The reason you love her is because you don't know her at all.*

*I am enclosing five dollars that I intended to give you for your graduation gift. Use it to get yourself a dress or a hairdo. At least when you ignore my advice and introduce yourself to Hattie, you should look like your grandmother raised you right.*

*Yours,*
*Daniel*

*PS: The letter of introduction will arrive in a separate envelope. Who gave you this idea? Vernice/Niecy? You want a job as a barmaid, not as a tutor. But it is on its way, my dear. Your wish is my command.*

---

*Dear Annie,*

*Raynelle Jemison is penning this letter on my behalf, because "Uncle Arthur" is bedeviling my wrists.*

*Thank you for the money. I will hold it back until Christmas-time. When you come back home, I know you want to find a nice meal on the table and a bundle under the tree.*

*You did not say who you have been running the streets with, but people talk. I know that you are with some relative of Mr. Daniel. I have to tell you in advance that I cannot raise any more babies. It's not just that my wrists and knees hurt so bad that I do not sleep at night. But it is also that I cannot take being left again and again. You children treat me as bad as the white children I used to get paid to take care of. You don't love me. You just need me for what I can do to keep you alive. Jesus is the only one that loves me and blessedly His love is enough.*

*I pray that you have found a church home over there in Tennessee. I also hope you will close your ears to the slicksters up there. The Adversary always wears shiny shoes. Stay prayed up so you can smell the devil, no matter how handsome.*

*If you see Hattie Lee, remind her that Jesus forgives us all and that I am praying for her the same way that I am praying for you. As you know, the wages of sin is death and I want you to enjoy eternal life with me and your grandfather when we put on our long white robes.*

*Your grandmother,*
*Irvina*

---

*Dear Annie,*

*I am not sure what to say. I am beyond relieved to hear that you are settled with a proper address. The postcard you sent in*

*June hurt my feelings. My best friend runs off in the middle of the night and all I get almost a month later is a postcard? News so bland that it doesn't even need the privacy of an envelope. Aunt Irene said that it was "proof of life," snapped it in her bag, and took it to your granny, who was so glad to see it that she gave a testimony at church. Just so you know, every old lady in Allen Parish is praying for you.*

*You and I are still best friends. The people in Atlanta are very interesting to be around and get to know, but those connections are only skin-deep. But I don't feel like we are the cradle friends that we were just this past Easter. Your letter was very informative and entertaining, but you know what you didn't say? SORRY. You, of everybody in this world, should know what it feels like to just be up and left.*

*When your grandmother asked me if I knew where you had gone to, I said NO in such a way that she would think that I was lying because I was just so embarrassed to be left in the dark. Everyone was so impressed that I was so tight-lipped. Girls called me "Fort Knox" because of how close I kept your secret. But the real secret was that I didn't know any more than they did.*

*Annie, I love you but you really need to think about how you treat people. I am happy that you have found true love and all of that, but I feel like you and me are on different sides of a waterfall.*

*Yours truly,*
*Vernice*

---

*Dear Annie,*

*Mama told me to send this letter to you, as she doesn't have time to sit down with pen and paper. Things are very busy on the property these days. There was a serious incident that took place last week. Your friend Shadrack, who fixed you all's car, well he got into a fight with one of the sirs and ended up dead. Luckily everyone involved was colored, but you know how polices are. They always want to harass Mama. They want to have barter for not arresting her. So now we have deputies around here making everybody nervous. Mama wishes the haint would come back and run these white men off. She says to tell you that you got out of here in the nick of time.*

*She also tells me to tell you that you should not read the Bible by yourself because it is only confusing when you don't have anyone to decipher with. She also says that you shouldn't read it with Bobo because reading the Bible with a man only leaves you chained to a stove somewhere. She says this means all men, even preachers. Now she says* especially *them. If you have made some new girlfriends, maybe read it with them. You don't want to open the Good Book with Babydoll. Mama still does not like her.*

*Lastly, she says that you should leave your mother alone and stop trying to climb back in her womb. She pushed you out and now you just have to live your life.*

*Sincerely,*

*Delia*

*PS: Mama says one more thing. She does not want to ever see you again, but you can continue to write to her if you want to.*

*Chapter 15*

# VERNICE

It wasn't just me; everyone was in love. This may just be the condition of being a very young woman confined in a dormitory. The girls who lived across the hall were smitten with a pair of brothers and were planning a double wedding, even though only one of them had even said as much as boo. But love, I learned, was the responsibility of the one doing the loving. The other person didn't necessarily have to make a contribution to the stew. Marylinda, of course, was in love with changing the world, and also Desmond, a reverend-in-training who studied at ITC—the seminary a mile down the road. He called himself a "Philadelphia Negro" because there was a famous book by that name, but he was from Delaware. Most people avoided him because he could hem you up in a corner at a party and not let you go until you agreed that Jesus was really a Negro. Whenever Joette saw him coming, she covered her ears and said, "Lamb's wool!"

He sometimes tipped an imaginary hat and said, "Mademoiselle Mouse."

By then, I had stopped fighting the nickname and all its variations. "Hey, Desmond."

"You are welcome to join the Movement at any time," he reminded me.

"I'll pray on it," I said, because that usually is enough for religious types.

"Just don't pray to no blond-headed Jesus. You don't want it delivered to the wrong box."

"Lamb's wool," I said.

"Amen, sister. Amen."

Being inside the joke marked my transformation into a coed. I was a caterpillar halfway to being a butterfly. Not yet magnificent, but way better than the worm I had been. It wasn't just the classes where I studied Victorian literature, or what Miss Jemison called "exposure," which included dealing gin rummy with daughters of doctors, watching plays by Langston Hughes, and raising my alto voice in the glee club. Of course, these experiences changed me. For one, I learned that there were so many words that I was pronouncing all wrong. I practiced them while I soaped myself in the shower. "Ambulance." Am-bu-lance. Libra-ry. Nobody could say that I wasn't a quick study.

All the new manners and ideas altered the way I *appeared.* But my feelings for Joette changed the way I *was.* My connection to her made me vulnerable to art, music, and beauty in general. Miss Jemison had tried to teach me the exact same sonnets by the exact same Shakespeare—some of them I'd even memorized. But how can someone appreciate "my love is a fever" until they have burned themselves?

Young love is not unprecedented. But closed in room 347, we touched each other like we invented fornication. In the night, we spoke to each other like we invented language.

This was all new to me, but Joette had been here before, when she had been a freshman herself. The girl had been heavyset, friendly, and hailing from some state where I didn't even know there were colored people. Nebraska, maybe. I didn't like to think much about her. I told Joette I didn't even want to know her name, teasing in the way that you do when you aren't joking at all.

"So, you just get tangled up with whoever they put you in a room with?"

Joette said, "No. No. No. She wasn't like you, Country Mouse. And it wasn't like this."

I didn't press her to say exactly what she meant by "like this." I was afraid that she might claim to love me, and I was afraid that she might not.

"Her mother pulled her out of school before Christmas recess," Joette explained. "She was in the habit of writing everything in her diary. The story on the street was that she didn't come back over money, but I think someone read what she wrote about us."

"I don't keep a diary," I said. "And I don't have anybody back home who would care, even if I had one." This wasn't a lie. Annie would have been interested, but she wasn't back home. I wondered what she would have to say about this impossible love affair. She had been free with that news that she and Bobo were shacking up. She set the words on paper trusting that I'd share in her happiness.

"I don't mean to scare you," Joette said into my silence. "Just be careful. You never know who can hurt you once they know how you are."

"This isn't 'how I am,'" I said.

"You know what I mean," Joette said.

"This can't go on forever," I said.

"Says who?" Joette said, making her voice lead lined. "Look at your aunties. The second they walked in the room, I knew what was what."

I didn't answer, but there were things that even I, the country mouse, understood. I didn't come all the way here to return back to Honeysuckle like Miss Jemison, to be some kind of small-town eccentric.

"Anyway," I said, "don't you want a family, Joette?"

"Naw," she said. "I don't want babies. And as we both know, there's only one way to get one. You been here six months and you haven't made a move in that direction."

"But that's because—" I started, but I couldn't bring myself to say the obvious.

"Exactly," she said. "Because you don't want to."

"But I'm going to," I said.

Joette pushed me away from her and I missed the heat of her body. "You a lie," she said.

---

Sisters Chapel, built in 1927, was the center of the campus. Joette let me know that it wasn't named for us, the sisters who attended the school, but the Rockefeller sisters—the wife and sister-in-law of John D. "Spelman was his wife's maiden name," she said with that contemptuous eye-roll that I had somehow come to love.

"Stop being so negative," I said. "It might have been named for two white ladies, but it belongs to us now."

"You got your hook and line," said Joette. "All you need is the sinker."

Joette couldn't understand the pleasure of belonging that I got from the Spelman sisterhood. She longed for the freedom of being an outsider, but only people who have never been shut out think this is how it works.

On April 11, we celebrated the origins of Spelman College. In 1881, the Civil War was just over and these two white ladies from New England had the idea to educate the women who had just been freed. The land we slept on every night had been the barracks for the Union soldiers. As Joette and I stood shoulder to shoulder waiting to climb the steps, I looked at the broad magnolia beside Reynolds Cottage, where the president lived. It was likely older than Spelman itself.

"It wasn't that long ago," I said to Joette.

She turned to me, ready to give her commentary, but the alumnae were heading our way. These were women who had graduated in the years prior. Alumnae, pronounced "alum-nee," like on your leg, not "alumni," like on your face. If you accidentally got it wrong, you were invited to go enroll where they had alumni—Clark College or Morris Brown, where men and women went to school side by side. Although coed education was the norm, the proposition seemed vulgar, like mixed restrooms.

Many alumnae, like Miss Jemison, had labored to earn their place in this league. They had made beds they never slept in, cooked meals they were not permitted to eat, diapered babies they fake-loved, and touched men they did not desire. Some had even sat in jail cells, accused of stealing silver ladles or imaginary heirlooms—all while taking one or two classes a year with their eyes on one day becoming teachers, nurses, secretaries, and of course wives who held babies with fingers purified by bands of gold. Of course, this struggle was behind them now. In their white dresses, hosiery, and black shoes, no one could distinguish them from the ones whose daddies had paid their fees, those whose mothers had soft feet.

These well-dressed women were who we would become in just a few years' time, cured in this kiln of respectability. We were beautiful, we knew, lined up before the chapel door. Our bleached dresses highlighted our coloring. Even Marylinda, pale as a dogwood blossom, glowed in white. I felt resourceful in clothes created by my own hand. My chin was high as the alumnae appraised us, sometimes pinching our legs to be sure we wore stockings.

The woman who discovered Joette's bare legs knew her by name.

"Joette Cunningham, why are you so ornery?"

"I'm not onery. I'm just bare-legged, Mrs. McHenry. It's too hot for hose and I'm too dark for 'suntan.'"

Mrs. McHenry sighed. "Please go to your room and dress appropriately. You know your mother is here."

Joette didn't make a move toward the dorm and the lady didn't try to make her. Instead, she bent and pinched my nylons. "Very good," she said.

I felt myself smiling under her approval. "Thank you."

Mrs. McHenry wanted to know where I was from.

"Honeysuckle, Louisiana," I said.

She clasped her hands in front of her face and beamed. "Did Raynelle Jemison teach you? She was a few years ahead of me. Did she refer you to Spelman?"

"Her and my aunt that raised me," I said.

"She and your aunt," she said, gently tweaking my grammar. "And we raise potatoes, while we rear children."

Joette rolled her eyes so hard that she could have permanently damaged her eyesight, but I found it all to be very charming.

When Mrs. McHenry moved on to inspect the other girls in line, Joette said, "You better be careful. She's searching for a wife for her crippled son."

She laughed and I did, too. Because you can't know what you don't know.

*Chapter 16*

# ANNIE

Spring had just sprung when Babydoll spotted a little hole-in-the-wall bar called the Elektra. There was a sign in the window that said, GIRL WANTED. We had passed the storefront with its painted-over windows I don't know how many times as we walked to the bus stop on our way to Firestone, where we worked with lampblack all day and came home so dirty that we stained the sheets, even after our baths. The fellows found jobs at Memphis Furniture, but they quit because they didn't want to make billy clubs for the cops. After that, they went over to Federal Compress, but Clyde couldn't take being around so much cotton and Bobo couldn't take the heat. Finally, Bobo got hired on at the Peabody hotel. It was a weird job that involved ordinary bellman work but also caring for the flock of mallard ducks that swam in the lobby fountain. For his part, Clyde made money here and there being a catch-as-you-can kind of person. Also, he was talented at poker, especially five-card stud.

When Babydoll saw that sign, she said, "Here go our new life." I pointed out that the sign said they needed a girl, not two. And she said don't worry about it, and ducked around the corner to tie off her blouse at her navel and plump up her bosom. "Come on," she said.

I didn't bother tying or plumping anything, because I am realistic.

The owner, Mr. Wilson, had a whole different mentality from Mr. Daniel. They both separated the world into hardlegs and softlegs, but where Mr. Daniel saw softlegs as trouble looking for somewhere to happen, Mr. Wilson saw Babydoll as a bag of cash money tied up with a silver string. After she told him her name, he said on the spot that she was hired. "Only thing better than a thick girl named Sweet Thing is one they call Babydoll," he said. "You get half of whatever tips you wheedle out of these drunk bastards. You got any friends?" She did, and that was me. He frowned at my flat behind. "You got any more friends?"

When Babydoll told him we were a package deal, I was touched. While she handed out drinks, I ran around with a mop.

It could have been worse. Hell, it had just recently been worse. Lampblack could have you hacking up blood like a coal miner. The colored restrooms were so disgusting that Clyde speculated that they must have hired someone to piss on the floors at night.

This is not to say that I enjoyed being a glorified janitor, but even when a girl got too far into her Cuba Libres and ended up puking in the sink, cleaning up behind her felt almost like a family affair. Besides, even though it wasn't Beale Street, the Elektra was a happening place to be. There was live music on the weekends, and sometimes on Wednesdays, too. On Friday nights, especially, the place was hopping because some people can't resist drinking up their pay. Plus, men who can't help spending money attract women who enjoy helping them do it. I didn't say it out loud, but the Elektra was the kind of place where you might meet a woman like Hattie Lee.

It was a joyful time for Bobo and me. He had his day job at the Peabody hotel, but he had fallen in with a jazz quartet and they played for parties all over town. These events were whites-only, which was a drag, but anyone who has ever loved a music man knows he is happiest when he gets to play.

On these nights, he came home feeling like a bandit. It would be so late, it was early, so I made us a breakfast of sausage, grits, and eggs. "When I sit at that piano, they have to give me my respect because they know can't nobody do it like we do." Then his mood came down just a little bit. "But as soon as the last note is played . . ." He ended that sentence by dusting his hands together with a loud clap. "I get the hell out before what is honey on my tongue goes rancid on theirs."

His pleasure was contagious. I didn't even wash the dishes before we landed in bed, full of food and full of love.

*Chapter 17*

# VERNICE

Mrs. McHenry explained that they were good Uplift people, lifting as they climbed. They belonged to the NAACP and many other organizations that contained the words "National" and "Negro" or "Colored." The father held degrees from the Big Three. After Morehouse, he went to Howard and Meharry both. He signed his name *Richmond McHenry, JD, MD.* He named his law firm McHenry & McHenry even before his sons were born. The oldest boy turned his tassel at Morehouse, but after Meharry, he decided that being a doctor was plenty. The middle boy left the United States completely, calling himself a writer. The youngest one, Franklin, had been sickly as a child but was blessed with the quickest mind. With his Morehouse BS and JD from North Carolina Central, he was the second McHenry on his father's shingle.

With her up-to-the-moment fashion and trim figure, Mrs. McHenry was an ideal wife for a doctor-lawyer. She was attractive, but not so much that it made her husband seem impractical. Her three kids proved that she was serious about motherhood, but she didn't have so many that you wondered if she thought she was living on a farm. When she opened her mouth, the perfect words floated out. Obviously, the immaculate grammar had come from somewhere, yet she didn't flaunt her education. She invited me to her home for tea with a smile that said, *Dear, this is how it is done.*

---

Her youngest son, Franklin, came to collect me at the ornate gate at the front of the campus. A magnificent magnolia tree, known as the Sojourner, dropped a heavy cone bursting with ruby seeds. It grazed my shoulder and I caught it as it tumbled toward the sidewalk. As I turned the spiky cone in my palm, it seemed significant. Each seed, jewel red, nestled in its own nook, tethered by a delicate cord.

Seeing the finned sedan idling on the curb, I let the cone fall. Franklin hopped out of the green Buick to open my door. As he hurried, I noticed the limp. Joette had exaggerated when she described him as "crippled." But she was a girl with money who resented people with money. I was a girl without money who wondered what it was like to have comforts that you didn't even know you wanted.

"Call me Frank," he said.

"People call me Niecy," I said. "Short for Vernice. Or you can say Mouse. That's my other nickname."

He frowned. "Maybe we should stick to our given names."

"All right, Mr. Franklin," I said.

He sighed. "Please don't be so formal."

I didn't respond right away.

"Let's talk like we're friends."

"I like to be called Niecy."

"Then Niecy it is."

We drove down Hunter Street, passing the library and Booker T. Washington High School. He tipped his head when we passed Mozley Park. "We used to live up that way."

"I'm not from Atlanta," I said. "I don't know what it means to live over here or over there."

"Fair enough," he said.

The McHenrys lived on Veltre Circle, "in enemy territory," Mrs. McHenry quipped with a trill of satisfied laughter. They were only the third Negro family to purchase a home in Cascade Heights.

"There are rumblings about them putting up a barricade to keep anybody else from moving in," she explained, slicing vegetables for our lunch. "Like a little piece of wall can stop the march of justice." She popped a juicy wheel of cucumber into her mouth. "The day we arrived, you should have seen us. My sons were unimpeachable, I tell you. You could cut yourself, they were so sharp! As the movers unloaded our furniture, those white folks almost passed out. When my Chippendale couch came off that van, they knew that a new day had dawned."

She laughed so hard, she nearly choked. "I don't know why I like that part so much. My husband says I'm obnoxious, but he loves it."

She untied her apron and fastened her surprisingly large hands around a pair of oblong plates—trimmed in the color I now knew was Spelman blue. In the corner of each was a depression to accommodate a short tumbler. She set them on a brass tray and pointed with her head. "Let's go to the sunroom."

I followed her as though I knew what a sunroom was. Turns out, it was just like it sounded—a lovely windowed space, ecru with soft gray trim. We situated ourselves at a wrought iron table, perfectly sized for a lunch of tiny sandwiches and tea.

"This is the most important piece of advice I can give you."

I leaned in.

"When you get married, make sure there is a place in the house that belongs to you. And I am not talking about the kitchen."

I nodded and wished I had brought a notebook.

"I like you," said Mrs. McHenry. "From the instant I saw you in the chapel line, you reminded me of myself. I am from a town in Alabama called Sunflower. You have never heard of it, have you?"

"No, ma'am."

"Consider yourself blessed." She laughed once more, but it wasn't as tinkly. "I made it to Spelman College by hook and by crook. My daddy chopped cotton, and my mother took care of the Mowad family.

"Mama took me to Mrs. Mowad's bedside on my graduation day. The old woman wore a fresh gown, but I could smell decay. She took my hand, saying I was smart, how proud she was, all of that. Finally, she said she wanted to help me because she loved my mother so much.

"Child! I knew her checkbook was right there in the nightstand. When she asked Mama to get her a pen, my face was on fire!"

Riding the wave of her storytelling, I was on the actual edge of my seat. One little tip to the left or to the right, and I'd have landed on the carpet. I hoped to one day be a woman like Mrs. McHenry, effortlessly keeping the room rapt while serving tiny cakes and sandwiches.

"Did your mother do domestic work?" she asked me.

I shook my head. "No, ma'am. My mother passed when I was a baby."

"Ah," she said. "My condolences."

To ease the awkward silence, she helped herself to a triangle sandwich of chicken salad. She nodded approval at her own handiwork as she chewed, then she selected another. Egg salad, this time.

"Are you not hungry?" she asked. "Don't be shy."

"Yes'm," I said. I picked one of the round sandwiches, curious about the dark-colored bread. The flavor was almost spicy.

"Rye," she explained. "My husband travels."

Once I had eaten enough so as not to offend her hospitality, she refilled our glasses from a painted glass pitcher.

"So, who reared you?" she said. "Someone had to teach you these lovely manners."

I smiled like babies do when you kiss them. "My aunt took me in."

"Did she work as a domestic?"

I frowned, a little offended.

"Did she clean homes? Don't be ashamed. I only want to get to know you a little better."

"Aunt Irene did housework. But not overnight."

"Well, that's a small grace. It's not easy being a child when your mother is tending to another family all day. It's among my theories that this has created a wound for our people. Our mothers were stolen from us. Someone should write a book about it."

Again, I itched for a pen. I wanted to remember everything about this day, and I wanted to tell Annie. What if we had been so carelessly raised because her granny and my aunt were just too exhausted to dote on us? What if it turned out that it wasn't personal after all?

"Forgive me," Mrs. McHenry said. "I got off topic. Where was I?"

"The lady was about to write you a check," I said.

She leaned forward and let out a harsh cackle. "I'm laughing now, but it wasn't even a little bit funny at the time. That lady didn't take a checkbook out of that drawer. Instead, she came up with a notepad and she wrote down a name and address. 'My dear cousin Shirley lives in Atlanta and they need a girl three days a week.' "

In the way of born storytellers, she paused to let it sink in before offering the moral of the story. "That's why I don't have a maid in this house. I don't want anyone making beds or fixing breakfast for my children. Any food that goes in their mouth was prepared by my hands."

Reaching for a cloth napkin, she asked, "Do you have a job?"

"Yes, ma'am," I said. "I help in the library on Wednesdays and Tuesdays."

"Who is your boss? Willard Riley?"

I nodded and cast my eyes to my plate.

She said, "I'll talk to him. When I tell him you are part of my family, he won't keep chasing you around the stacks."

I was so startled that I spilled the honeyed tea on my skirt. How did Mrs. McHenry know about the times that Mr. Riley trapped me in the corner, pressing his hard hips against me, pleading for "a little trim"? "He's terrible."

"Indeed," said Mrs. McHenry. Then she smiled like she was glad she'd gotten that handled. "What else?"

"What else?"

"What else do you need?"

I shrugged because I didn't even know how to approach such a question. What did I need? Money, of course. Most everyone would be better off with a bit of spending change. Aunt Irene sent me two dollars every few weeks, but I dreamed of being the one sending money to her.

"My aunt up north provides for me."

She clucked her tongue and bounced her left leg. "Good woman. You have to admire the resilience of colored ladies."

She picked up a wedge of lemon, squeezed the juice into her glass, and stirred the ice with her finger. "Look at me. Just talking, talking, talking. It's your turn. What do you want me to know about you?"

I was stumped. I don't think anyone had ever, point-blank, just asked me about myself. "You already know I come from Honeysuckle," I said. "I already told you about Aunt Irene . . ."

"Begin with your mother," she said. "How did she come to die so young?"

"My daddy killed her," I said. "Then he killed himself." After the words came several heavy breaths as I recovered from the sheer exertion of telling the truth. As I filled my lungs and cleared them, Mrs. McHenry watched me, bobbing her head in staccato nods.

"Candor is a virtue," she said to me. "I like you more now than I did even an hour ago."

After we finished our sandwiches and the tumblers were empty, Mrs. McHenry poured what she called a "spot" of sherry. Then she offered a "splash" of whiskey. After that was just a "swallow" of limoncello brought back from Italy.

"Are you enjoying yourself here in my home? Do you want to continue chatting?"

"Yes, ma'am."

"Because I have so many questions," she said. "I am intrigued by you! How many children?" she asked me, her breath citrussy and hot.

"I'm an only child," I said. "Remember?"

"No," she said. "How many children are you willing to mother?"

"I want a boy and a girl." The answer came quickly, as I had been rehearsing it all my life. If you had asked me when I was just a kindergartener, I would have said the same thing.

"Just the two?"

"Well, I could go up to three," I said.

"Shoot for two. Everyone always ends up with one more child than they were counting on. That's just the law of nature. My baby boy, Franklin—he was determined to get here. Precautions be damned."

"Mr. Franklin, he seems like a nice man."

"Don't 'mister' him. He's thirty-one. Barely more than ten years ahead of you. Trust me. You want a husband that is a little bit older. My husband is seventeen years my senior. One day I will tell you that whole story. Don't listen to a word that Joette Cunningham tells you."

The mention of her name gave me a jolt.

"We're close," I said.

"Oh, I know," Mrs. McHenry said. "I know everything."

My lunch flipped in my stomach. "Ma'am?"

"Joette's aunt was my friend in school. She frowned on me because I was from the country, and she was envious of me because I was clever. And when I was the one to marry a McHenry, she was fit to be tied. Me, ending up with all of this!" She laughed and clapped like a drunk seal. "My husband says I am obnoxious, but he loves it."

"Joette is nice," I said.

"That's fine," she said. "I'm just telling you not to believe what she tells you about my family. It's all lies."

"Joette doesn't lie," I said.

"She might not be a liar, but she comes from a lying lineage, so anything Joette thinks she knows, well, it's a lie. You don't have to be a liar, per se, to lie."

Once we were done with our meal, we gathered our plates and returned to the kitchen. I washed the snack sets with a soapy sponge. Mrs. McHenry rinsed the delicate plates in a basin of cold water.

She smiled a loving smile. "Franklin will drive you home. He's a good man. He will give you a good life."

"I—I don't even know him," I said with a stutter.

"But I do," she said. "And listen. I know that with your background you may be apprehensive about men. But I can promise you this: my son will not kill you."

That promise unfolded its petals inside of me. Her words assuaged a fear I hadn't even known I was harboring until she chased it away.

"I love you, darling," she said. "I know you will think it odd, but I am a woman who expresses herself. The Lord did not see fit to bless me with a daughter. But he has brought us together now. Scripture says, 'But let him ask in faith, nothing wavering.' "

She took my hands, warm and sudsy, and plunged them into the cool rinsing basin.

"Do you feel it?" she asked.

"Yes, ma'am, I do."

*Chapter 18*

# ANNIE

By the time December rolled around and the Elektra was decked out with foil tinsel and popcorn garland, I was seeing Hattie Lee everywhere. Every morning, I consulted the creased photo in my wallet. I studied her sweet face, identifying the things that don't change over time—thick eyebrows, broad nose, slender neck. The photo was black and white, but her skin tone looked about the same as mine and Granny's. It wasn't much to go on, but I believed that blood called to blood.

The first time it happened, I was busy with my mop, sopping up a spilled splash of beer. A man wearing velvet trousers was making the case that the bartender should replace the wasted pint, free of charge. At the Elektra, people believe that nothing beats failure but a try. If the skinny young guy was pouring, he might have gone ahead and filled the empty mug. But on this particular evening, Mr. Wilson himself was presiding and any free booze came out of his bottom line. The man was tight as a skeeter's teeter. If I filled the peanut bowls too high, he grabbed a few off the top and shoved them in his pockets before threatening to sock my little paycheck.

As I mopped up the mess, Velvet Trousers whined, "Come on, man. Wasn't my fault." He pointed at a woman coming out of the bathroom stalls. "She knocked my beer over with her elbow. I was only half done."

"Well," said Mr. Wilson, "you best ask her to replace it."

The woman, wearing a pink minidress with a red stripe, slid her shapely hips onto the bar stool, as if she had no idea what the men were squabbling about. With a shrug, she smiled in my direction.

My blood knocked in the side of my neck. She was the same brown as me and her eyebrows were downright luscious. And that neck—long and fragile, like the stem on a coneflower. Inching forward with my mop, I managed to get so close that I could smell the sweet oil in her pressed hair. It was the aroma of home.

"Are you Hattie Lee?" My voice caused her to spill what was left of her whiskey sour. She twisted in my direction, and we butted heads so hard that we both cried out. My fingers went to my forehead, and hers did the same. It was like looking in a mirror.

"What the hell is wrong with you?" She used four polished nails to put some air between us.

"Aren't you Hattie Lee? I'm Annie. I'm Annie Kay!"

Her face said that as far as she was concerned, I was Boo Boo the Fool.

"You made me waste my drink," she snapped. "Somebody owes me another whiskey sour."

Mr. Wilson had watched the whole thing with annoyed concern. He kept his eyes on me as he mixed her replacement, but only half strength.

The anger in her voice shamed me as the annoyance on my boss's face sent me scurrying out the back door to rinse and wring the mop. I wet and squeezed that mop so many times that the water streaming over the concrete was clear as window glass. I would have stayed out there all night if Babydoll hadn't come out back to get some air.

She made a face like a jack-o'-lantern.

"What's wrong?" I asked her.

"Why do you reckon Clyde hasn't married me yet?"

I shrugged, assuming that she was in a better position to know this than me. "Some men don't like to be tied down."

"But he don't have any trouble doing the tying. Meanwhile, he got me out here without a ring on my hand. It's like I'm in the lion's den with T-bone drawers on." She showed me her knuckle, red and angry. "I poured ammonia on it because this fool in the back licked his tongue up and down my hand talking about he can taste metal if a woman has been wearing a ring."

"What?"

She fisted her hair and pulled at it. "I told him I was married so he would go away. But instead, he put my finger in his mouth! I hate this job and if he don't shit or get off the pot, I am going to start hating Clyde, too."

Babydoll slid three fingers into her pocket and produced a stick of gum and a butter mint. She unwrapped the Wrigley's and folded it in two before adding it to the wad already in her mouth. I accepted the butter mint; the creamy sweetness took me back to my life in Honeysuckle. I wondered what my granny was up to now that she had the A-frame house all to herself.

"You looking a little peaky yourself," she said.

"I just got mixed up," I told her. "From the side, that lady in the pink, she looked just like Hattie Lee. I was excited is all. She reported me to Mr. Wilson."

"You might be losing it," Babydoll said, the same way she might say, *You might be catching a cold.* "The same thing happened to my mother when she thought that my daddy might come back."

---

When I got up to our rooms, Bobo was waiting on me, since he didn't have a piano gig that night. He pouted, as he did when there was nobody to listen to his music. I had tried to convince Mr. Wilson to let him perform at the Elektra from time to time, but Mr. Wilson had been in the nightclub business too long. "I don't like none of that boyfriend-girlfriend stuff on my payroll.

Next thing you know, somebody ends up getting shot, and after that, this whole place will end up shut down."

Bobo's eyes were heavy, like he had been catching a little rest but trying to stay awake for me. I was exhausted and rattled at the same time. What if the lady in the pink lipstick really was Hattie Lee? I was wrong to just throw myself at her like that. Of course she denied it. In the movies, it's exciting for truths to be revealed in public, but it would have been more fitting for me to introduce myself in private. I tried to give myself some grace. When I took into account how long I had been searching, it was only natural that I was a little less than ladylike.

"I'm embarrassed," I said to Bobo. "I made a fool of myself."

After he heard the whole story, he looked puzzled. "Tell me again from the beginning."

I did, but the details didn't clear it up for him. "Now, why did you think she was Hattie Lee? Her eyebrows?"

I pulled out some cold cuts and cut slits in the bologna so it would stay flat when I fried it. I cooked enough for the both of us, even though I didn't appreciate his tone. "I can't put it into words," I said.

"There are words for everything," he said. "If you want to express yourself badly enough."

I guess I didn't really want to talk about it, because my tongue sat heavy and still in my mouth.

Bobo, as always, had big thoughts and all the words to share them with.

"I despise my job," he said. "I'm considering severance."

I made like I was pondering, but the choice was clear when the options were paying the rent and getting kicked out. Besides, he had the softest gig out of all of us.

"Nobody likes their job, Bobo. That's why they pay you—because they know otherwise you wouldn't come. If you liked it, if you wanted to be there—well, then you would have to pay them, and call it a vacation."

I chuckled, pleased with my own way with words.

"You're right, you're right," Bobo said as I slid him a sandwich on a chipped plate. "I'm just tired."

As I changed into my nightclothes, he said, "In the daytime I dress up like an organ grinder's monkey and shuck and jive with a half dozen ducks that eat better than we do! Then at night I'm twisting the blues into Rat Pack. Sometimes I just want to go on back to Louisiana and work at Standard Oil. At least then I could bring money home to my parents."

Kneading my tight shoulders, he told me that the Peabody hired colored women who sat on gilded benches all day in the ladies' room, handing out linen towels and peppermints. By almost any measure, it was a better job than the one I had now. The wage was a smidge higher, the hours more civilized, and I could eat lunch on the roof with Bobo. He said he could put in a word. "You could be a sunray for me," he whispered into the nape of my neck.

When I said I would think about it, he sighed.

"It's okay, Annie. I'm just being selfish."

"No," I said. "I would love to work alongside you, carrying our lunches in the same paper sack. It's just . . ."

The sentence, incomplete, hung in the air as I stroked his narrow back.

"You come work at the Peabody," he urged, "you won't have to worry about drunk men taking liberties. When I run into Babydoll after work, I swear I can see fingerprints all up and down her thighs."

I tangled my legs around Bobo and pressed my lips to his neck. "That's why I can't leave Babydoll at the Elektra by herself. It ain't safe, you know."

But the truth of the matter was that Hattie Lee could have been almost anywhere in Memphis, but one place that I knew she wasn't was the Peabody hotel. Even if I had been chasing a wild goose tonight, the next woman with sad eyes and a taste for brown liquor could be the one I had been waiting for.

"I hear you," Bobo said. "I'm just being greedy. The only

thing that loves company more than misery? A bluesman working a day job." He tried to laugh, but what came out was a groan. "You get what I'm saying?"

As we moved in the private dark, I took comfort in knowing that I shared my bed with a very good man.

*Chapter 19*

# VERNICE

Sundays became what Mrs. McHenry called a "standing engagement." I attended the 11 a.m. service at Friendship with the entire family, and then we repaired to Veltre Circle for dinner and fellowship. Each time, Mrs. McHenry kept me a little longer after the meal, as though she couldn't bear to relinquish my company. It was only a matter of time before I missed curfew. Nibbling on a French macaron, I yelped at the angle of the hands on the kitchen clock. Franklin pulled the car around faster than you could say "expelled." I hopped in the passenger side before he could make it around to open my door. His mother, loopy from her sherry, shouted, "Charge!"

Even though he drove at a brisk pace, it was clear I'd be a good fifteen minutes late. My nervous fingers tatted on the half-open window.

"You won't be punished for what isn't your fault," he said.

My mind went to my mother, as it did so often. In what universe did he live where punishment was only meted out to the guilty? And then my mind went to his mother's promise. Franklin didn't seem the type to kill anyone. But had my father? Once everything was done, a couple of folks swore they smelled it coming, but had they? Or had he seemed to be an ordinary man with average anger and mundane expectations? Certainly, if he had behaved like a murderer, they wouldn't have let him live in the house with someone as young and vulnerable as Arletha. But even those who claimed to have been surprised—and these were those close enough that they could have intervened—even they didn't say that he seemed like he *couldn't* kill his wife. They just said that he seemed like he *wouldn't.*

"Girls get expelled for missing curfew," I told Franklin.

"But not you," he said. "I'll tell your dorm mother you were with me."

We idled at a red light that I wished he would run. "Telling them I was with a man will not help."

Franklin smiled a lazy smile. "Progress," he said. "At least now I got you to admit that I am a man."

Before the light changed, he reached over and stroked my cheek. "I am prepared to wait. That is my primary virtue, that I understand the value of patience. When I was a boy, I more or less lived in hospitals. Polio, as I am sure you have heard."

I nodded. "Yes, sir."

"Don't 'sir' me," he said. "I am indeed a man, but I am not your sir."

As we sailed down through the Atlanta streets, it saddened me to think of how little of the city I had seen at sunset. I cranked down the window to feel the darkening air. I opened my mouth just a little to taste it. While my head was turned, Franklin took my hand and pressed it to his lips.

When we arrived at the formidable gate of Spelman College he said, "Vernice, do you think there is the potential for love?"

Flabbergasted, I moved my lips but was silent as a fish.

"Potential, is all I am asking for. I know you likely have fellows coming around."

"No fellows," I said too quickly.

But he ignored me. "Fellows are natural. It would be wrong if you didn't. But I want you to consider me, too."

He made a move to leave the car. "When I come around to open your door, go ahead and stare. Watch how I drag my left leg. But when you take me in with your pretty eyes, think about me not as the crippled McHenry. Remember that I survived the iron lung and taught myself how to breathe again. Never forget that I am the one that the devil tried to snatch."

As he walked around the Buick, I did as he said and filled my eyes with the sight of him. His strong right leg led every step as the left leg let the rest of his body pull it along. He rolled his lips together, uncomfortable under my gaze, but he let me watch. I don't know that I had ever gawked at a man, assessed his body, his gait. The journey from the driver's seat to where I sat was a show, as the golden glow of the headlights turned the road into a stage. Franklin didn't hurry. He dragged his left leg and held his head high to greet the rising moon.

He opened the door and offered his hand. I took it and he assisted me with a gentle competence that I would come to love. Once I was on my feet and my skirt smoothed, he surprised me by circling my waist with his strong forearm. Some instinct guided my arms to rest on his shoulders.

I have never thought of myself as a delicate person. My mother was as slight as a promise. In photos she looks like she stands only by some miracle of physics or maybe God's grace. Perhaps it's just because I knew what I know, but I could look at her and know she wouldn't survive this man's world. I was built to last. Skinny but strong, like a pole made of steel. I took after my father's people, if only in body. I never once in my life had to pick cotton, but if it had come to that, I am sure that I could have.

When Franklin closed the space between us with the strength of his body, it wasn't by force. I didn't resist. There wasn't time, nor was there inclination. But the energy and the power belonged to him and he displayed it the way other men display their wallets.

"It has been a pleasure, Miss Niecy," he said, releasing me as abruptly as he grabbed me.

"Likewise," I said, embarrassed at how much breath there was in my voice.

He opened his jacket; from the inside pocket he produced a card that displayed his full name in calligraphy. *William Franklin McHenry, Esq.*

"Give it to your dorm mother in case there is friction."

The card was heavy, as though it were made of cast iron rather than rich card stock.

"Goodbye," I said over my shoulder as I crossed the gate back into campus. I could feel him watching me, just as I had watched him. It was not the first time I had felt a man's eye-heat. Even cloistered at Spelman, there were men around—gardeners, janitors, guardsmen. And of course, there was the slimy librarian. Monsieur Johnson, who taught French, wasn't much better but he constrained his lust to stares and wet lips.

Franklin watched me, but he saw me, too. Nothing escaped his attention. A man who had faced down the devil could sense what his eyes could not. I walked across the grassy oval feeling delivered like Daniel. As I passed the dogwood tree, I pressed a palm to her knotty bark. "Tell me what to do." I spoke the words aloud into the branches. "Please ask my mother to visit my dreams."

Under the portico, I gripped Franklin's business card, ready to wield its power, but somehow the heavy oak door was unlocked and the lobby empty, but for Joette.

"I was worried," she said. "It's after curfew. You could get expelled and end up on the next bus back to Loo-zee-ana." There was a meanness in her voice I had never heard before. My desire was to take her hand and hold it to my busy chest, but we were walking down the buzzy hallway. Girls wearing pajamas asked, "Where you been, Miss Lady? What have you been up to?"

"Nothing," I said.

"Oh, that's what they call it these days."

The laughter was good-natured, maybe even relieved. On more than one occasion, I had helped my classmates climb into and out of Marylinda's window on the ground floor, after which they exchanged their warm bodies for the cold pile of pillows that was meant to impersonate them while they were out—mostly with men, but sometimes doing virtuous work with the Movement. But mostly with men. Sometimes Movement work with Movement men.

"You already know Jesus loves you," said a girl from Detroit who was spared expulsion because her daddy was a big-time numbers man who paid four years of tuition, room, and board in a single cash payment. "But now you know He also *likes* you. The dorm mother is running the streets herself; the door is open because she didn't want to lock herself out."

"Even the righteous shake a tail feather," piped in her roommate. "They calculate it by the moon, like Easter. Nice girl's night out is a different day every year."

"Don't lay down," said Detroit. "You need to keep yourself upright for two hours. Word to the wise. Let gravity be your friend."

Joette said, "Don't be so stupid. First, that's not what she was doing, and second, that's not even how the body works."

"Ooh," said the roommate. "Somebody jealous!" More laughter. "You could get some action, Joette, if you gave our Morehouse brothers a chance. Let somebody put a smile on your face."

I delighted in the attention and whistles as we made our way to the end of the hall.

Back in our angular room, Joette shut the door gently, as though she were not furious. She pressed herself against it, her body a barricade.

"Mercy, Vernice," she said. "He marked you like a dog. That's why everyone is hooting and hollering. They can smell that man on you."

"Joette," I said, "I don't know why you even waste your air talking nonsense."

As she prepared the room for sleep, I gathered my toiletries and removed my clothes. As I unhooked my nubbly robe from the hanger, I felt eyes on me for the second time in the last hour. Franklin had watched me with curiosity and with wonder. His imagination did most of the lifting. But Joette knew this body like you know your favorite song. If my body was the record, her gaze was the needle that made it sing. I faced her before I belted the robe closed.

"See? No marks."

She shifted her attention from her work of bringing our two

narrow beds together. The metal feet of the bed glided on felt pads. She clucked her tongue. "You just like having people look at you."

Chastened, I tied my robe and mumbled a sort of apology.

"What are you sorry for?" Joette asked as she arranged the blankets, smoothing the satin trim near the pillow.

I sat on the bed, which sank soundlessly on its oiled springs. She sat next to me and nuzzled my shoulder. "What did you do?"

"I didn't *do* anything."

I took deep breaths to keep my body supple and relaxed under her relieved caresses.

For the first time in the half year we had been lovers, I felt like the wise one who could somehow see around corners. Sure, Joette had seen the world, but it was as though she didn't understand basic tenets of reality. She had such contempt for the McHenrys but she was more like them than she would have liked to believe. She was naïve, like Franklin promising me that I wouldn't be punished.

Joette divided my hair in two, pressing her face into the part. Her breath was warm upon my neck. "I was terrified you would come back engaged."

I said to Joette, "I have to marry somebody. We both do."

She didn't reply with words. Instead, she encircled me with her familiar arm.

## *Chapter 20*

# ANNIE

*Dear Niecy,*

*Friend, start from the beginning! You have not one boyfriend, but TWO. Two? Like 1 plus 1? Like you have one man and another one? When I read your letter, I almost choked on the pralines that Granny sent me. (I should ask her to send you some too.) You got sent to an all-girls school and found yourself more men than you know what to do with. When you went there, did you know that MOREHOUSE COLLEGE WAS RIGHT ACROSS THE STREET? I know your aunt is free-minded, but Granny would be UPSET if she sent me to what she thought was a nunnery, but it turned out to be a juke joint with books. But back to the matter at hand—*

*So, let me get this straight. Boyfriend #1 lights your fire. Welcome to the club of people who are burning up. I think that's why Granny and them always warned us against it because once you do it, you kind of want to do it all the time. Or at least at first. Me and Bobo are not as hot as we used to be, but it's plenty warm. I do, sometimes, wonder what is the next step for us, but we can talk about free milk and cows in the next letter. What I want to talk about is YOU.*

*So, Boyfriend #2 is a stand-up sort of person. A lawyer! Now, this doesn't happen every day. It seems, tho, that since you met #1 at college, he could become a lawyer in due time. So, I think he should get some points for potential. Plus, the fire-lighting. But I can also see what you mean about Boyfriend #2's nice family, especially his mother. Do you wonder why she is so much "welcome to the nest"? A lot of women are very snooty with girls that come after their sons. Did I ever tell you that Clyde's mother tried to fight Babydoll in their front yard? I wasn't there, but I have heard the story.*

*Bobo has not said word one about me meeting his mother. He was a change-of-life baby so his folks are up there in years, nearly as old as Granny. He talks about them and he says they know about me, but he hasn't said exactly what it is they know. I guess this pot might as well go do-si-do with the kettle because I haven't exactly dragged him to meet Granny. But that's not because I am shamed of him, it's that I am sort of shamed of myself because of living with him without even being engaged. If I was wearing a left-hand ring, we would run all over Honeysuckle, come Christmas!*

*But too much about me. Back to YOU, young lady. I am very snoopy as to why you are not calling any names. Are you worried that someone might be reading your mail? I know it can't be because you don't trust your old cradle friend. For one—who would I tell? I don't know these people. And for two—you know that I have never not once betrayed a single secret. So, in your next letter, just spit it out!*

*Love,*
*Annie Kay*

*Chapter 21*

# VERNICE

According to city hall, Atlanta was "too busy to hate." Maybe they didn't have time to hate—like in Birmingham—but they had enough time to dislike. Everything was separate, but nothing was equal. But that said, the colored sections in Atlanta were better than what they had set aside for white folks back home. In Honeysuckle, we had a movie house called the Delta Grand. Down on the first floor was whites only, with worn red carpet and velvet-covered seats that were supposed to snap into place when someone stood up like a soldier springing to attention. Half malfunctioned, marked off with common rope. The rest of us had to watch the show from the "crow's nest," which is what they called the balcony. And up there, there was no place to sit, even though we paid the same freight to get in. We didn't go often. Besides the obvious reasons, it was hot up there. But there's nothing quite like a good movie and two sticks of licorice.

Like everything else in Atlanta, the Fabulous Fox Theatre lived up to its name. Situated on the corner of Peachtree Street and Ponce de Leon Avenue, it sprawled the whole block like a rich man's girlfriend stretched out on a chaise. Later, I learned that

Fox Theatres were common as oak trees, anchoring downtowns all over the country, even in places as uninspiring as Hutchinson, Kansas. Somebody said that they even had one in Bunkie, Louisiana, but there is only so much I am willing to believe. I suppose it doesn't matter if the building wasn't "one of one," because it was singular to my mind.

When the *Atlanta Journal* mentioned it, they didn't say "movie theater," they said "Motion Picture Palace," and who could argue? The roof was sculpted into peaked domes à la *One Thousand and One Nights.* On the Peachtree side, the word FOX was positioned vertical and formed with what had to be a thousand red and gold lightbulbs. The electric bill alone must have been obscene. Inside was equally arresting. The arcade entrance boasted floral carpet stretched through the lobby, giving the impression of an enchanted prairie, at the center of which stood a circular concession stand dispensing popcorn, candy, and cold drinks. A good nine or ten people served behind the counter dressed in red vests that picked up the flower pattern from the carpet.

Not that we were allowed downstairs to set foot on the carpet or buy ourselves a high-end snack from the round counter. Whatever familiarity we had with the décor came courtesy of the press. Segregation was still the law of the land. The only concession for us was a porcelain fountain that offered water in a feeble arc.

Wearing his good camel-hair coat, Franklin spent his attorney money to buy our tickets at the colored box office. While other couples took the stairs to the crow's nest hand in hand, Franklin and I made the journey single file because he needed both the banister and his cane. Behind him, I was chatty and maybe a little too loud until we finally reached the keyhole doorway. Effort beaded his forehead, but he held the door for me like the gentleman he was.

Even the crow's nest was elegant. There were proper snap-up seats with sturdy rests for your arms. We ladies were okay up there, but if you had a tall boyfriend, like I did, he might hit his head on the ceiling. Despite all that, it was a lovely opportunity to wear fine clothes and hold hands in public. Once we got settled in our seats, we watched the movie in contentment, purposely forgetting the world down below us.

As we watched *Some Like it Hot,* Franklin's heavy fingers rested on mine. His thumb made slow circles below my knuckles. In the dark, I shot him a smile and he sent one back, lighting the space with the glint of his teeth.

At intermission, I stood to stretch my legs and peer over the balcony rail to catch a glimpse of how the other half lived. For the most part, they didn't turn their faces our way. I didn't blame them. If I were a white person enjoying a matinee, I wouldn't want to worry about the colored people in the attic. I would enjoy my popcorn and Hershey bar in stubborn obliviousness. Leaning so far over the rail that I could have fallen over, I tried to determine if the red flower pattern on the carpet was meant to be a poppy or a camellia.

As I squinted, my eyes landed on a burgundy fur collar. The man beside her was bald, but for a fringe above his ears and around the back of his head. Even from the balcony, I could see the strawberry birthmark I had heard so much about.

I beckoned to Franklin, and he raised himself from his chair and ambled over with his cane. With his shoulders hunched, so as not to bump his head, he followed my pointing with his eyes, worried.

"That's Marylinda," I said. "Joette's cousin."

Franklin squinted and clucked. "Good ol' Harold Freeman felt a little homesick."

Franklin led me back to my seat and took my hand again, but not with the slow, sexy thumb caress. This time, he spoke like he was addressing a child.

"You know her father is not truly colored?" Franklin said.

"Are you sure he's not creole?"

Franklin chuckled. "Now I see why they call you Country Mouse. That man is from Brooklyn, New York. And Freeman is not his real name. I forget what it used to be. I know there was a Z in there somewhere. Do you follow me?"

I did not.

"It's the greatest love story in all of Atlanta. But you didn't hear it from me."

I stood up again and peered at the back of Marylinda's head. Her black hair was tied tight so as not to reveal a hint of curl. The set of her shoulders had changed, a subtle shift in the body language, an accent of the spine. It was like the way you could tell the race of a person on the other end of the telephone line just from how they said hello. I couldn't explain it to anyone, but Marylinda sat in the chair just like a white girl.

"But she is the main one talking We Shall Overcome."

Franklin shrugged. "People are complicated. America is complicated."

I watched the rest of the picture without really taking it in. When the names of all the actors rolled across the screen, I hardly noticed. Franklin stood too quickly and tapped his head on the ceiling. As we left, he offered his arm to me, although between stooping and dragging his leg, he was unsteady. It took us several minutes to make it down the metal staircase while the white folks flooded through the ornate front doors. His fine car was parked on Spring Street, but I walked in the opposite direction. I wiggled away, knowing he would be hindered by his handicap and also his habit.

I scanned the faces of all of the white people, some of whom gave me a wide berth, others of whom pretended I wasn't there at all, knocking me with their shoulders. I knew I probably wouldn't find her. But had the odds been likely that I would spot her in the crowd at all? Certainly, she had considered the chances when she headed out with her father.

To her credit, Marylinda spotted me first, and yet she still spoke.

"Vernice," she said, calling my real name like we weren't friends.

The man beside her had a kind face, but it was definitely a white one. He smiled sheepishly and fingered the strawberry birthmark on the back of his head. "Nice to meet you."

I felt the eyes around us appraising the situation.

“This is my daddy,” she said.

Franklin, at last, made his way to me. “Hello, Harold.”

“Hey, Frank, brother man! How are your folks?” His voice was deeper than I anticipated and undeniably colored in the timbre of it.

Marylinda shrugged at me and said, “Daddy likes to go to the movies.”

“Nothing is wrong with a good time,” Franklin said.

With that, we parted ways. I didn’t look over my shoulder to see if Marylinda and her daddy turned back into white people once we were gone. On the way back to campus, Franklin laughed at my agitation.

“This is Atlanta, baby. I won’t say nobody is what they seem to be, but in this town, you got to double-check everyone and everything. You ever seen an old person bite a piece of jewelry to be sure it’s real? That’s how you have to do people around here. Just test them with your teeth.”

I wasn’t so country and out of it that I had never heard of passing. *Imitation of Life* had played at the Delta Grand; not even Aunt Irene could hold back a tear when the white-Black girl cried, *Mama mama mama.* But never in all my life had I heard of anybody passing backward.

Franklin laughed again. “You won’t see it twice,” he said. “I told you; he gave it all up for love. He got on that train at Penn Station and when they crossed the Mason-Dixon, he followed his lady to the Jim Crow car and never looked back.”

“Well, apparently he did some looking back this afternoon,” I said.

“Vernice,” Franklin said. “Everybody needs to take a break sometimes.”

Were his words in my ears when I spoke to Joette just three nights later?

“I need a break,” I told her as she began the evening ritual of joining our beds.

She paused, her cheeks clean of rouge and her lips shiny with Vaseline. “Come again?” she said.

"I just need a break. It's too much, all this back-and-forth. Franklin is my boyfriend now. And this . . ." I gestured to the two beds on gliders. "It doesn't seem right."

She sat on her bed and crossed her legs as though this was story time. "What's not right?"

"It's not right for us to sleep in the same bed."

"Is it the sleeping?"

"The everythinging."

Joette unfolded her legs and eased her bed back to its original spot before looping an orange and green scarf over her pin curls. "You can't take a break from love," she said.

"I have a boyfriend," I said, hoping to sound firm.

"Does he know you have a girlfriend?"

*Chapter 22*

# ANNIE

It didn't happen every shift, or every week. I was not losing it. If the women were too old, too young, too bright, or too dark, I let them be. My attention was trained on those who could reasonably be my mother. One night, my eyes were drawn to a woman wearing tangerine lipstick so thick it split like drying clay. She had the coarse skin and dark lips of a longtime boozer, yellow eyes, too. Whatever beauty she'd ever had was faded, but there was an appealing glimmer when she smiled.

I set a bowl of peanuts in front of her, even though I knew Mr. Wilson didn't like me dishing out nuts until after the person had placed a drink order.

"Thank you, baby," she said.

"Yes, ma'am," I said.

"Can you tell the bartender to get me a rum and Coke?"

"Yes, ma'am," I said, even though taking orders was Babydoll's job.

She used her back teeth to split the shell before flipping the nuts out with her long fingernails and letting the empty husk fall to the floor like people do in the country. She had cleared out the whole bowl before Babydoll served her drink. She shook the bowl like a tambourine. At her service, I topped it off at the barrel.

Mr. Wilson snatched it and shook out half the contents. "People not supposed to make a meal out of my peanuts. If she's hungry, let her order a sandwich."

The lady took the second bowl of nuts at a more measured pace, but she threw that rum and Coke back like she had been waiting for it all her life. She set the empty glass down and twisted in her chair, hoping to catch somebody's eye with her smile. It didn't work at first, so she fiddled with her glass, shaking the ice and sucking off whatever liquid may have been released.

When Babydoll went for her break, I followed her.

"Hear me out," I said. "Just hear me out."

"Green dress? Orange lips?" she said, bending down to unlace her shoes.

"You got to admit that she marks all the right boxes."

"How old is Hattie Lee, again?" Babydoll said, peeking through a crack in the door.

"Thirty-six," I said.

Babydoll squinted. "Could be. Could be. That chick looks like thirty-six the hard way."

"That's not nice," I said.

"I'm just saying it checks out. You can tell she'd do whatever you ask for another drink, especially if you make it a double."

"It's because she misses me," I said. "I need to tell her who I am."

Babydoll shook her head and clucked. "There are a lot of sad, drunk colored women in this town." She added another half stick of gum to the mess she was already chewing. "In the *world* even."

"When she came into the room, the air changed. I felt it," I said. "And you've seen her picture."

I looked at Babydoll, waiting for her to say the word, but she wasn't convinced. She made her voice soft as cotton candy.

"You don't want to lose this job, do you? Because ladies have complained. One thing Mr. Wilson can't have is you running women away. A bar without enough women is a tinderbox."

I sat down on an upside-down bucket and gave myself a couple of sharp slaps on the face. "Am I that bad?"

Babydoll nodded. "You come off as crazy."

"Am I?"

"Naw," she said. "You are just damaged."

That night, when Bobo got off from work, I was pacing the floor. At 2:30 a.m. he was beat but handsome with his collar unbuttoned and tie hanging loose. On his head was a close-fitting leather cap, turned to one side. His eyes, glittering with strong liquor, made me self-conscious walking the floor in a dingy gown.

"Hey, baby," he said. "You waited up?"

He went to the sink and pulled himself a glass of water, finishing it in one gulp. He refilled it, prattling away about who all had been at the jam session and how he might get a chance to play on a record. He waved his hand that wasn't holding the glass like he was washing windows until he finally realized that I wasn't paying him any mind. He shut up midstory. "What's wrong?"

"Am I crazy?" I asked him. "Tell me the truth."

"Oh lord." He removed the leather hat. "What happened?"

I told him about the woman with the tangerine lipstick. "I know I should have introduced myself. I let Babydoll talk me out of it and when I got back in the bar, she was gone. It could have been my last chance."

I plunked down on the bed and moaned into the cave of my hands. "The whole reason I came here was to find her and then I let her slip away."

"Honey," Bobo said, kneading my heaving shoulders. "You don't even know that it was her."

"Yes, I do," I snapped. "Why can't you believe that I know what I know?"

He pressed his lips together in a tight line, trapping whatever words sprang up. Then he opened his mouth, but instead of talking, he brought his teeth back together with a click. This was the first time that he didn't tell me what was on his mind. With the fever of anger, it felt like a victory. I imagined myself like Babydoll, who could shut Clyde down with a cut of her eyes. Drunk on this watered-down swallow of power, I tied my headscarf on with triumphant tugs, climbed into the bed, and turned my face to the wall and my back to my man.

Bobo sat at the little breakfast table for another hour or so, swallowing glass after glass of tap water. A couple of times, I heard him gasp like he was winding up to speak, but he let it out again as a sigh. Finally, he rinsed his glass and set it on a towel to dry. After washing himself at the sink, he slid into the bed beside me.

"Annie," he said, "it's not that I don't believe that you thought you saw Hattie Lee; it's just that you don't even know for sure what she looks like. You don't even know for sure that she's here in Memphis. Hell, you don't even know if . . ."

He let the sentence hang there, but I could fill in that ugly blank. "You don't even know if she's even alive."

Lying on my side and suddenly cold, I drew my legs close to my torso. This rang a bell from my childhood. I had been three or four. The seasons had just changed, but Granny hadn't yet added a quilt to my bedclothes. Shivering, I had curled myself into a ball, as I was too little to know how to get un-cold. I pulled my legs into my trunk and folded my arms so that my fists rested under my chin. Then I cried in the quiet way that children do when they know that nobody cares about their tears. I don't know how long I lay rattling in the shell of my own body, until finally, I fell into sleep so deep that Granny couldn't wake me for Sunday school. The doctor declared that I had scarlet fever, leaving a bottle of horse pills to feed me twice a day.

I wanted to tell this to Bobo, but I wasn't ready to make up with him. Beside me, I felt him turn his body toward me. His torso was warm against my cold back.

"Annie," he said, "I hate to see you hurt like this."

---

The lady in the tangerine lipstick didn't come back to the Elektra not once that winter, or even when spring brought the drinkers out in their bright getups. Though I was disgusted with myself for letting her get away, I had at least stopped seeing my mother's face in every woman who asked for a double whiskey.

And since I no longer behaved like a crazy person with a hostility to makeup and other features of femininity, Mr. Wilson let me put my mop aside and wait tables. I couldn't pull in big tips like Babydoll. Some women are sexy and others are not. But I did all right because I was helpful and that was worth an extra nickel or dime from most people. Most of the money I received from women, who pulled the coins from their purses, after their men had settled the bill.

Near around Christmastime, Mr. Wilson let us all have a little nip before work, so we could better spread the holly jolly. This was how he'd discovered that I knew how to mix cocktails. For the most part, the staff kept it simple. People in Memphis were used to dark liquor with basic chasers—drinks that Mr. Daniel used to call this-plus-that. But sometimes I might mix a New Orleans drink like a mai tai or Sazerac. The fancy drinks were for Mr. Wilson because he had a curious palate and anyway, our staff freebie could only contain one shot of booze.

All the waitresses attached tufts of silver tinsel to bobby pins and fastened them just over our ears. Even the fellows got into the spirit, letting the silver dangle from their shirt pockets. Multicolored lights rimmed the blacked-out windows and sprigs of holly hung from the ceiling, standing in for mistletoe. By the end of the night, we were all drunk—workers and customers alike.

My nickname in those days was "Spoken For" because this is what I said when a man asked me anything. I didn't care if he was wondering about the weather.

---

The Christmas party held after hours was strictly for staff. The weather was perfect—chilly enough to feel the season, but not so cold that you had to wear ugly clothes. It was the first Thursday of the month, so everybody had a little extra money for sandwiches and chips to sop up some of the liquor we poured down our throats. Add to that, it was Mr. Wilson's birthday and he was in the mood to celebrate. And last but not least, it was a good day for the Negro race, at least locally. A young man from Manassas High School had been accepted to Northwestern University.

The announcement in *The Tri-State Defender* made everyone so proud, like it was our sons who had been certified as algebra whizzes.

"Spoken For, mix me one of those Bourbon Street drinks!" Mr. Wilson called, sitting at the bar for once, rather than tending it.

I usually chafed at the silly nickname, but it was the man's birthday. Also, I jumped at any opportunity to display my skills with spirits. My hope was that he would decide to take a chance and let a woman tend the bar, if only on Wednesdays. I squinted at the assorted bottles and picked up a bottle of something yellowish green. With a sniff I put it in the same family as anise. It might taste good in a Manhattan. As I stirred it around in a pint glass of ice, I heard Mr. Wilson say, "We closed. Can't you read?"

I followed his voice and there was the lady in the tangerine lipstick. Her waist-length jacket looked more like a hide than a fur.

"C'mon," she said. "Let me join the party."

She was drunk as four skunks and a rhino. Her words melted together like crayons in summertime. "Please, Wilson. It's cold outside."

"Nope," he said.

She turned her face to the left, revealing a wide bandage, stained pink. "I'm having a hard time."

"Well," said Mr. Wilson, "go have your hard time someplace else. I don't want whoever sliced your face coming here for more trouble." He used his body to herd her toward the front door as one of the bouncers held it open.

By now, I was crouched to duck from behind the bar. "Here I am," I called. "Hattie Lee! I'm right here." I sprang up too fast and banged my head, upsetting a bottle of maraschino cherries and a shot glass filled with toothpicks. With my hand on my throbbing brow, I pulled myself upright, then scrambled in the direction of the door, but Babydoll blocked my way.

"Annie," she said. "Act like you have some sense."

I stepped to the left to get around her, but she moved when I moved, like we were dancing. Babydoll gripped the sides of my face. She looked *into* my eyes, but I just looked *at* hers, training my attention on the mascara waxing her lashes. "You don't even know—" she started, but I did a feint to the right and got around her, expecting some interference, but all the drinkers just parted like the Red Sea. I thumbed the dead bolt and finally, finally made my way to the sidewalk.

The street was quiet but not silent, sparsely populated but not deserted. An old man made his way, leaning on a silver-tipped cane. A working girl headed toward the stop sign, happily alone, swinging her shoes from her left hand. There were a few other people, nobody memorable, and nobody wearing too much lipstick or a mangy rabbit coat. "Hattie?" I called. "Hattie Lee?" But if there was anyone within the sound of my voice that answered to that name, they didn't call back.

I sat down on the curb and waited for someone to come and see about me. Through the shut door, the laughter from the bar workers' party seeped out, like a sweet perfume that I happened to be allergic to. My chest tightened and my eyes watered. My dark clothes and my dark skin must have melded with the night because no one noticed that I was on this earth, breathing in air and taking up space. I sat there just a few minutes more, enjoying the pain of self-pity like a tongue teasing a rotten tooth.

Sure that no one was coming to save me, or to love me, I patted my hair and went back inside. A couple of people lowered their heads and raised their eyebrows, peeking over invisible reading glasses. Babydoll stood in my spot, straining the drink for Mr. Wilson. She shook her head at me like *Poor thing.* Then she plopped in some sugar water, which ruined the whole cocktail.

Once I had reclaimed my position, she squeezed my wrist hard enough for it to hurt. "You really are losing it," she said with eyes so soft, I thought maybe she would kiss me.

On our walk home, my top lip was swelling a little from sloe gin, but I didn't care. Babydoll had swallowed a little more than her share, but it didn't make her bubbly. The drinking pulled her down like those little weights they sew into the hem of curtains. We both had a little bit of a slur in our walk, so we hooked our elbows together to assure each other that we were still friends and also to stay upright.

"Why?" she asked me. "Why do you keep running after every wench that looks like she might abandon her kids?"

"Why?" I asked her back. "Why are you so set on being a bitch to me?"

"Because, I have to cover for you every time you lose your mind. When you look crazy, it makes me look crazy because everybody knows we're friends."

"That's not true," I said.

"Yes, it is," she said. "Everyone knows we're a package, and you are not holding up your half of it. I am tired of carrying you."

She was quiet-boiling with irritation and I stared at the dark sky considering what she said. "You have been carrying me?"

"Look down," she said. "You ain't going to see but one pair of footprints."

---

When I got to our room, Bobo wasn't home. It was late, after 2 a.m., and there wasn't any reason for him not to be sitting at the kitchen table eating the buttered cheese sandwich that I set out for him as I left for work. Things had been odd between us for a few weeks now. It was like he was standing on the other side of a sheer curtain, the ones you use when you don't want people peeking right in your house but you want some light to come in.

I stripped down to my panties and took a whore's bath at the sink. My hair stank of cigarettes but it was too late to do a full shampoo and plait. After my wash-up, I smelled under my arms and other spicy spots and decided that I was decent, but I knew that Bobo wouldn't be in the mood for affection. I ate the sandwich and washed it down with a small can of orange juice, tart but cold.

*Dear Niecy,*

*I am sitting up at my table at 3 o'clock in the morning. You are probably wondering where Bobo is, but I let that wave roll back to the sea a couple hours ago. Where he is doesn't matter. Where he's NOT is the point. And he is not here.*

*You have never lied to me, so I am seeking your opinion.*

*Am I crazy? Am I having a fixation? That last one is a Bobo word, if you couldn't tell already. He threw it at me on Friday of last week. He had a gig at the Eureka, what they say is Memphis's "Oldest and Best Colored Hotel." (They also say Duke Ellington stayed there and wrote "Sophisticated Lady" after one glimpse of the owner's wife painting her nails.) Bobo is very gifted, Niecy. I am mad with him right now, but I have to give him that.*

*It is a nice place, so I fixed myself up in a red dress with sparklies around the neck. He was playing "They Can't Take That Away from Me" when a well-dressed woman caught my eye. She was built sort of like me, but I thought she was too tall to be Hattie Lee. But then I saw that she had on some sky-high heels. She had a man with her, he seemed in league with your Franklin. His shoes alone let you know he was an Esq. I was cool, calm, and collected the whole time. Then the two of them asked to join me at my table. So let the record show that she came over to me.*

*Niecy, my everything was beating! It felt like I had swallowed a frog. I did not, I repeat, I DID NOT ask her if she was Hattie Lee. I just mentioned some other things to rule her in or out. Halfway through Bobo's second set, her and her man got up and went to another table that had just emptied out. I thought it was because they wanted a better view of Bobo. Since they shared my table all that time, it made sense that I should have been able to share theirs, right?*

*I stood there with the chair pulled out about to sit down and they asked me to go on back to my original table. And they didn't say it nice. And the man didn't say it quiet. It was like they had slapped me. I went on back to where I was, with shame on my face. When the band took a break, I was ready to tell Bobo how rude those people were. But he had the nerve to be mad at me.*

*Told me that I embarrassed him. That was when he used the word FIXATION. So, I just walked out. And he didn't even try and chase me down.*

*Niecy, all I want is to find my mother. Bobo talks about how I am not normal, but I think wanting to find my mother is the most normal thing in the world.*

*Your cradle friend, who is not crazy, who is normal as butter on a biscuit,*

*ANNIE KAY*

*Chapter 23*

# VERNICE

In the early months of the New Year, Franklin often drove me to Piedmont Park, northeast of downtown. He enjoyed walking more than going to the picture show or sitting on the bleachers watching baseball. Even when it hurt him, he was eager to travel on nothing but his two feet. He took pleasure in all weather, even cold damp afternoons.

I was bundled in a heavy wool coat, and a felt hat to protect my hairdo from the moist, frigid air. My neck was wrapped in a cashmere scarf he had given me for my birthday. The color, the moody pink of June hydrangeas, was his mother's signature shade, but I didn't mind at all that they had collaborated. Did he suspect that Mrs. McHenry had guided me in selecting the silver tie clip that I had slipped into his Christmas stocking?

After about a half hour of strolling, we reached the base of the ghost stairs, a mysterious series of broad steps, about ten or twelve feet across, leading up the side of a grassy hill, for no apparent reason at all. Large urns, constructed from the same stone, flanked each side of the construction, housing wild rosemary that gave a savory quality to the environment. Our habit was to sit on the third row to allow him to rest his legs and to steal a kiss or two.

I refused to compare his touch or his talk to Joette's. My two lovers occupied different rooms of my life. In biology class, our teacher led us in dissecting a fetal pig. Discovering the four chambers of the heart seemed like discovering a message sent from God. The professor explained how the structure of the organ kept the vascular system organized. Dirty used blood darkened, traveling by veins, while clean, capable blood was bright red, like lipstick coursing through sturdy arteries. Tracing a diagram into my notebook, I finally understood my life.

Franklin's arms were muscular and shapely. I enjoyed the power of them pressing me close. When he spoke my name, my body tingled in anticipation. I perched in my place on the stairs, ready for his touch, but instead, he wanted to talk.

"When I was a boy, I sometimes looked out the window and saw my brothers horse around in the yard, not a thought in their heads or a care in their worlds," he started.

"That's how I feel sometimes about people who were raised by their real parents," I broke in. "Like Joette. She's so careless with her folks. She doesn't even see—"

He cut me off by sliding my glove off my hand, directing it to his chest so I could feel the vigorous thud. I imagined the blood, thick and red streaming through veins, arteries, ventricles. So much activity in these bodies that seem still.

"I never resented my brothers," he said. "I felt sorry for them. All that running and jumping and not one second to reflect on what a gift it is. Every time I take one step—anywhere or for anything—I am struck by God's glory. And I see that glory in you, Vernice. You don't know the marvel that you are. But I want to spend the rest of my life helping you see it."

We come to love people in many ways. Much is made of the burning love that hits like a smoldering remnant of a star hurled down to earth. Yet this is not the only type of love any more than the camellia is the only flower. There is the love that blooms from decency, and from that love, passion. On that cold day, I wanted to feel the marvel that was Franklin. I wanted to see his entire body, including the leg that he dragged on his left side. I wanted to feel the man that the devil tried to snatch.

"I love you," I said.

He startled, and I likely did the same. My lips and tongue formed the words without my permission.

Franklin laughed with a joy and pleasure you will only hear once or twice in this life. It marks the arrival of good news that has no downside, at least none that you can see.

"That's supposed to be my line," he said.

"I never do anything right," I said.

"You are doing this just perfect."

The three small diamonds were housed in braided gold. The stones were cloudy, but they were real. The engraving inside said *1863*. Franklin's grandmother was the last in that family to be born in chains. Her name was Agatha Marie and she earned money even before Emancipation as a seamstress. When she sewed uniforms for Confederate soldiers, she didn't reinforce all the seams, enjoying the idea of them squatting to take aim and ripping their trousers across the seat. One day, a Union soldier, dressed in a uniform that was worn but well made, crawled into the dirt yard before her hut. He asked her if she would allow him to come inside her place to die. She didn't say yes right off the bat because she was so taken aback at the idea of a white man asking her permission for anything. (And that means *anything*. Where did I think the McHenry boys got that wavy hair?) He said, "Please, ma'am. I can't bear the idea of dying out of doors." It was the "ma'am" that touched her. Fearful as she was, she half dragged him inside and let him lie on the buckwheat mattress that she had constructed herself. She did what she could for his pain, but mostly she just offered him a roof that he could die under. Before he breathed his last, he gave her a ring intended for his beloved back in Pennsylvania.

There is a picture of her on the McHenrys' mantel and you can make out this very ring dangling from a cord around her neck. All this, Franklin explained, kneeling before me, despite the pain on his left side.

"Say yes," Franklin said. "Vernice, be my good thing."

Words snarled in my throat. So, I could only nod. Be a good thing. Accept a good thing. Join a good thing.

"When?" I said.

"June?" he said. "Aren't all weddings in June?"

"After I graduate. Please let me finish school," I said.

The pleasure on his face made him glow. "Of course."

I helped him to his feet and he kissed me hard, with all the urgency of what was to come. "I wish we could go on and get married next week, because you are driving me crazy."

And this time, I felt it too. My breath came quick as I enjoyed his hands roving over the nice underthings Mrs. McHenry had brought me back from a trip to New York.

"But I can wait," he said. "I can wait and do it right."

---

When I returned to Abby Hall, well before curfew, no one paid any attention to me. All the girls knew I had a suitor, that he was an attorney, but he was older and one-sided. The peanut gallery had opinions about how heavy our relationship was, but I was tight-lipped. But Joette grasped all that I believed I kept to myself.

"You went and did it," she said. "Let me see your hand."

I held it out and she shook her head. "Why do you have to be so timid all the time? Why do you have to do what people tell you to do? There are other ways to live. We could go up north . . ."

I turned my eyes toward the ceiling.

"We could move to DC," she said.

"Move to DC and do what?" I asked.

"Work," she said. "Live. Be together."

I shook my head and shifted my eyes on my ring.

"What did they promise you?" Joette asked. "Tea parties and cotillions? I've lived that life, and let me tell you, it's not all it's cracked up to be. Take my mother, is that who you want to be? Ask Patty McHenry, who has your nose wide open, ask her why she drinks so much."

"I don't care about tea parties," I said. "You know me better than that."

She stopped pacing.

"Don't do this," she said. "Please. Mouse. Don't."

"You know my daddy killed my mama," I said. "And my aunt who raised me—she loved me, but she didn't mother-love me. You know all this already. But . . ."

Joette turned her head to one side and pulled her eyebrows together like she was doing long division in her head. "But?"

"I been through a lot," I said.

"And if you marry these people, you are about to go through some more."

"Like what?" I said. "Like having my own family? Like my own house? My own children?"

When Joette was mad, she didn't make her voice loud, but she let it go deep. "Please don't tell me all of this is because you want someone to call you 'mama.' That won't fix you."

I waved my arms to encompass the tiny dormitory with its slanted dormer ceilings and hers-and-hers desks and dressers. "Joette, in real life people get married. Have children. You never wanted a baby? Never for one second? Admit it. It's just natural."

Joette nodded. "Of course, I considered it when I was young, not knowing that a person had a choice in the matter. Trust me. There is nothing like an incompetent mother to convince you that you could do it better. So, I thought about it, sure. But I never wanted it."

"Well, I do. I want it so bad. And you can't give it to me."

---

I should have been the one forced out of our slanted sanctuary, as I had committed the heartbreaking. The fact that I, too, had cried myself to sleep was beside the point. Yet in the shadow of all the unfairness in this world, I was the one who had nowhere else to go. So, Joette moved back into her parents' home, confessing to a profound romantic disappointment, and allowed her parents to celebrate when it became clear she wasn't pregnant.

I lived alone for the rest of the term. Joette's space was stripped like a plague of locusts had eaten away any evidence of her: the lavender tiebacks and matching linens, the orderly stacks of books, and even the unruly potted plants. My bed was bare of the purple spread that I had come to think of as my own.

I didn't see her again until Founders Day. Like the other seniors, she was cloaked in her dark baccalaureate robe and prim collar. Since she had dressed at her mother's house, I knew she wore the full complement of foundational garments. It was particularly humid that spring, and her pancake makeup shone as she processed down the aisle. The only evidence of her rebellious spirit was her busy jaw laying waste to a wad of gum. As she passed me at the head of the pew, she extended her pinky, letting the oval nail scrape the back of my hand. Her expression was an unpleasant mixture of sorrow and rage. "Look what you have done to me," she said, and paused. "Look."

When I did, I saw a young woman poised to take flight. Joette had the itchy readiness of a bullet in the chamber. I admired her in that moment as much as I had the day I met her, when I was just a country mouse toting a carpetbag.

Joette Cunningham was "one of one" like the Ohio Man—the likes of which I had never seen before, and, I suspected, something I would never see again.

*Chapter 24*

# ANNIE

Bobo didn't say that he was leaving if I didn't stop searching for my mother, but it was clear that he was irritated. Any time I opened my mouth to say "Hattie Lee," he let his eyes linger just a little bit too long on the closed side of a blink.

"I just want to see where she lives," I said. "You know that's why I moved here."

"Babydoll told me how you have been carrying on at your job, and I saw it with my own eyes at the Eureka Hotel. You need to just let this Hattie Lee thing go." You know how people say they "threw up their hands" when they mean they were irritated? Well, Bobo actually threw up his hands. He did it without thinking, forgetting about his half cup of Nescafé, which went flying and ruined the shirt I had ironed for him. "Goddammit, Annie," he said like I was the one tossing coffee around.

I got him dressed again in another clean shirt, leaving the dirty one in to soak with salt and baking soda. Then I crossed the hallway and knocked on Babydoll's door.

Clyde answered, dressed in khaki coveralls for his job. This was a new gig. For the last one, he'd worn green. That man was good at getting jobs, but keeping them proved to be a challenge. His side of the narrow closet was probably stuffed full of twice-worn uniforms and caps to match. He smiled, flashing all those crooked teeth. "You must want Babydoll."

She popped out from behind him. On her, his undershirt fit flirty, like a sundress.

He pulled his lunch bag from the table, gave us a quick salute, and slipped out the door.

"Girl, I love that man." Raising her arms to stretch, she gave me a glimpse of the side of a breast that was full and compact at the same time. I envied her, so relaxed and freshly fucked. I could barely get Bobo to help me unzip my dress.

"Today is the day," I said. "I'm ready to do it."

"Do what?"

I slapped the paper with my mother's address on the table like it was the high joker cutting the ace of spades.

She chuckled. "Bobo had enough of you carrying on like Dick Tracy?"

"He said something to you?" I asked.

"Naw," Babydoll said. "To Clyde, but I didn't even hear it. Clyde asked me what 'incorrigible' meant. I checked the dictionary and I put two and two together. What did you do?"

"I thought I saw her at the Eureka Hotel," I said.

"So, you want to go on over there, grab this bull by the balls, and get it out of your system?"

"I don't want to lose my man," I said.

"No," said Babydoll. "There ain't nothing worser than that."

---

I'll never forget that day. It was the fifteenth of May. It had rained all morning, so the air was steamy and thick, like the devil's waiting room. Even without a mirror, I knew my face shone like a beacon in the night. Even pretty Babydoll looked a little melted. She had her hair snatched up into a ball on the top of her head, but little beady-bees had formed at her neckline.

We stopped to drink from a hose at a filling station. The water was refreshing, despite being warm and tasting like pennies.

"Here's a tip," she said, dabbing the corners of her lips. "Mothers are not all they are cracked up to be."

I rolled my eyes because I had heard this before—from everyone who had a mother but wasn't yet a mother.

"No," she said. "Listen to me. You know why Lulabelle at the ho farm didn't like me?"

I could feel myself getting my back up. Babydoll and I had agreed to disagree about Lulabelle.

"She don't like me because I know what she is. And I know what she is because my mama is just like her."

"What is she?" I said. "She let us stay at her place for months. She gave us somewhere to sleep. Food to eat . . ."

"She's a pimp," Babydoll said. "A pimp will always give you what you need to stay alive. What's a pimp going to do with a dead whore?"

"We weren't whores," I said. "She never tried to get us to go with the sirs."

Babydoll shook her head. "You best be glad Bobo saw that ghost and got us run out of that place. Two more weeks and you would have been screwing for your red beans and rice. She had you wrapped around her finger. But not me."

We walked for a couple more blocks without saying anything to each other. When we approached Carver High, we had to make a left, which meant I had to speak to tell her so. Soon as I broke the seal on the silence, Babydoll kept talking.

"What I am telling you is that my mama saw a girl child as a way to make money. She figured she made me and I belonged to her. I was so jealous of you with your precious little cherry that you presented to Bobo like it was the Nobel Peace Prize. My mama swapped mine for a felt hat and a pair of gloves. That's why you will never see me with a hat on my head. I don't care if it's a funeral. Fuck a hat."

She knelt and picked up a chunk of rock, smooth and gleaming. With a flick of her wrist, she sent it flying against the side of a wood house. The sound put a dog to barking.

"Shut up." She picked up another rock as the dog strained against the rope around his neck. I didn't know what kind of canine was what. I could only tell if it was big, medium, or little. Or if it was a biting dog or a playing dog. This was a grayish-brown animal, medium-big and biting. Babydoll held her arm back like a threat, but the dog wasn't impressed. She was right about to send a rock right between its crazed eyes when a man opened the front door.

"Why you messing with Apollo?" he said. "He used to be a police dog, so you know his favorite food is Negro ass."

The man was older than us by a good bit. Maybe he was about the age of Mr. Daniel.

Babydoll said, "You need to ask Apollo why he is messing with us. We were minding our business."

He shook his head and said, "Save that lie for the white people. Why are you out here picking a fight with a guard dog?"

"Sir," I said, "we are looking for your neighbor? Her name is Hattie Lee? She's about yea tall," I said, tapping my forehead. "Skinny neck?"

"Drunk all the time?" he said. "She owe you some money?"

Behind him, the screen door opened, allowing another man onto the porch. He was tall, lanky, and yellow—putting me in mind of a number-two pencil, which put me in mind of school, which put me in mind of Niecy. He waved and I waved back before I realized he was waving at the dog, who settled back on his haunches.

"What's going on out here?" His voice tipped up at the end, like he was interested. "I'm Isaiah," he added in case we were wondering.

"They looking for Hattie Lee."

"Hattie Lee?" Isaiah turned his eyes to the sky, as though her name were written up there in cloud letters. Then the men faced each other for a few moments of silent communication.

"She owe you some money? You not going to get it."

"No," I said. "This here is a social call."

"Well," Isaiah said, "I regret to inform you that lady has passed away."

"She dead?" Babydoll didn't like anything left murky.

"About a month now," Isaiah said.

"A month," I said. "I missed her by a month?"

---

Let's blame it on the heat. Let's fault the dog that had given me such a scare. Let's say it was because I hadn't eaten breakfast. It might have been because I was nervous. But my body shut down in a slow extinguishing of my spirit. I was a drugstore and the lights were cutting off one section at a time until the whole place was dark. It took a while, and it was like I was watching myself die. I looked up at the sky to see who waited for me, but I didn't know anybody else who had passed, except maybe Niecy's mama, but she didn't know me. On my way down, I shut my eyes hard in case the haint from the farm had spit into the pot; I didn't want to see the eyes that had frightened Bobo until he quivered in my arms.

Babydoll said it took less than a second. Isaiah said, "No money for a funeral," and next thing, I was on the ground. Both men came rushing down and carried me up onto the porch. The tough one, who I came to know was called Sweet, held two fingerfuls of Vicks under my nose, while Isaiah dabbed my face with a cold cloth. All this time Babydoll called out rapid-fire Hail Marys. Apollo went into his doghouse, avoiding all the commotion.

"How?" I said with a tongue so big it seemed like it wouldn't fit between my lips.

They had put me in a cane rocker. The seat was worn and I felt my bottom droop so low that it might graze the cement floor.

"She wasn't ailing," Sweet said, shaking his heavy head.

"Pretty much anything that goes on in that house over there, we privy to. From my living room window, I can see right into theirs. It's better than TV because we don't get good reception out here," Isaiah put in.

"You don't need rabbit ears when you can just spy on your neighbors for free," Babydoll offered in an understanding tone.

"Exactly," Isaiah said.

Sweet asked Isaiah to bring out some sun tea and butter-baked crackers. Once we were each situated with three salty rectangles and a glass of tea so strong it made my teeth hurt, Sweet bowed his head for a few seconds. Whether he was blessing the modest snack or if the words were to sanctify the information he was gearing up to share, I couldn't tell.

"I was born in this house," Sweet explained. "But Isaiah has been here only about five years, so everything is interesting to him."

"Just y'all two?" Babydoll said.

"We cousins," Isaiah lied.

"Babydoll, get out of people's business," I said.

"But you are here to get all in Hattie's affairs," Babydoll snapped.

"Ladies," Sweet said. "Simmer down."

"It was Sweet really who was her friend," Isaiah said.

Sweet shrugged, taking his massive shoulders up to his ears. "She was nice to the dog. Unlike some other people," he said, pointing his words at Babydoll.

"I already apologized," she said.

Sweet lifted a cracker from Isaiah's plate. "Either one of you have a spiritual gift?" he asked. "I received a double blessing. Speaking in tongues is one. That's how I met Isaiah, because his gift is interpreting tongues. We grew up in the same congregation over nearby to Tupelo. But my other gift is discernment. So, I don't hardly ever get got. This is why your mama hurt me so bad."

The cold tea was suddenly warm in my mouth. "I didn't say she was my mother."

"You didn't have to," Sweet said.

Sweet looked at me and then to Isaiah.

"Spitting image," he said. "Let me touch your hair."

He sounded wistful. "She reminded me of my grandmother in a lot of ways. That chick-feather hair . . ." He put his big hands on my head.

"And that forked tongue," said Isaiah.

"It's not your business," Sweet said. "Me and you don't mingle our money. So, if she stole from me, she stole from me and me alone."

"How much did she get you for?" I asked. "I might be able to help you get whole."

Sweet said, "You are tenderhearted, just like your mother."

It was the first time I had ever heard anything spoken about my mother in a complimentary way. It hurt sweet, like kind words spoken over a coffin. "She lived over there a nice little while," Sweet went on. "Before I would rent to her, we had to have a little how-do-you-do, so I could use my discernment. I was impressed first off that she told me her Christian name. Just as a word to the wise, be real careful. With your true name, the one wrote down in Saint Peter's book, somebody can spell you."

Babydoll nodded as if she had considered this all before, but the concept was new to me. I thought about all the people in this world who knew my name. I even wore it pinned to my blouse at the Elektra. Who knew this was giving away the keys to my city? Before I could spend any more time worrying over it, Isaiah put his two cents in. "Not everybody in this house believes in spells. I am washed in the blood of the Lamb."

Sweet said, "You say that now because you are enjoying the safety of your own home. You can be saved and still guard yourself against demons. That is just common sense."

"Oh Lord," Isaiah said. "Get on with what you have to tell her."

"I want their names first," Sweet said. "I got the gift of discernment; I need to hear how they say their names."

"I'm Annie Kay Henderson." Even though I had told my name to countless people, pronouncing it made me feel vulnerable as a snail pried out of its shell.

The men regarded each other again in that way that made me think maybe they did have some kind of talent from above. Isaiah repeated the syllables under his breath. If he hadn't just declared himself to be a Christian, I would have sworn he spelled me. Then he turned to Sweet, and with just that glance they fought, called a truce, and came to some middle ground they could both live with.

"And your name?" Sweet said to Babydoll, returning his attention to the here and now.

"Babydoll," she said.

"That's what the King will say when he sees you?"

“Why you so sure I am going to heaven?” Babydoll said.

Sweet laughed a wide laugh. “Ruthie Mae,” he said, “you have nothing to fear here.”

Babydoll looked like she was going to be the next one to pass out.

Isaiah said, “Sweet, why do you have to keep scaring people like that? God might snatch that gift away from you if you keep using it for malice.”

Babydoll sat next to me on the double-seater and I hugged her to me.

“I’m Ruth Ann, not Ruthie Mae,” she said. “Almost don’t count.”

Sweet smiled and adjusted his undershirt on his healthy shoulders.

“Hattie Lee was here, what? Three years? Four?”

“Thereabouts,” Isaiah said. “When she came, young gal was bone skinny, but by the time they left, she was coming into being a young lady. And how old was the baby?”

“Who had a baby? Not Hattie Lee?” Jealousy threatened to shut my lights out once again.

“No. The gal was the one who got herself with child, like they say at Christmastime. Pretty little girl and the baby was just as cute as can be.”

“So, who was the girl?” I said, imagining Lulabelle and her maid.

“She didn’t say,” Sweet said, “and I didn’t ask. I try to stay out of people’s relational business. You see I didn’t ask you ladies how you knew each other.”

Babydoll said, “I thought you didn’t have to ask, that you could just *discern.*”

“Blaspheming is not cute,” Sweet said.

Isaiah topped off his iced tea and said, “I’m getting tired of both of you.”

“We first met Hattie Lee when she knocked on this very door, saying somebody at her church said this was a safe place to live and that I was a good Christian man and all of that.”

"See, that's how you should have knew she was lying," said Isaiah. "Ain't nobody at Christ the Redeemer sending people to you!"

"Maybe they might would," Sweet said, hurt. "I've been the organist for years."

"How did she look?" I said. "Healthy?"

"She wasn't ate up by liquor if that is what you are asking. She looked like a regular person that was working too hard to keep the roof overhead."

"What was she like?" I asked.

"I liked her," Sweet said. "Isaiah was on the fence but I took to her. For Christmas she brought us a bowl of nuts and two pieces of fruit. She didn't have to do that. It's just that the whiskey had her by the throat. I believe that some people are born like that."

"Did she tell you she had a daughter back in Louisiana?"

"Louisiana? She told us she was from Meridian."

Sweet shook his head. "Sometimes the Lord sends people in our lives to get us humble. Even if you have discernment, He has to let you know you ain't no fortune teller."

"Hattie Lee was born and raised in Honeysuckle, Louisiana." Optimism poked its head up like a groundhog. "So maybe we're not talking about the same person." I unsnapped my handbag to produce the creased school-days photo. "This is her."

Sweet stared at the gray rectangle that I placed in his palm. "Oh, Hattie," he said. "You was a girl once."

Isaiah peeked at the photo himself. "That's her for certain."

Sweet held his palm close to his face. "Oh, Hattie."

He passed his hand over his eyes and then held the photo close to his lips. "She never told me about a girl back home. Was that where her money went? She didn't tell me she had other mouths to feed."

Isaiah said, "You can't be held responsible for what you don't know."

"I feel so terrible," Sweet said. "I was fixing to put her out. She said she couldn't stand to be outside again. She begged me to let her stay, claiming she could come up with the money, but she didn't no ways tell me how."

Isaiah petted his back. "You are a landlord, not *the* Lord. Folks want to stay, they got to pay the rent."

Sweet said, "I just hate that the last words I said to her were cross."

---

For my birthday, Bobo had given me a glass candy dish with a lid. Instead of peppermints or gumballs, it was home for two tiny cactuses growing up from three kinds of dirt, positioned so it resembled a layer cake. On the bottom were rocks, atop that was rich black soil, and just under the plants, sand so the cactus would think it was back home in the desert. Bobo called the whole contraption a "terrarium" and grinned to let me know he had made it himself. I wasn't sure what to make of the gesture. I had been hoping for a ring but would have been satisfied with long-stemmed roses. Niecy said she had received a whole dozen from her fiancé. I knew Bobo didn't have Franklin money, but Babydoll said you could buy the roses one by one.

"Do you like it?" Bobo asked, worried.

I didn't, but I loved him, so I nodded. "It's pretty."

"And it will last," he promised.

When I returned to our rooms after learning that my mother was dead, I found Bobo ladling two tablespoons of water over the cactus. He was dressed only in the snug black trousers he wore when he had a gig. Setting the spoon down, he scratched the soft carpet of hair rimming his chest. "Everything requires water to live. But not too much. That's the paradox of water. You need it, but it can kill you."

When I didn't comment that this was interesting or that he was so smart, Bobo nestled the lid back into place and looked up. "What's wrong?"

"Hattie Lee is dead." I didn't use any of the soft words that we favored in Honeysuckle—"passed," "gone to glory," "deceased." I didn't even say she had died, because that was something a person *did.* A person lived; a person died. I said she was dead because that's forever. That's what she was. My mother was dead.

Bobo didn't rush to put his arms around me like I expected

him to. Instead, he jutted his bottom lip and asked, "How do you know?"

Gripping the terrarium, he made himself open as a bowl, holding whatever I poured.

"How do you feel?" Bobo asked.

"Like I'm always too late," I said.

"That's not a feeling," he said. "Tell me in one word."

I sat at the breakfast table and let my fingers follow the scars on the wood. I wondered about all the people who had lived in this room before us. This little table had never done anything to anyone but give them a place to rest their plates, play their cards, and support their elbows when they balled their fists under their chins to think—and they treated it any old kind of way, scarring it with hot mugs, peeling the varnish, and scratching their names with keys.

"I feel spelled," I said.

He bobbed his head. "You feel like you are at this moment spelled, or you feel like you were spelled in the past?"

"Both," I think. "She was a tapeworm inside me eating my life."

"And now?"

"I can't search for her anymore."

Bobo didn't smile. He was too good of a man to celebrate Hattie Lee's death. And maybe I didn't have the prophetic gift of discernment, but I knew that he circled this day on the calendar in his mind. This was the day that he and I would start anew. The day when we could be two regular people in love, a couple where neither one of them is crazy.

"But . . . ," I sputtered.

He gripped the terrarium like he wanted to throw it. "You want to find her grave? Save up for a headstone? Make a pilgrimage?"

I almost apologized for being so messed up, but he knew who I was when he first said he wanted to love me.

"I'm grieving," I said. "I have a right to that. And grief is a kind of spell."

He released the terrarium. "Forgive me."

*Dear Granny,*

*I write with terrible news. This is the sort of message that should be delivered by telegram but I don't have the foggiest idea how you go about sending a telegram. I bet Niecy does. Granny, she is the queen of all Atlanta. We are close as sisters, but it is true what you told me so many years ago. I miss her.*

*But I am stalling.*

*I went to the address that Mr. Daniel gave us for Hattie Lee. I am afraid that I waited too long. I wanted to go see her when I thought that I was someone she could be proud of. I wanted to walk up to her door as her child, but not childishly. I had some money saved, but not enough to impress somebody with. I have a gentleman friend but not a fiancé yet. I have a job, but not one that you wear pantyhose to. I think you can understand what I mean and I am hopeful you will see why I was shy to go there at this particular fork in my road. But, Granny, I went ahead and went because I was in certain danger of losing my mind.*

*So, I went to the address and I met her landlord, who told me that our dear Hattie Lee is no more. They said it happened at her job, but I am not sure anyone winds up dead fixing plates at a meat-and-three. The people who told me were not eyewitnesses, they just heard it through the grapevine. The details were soft but the basic facts were hard. Hattie Lee has gone home to be with the Lord. I do not know where she was buried. It strangles me to think of her buried in a potter's field, but I believe that this is where they laid her down.*

*I have known this for one month now. I am sorry not to write earlier, but I couldn't get my fingers to hold the pen. I am sending a five-dollar bill. If it is not here, then someone stole it, which would be very sad. If there is a collection at the church to send any young lady to school, please put a little something in the plate. Let her go and have a chance to be like Niecy and not like me and Hattie Lee. One heartbroken and the other one dead.*

*Your loving,*
*Annie Kay*

*Chapter 25*

# VERNICE

The whole year I had been with Franklin, I had never asked him for one cent. Marylinda teased me that this was because he gave me whatever I wanted before I could even think to file a request. But this isn't the case. It's true that he kept me surrounded by lovely trinkets like beaded handbags, perfume compacts, and aquamarine jewelry that made me resemble his mother. But I was still the girl who worked in the library to earn money to buy tooth powder and sanitary products. I wore the dresses his mother selected for me, but my slips beneath them were darned with my careful needlework. Being as our engagement was public, I was all but a McHenry. It wouldn't have been completely inappropriate for me to seek a small allowance, but I couldn't bring myself to do it.

This was the end of my second year at Spelman. The previous June, I'd lived with an alumna who needed a girl to look after her mother. Mercifully, no one used the word "maid." Aunt Irene extended a feeble invitation that I could spend the recess in Ohio, where she had resumed the life she enjoyed before fate hung a baby around her neck. How could I accept? She had done right by me, but there were limits and I knew what they were.

I am not completely certain whose idea it was that I should summer with Marylinda. When she suggested it, I asked, "Did

Mrs. McHenry put you up to this?" This sort of arrangement was right in her wheelhouse. But Marylinda shook her head. "Lord, no. It was my idea, Mouse. You don't want to spend the summer in the country, do you?"

In short, it was an offer I couldn't refuse. Room, board, and company for the whole summer? They lived just a half mile from Franklin, as Marylinda's folks were NAACP types, too. There was nothing they enjoyed more than integrating. (If they weren't hoping for their daughter to find a husband in college, they would have sent her up to Athens to kick in the door at the University of Georgia.) The baby boy studied art history at Oberlin College and would be home for the summer. The older brother and sister both were working toward doctorate degrees at Cornell University, living in Ithaca year-round. Because of this, the family had more bedrooms than children. Without paying a dime, I would have a room to myself, just across the hall from Marylinda.

My only reservation was Joette. Marylinda's mother and Joette's were sisters, and by all accounts very close. I hadn't seen Joette since Founders Day and I would have liked to let a little more water slosh under the bridge before we encountered each other again.

Marylinda's mother, Mrs. Freeman, opened the door when we arrived with our suitcases and cardboard boxes. She was a tiny woman without an ounce of excess fat on her body. On some women, tininess makes them seem fragile, but Mrs. Freeman just struck me as incredibly efficient.

"You're here," she said.

"Apparently," said Marylinda.

"Yes, ma'am," I said.

Mrs. Freeman smiled, flashing a resemblance to Joette so striking that my eyes watered. "Of course you are the picture of manners," she said. "Patty McHenry has impeccable taste."

"Ma-muh," Marylinda said, drawing the words out.

"Thank you for allowing me to stay here," I said. "I appreciate your generosity."

Mrs. Freeman let her face soften. "Welcome, dear. It is not your fault that your mother-in-law is so unpleasant."

"Ma-muh," Marylinda said again. "Can we not keep litigating the Depression era? We are not colored Hatfields and McCoys."

At this point, Mr. Freeman strode into the living room, every bit the white man he was pretending not to be. His smile was framed by blade-narrow lips. I searched for any hint of Negrodom, but I came up empty-handed, which is highly unusual because you can inspect anybody close enough and notice some feature you can take to the bank as proof of mixing. But Marylinda's father didn't have anything from this side of the tracks except his voice, which was as big and certain as a CME reverend's. He pumped my hand and boomed, "You are the McHenry girl, am I right?"

"Not yet," Marylinda said. "They are only engaged. Besides, she has a name. Vernice Davis. She is majoring in English. Also, she is a Movement girl. She integrated a Trailways bus and spent a night in jail!"

I squinted at Marylinda. Fair enough, I had not disabused her of the idea that I was a sit-inner, but I never claimed to have been arrested, let alone put behind bars.

"I see," said Mr. Freeman. "I am not surprised. Franklin McHenry is a man of impeccable taste and sound judgment."

"Dad-dee," Marylinda said in the same tone she used with her mother. "She is a person in her own right."

Mr. Freeman chuckled. "Our daughter thinks that we are Neanderthals." He put his arms around her shoulders and placed a kiss at the part in her heavy hair. Then he gathered up my suitcases and disappeared down the hallway.

"So patronizing," she mumbled.

---

Atlanta is a Negro soap opera. By the time we sat down for dinner, I wished I had a notebook to keep up with what was what and who was who to whom. To my left was Marylinda, who looked as white as Shirley Temple. To my right was her brother, Morris, who looked exactly like what he was—a light-skinned boy whose mother believed him to be adorable. Straight across from me was Mrs. Freeman, who shared a face with Joette, whom I missed so much that I could taste the salt of her sweat. And at the head of the table was Mr. Freeman, white as J. Edgar Hoover but holding court like he was Dr. Martin Luther King himself, full of opinions about what all "we" should do to end segregation.

When the topic of Malcolm X came up, he smacked the table so hard that the lemon fell from the rim of my glass of sweet tea.

"What is his contribution?" Mr. Freeman boomed. "How is he helping a sharecropper in Mississippi with all this 'white devil' this, 'white devil' that? Besides the automobile, what good has ever come from Detroit?"

Marylinda laughed right in his red face. This wasn't the tinkling, playful laughter that I knew from dormitory life. This cackling vibrated with an undercurrent of scorn. I turned my attention to Mrs. Freeman, feeling like there was some connection between us because neither one of us was a white person, or could be mistaken for one. Who ever heard of a Black girl laughing in her father's face? I knew this, and I didn't even have a father.

"Daddy," she said, once she turned off the chuckles, "what have you done for any Mississippi sharecroppers? Not just you, any of us?" She waved her hand to indicate all of us, and maybe the neighborhood, too. "Mouse might get a pass because she is from the country."

"I was never a sharecropper," I pushed back. "We had a house."

"Oh, Mouse," she said. "You know what I mean."

Mrs. Freeman broke into the conversation with a tone that I recognized. "I don't care what anybody means. We are going to eat this dinner like civilized people." To demonstrate, she took up her knife and fork and sliced into a chicken leg.

When I sat down that night at the prim writing table in my room, the letter I planned to write Annie could have written itself. But there on the desk was an envelope that must have come in earlier in the day. There was Annie's penmanship, but the letters were shaky, as though scribbled by a pen unsteadied by fear, or worse.

---

*Dear Niecy, The very worst has come to be. Your loving friend, Annie Kay*

---

The years had sent us in different directions, there was no denying that. Each time she wrote that she had possibly found Hattie Lee, my heart felt bloated, my chest crowded and overfull. Annie and I were two motherless girls who grew into motherless women. Who would we be to each other if Annie and Hattie Lee connected? Yes, we would always have our childhood in common. But what if Annie repaired the hole in her dam with concrete and straw, whereas I was still using my finger?

Tiny, living particles of guilt flooded my body like tadpoles in the puddle of muddy water. Yet even when I feared being left alone in my condition, I never rained on her parade or discouraged her search. When she wrote about all her near-brushes with Hattie Lee, I replied with enthusiasm—exclamation marks all over the place. But was I pure? When I wrote, *Oh, I hope it's her!*, did I? But on a stack of Bibles, on my mama's headstone, I never wished Hattie Lee dead. I confess that I wished her forever out of reach, but never cold in the ground.

---

Mrs. Freeman allowed me to keep company in my bedroom. When Franklin came calling, his cane made a soft noise like frying potatoes against the thick carpet in the hallway. He made himself comfortable on the desk chair, and I sat at the edge of the bed. We had been engaged six months by that time, but we had never been alone behind a shut door. The privacy made me nervous. I wished that I had taken more time grooming myself. My skirt reached my calves, but my knees above the hem were ashy.

"Can I sit closer?" he asked.

"Of course," I said.

He supported himself with the wing chair and transferred himself to the slender mattress covered with a chenille spread. Lying back onto the stack of pillows, he whispered, "Let me put my arms around you."

I arranged myself so that my head fit into the space below his chin.

"You know I go out of my way not to trouble you with my work." He waited for my agreeing nod before he continued. "And I won't. Not without your permission." His touch was urgent, but not intense as it had been on the ghost stairs, the day he offered me his grandmother's ring.

Franklin and his father had been on the cover of the *Atlanta Daily World* twice, due to their fight against city hall. McHenry & McHenry were filing motions left and right to stop a freeway from cutting through Old Fourth Ward, splitting Sweet Auburn in two. It was a lost cause, everyone knew, but they came at it hammer and tongs.

In addition to saving neighborhoods, as Race Men, they represented folks denied money, access, or humanity in the public square. A month or so ago, he'd secured a three-hundred-dollar settlement for a gentleman who was forced to ride from Wilmington to Washington in the restroom of a passenger train, despite the fact that he held a first-class ticket. The old man arrived for his grandson's graduation reeking of piss and humiliation. My Franklin had argued that case and won a solid egg for the family's nest.

His chest, against my ear, rose with his question. "Do I have your permission to tell you what weighs on me?"

"Yes," I said. "I love you, you know that."

"At the NAACP, they get letters," he said. "There's a girl whose job it is to keep track. The ones she thinks we can help with, she delivers. A lot of them end up in the file cabinet—labeled, dated, sometimes rewritten if the original handwriting is hard to read. We can't help everybody, but we take note of every single one. A new girl just started last week after the one before her quit. It happens. Sometimes the letters can just be too much. You follow me?"

I nodded, hoping I didn't smear my rouge onto his shirt.

"This new girl put a letter in the inbox that should have been filed away because there wasn't anything we could do for these poor people. There I was at my desk, having my lunch, flipping through the mail. I was half-hoping for one of these frilly notes you send me from time to time."

Above me, he angled his chin down to kiss my head, his lips landing on the hair clip above my ear.

"My father never brings his work home to my mother. Says it's so as not to dim her sunshine. He said, 'Your wife brings the light to your life. If you put out that flame, the two of you end up just sitting in the dark.' "

"He underestimates your mother," I said.

His crisscrossed arms held me fast. "You understand me. Do you know how good that feels? I hope I can understand you in return. I know I don't, not yet. But I am learning you."

"Tell me," I said. "Tell me what's got you so strange today."

"Louise Neville was a woman who was raised up in Oscarville, before they built the dam and flooded the whole town. It was a nice place, too. But the state decided that it would be better off as a lake, so *whoosh*. The whole town just gone. So, she moved to live with some relatives in a town close to Augusta. She got married, had three children, all under ten. Well, she was in a corner store and she made the mistake of handling some walnuts in a barrel. When she went to the counter to have her bundle weighed, the shopkeeper's wife accused her of stealing. One thing led to another and Louise ended up leaving in a huff. She didn't get to the street before the shop owner came out behind her with an axe handle and clubbed her to death in front of God and her children. He beat her face off her head."

Franklin's voice strangled a little and he coughed it clear. "The letter detailed the whole thing. The signatory was her pastor. But he included a sheet of lined paper from a school tablet. Just a sentence printed with such care that I could tell the child who wrote it is at the head of the class. It just said, *We are motherless and naked like peas without a pod.*"

Then he let out a sound that was akin to a laugh. "When I hear myself saying it, it sounds rather maudlin. But if you could see the lines and feel how soft the paper is. Vernice, I put my head down on my desk and wept."

I struggled to release myself from his tight hug and pulled myself upright. I searched his face to see if tears stood in his eyes to match the anguish in his voice. I was nearly twenty and Franklin was thirty-three. His eyes, pleated at the corners, shone with empathy for these children.

I recalled Annie and me harvesting crowder peas on her grandmother's land. We pinched the pointed hull until it burst, then we drove the damp, vulnerable peas out with our thumbs. It seemed cruel now, like pouring salt on snails.

I opened my mouth to reassure my fiancé, to remind him that the work that he did for weary travelers, busted blocks, and defiant students was more than his share. But when I tried to speak, my throat gave me plenty of air but no voice.

His arms were around me, once again, returning me to their nest. "I was crying for those children, but not just them. I thought about you, and your mother."

Nobody, not Joette or even Annie, had shed tears for me, a naked pea without the safety of a pod. I touched his cheeks in the way of the blind, learning his face by feel, searching for the damp promised by the quaver in his voice.

"Could you cry for Annie? Her mother is passed now too."

I rubbed his tears on my dry lips and verified their authenticity by taste.

"I want to marry you today," I told him. "I want to be yours for the rest of my life."

"You mean it," he said. "You want to be my wife."

"I do; I do; I do."

*Chapter 26*

# ANNIE

I grieved twenty-eight days, from one monthly through to the next. For those weeks, I washed my hair only when the smell of stale oil caused my pillowcase to reek. I worked every day I was scheduled, but I didn't shake fancy cocktails the first. I didn't allow Bobo to touch me, not even in the morning, which was our favorite time to be together. He rested two hopeful fingers on my hip, but I just wiggled myself out of reach. "My mama is gone," I said in a whisper sharp enough to debone a chicken. "I apologize," he returned, sounding truly ashamed.

One Wednesday evening, as I mopped up spilled beer with a sour sponge, the woman with the tangerine lipstick sashayed in. She looked better than she had in the days when I had mistaken her for Hattie Lee. Her cheeks were fuller and the lipstick was square on her lips, carefully applied to accent the little dip at the top. The same color shone on her eyelids. Propping herself up on the bar, she fished a dollar bill from her cleavage. It was folded back and forth, like a notebook paper fan.

"Give me a Cuba Libra, because that's my sign. October seventeen."

I pulled down a highball, but she tapped the bar. "Short glass. I like more Cuba than Libra."

I mumbled an apology and got back to work.

"What's wrong with you?" The high note in her voice said this wasn't her first stop of the evening.

"Grieving," I said.

"She lost her mama," Babydoll explained.

"Oh, you poor little thing," the lady said, half-rising from the stool and grabbing on to my busy hands. "Oh, you poor little baby."

This was the tone of voice ladies at church always used with Niecy. The lady stood on the bar rail, which allowed her to tower. Like a child, I looked up at her.

"You poor sweet little thing. But you have an angel now. Maybe she is up there right now with my mama, dealing bid whist. When your mama is in heaven there is nothing to stop her from loving you—not a man, not a job, not whatever she wanted to be doing but she had kids instead. When the sun shines, you can feel that pure love on you. It tastes like sugarcane."

That next morning, I woke up to the sun warming my oily face because I had been too sad to bother pulling the shade when I went to bed. The lipstick lady was right. That light on my face had the woody sweetness of fresh cane. It was alive in my mouth and my nose. I turned toward Bobo, who had taken to sleeping tucked into a tight ball, like a pill bug under threat. I set my two fingers on his body in invitation.

"You back?" he said.

I let my answer reach his ear as a hum.

---

Bobo called these our "salad days." They were the happiest of my life. I don't know why I am so intent on having my life up on a scoreboard. Bobo said that I should always say, "This is the best *so far* . . ." Because you never know what God has tucked away in his back pocket. Fair enough, but I am not a greedy person. The pleasure given to me in those months was enough to remedy all my life's sadness. The four of us pranced all over Memphis like the whole state of Tennessee was created for our enjoyment.

For the first time, we had some real money.

Bobo was still at the Peabody with his web-footed friends, but the Duckmaster went on back to his hometown to finish getting old, and Bobo was moved up in the ranks. Now he had a kid to train, and he let the youngster do most of the *yessuh* parts of the job. Not only that, but he found a blues singer in need of a piano player, so every Thursday he had work that paid like a job but didn't feel like one. To make it even sweeter, Mr. Wilson let Bobo's band play on the last Saturday of the month. Now when people called me "Spoken For," they could see by who.

As for Clyde, he found himself a job he could keep. There was still broom-pushing, but his boss was a colored man who played the role of a kind father. Babydoll was pleased because Clyde's boss was married and urged Clyde to go on and seal the deal.

Two-plus years at the Elektra had earned me and Babydoll some seniority. She only took care of the high-top tables and booths. Occasionally, Mr. Wilson pulled me off the floor if enough customers requested the expensive cocktails that I had turned them on to. When the liquor truck included a fifth of triple sec along with the usual spirit delivery, I knew that I had made my mark.

I don't mean to give the impression that I danced on Hattie Lee's grave. Everyone can tell you that I mourned like a widow. If I had owned black clothes, I would have worn them. Yet I felt unburdened. Now, when anyone asked me about my family, I said, "My mother passed just this year." It was normal to be a grown woman and to have buried your mother. Next time I saw Niecy, I was going to ask her if she was glad, finally, to be old enough to tell people that her mother was dead and not rustle up a herd of wild speculation. In those months that my mother was with God, I was normal, for the first time in my life.

---

On the last Saturday in February, Bobo's band played the Elektra. The front man, Luster Lee Lockhart III, was known for what they used to call swamp blues. (Imagine if Louisiana and Mississippi had a baby.) I loved it, but Babydoll said it sounded to her like zydeco with the flu. But even if you didn't like this particular style of music, you couldn't help but love the energy. People drank and danced, and Lordy, did they tip.

Luster Lee took a shine to Babydoll, but lots of people do, especially after midnight. On this particular night, things were a little bit more complicated because Clyde was in the house, seated at a two-top, just to the right of the platform where the musicians set up their instruments.

Babydoll's tips looked good on him. Wearing a shiny red shirt and a necklace that may have been real gold, he was something to see, like a visitor from a hipper planet. He puffed on a store-bought cigarette and let it keep burning in the ashtray to let the world know that he had money enough to buy another pack. As Babydoll crisscrossed the room serving cocktails and making money, she shimmied herself against his back when she passed him. The smoke rolled into a halo above his head as he grinned with all those mismatched teeth, pleased as punch.

Halfway through the second set, Luster Lee came down with a coughing fit. He doubled over and hacked, but graciously turning away from the crowd. Wiping his mouth with his sleeve, he extended the microphone to Babydoll.

"Come on up here, angel. Sing a couple of songs while I get my act together."

Babydoll managed to make herself look surprised and shy as she stepped up to the platform. "I don't sing Cajun," she said.

Bobo tickled the keys. And to everyone's surprise, even Clyde's, she sang the quiet opening line to "Don't You Know." I had seen my friend sing in church, but that was different. She was still dedicated to the Virgin, but here in Memphis she worshipped according to Clyde's tradition—Sanctified. At their church, the music was loud enough for God to hear it all the way in the upper room. On the little platform stage, she confused us all by being prim and proper like Della Reese herself. She sang that song like she and Clyde were alone. "Can't you see, I'm under your spell." My heart squeezed tight for her, exposed like this in front of everybody.

For the next song, she popped her fingers at Bobo to up the tempo. The bass player hopped in and nearabout everybody was on their feet dancing to "I Just Want to Make Love to You." This time she used her got-the-spirit voice. That girl was putting the electric in the Elektra. Luster Lee bounced up from his chair and sang with her. His voice was raspy and hers was sweet. She bumped and he grinded. She was dressed for work in her black button-down and simple trousers and he had on a shirt that could have been stolen from Elvis. I could hardly keep up with all the raised glasses in the room wanting another round.

It was a great performance, and I understood it for what it was meant to be. Bobo was all over that piano, caught up in the rapture of the music and counting out his share of the tips in advance. Babydoll preened, enjoying all the eyes upon her. Luster Lee was feeling horny, show or no show. Clyde Alexander Robinson was mad as hell.

Until now, I had only known him to be easygoing. This was part of why it was so hard for him to stay employed. He just couldn't bring himself to be unhappy, and unhappiness was the backbone of most jobs. Not once had I ever heard him raise his voice to Babydoll, let alone his hand, even though she got so frustrated that she came at him with screaming voice and scratching nails. When she was at the top of her rage, he would just flash those crooked teeth and say, "Baby, why you so mad?"

On that fateful Saturday night, Clyde snapped up so hard that his chair fell over before mounting the stage in one powerful step. The whole room got quiet, unsure if this was part of the act or some real-life showdown.

"That's my woman," Clyde said. "Everybody in here knows we together."

All the liquor in him caused his words to get snagged on his lips.

Luster Lee acted baffled, like he didn't notice Babydoll hooked in his arms with her rump on his belt buckle.

Bobo, for his part, kept on the piano, trying to mellow the

situation, but when Luster held up his hand, he had no choice but to let the ivories go dead.

"This here is your wife?" Luster Lee asked Clyde. "If so, I offer my apology most humble."

Clyde stood there, swaying drunk, thrown off by a trick question.

"If she ain't your wife," Luster Lee went on, "then you need to take it up with the lady when we done with this song." And with that he gestured for Bobo to play, but my man hesitated, fingers still above the keys.

"Clyde is my cousin."

This whole time, Babydoll lived up to her name, like a child's toy up under the Christmas tree. When Bobo started playing again, she let her body be spun when Luster Lee wanted her to twirl. He bent his knees, she bent hers. I turned my eyes to Bobo, who let his fingers do what they needed to do, but his whole attention was on Clyde, who was stock-still in front of the stage.

The mood in the room was green around the gills. The dancers had returned to their seats. Clyde's cigarette in the ashtray burned down to gray powder.

When Luster Lee had Babydoll spinning like a top, Clyde called out, "We engaged!"

Now Babydoll stopped dancing. "We are?"

Clyde sank down to his knees with a thunk that must have hurt. "If you'll have me."

Everybody in the room roared with approval.

Luster Lee stepped back several paces, like he thought matrimony was contagious. Bobo and the bass player improvised a funky version of "Here Comes the Bride."

The number runner in the back left corner let all his rings catch the light. "Get us a round for everybody!"

Like I said, I am not a big drinker, but we all drank big that night. The men raised their glasses to Clyde's boldness, while we ladies raised our glasses to romance, saluting the rare occasion of seeing someone be so lavishly loved.

Some women want to get married so bad that it makes their teeth ache at night. Niecy's letters were full of reports of girls like that, seeking their "Mrs." degrees. She said they sometimes didn't even finish their diplomas, and their families didn't even get mad about all that tuition not buying them a certified college graduate. When I read those notes aloud to Bobo, he clucked his tongue and said, "Some people are just determined to believe in Santa Claus." Watching Babydoll and Clyde slow-drag across the sticky floor, the sparkly shadow on her eyes twinkling like pixie dust, it made me a believer, too.

We stayed out so late that by the time we walked home, the saints were suited and booted as they made their way to church. Arm in arm with Bobo, I delighted in the women's pinched brows and the men's wistful lips. The sidewalk was littered with playing cards, causing a lady in a brown hat to take clumsy steps to avoid touching them with her suede shoe.

Spying an ace of spades, Bobo bent down, picking it up for luck. He slid the card in his pocket but didn't rise.

"Annie Kay," he said, "what about us? How about we get married, too?"

Back at our place, we were happy, joyful even. We might not have ripped each other's clothes off, but it was only because we were worn out. I was too sleepy to tie up my hair and he was too beat to wash his face. We hit the hay, promising each other we would properly celebrate tomorrow. Bobo licked a kiss between my shoulder blades to prove his intentions.

We were asleep, tangled together like a pair of puppies, when a tap at our door stirred us. My eyelids were so tacky with mascara that I had to pull them apart. Bobo just grunted but didn't quite stir. I waited until there was a second tap before elbowing him awake and calling out, "Yes?"

Bobo, with the anger of an interrupted dream, demanded, "Who is it?"

"I'm looking for Annie Kay." It was a man's voice, but not

menacing or sexy. "Annie Kay Henderson," the voice continued like there could be another Annie Kay laying up in the room.

"This is Annie," I hollered, climbing out of bed, reaching for a brassiere and a muumuu.

"It's Isaiah," he said. "I don't mean you any harm."

"Isaiah?" Bobo said, pulling on some trousers without the decency of underwear. He was barely clothed when I pulled open the door to find Isaiah's voice and rubber-eraser hair linked to a face I could hardly recognize.

The six months and change had gotten to Isaiah like a hive of termites. The apples of his cheeks had rotted, and the weight of the empty skin pulled his mouth down at the corners, announcing his sadness.

"Is it Sweet?" I asked, ushering him to the little table. "Something happen to him?"

Bobo stood shirtless and suspicious. He reached behind him, found his hat, and pulled it on.

I spooned some Nescafé in a cup and put the kettle on even though Isaiah said I shouldn't bother. "I ain't worth a cup of coffee."

"What exactly is going on here?" Bobo frowned at me.

"I have sinned," Isaiah said. "The Lord has stripped me of my gifts. Me and Sweet know some congregations won't have us, but we have a relationship with Jesus, separate and together. God made us and He loves us how He made us."

"I'm following," said Bobo.

"But now," Isaiah said, spreading his hands, "He done took it all from me. Sweet caught the spirit and started speaking in tongues. It's sacred, you know, when God gives you His language."

"Glossolalia," Bobo said, because he has a word for every occasion.

"Sweet is a big man, but when Spirit touches him, he doesn't writhe or flap around like some of these other people. He's light like a leaf in the wind."

Isaiah didn't touch his coffee so Bobo reached toward the cup. "May I?"

"Take it," Isaiah said. "Everything else has been snatched away."

Bobo chuckled. "Oh, I know that feeling."

Now Isaiah buried his ruined face into his hands. "Today, the Lord was moving through Sweet like nothing you will ever see. The choir was singing, the preacher was dancing, an elder was testifying. You know how it is when the sanctuary is just full of spirit. It got so tight in that room that you knew that somebody was going to bust, and this time it was Sweet. The Lord's words in his mouth used to be like music to me. But not this time. And not the two times before that. Now when he talks in tongues, all I hear is baby babble. I was gnashing my teeth and rending my garment—calling out to God and asking why He is doing this to me. Everybody around thought I was crying because I was caught up in Spirit, but I was crying because I was caught *outside* of Spirit. And then, for one second, He let me hear what Sweet was saying, then shut it off again. And I knew right then that God is angry with me because of what I did to you."

"You did something to Annie?" Bobo said, getting his back up in a way that flattered me a little bit, nearly distracting me from whatever matter was at hand.

"No," I said. "Isaiah is the one who told me about my mama."

"No," he said. "I'm the one who lied about your mama."

"Oh shit," Bobo said, sucking down that lukewarm coffee to fortify himself. "I knew something wasn't right about that story. How did she pass?"

I stood close to Bobo and he hooked his arm around my waist as I whimpered a little, frightful about whatever detail Isaiah was set to reveal. "Did she suffer?"

Bobo, always so reasonable, said, "I am sure that God understands that whatever lie you told was just to spare Annie's feelings. He wouldn't take your gifts over that." Then, staring in the coffee cup, he added, "Not that I can read the mind of the Lord."

Isaiah shook his head. "You think I'm that simple?"

"No," I said. "Bobo don't mean any harm. Please stop crying. It's scaring me. Just tell me what you came to say."

"Annie Kay," he said, "Hattie Lee is not dead. She lives on South Lauderdale."

"Oh, hell no," said Bobo. "Why—"

"I didn't want to lie to you, Annie. The falsehood was intended for Sweet. He was so fond of Hattie Lee and it would have hurt his tender heart to know that she was the one what broke into our place and stole the money from the coffee can, then lit out—knowing good and well she owed Sweet three months' rent."

"So, you told him she was dead? Didn't that break his 'tender heart'?" Bobo asked.

"Well, yeah, but it was different. Besides, if he knew she was living, he might try and find her."

"Trust me," Bobo said, "I get that part. You do not want to cohabitate with anyone hell-bent on finding Hattie Lee."

I gave him a glare and he put his hands up. "No offense."

"Anyway," Isaiah said, "here go the address she left in the coffee can, where the money used to be."

He gave me a sheet of notebook paper, ruffled on the edge where it had been ripped from the spiral binding.

I snatched it from him, greedy to touch something that had been handled by my mother. I reached in the front of my shirt and tucked the paper between my breasts. The paper gave a satisfying scrape against my skin.

Then he turned and got on his knees in the same way that Bobo had done yesterday when he said he wanted to get married.

"I beg your pardon." He grasped my hands in his and gazed up at me.

The pressure of his strong fingers made me really hear the words he was saying. *I beg your pardon.* I don't know that anyone had ever begged me in my life.

"Please forgive me," he said.

"Oh no," Bobo said. "We can't go back to square one."

Responding to the heat in Bobo's voice, Isaiah aimed his apologizing at my man. "I am so sorry. As soon as Annie walked away, I could see that she was grieving her mother hard; as a Christian I should have given her comfort. Instead, I chose to be selfish and vain."

"You are being selfish right now, motherfucker," Bobo said. "She had moved on. We had moved on. And then you come over here crying and whatnot and send Annie right back to where she started from? Just because you think you're not catching the Spirit like you want to?"

"God sent me here," Isaiah explained.

"No, He didn't," Bobo said. "Stand up and get the hell out of here."

Isaiah got to his feet, unfolding himself to his full height, at least six inches over Bobo. "Can we pray together before I leave?"

"Hell no." Then my man, who never as much as stomped a roach, hauled off and punched Isaiah under his chin.

Isaiah was addled at first, like he couldn't understand why his head was hurting. Then, I guess he decided that whatever punishment he had come here to receive was not an ass-whooping, and he swung back. The sound of it was horrible, the smacking of skin on skin and the grunts of angry effort. The men were evenly matched, so no one was going to claim a fast victory. As they twisted, twitched, and twined, the table was knocked over, sending the thick stoneware mugs to the ground. Spilled coffee glistened on Bobo's shoulder blades and ruined Isaiah's shirt.

I sprinted into the hallway calling for Clyde and Babydoll, who were already there, wearing their same clothes from last night.

"What the hell?" Clyde said, crossing our threshold to find Isaiah and Bobo each holding the other too tight to move.

"That's Isaiah?" Babydoll said.

Realizing they had an audience, the men released each other. Bobo, flustered, seemed like he wanted to explain.

Isaiah said, "You can't just haul off and sock me like that. I'm still a man, you know."

"I'm a man, too," said Bobo.

"Just go on," Clyde said to Isaiah.

Isaiah made his way to the door, ass-first like he didn't trust us enough to offer us his back to stab.

"I apologize, Miss Annie," he said again.

At the doorway, Isaiah pivoted to sprint down the stairs. Bobo ran to the door and yelled down the corridor, "Ain't no such thing as speaking in tongues!"

Babydoll turned the table and chairs upright, serene as a cloud. Bobo flexed and unflexed his fists. I fondled the folded paper as Clyde fired off questions that might explain how his book-smart cousin turned into a madman.

As fights go, I suppose it wasn't too serious. We had seen much worse in the Elektra. No blood was spilled, but Bobo was going to be sore by bedtime.

"Give me the scrap of paper," Bobo said. "We're not going through all this again. Give me that paper and we are going to act like this never happened."

I shook my head no. "It's mine."

By then, Babydoll and Clyde had gotten a sense of the entire episode. Clyde let his mouth swing open as Babydoll sucked her teeth and tapped her foot. Bobo let go of the dictionary words and cussed like a mill worker.

"Let's take a vote," Bobo said. "Who all thinks Annie should just leave well enough alone?"

All three of them raised their hands. They did it quick, like there were not at least two sides to this particular story.

---

That night, Bobo and I lay in bed on our backs. The bedside lamp lit the room enough for me to study the water marks, like a child searching for animals in the clouds. Little grunts let me know he was feeling the effects of his tussle with Isaiah. I wanted to feel sorry for him with his puffy cheek and tender shoulder. After all, in his mind, he had been fighting for me.

"Piano players are not supposed to fight."

"Nobody is supposed to sucker punch somebody just doing the right thing."

"How is this right, Annie?" Bobo said. "You can't tell me that your life hasn't improved since you gave up hunting down your mother."

"I didn't give up on her," I said. "I thought she was dead."

"You completed your mourning. Baby, that sorrow had been weighing on you since I first laid eyes on you. When a girl is a little stormy, a man like me wants to follow behind you with an open umbrella. But I am exhausted now, and wet."

"She's my mother," I said.

"Tear that paper up, Annie. You grieved your mother. You did all that work, all that crying, all that understanding. What was your prayer?"

"I prayed for her to be at peace."

"You can keep praying that prayer. But pray it for yourself too."

"I can't rest knowing she is out there. Knowing she is just a couple miles from where I lay my head."

"Maybe you could," Bobo said. "Maybe you could try. This is what I learned working for Daniel. I wrenched my back lifting a case of Buffalo Trace. Daniel gave me two pieces of advice. He said, 'Stay in school, young man, because you are poorly suited to manual labor.' Then he gave me some guidance I could use on the spot. 'Lift with your legs, not with your back.' Then he demonstrated how to haul something heavy."

I lay there with the blanket tucked tight under my arms, looking for the meaning in this puzzle.

"Hattie Lee is heavy like two cases of whiskey," he said. "And I understand that she will be with you for the rest of your life. But you have to lift her with your legs, not your back."

*Chapter 27*

# VERNICE

"When you move your wedding date up, everybody thinks they know why," Mrs. McHenry said sotto voce as we walked down the front steps of Marylinda's house to the finned Buick. "Claudine Freeman had the nerve to ask me if she should be knitting a pair of booties for your bridal shower."

I am a smart person, but sometimes I am a little slow. Mrs. McHenry had whipped herself into a fine frenzy of innuendo and implication before I figured out what she was talking about. By then, she had ticked her way down a whole list of her neighbors' sins that she had overlooked. "Starting with the fact that her husband is a Jew! Not that I have anything against them. Half the Freedom Rider kids are of that persuasion. But they don't walk around pretending to be Negroes and then have the rest of us have to go along with it—like we don't have eyes in our heads. But I never not once said anything about the fact that it's usually a fly in the buttermilk, not the other way around. Why? Because I stay out of people's business."

We were halfway down Gordon Street before I could even get a word in.

"I'm not expecting," I said.

"You're not?" she said.

"No, ma'am."

Mrs. McHenry laid on her horn with three triumphant toots. "Of course you're not. I just figured that since you and Franklin have been keeping company so long . . . My son is a handsome man. I know how one thing can lead to another."

I opened my mouth to object but she waved my mouth shut. "Didn't I just tell you I stay out of people's business? But I should have known that even if you two were getting better acquainted, you are wise enough to take precautions. It's so much better now that the doctor can fit you for a diaphragm. In my day, pull-out and prayer were all we had." She shook her head.

For my part, this conversation had me blushing so hard that even my lips felt warm.

"Oh my word," she said, to my distressed face. "This is why my husband says I am obnoxious."

"But he loves it," I finished for her.

"He does," she said. "That's what you want. My Franklin is crazy about you. He would marry you tomorrow, if I would let him."

"It's mutual," I said. "That's why we want to get married in the fall. We don't want to wait."

"No, ma'am," she said. "I am not throwing together a wedding in two months. Besides, we need a date far enough in the future that nobody expects to see your daddy with a shotgun. You will be a June bride."

Rich's department store sat at the corner of Alabama Street and Broad. The six-story triangular building seemed like it was there first and then they built the street around it. Just above the front door, a large clock let us know it was about lunchtime, although my stomach had long since sounded the alarm on that appointment.

Mrs. McHenry paused before pulling open the door. "I am so proud of our young people," she said. "They stood their ground."

I looked at my shoes at this. Marylinda and the other Movement girls were especially pleased with this victory. Why hadn't I come along when I had been invited to take part in history?

The answer, of course, was Joette. She hadn't thought it was wise and I had done whatever she advised me to do, just like a little mouse.

At the time, it made sense. Even though my run-in on the Trailways bus was well behind me, I still remembered how the bus driver's spittle smelled of Sen-Sen and ashtrays. So maybe I demurred because I was afraid. And because I was too poor to be thrown out of school. Whatever my reasons were, I didn't have anything to be proud of. Crossing the threshold into the clean, well-lighted department store felt like riding a train using a stolen ticket.

"It's going to be all right?" I asked.

In New Orleans, they had a nice store like this, Maison Blanche, but I had never crossed the threshold, even when they started hiring colored clerks. There are two kinds of signs to keep a place segregated—the one that says NO COLORED, and then the ones that say how much things cost.

"To the Magnolia Room!" Mrs. McHenry announced, like she was leading an army to the escalator.

I took the ride like a tourist, gawking at the mannequins, blank-faced and slim, that displayed up-to-the-minute dresses. Amid them, shoppers wore the latest fashions with ease. And by "shoppers," I mean colored and white both. I was a little shabby in the buttercup shift I had been so pleased with when I finished sewing it. Mercifully, no one held it against me. The other shoppers seemed almost like teachers who never judge their pupils.

Just before the hostess stand, Mrs. McHenry ran into a woman whom she greeted with a smile that didn't reach her eyes. The lady's dress was a work of art. Boning corseted her middle, but under the nice summer-weight wool, no one was the wiser. As Annie would say, "money's mammy."

"Tina," Mrs. McHenry called, and kissed the woman so lightly only the lightest lipstick scar landed on her powdered cheek.

"Is this your daughter-in-law?" she asked. "I hear you're rescheduling the nuptials."

"Well, you heard wrong. Franklin is itching to say the I dos, but Vernice insists on finishing her degree. These girls today are more savvy than we were."

"Fair enough," said this Tina person as she scanned my middle. "It's a nice problem to have. I spend half my time convincing my daughter that it is not appropriate for her to take over my husband's business."

Mrs. McHenry gasped. "My word. Why doesn't she just tell you that she has no intention of getting married?"

With this, Tina cut her eyes hard.

"I'm joking," said Mrs. McHenry. "I'm joking."

"Well," Tina said, "this isn't common knowledge yet. But since we're friends . . ."

"Oh, Tina," Mrs. McHenry said. "Jesus said, don't be such a tease."

"You are not the only one with a wedding to plan. Joette and I are here to choose a china pattern."

Now it was my turn to gasp. "Joette Cunningham?"

Mrs. McHenry clasped her hands in mock-shame. "Forgive me for assuming that everyone knows each other. Vernice, meet Albertina Cunningham."

I held out my hand and Joette's mother accepted it with grace. "You girls were roommates for a while, correct?"

"Yes, ma'am. But we haven't been in touch."

"Tina," Mrs. McHenry interrupted, "enough chitchat. Who is the lucky gentleman?"

"Thomas Donaldson, Jr." Mrs. Cunningham spoke with such careful diction that I could hear the comma between "Donaldson" and "Jr."

"So it's a merger," said Mrs. McHenry.

"Why are you so obnoxious, Patty? I am not your husband, so I do not love it."

"I'm sorry," said Mrs. McHenry. "My attempt at humor obviously landed all wrong. Congratulations. Sit with us. We'll have champagne with lunch. Where is Joette?"

---

So this was the Magnolia Room, the restaurant that Marylinda was willing to go to jail for. Of course I understood that it was a matter of principle and not the flank steak and potatoes au gratin that were worth the fight. Yet I expected more grandeur than the four-top table, covered with a white tablecloth and ornamented with a large daisy leaning inside a bud vase.

We had been seated several minutes and placed an order for three Coca-Colas and a sweet tea before Joette materialized. Her face was damp, like it had been recently washed. She was maybe two words into her apology to her mother when her eyes caught mine.

In a year, Joette had put on some weight and was curvy like a *Jet* magazine Beauty of the Week. Her body was solid and unmoving, evidence that under her neat skirt and blouse was a long-line girdle. An unkind smile parted lips painted a deep magenta as an annoyed glance upward drew attention to the false lashes rimming her round eyes. She looked like an entirely different person, but when she opened her mouth, the real Joette offered proof of life.

"Oh hell," she said, either to me or about me.

"Hi, roomie," I said. I made my voice kick up a little at the end, hoping to sound girlish and excited. "Your mother just told us that you are engaged."

She sat heavily in the chair. "Mama," she said, "when they run the announcement in the paper, everyone will already know."

Mrs. McHenry chuckled. "You don't sound too excited."

"No," said Joette. "I'm excited. I'm elated."

"Me too," I said. "I'm elated, too."

The china display was only a small portion of Rich's. A few plates propped up on stands were there for you to get the basic idea. But dinner plates were only the half of it. A bride needed bread plates, soup tureens, gravy boats, spoon rests, and several other pieces. We were here, Mrs. McHenry explained, to establish my registry—a list of what I preferred. Wedding guests would come to the store, give my name, and receive a list.

"Still the same country mouse," Joette said, reading my face.

Joette's mother touched me with a gentleness I didn't expect. "Don't mind my daughter. All of this is new to most of our people."

The four of us stood before the shelf of dishes. I can't say that I was particularly moved by any of it. I didn't want to embarrass Mrs. McHenry, so I touched my finger to a design featuring plump peonies that were the precise shade of mauve as the inside of Joette's lower lip.

Joette's mother shook her head like she was my coach. "No husband wants to eat off a pink plate."

Joette offhandedly pointed at a simple plate banded with silver.

"Ah," said her mother. "Such expensive taste!"

When I finally chose an appropriate pattern, Mrs. McHenry beckoned to the salesgirl. She was white, about my age.

To her mother, Joette said, "Me and Mouse need to go downstairs and look at dresses."

"Not wedding dresses!" said her mother. "We agreed that you'll wear mine."

"And Vernice is wearing mine," piped in Mrs. McHenry.

"We just want to see what else is out there," said Joette, striding toward the elevator, confident that I would follow. And I did.

On the first floor, well-dressed women extended jeweled atomizers and asked if we wanted to try their perfume. Joette waved them away and strode toward the front door with determination. Her heels clicked against the tile floor with every angry step. I paused to accept a mist of gardenia and orange rinds.

"That's so nice," I murmured, taking note of the words looped across the bottle. I held my wrist to my face and filled my nose and lungs with the beautiful odor of opportunity. I wanted to climb inside the bottle, stoppering myself inside like a genie.

At the door, Joette glanced over her shoulder, a question on her face. She spoke my name and held the door open to the busy street.

"I have to go," I said to the saleswoman, who responded with a disappointed shrug.

Outdoors, Joette waited on the bench of a bus stop. To her left was a man wearing a billed cap, a white undershirt, and worn trousers. The sole of his left shoe had come free, revealing a striped sock. He nodded hello as he munched on a handful of peanuts. This was the center of downtown, where five streets came together. Street signs cautioned which way drivers were allowed to travel and what sorts of turns were allowed. The smell of my perfume mingled with car exhaust, causing my stomach to bubble. To Joette's left, the space was so narrow that our hips touched when I sat beside her.

"I can't take it," she said.

"You've been knowing I was engaged," I said.

"Not *you* getting married," she hissed. "*Me* getting married."

The bus stop was crowded with folks getting off from work. It was a mixed crowd but mostly colored. The man in the undershirt got up and gave his seat to a pregnant lady who sported a sailor dress trimmed with ribbons and buttons shaped like anchors. Joette frowned and turned her face away.

"That's never going to be me," she said.

Joette knew how much I wanted to be the pregnant lady everyone smiled at. But only after I was married. Steps must be taken in their proper order, or what would be the point? Franklin had chosen me, proposed fair and square. Like his mother, I had earned my way into the McHenry family.

Joette consulted her watch, then a grid fastened to the pole. "The bus will be here in three minutes. Let's get on it. Just get on it and ride somewhere so we can talk."

I shook my head. "Ride it where? Across town? And talk about what?"

Joette said, "Talk about how we still love each other."

"That's not real life," I said to her. "You know it, and I know it."

"Are you saying you don't love me?"

I sighed. "I am saying that I am engaged to Franklin. And you are about to marry into the Donaldson family—"

"He doesn't want to marry me either," she said. "Everybody in Atlanta knows it."

The pregnant lady's eyebrows twitched and she shifted her weight, like she was leaning a little closer to the radio to hear the stories. But nobody else was studying us, looking like two college girls. Still, I lowered my voice to encourage her to do the same.

"Don't ruin your life over rumors. You have to—"

"Marry somebody," she finished the sentence for me. She repeated herself in an exaggerated country accent that hurt my feelings. "We have to marry somebody!"

The bus pulled up and the doors opened with an exhausted hiss. Joette stood. "Let's just take a ride. We can figure it out later."

I stood, and she smiled with real relief. Even with the new hair, new body, and new clothes, I could read her like the Bible. I spared myself her face and whatever promises were written there as I turned away and walked back toward the department store, leaving a trail of floral and citrus behind me.

*Chapter 28*

# ANNIE

*Dear Niecy,*

*I may be engaged and my mother may be alive. I know that a normal person would be certain, but I have never led a normal life. You either, although it seems like you have one by the tail these days.*

*The engaged part should be simple, but it is not. Bobo proposed, but he has not presented me with a ring. This is not what makes me unsure if we are fiancés. Plenty of people in Honeysuckle don't see gold until they stand in front of the preacher. (Your lawyer man is cut from a different bolt of cloth.) Anyways, the question was popped and I said yes. But this is where the story about my mother and the story about my man get thorny and—truth be told—ugly as the bottom of my foot.*

*Bobo and Hattie Lee have never gotten along. True, they never met, but he has always been jealous of how much space she takes up. His claim is the same as your auntie's—all about how she had never come to find me, so why should I go looking for her? Blah, blah, blah.*

*But, I think it's because he wants to have me all to himself. It's not right. He sends money to his mother every week and once a month, she goes to the general store to call him and he goes downstairs to take her call. I never complained. I never whined about how that money could be used to help us get a real place to live instead of living in this one room with a little nook to sit and eat. I accepted that he has a mother and he has a responsibility.*

*When I was told that Hattie Lee had passed, I think he was happy. Not dancing a jig, but glad in the way you are when you can finally get some sleep.*

*This is not to speak against Bobo. He's a quality man and probably should have gone to college. I bet that the people from his church would have passed the plate to send him. He is intelligent, reads a lot, and is kind to everyone that he meets. I could see him becoming a college teacher, or even some sort of businessman that helps the colored people who don't know how to speak proper English. Granny could have used somebody like him when she had all that trouble with her property tax. But he is determined to be a musician, and he is good at that, too. I guess it must be hard for someone like him that is good at so many things. I don't know that I have any particular talent. I am smart enough, I believe. But we both know that I am not pretty. I am clean, but I will never be the kind of wife who stays home and makes things elegant. (Babydoll could, but she is not the type of woman that men like that want to marry.) It seems like you are headed in that direction, and I am pleased for you. I hope to meet your Franklin very soon.*

*So this is why I said YES when he got down on that knee and asked for my hand. Like Granny would say—he wanted to buy this cow after all, despite all the free milk.*

*Well, not one full day after he got down on bended knee, I discovered that it was all a big misunderstanding. It's too much to go into, but I was lied to and then that lie was undone. HATTIE LEE IS ALIVE.*

*Yours in wonder,*
*Annie*

---

*Dear Annie,*

*Your news of Hattie Lee has me reeling. Why is life like this? Up one day, down the next? I have shared your story with Franklin. I hope you won't mind that but I couldn't truly explain to him who I am without telling him about you. He is a trustworthy person and will never betray you or me. This is why I am marrying him. Also, he is handsome.*

*When I told him about Hattie Lee rising from the dead he asked me a strange question. He said, "Is this good news or not?" I surprised myself by not being able to answer right away. Of course I did not want your mother to be dead. But I was wondering how you were feeling about all of it.*

*If I were to discover that Arletha had somehow been living all these years, what would I feel? I suppose it's foolish to even wonder. My dead mother is the only way I know who I am. And I guess your gone mother is the same to you. So I told Franklin that maybe you can feel like yourself again. And he asked me again if this was good news. He is an intelligent man. He reminds me of your Bobo in that way. He gives me so much to think about.*

*You have not yet told me if you will be my bridesmaid. Please say yes. I can't say I do and mean it without you right there.*

*Love,*

*Niecy*

---

*Dear Niecy,*

*I promise you that I have tried to listen to Bobo, Babydoll, and even your Franklin, who was trying to give me advice by asking you that question. Babydoll has been giving me a lesson in how to be mad at Hattie so I will finally work up the gumption to get rid of the paper with her address on it. I even let her take it to her home for safekeeping, but of course I had it memorized.*

*For Christmas, Bobo gave me a bus ticket to come to Atlanta to see you and help you get ready for the wedding. I am sure you must be busy with the big day just a couple of months away, so please tell me if what I am about to ask you is out of line.*

*Will you come to Memphis for a day or two? My idea is that you can use the bus ticket. I will make Bobo stay over at Clyde and Babydoll's place and me and you can sleep head-to-feet like the old days.*

*You and I have known each other since Moses was a little boy.*

*Your first word was "mother," and I think it will be the last one I say before they put me in the dirt. Being a motherless child is so bad that they wrote a slavery song about it.*

*Arletha is gone, and it wasn't her fault, and she is never coming back. But what if you found out she was really living about a mile away? We both know what you would do—whatever it took.*

*It tears me up, I won't lie. I am in pieces inside. But if loving my mama is going to cause me to lose my man, I need to at least lay eyes on her. Or else I will be stuck with no man, nor mama.*

*So please write me back and say that you are coming. Please write me back and say that you love me. It is all one and the same.*

*Your cradle friend,*

*Annie Kay*

*Chapter 29*

# ANNIE

Bobo didn't appreciate me swapping out the ticket he saved to buy me. "The idea was for you to get away and spend some time with your friend, not for you to invite Niecy up here to participate in your madness."

This was three days before Niecy was scheduled to arrive. Because I knew he wouldn't think much of my plan, I had put off telling him. We were still a couple, but held together by a cord as fragile as spider silk. Nobody could say I didn't make an effort. I went out of my way to be sweet-smelling and soft when he got home from work. When he was late, I didn't ask any questions. I even employed some of the loving tricks that Babydoll told me about. When he walked in the door, I was as docile as a bottle of Coke and he had the church key on his ring. He took what I offered but didn't enjoy it much.

"I love you; I love you," I whispered as he labored over me, but he didn't say it back.

An "I love you" that is out in the world unanswered bedevils a space, like the ghost of a whore in Mississippi. It's lonely, then miserable, then angry. My words, left hanging, swung all over our freshly painted apartment. When I separated two plates, they wafted out like an odor. In the closet they hid in the toes of my shoes like pregnant spiders. It was terrible. Bobo never said anything about it, but sometimes he slapped his neck, then examined his palm, mystified that there was nothing there.

---

At the end of March, I took a city bus to the Greyhound station and waited for Niecy in the colored waiting area. I took a seat beside a woman dressed in a striped shirtdress who cradled a little girl decked out to match. The mother's hair was pressed to silk, but the child's hair was brushed into thick wooly buns decorated with fluffy bows.

"Hello," the girl said in that odd accent that all children seem to have, like they are only now forgetting the language they spoke before they were born.

"Hello," I said, and returned her little wave.

Her mother smiled with tinted cheeks. There was no road leading from my life to hers. Even if I were to marry Bobo and we had ourselves a daughter, I could never pull off the magazine perfectness that this lady displayed so easily. I studied her and she watched me back and I wondered what she thought of me in return.

Since none of us carried lunch bags, I figured they were here waiting on someone just as I was waiting for Niecy. I covered my eyes in peekaboo until the little girl laughed. I was touched by the music of it. I wondered if I had been cute as a small child. I wondered if I made women wish for babies of their own.

Buses are sometimey. They get here when they get here. I don't even know why they bother with a schedule. I was at the station right on time, because you never knew, but after an hour and twenty-five minutes, I wished I had brought a lunch bag for myself. The mother clearly had thought ahead, and fed her little girl raisins with one hand and read a book of poems with the other. The child pranced around singing "The Itsy-Bitsy Spider." The word in the air was "precious."

Around the two-hour mark, the little one shifted her weight from leg to leg.

"Mommy," she said, and we all knew what it meant.

The mother surveyed the room but the man sitting quietly in the corner shook his head no.

I turned, hoping for a sign that said COLORED TOILETS. After all, there was a colored water fountain. If someone had the foresight to see that colored folks got thirsty, certainly they knew that we needed to pee. When I was little, before we set out for town, Granny would sit me atop the toilet stool and wait for me to empty my bladder. If she wasn't satisfied with the amount of water I let go, she waited until I had to go again.

Everyone in the waiting area was gripped with panic, even the men. We did not want this baby to spoil her clothes. We did not want her father—whom we pictured to be as elegant as the rest of the family—to emerge from the back of the Greyhound and find his child soaked in urine.

"Carry her out back," one woman suggested, her voice high with worry. "Just let her squat by the bushes."

The man wearing the red shirt produced a handkerchief. "You can clean her with this."

"I'll watch your stuff," I offered, like the little drummer boy, just doing what I could.

The mother rose and, jerking the little girl's arm harder than she needed to, rushed from the room, snatching the handkerchief as she made her way. Everyone breathed in relief. Conversation started back up, with people swapping who they were waiting on and for how long it had been. I spoke Niecy's name.

Then we heard the little girl crying and we knew her mother had swatted those short chubby legs with a green switch, and we got quiet again.

When they returned, the little girl clutched the pissy handkerchief like a comfort blanket. "My husband will pay you for the handkerchief."

"Naw," the man said. "I didn't aim to sell it to you."

To me she said, "Thank you very much."

Somehow the child had lost one pink ribbon and her ruffled sock was scrunched under her heel. I covered my eyes in peekaboo, but she didn't want to play.

. . .

The bus arrived at the station fewer than five minutes later. The girl was too young to understand that if she had only held on a little longer, she could have avoided the contagious humiliation that had the whole room hangdog and quiet. We sat there after the announcement, giving all the white folks a chance to hug their relatives on the other side of the wall. The lady swinging the broom had confided that there was nothing special over there. The only halfway-luxury thing was a large clock with curlicues for hands. "And to tell the truth, it's hard to read."

Finally, the colored folks trickled in, drained from the trip but glad to be where it was that they were going. The lady's husband was dressed in jeans, starch-stiff. He dipped his wife and kissed her like that one soldier did in *Life* magazine. Then he picked up his daughter, who looped her arms around him like he was a life preserver. Despite everything that led up to it, it was nice to watch.

Niecy must have been in the back of the back, because she was nearly the last one to enter. Three years had put some weight on her, and some age, too. A filmy scarf the color of honey covered her head, and cat-eye glasses made her seem stylish and suspicious. It wasn't until I recognized my crab-blue graduation dress that I believed this sophisticated stranger was the person who knew me best in the world.

"Annie!" she said with a voice that hadn't been altered one iota by whatever had happened to her in Atlanta.

"Niecy!" I hollered back. Then we were hugging each other like two people freezing to death, each one using the other one like a heating pad.

We walked, holding hands like children. With my free arm, I carried her baby-green suitcase, and with hers she carried a matching shoulder bag that looked brand-new. After being apart so long, I thought we would be chirping at each other like a couple of chichi birds, but after our scene in the bus station we were suddenly shy. Doubt threatened to choke off my air, but I noticed that whatever hesitation we were feeling was mutual.

Like a question, I squeezed her hand. And like nodding, she returned the pressure.

"We're nearly there," I said. "You must be tired and hungry, too. I know a place where we could get some catfish."

"That would be nice," she said, just as prim.

I steered her toward the front steps of the church where me and Bobo went when we first got to Memphis and were stuck in the rhythms of where we came from. We sat down on the stone steps. The day was bright, but there was a nip in the air. Easter was early that year, so little girls would have to wear sweaters over their frilly dresses. The thought of it made me sad, for no real reason at all.

"Niecy," I said, but didn't have the words to say what I was feeling without it sounding like I was mad. "You are the first person I ever met in my whole life."

"I know," she said.

"So, tell me what's wrong," I said.

"I just don't like riding on buses."

Since she wasn't about to tell me what was wrong with her, I offered up what was wrong with me. Leading by example, like Miss Jemison used to say.

"I think Bobo is about to quit me."

"He better not," she said. "He better not break up with you."

"I'm already broken," I said, feeling the weeping coming on in the same way that a woman can feel her cycle starting, that rearranging of the furniture inside you. "I've been broken since the day my mother left me with my granny. Why can't he accept me like I am?"

Walking people slowed. Some to gawk. Some to offer help. Niecy shooed them away with the arm that she wasn't using to hug me close.

"Me too," she said.

"Heartbroke?" I asked, searching her face through the blur of my tears.

She nodded. "Not yet. The rainbow is bending my way, but I can smell the devastation in the air."

I started to say, "You can't see the future," but I didn't know for sure if that was true or not. Instead I just said, "You could tell me. What are you so nervous about?"

She said it was the somebody before Franklin. Somebody that she wasn't supposed to be with. She told me she cut it off and burned the field so it wouldn't grow back, but what is done in the dark always comes to the light. I didn't ask for a name because it wouldn't make no never mind. I didn't know a soul in Atlanta. And I didn't ask what made this lover so wrong for her because I was scared she would say something that reminded me too much of myself, Bobo, or Clyde.

"Don't fret," I said. "It's so many things worse than not being fresh. And Franklin won't care about anything that happened way back before. You have been true to him since he asked you, right?"

She nodded.

"You love him, don't you?"

Another nod.

"You don't love the other one, do you?"

She didn't nod or shake her head either. She was upright as twelve noon.

"I hate the way we always have to choose," I said.

And then we unscrewed the cap off our feelings and we sat there on South Main Street, two cradle friends, with me weeping like Mary and her moaning like Martha. My sorrow was for what had already happened and hers was just around the bend. It was how we were as friends. Not the same, but still the same.

I woke the next morning to the murmurs of Niecy's prayers. She knelt beside the bed with her folded hands tucked along the curve of her neck, knuckles pressed against her chin. I couldn't make out the core of the appeal, but the word "please" floated on the air again and again. When she finally did her amen and opened her eyes, she found me awake.

"It's Palm Sunday," she said, like that explained her desperation.

I fixed us a little breakfast on the hot plate—cornmeal pancakes, sausage patties, and dark Karo syrup. On the side was a cup of strong coffee lightened with PET milk and softened with a heaping spoon of sugar.

Niecy laughed after tasting the meal. “How did you turn into your granny?”

“Well,” I said, “you know I have a man to feed.”

Just mentioning Bobo sagged me. He had vacated our place to make room for Niecy but I didn’t know where he had gone. I only knew that he had been glad to leave.

“He’ll be back,” Niecy said. “If only for these hoecakes.”

I made myself smile.

As I rinsed thick syrup off our empty plates with water hot from the kettle, there was a knock at the door. Niecy smiled, thinking it was Bobo—because she thinks that life is like the movies.

Of course, it was nobody but Babydoll, with Clyde in tow. Since he’d proposed, she was pushing him to go Catholic. I wouldn’t go so far as to say Clyde was miserable, but it was clear he would rather have been back in his bed, preferably with Babydoll.

“Hey, Niecy,” he said, smiling with all those jumbled-up teeth. He at first made like he was going to hug her but then decided on a handshake. Right when Niecy reached for it, Babydoll extended her hand instead. “I’m Ruth.”

Of course, Niecy knew all about Babydoll from my letters, but she played it cool. “Nice to meet you.”

Poor Babydoll was so jealous that she didn’t know what to do. She didn’t appreciate that Clyde almost hugged Niecy. She didn’t like that Niecy was here as my cradle friend. As she eyed Niecy’s Thom McAn penny loafers, black instead of oxblood, and fitted with dimes, she looked like she might cry, or fight.

But Niecy has a way with people, and the manners she learned in Atlanta just made her that much easier to love.

“Gorgeous dress,” she said to Babydoll. “I wish I could look so elegant in a peplum.” Then she made herself seem sad for lack of a peplum, whatever that was.

Babydoll smiled, appreciating the compliment, all the way down to her bones.

She explained to Niecy her personal dedication to the blessed Virgin. Niecy already knew, but she let her mouth open just a little to show that she was intrigued.

This is what people learn in college. You learn how to act. I had seen it in a few people back home, namely Mr. Daniel and Miss Jemison. In just over a year, Niecy's jagged edges had been filed away. Not that she was ever a rough character. Miss Irene taught her all the manners, the "yes, ma'am," the pleases and thank-yous. I had them, too. Granny didn't raise me in a barn. But Niecy had class about her now. I tried to put my finger on what had changed about her. Was it that she had words for things that I never knew needed talking about? I listened to her back-and-forth with Babydoll and came to understand that the difference was in the way that she talked. She spoke slowly, tasting every letter, like she was teaching you how to spell it. They were chatting, I realized. *Chatting*. It was a word I had seen written on paper. Chitchat was a conversation that you were meant to have with your pinky sticking out.

Finally, Babydoll noticed the time, stood, and tugged the little ruffle at her waist. Following her lead, Clyde also sprang up.

"It's good to see you, ma'am," he said to Niecy, who gave him a soft smile that didn't show teeth.

"I mean to say Niecy," he said, after his own words hit his ears. "I don't know what's wrong with me."

---

We hadn't walked half a mile before we encountered a throng of good people, fresh from church. The Easter snap was snapping, so folks moved hurriedly. Each hand jutting from the cuff of a winter coat clutched a palm frond. Niecy looked wistful and I matched her. When we were little, it was our job to help Granny loop and crease the leaves into the shape of a cross. By the time we had made enough for the congregation, our knuckles were sliced and sore.

"Hosanna," she said softly.

"Blessed is He who comes in the name of the Lord," I finished.

A tall woman who wore no coat at all offered fronds to us both. "Hosanna."

We accepted and kept toward my destiny, the palm crosses before us like pinwheels.

"What are you going to say to her?" Niecy said.

"Whatever Spirit moves me to."

"When I was a child, I couldn't wait to see my mother in heaven." Niecy shook her head. "Aunt Irene said, 'Nobody else around here can die.' "

She had told me this story more than once, but each time her voice cracked like a hot glass touched with ice water.

"Granny shook me like a rag doll when I said I missed my mama. I was about six or seven. She could have broken my neck, all the while talking about 'after all I have done for you.' "

I, too, had shared this memory before. And I also had a voice full of shards.

---

Two twenty-five South Lauderdale was the mirror of 485 Rawlings Street. Same frame house with the same crooked patio. I walked slowly, half expecting to see another friendly landlord, protective German shepherd, and chatty "cousin." But this street was mostly quiet.

"We may as well be back in Honeysuckle," Niecy said.

I let myself take slow, full-chest breaths as I registered the details of the run-down but tidy home. A couple of lightbulbs gave a faint glow in the daylight. "Somebody is in there."

Niecy nodded and I appreciated the fact that she didn't ask me if I was sure this was the address. She trusted me to know what the hell I was doing. Maybe that was what friendship was. I hadn't seen my Niecy in three years, yet for most of my life I had seen her every single day. Three years was just a blip in a connection as long as ours. She may have been newly classy, but she was the same Niecy.

"This is the point of my whole life," I said to her.

She shook her head. "It can't be. This can't be the point of your whole life."

"Why?" I said.

"Because your life isn't even half done. You can't be at the whole point today. And . . ." She let her voice trail off the way you do when you stumble to the lip of a cliff and have to jump back a couple of paces.

"And what?" I said, hoping to sound gentle, although I felt a little less understood with every pound of my pulse. "You are not about to tell me to get ready for my mother to be a stranger, are you?"

"No," she said. "I was going to say that if meeting your mother is the point of a person's whole life, like you said, then what does that leave for me?" Her eyes were dry and red-streaked. "It's Arletha's birthday this month. So, this makes three times that she is lying in the ground back home with nobody to fill the vase."

So, there we were, kitty-corner from Hattie Lee's address, each one of us eating her heart out over her whole motherless life. We were also fatherless, but this didn't bite the same way. When you don't have your mother, you don't really know who you are. Even if you have a bad mother like Babydoll had, you can use her to know what you are not.

Niecy thumbed away my tears as the door before us opened. A girl, about fourteen, peeked out. She shut the door behind her and padded down the three steps in just her socks. Her hair was neat on the left but sleep-wild on the right. Jerking her head at a noise, she tipped back up the steps and cracked the door to let a round-cheeked little boy join her on the porch. She swung him up on her hip like a grown woman.

"Y'all missionaries?" she called. "Because everybody in this house is already saved."

Niecy and I gathered ourselves in the second it took the girl to meet us at the curb.

"No," Niecy said, handling the palm frond as though she had no idea where it came from. "We are trying to find somebody."

Now the girl was suspicious. "Are you truancy? Because I didn't get a chance to start yet, but I am fixing to. I'm smart with math. When I get to that school, they will tell me to sit in the front."

"What's your name, sweetie?" I asked her. "Maybe you can help us."

"Annie Kay," she said, bouncing the baby. "This here is my little brother, Bobby. Can you believe some people think he's my baby? People keep their mind in the gutter."

She talked like she was on a stage by herself, but I was caught up on her name. So caught up that I sat down on the curb.

"Is your mother available?" Niecy asked.

"She sleep," the other Annie said. "She works at night. I got everybody ready to go to church."

"Who all is everybody?" I asked.

"Me, Bobby, and Danny. I fixed breakfast, too. My teacher at my other school said I was a very capable person."

Her smile called up dimples so deep you could lose your finger in them. Her clothes were too small and a little bit raggedy, but she carried herself in such a way that it broadcast that she was a well-loved child.

"Your mother is Hattie Lee?" I asked, praying to God above that she would say no, that the person who loved that smile on her face was some other mother, some other woman who didn't raise some of her children and throw away the rest.

She flattened out her expression into something that was a little bit more adult. "I didn't say her name. How you know who she is?"

Niecy straightened her spine, ready to dance to whatever music I wanted to play.

"I know her from back home, is all," I said. "I was in town and wanted to say hello."

"I told you she was sleep," said the other Annie.

"Tell her I stopped by, hear?"

"You didn't tell me what your name is," said the other Annie.

"Annie, just like you." I tried to seem easy, not like I was this close to vomiting on the pavement. "Tell her Ms. Irvina is my granny."

The other Annie nodded, and moved her lips over the message so as not to forget. "That's all?"

"Tell her that she don't have to worry about me coming back."

The other Annie looked over her shoulder, sensing the hand peeling the newspaper from the window at the corner of the house.

"I gotta go," she said. "It's time for Bobby to eat some oatmeal. I'll tell my mama what you said."

Those two words, "my mama," tumbled so effortlessly from her mouth.

As the other Annie climbed back up the porch steps, I made sure to keep my face in view of the pulled-back corner of newspaper. The palm frond bounced with my nerves. I was older now, but maybe she would recognize me, my face so close to her own, and so far from the Annie she chose to love. When the door clapped shut, my mother smoothed the newspaper back in place. Her child was closed inside her house and she didn't care about anything beyond that.

---

Niecy was three days gone back home before Bobo returned to our room. He smelled clean, like barber soap, and guilty as sin.

"Annie," he said. "We need to talk."

"No, we don't," I said. "Whatever you have come here to say, I don't need to hear it."

He took off his newsboy hat and massaged his forehead. "You know I love you, Annie."

This didn't feel like the return of the "I love you" that had floated around this room for months. This "I love you" was in another category of declaration. This was an "I love you" like the one that Granny gave, like the one that Hattie Lee might have offered had I given her the chance. This kind of "I love you" was a bell without its clapper, a check with nobody's cursive name on the bottom, a winter coat without buttons.

"No," I said, sitting myself in the kitchen chair to keep from falling at his feet. "You can't replace me. Please don't tell me that you are replacing me."

Bobo fished his billfold from his pocket. "I could leave you enough money to pay on this room for another month."

He placed the bills on the table and I swept them to the floor. "You been saving up to leave me?"

The two of us sat at the table, looking at the money like it was only scrap paper.

Bobo cleared his throat. "Will you let me talk?"

I nodded. "Don't say what you practiced. Say what's real."

I got myself ready to hear one of his complicated statements, embroidered with ten-dollar words. When he talked like that, I listened to the feelings up under the words to tell me what he meant. The dictionary gave me the details, but the vibration of his voice is how I understood. When we first moved here, I touched his voice box to feel his words on my skin. But as we sat three feet apart at this table, whatever he wanted to express would come to me on the air.

"I'm ready," I said.

"Annie," he said, "I'm not fulfilled."

Three words. And how could I dispute it? If he had judged me, I could have defended myself. But instead, he spoke for himself and there was no denying it.

"Don't leave today," I said. "I can't take this back-to-back."

"Back-to-back?"

"She replaced me," I said.

Bobo may have been ready to walk out the door and leave me with four weeks' rent and a useless "I love you," but still, he was a solid person. He wasn't raised not to step up when somebody is wounded.

"What happened?" Just that question, spoken with caring, settled the room.

I didn't answer him with only words. I told him with my face, my arms, my thighs. "Oh, Annie," he said with condolence and consolation. "Oh, Annie," he said, angry when I was. "Oh, my Annie," he said with disappointment to match my own.

"I should have accompanied you," he said. "It was my role to stand beside you."

"It's okay," I said. "I know I haven't been easy to stand beside here lately."

"Regardless," he said, "I let you down."

I forgave him in the long tradition of women who have only known one man. He was singular in my bed and in my spirit. And he was sorry. And I was sorry too.

*Chapter 30*

# VERNICE

From the start of May through the eve of my June wedding, ivory-wrapped boxes arrived at the McHenry home. Each gift I'd selected at Rich's had sold, and the list at Davison's was half-cleared, too. Mrs. McHenry recorded the givers' names before adding the wedding presents to the impressive display. Each bore a tag reading *Mr. & Mrs. Franklin McHenry.* Therefore, until June 16 at two o'clock in the afternoon, these extravagant gifts belonged to a couple who did not yet exist.

We did marry on the appointed day at the appointed time. At the first note of the steeple bell, I set my left foot on the aisle of Danforth Chapel, on the campus of Morehouse College. His mother had once worn the dress that I starved myself to fit. Decades of optimistic storage had yellowed the lace. The result was heirloom ivory, not the compromised ecru required of women with pasts.

Along the back of the gown were thirty-eight pearls, each paired with a fragile satin loop. Dressing me, Annie's fingers were butterfly kisses along my spine.

"Girl," she said, "if you so much as think about a piece of pound cake, you will pop out of this dress and pearls will go flying."

"Have you ever heard of anybody fitting into a wedding dress with ease?"

Annie situated a couple more pearls, considering. "I don't think I know much at all about weddings."

I fought the urge to apologize and draw attention to my faux pas. It was easy for me to lose track of all the ways that Annie and I traveled different roads. These misspeaks didn't seem to bother her, but my comments made me feel as though I were putting on airs.

"Thank you for coming," I said. "I know it wasn't easy to get here."

She had arrived the night before with Bobo, Clyde, and Babydoll in tow, missing the rehearsal dinner entirely. They had rolled into Atlanta in the Packard that they called the Miracle-mobile because it was constantly on its last leg. That morning, I'd overheard my mother-in-law on the telephone. "The maid of honor washed up on our lawn after midnight. We put them up at Forrest Arms." I don't know what was said on the other side, but it earned a low chuckle.

"Did you sleep well?" I asked her.

"Like a rock. The rest of them went out to hear some music, but I had to get some beauty sleep."

We sat for a few moments, gazing at our reflections in a brass-framed mirror. Annie's dress had been made to order but managed not to fit her, straining over her bosom and buckling at the waist. Yet the color, the bold blue of her graduation dress, amplified her familiar beauty. I had let my mother-in-law choose many of the details for the day, but I could not be budged on Annie's gown.

I enjoyed the quiet the way Annie and I used to enjoy the dregs of summer when we were children. I was always torn on those dog days. I wanted the unstructured days to continue, but I was also eager to see what the New Year would bring. Annie was always melancholy in August. She didn't enjoy school like I did—not the books, or the clothes, or the socializing. She was a person built for the summer—the heat, the fruit, the adventure.

"You ready?" she asked me.

"It was in the paper," I said. Before this, my name had never been in print, outside of the mimeographed program for graduation in which a careless typist had transposed two of the letters. This meant my true name had never been published. And now that I was getting married, my name was news. It would appear in the *Daily World* and the *Inquirer* both.

"But how do you feel?" she asked. "Like really really feel."

"Blessed," I said. "Blessed and lucky."

"Then it's what I want," Annie said. "If an angel came down from heaven and told me that she didn't have but one cup of happiness, I would tell her to pour it over you."

She didn't have an ivory box to add to the ones heaped on the table. I hadn't even told her about the registry. But this gift, the imaginary offering from an imaginary angel, was more meaningful than china and flatware bound with gold-wired ribbons.

"And I would give it back," I said. "Nobody deserves to be happy more than you."

Mrs. McHenry interrupted us in a cloud of perfume and limoncello. Dressed in moody pink, she radiated uncomplicated joy that verged on victorious.

"Simply gorgeous. The second time's the charm," she said, reminding me that the dress had been hers. "Take care of it. Maybe my granddaughter will wear it too. But I am always ahead of myself. My husband loves it."

Annie said, "You look so pretty, Mrs. McHenry."

She fluttered her eyelashes because she could never resist a flirtatious response to a compliment. "You aren't too bad yourself, Annette!"

In the mirror, Annie and I raised our eyebrows.

Tugging the bodice to center the dip of the sweetheart neck, she said to Annie, "I love this little girl so much." She squeezed my shoulders like she couldn't stand the idea of not touching me.

"Mrs. McHenry—" I began.

"Vernice, the instant you walk out of the church, you must call me Mother!"

The lemon on her breath mingled with her perfume, creating a fragrance that made me smile.

"That was her first word," Annie told her. " 'Mother.' "

"Well, here I am," she said. Popping open her beaded bag, she handed me a small velvet box containing a simple pair of pearls, perched in a nest of gold wire. They were lovely, but I was already wearing the paste pearls that Annie had left on the chifforobe when she left for Memphis.

When I met my friend's eyes in the mirror, they were no longer amused.

"I already have earrings," I said.

Mrs. McHenry said, "But these are my gift to you. Put them on."

Annie piped up. "But she needs something old, something new. Almost everything she has on is new."

"My dress is the something old," she said.

"These are . . ." Under Mrs. McHenry's gaze, all the wrong words came to mind, like "fake," "coarse," "cheap." The earrings were all these things, but they were more. "They are from my family."

In the mirror, Annie's eyes smiled and mouthed the word. *Family*.

"Very well," said Mrs. McHenry with a sigh.

I closed my eyes to focus on the sensation of the earrings, screwed on tight. I'd keep them always, but I knew I would never wear them again.

---

The older McHenry brothers had both married in the churches where their wives had been baptized, large houses of worship that could accommodate bridesmaids, groomsmen, flower girls, ring bearers, and even a holy light brigade for the candles. Danforth was an enchanted jewel box. As with the Fabulous Fox Theatre, I was unaware that there were several chapels by this same name, sprinkled throughout the land. And just as before, it didn't matter because no matter how many Danforth Chapels there were, only one ushered me into the life I deserved.

At the opening chords of "Here Comes the Bride," the guests took to their feet. The ten wooden pews on each side were filled with people gathered to bear witness to my good fortune. Aunt Irene twisted in her seat to catch me at the threshold. Ohio suited her. Spiral curls hung from her temples, festive and somehow girlish. Clad in peach and lace was Miss Jemison, and beside her were the three Louisiana refugees—Clyde, Bobo, and Babydoll.

Annie and Marylinda waited at the altar. Annie's face, colored only with a swipe of lipstick, was wide open and gracious. Marylinda could have upstaged me, but she had refused the services of Mrs. McHenry's hairdresser. Instead, she copied a coif inspired by the women of Senegal—two cornrows tracing her hairline and festooned with wooden beads. The thick hair in the back was back-combed until it was sort of next door to an Afro. Franklin would later say she looked like a radical dandelion. Her father, long, lanky, and kind, stood in for my long-dead, murderous daddy.

Between his two suave brothers, with their wet-comb waves, stood Franklin, without the aid of his cane. Where they seemed lacquered and set, he looked flexible and sweet as saltwater taffy. How I wished I could have watched him travel the distance of the pews, one hard-earned pace at a time.

I processed the melody that emerged from the upright in the corner. It occurred to me that the piano was a percussion instrument, the music pounded out, not blown or strummed. It was an observation I would have mentioned to Joette, in those days when we talked about everything. With this thought, I swatted my mind like it was a naughty child. I focused my attention on what awaited me at the altar—a miracle of a man, swiping at his eyes with the back of his hand.

---

The next time I thought of Joette, it was not the fault of my wandering mind. It was because she sat in the pews, thigh to thigh with her own fiancé. Together, they embodied the solidity that comes about when two rich people decide to get married.

"She doesn't love him, though," Marylinda told me once.

"She told you that?"

"No," said Marylinda. "I just happen not to be blind."

I wasn't blind either, and I could see that Joette Michelle Cunningham was miserable. Some women are made radiant in their suffering, but not Joette. Her emerald necklace was stunning, but her face was casket-ready. I reminded myself that I had no real evidence as to the source of her sorrow. Life, even for those with advantages, was rife with all manner of disappointments. She could very well have been devastated over some other girl. After all, a person could get a lot done, love-wise, in a couple of years. Who was I to assume that all this sulking was about me and the time we had spent together in that slanted dorm room?

Still, I knew her well enough to know that Joette wanted to be in this chapel on the day that I made my promise to Franklin. Just as she didn't say what she didn't mean, she didn't RSVP yes when her mettle said no. If she became a Donaldson bride, it would be because she chose to, even if the reason was not love. She was present at my wedding, even if the reason was not to wish me well.

---

The reception was at Paschal's, a mile or so away, on Hunter Street. The ceremony itself was limited to who could fit in the tiny church, but for the party, Mrs. McHenry invited every Negro in Atlanta who had two dollars to rub together. Doctors, lawyers, pastors, insurance salesmen, undertakers, educators, and anyone else who moved the needle in the direction of progress. By this, Aunt Irene was especially tickled. It turned out that she knew Robert, one of the Paschal cousins, from all those years ago in Jacksonville. In those days, he was pretending to be a fortune teller, but now he had gotten saved and rich, too. She charmed him into standing beside her in the foyer as she took her place in the receiving line. The air trembled with her throaty laughter and his chortle, which sounded like a heavy clap on the back. If you didn't know better, you would have thought they were married.

Annie and Marylinda remained in the ballroom long enough

to see me and Franklin dance a few steps to "The Nearness of You" as everyone roared with approval. As I pivoted on the balls of my hand-dyed pumps, I watched them slip out the back of the hall. Joette joined them, holding hands with Marylinda like the girl-cousins they were. It felt like a page turning on my life, more than the moment when I promised to love, honor, and obey. This was the line between what was and what would be.

I admired their bodies as they left. Marylinda was built like a cello, Annie like a graceful egg. Dear Joette was lean and functional like a lightning rod. Returning to their lives of girlish uncertainty, they were three misses and I, on this side of the doorway, was Mrs. Franklin McHenry. A person could refer to me now without speaking any of the names I had been born with. The door opened again, and Annie tipped in and retrieved her cloth purse. Without a backward glance, she left again, a vision in that intense shade of blue.

Franklin appeared at my side. I expected a cliché like "Hello, Mrs. McHenry." But instead, he asked, "How is your heart?"

I took a moment to take inventory of myself. How *did* I feel? My ribs registered the pinch of the corseted whalebone bodice, but it was merely my body that felt trapped and molded into an unnatural form. How did I feel? I took in as much air as my compressed lungs allowed and circled my tongue over my teeth, searching for the taste of my own mouth. I shut my eyes and tried to register a pulse of life from each segment of my anatomy, starting with my tiniest toe, wedged into satin pumps, up to my ankle beneath smooth silk stockings. I paused at the place where my legs came together, shrouded behind pale lace panties—something blue—and there, I was aware of a quiet thump of anticipation. Beside me, Franklin waited through this entire bodily roll call. Finally, I stood straight.

"Mouse is gone," I said. "I'm Vernice all the time now."

I spun around. In my heels, our faces were level, and I kissed my husband. "What about your heart?"

"Overjoyed," he said, speaking the word directly into the air I breathed. "Overjoyed."

. . .

He was an easy man to love, and love him I did. This was the difference between me and Joette. She was the sort of person who knew only one way to be satisfied, setting her mind on what or who she wanted and nothing else would do. It was a rich-girl thing, had to be. I couldn't imagine me and Annie back in Honeysuckle being so brittle. We did with what we had, and the pleasure that warmed our chests was real. When Franklin dipped me to the cheers of the room, the happiness stretching my face and crinkling my eyes was as genuine and hard-won as the cloudy diamonds on my hand.

---

Back in the bridal suite, I struggled to undo the line of pearl buttons. Everybody wants to help the bride get ready, but nobody wants to help her remove the finery, except maybe the groom, but Franklin was downstairs enjoying this occasion with his brothers. As I contorted, fussing with the various fasteners as best I could, the door opened behind me.

"Annie," I said. "I thought I would never see you again."

She pressed her face forward, as though getting a better look at me. "Are you losing your mind?"

"I love you," I said. "You know that, right?"

"Hold still," Annie said. "Let me help you."

With the release of each hook and eye, my lungs spread a little more. "Annie," I said, "you are a good friend." Maybe it was the champagne, but her assistance felt like a gift unmeasurable. The dress had me fast, and out of nowhere here was Annie, who had been baptized with me in the same pool of water, Annie, who was there when the grocer had tried to slip his hands where they didn't belong. He offered us fifty cents. Annie took the money and then kneed him right under his belt. She gave me a quarter although I hadn't done anything to help. Annie was my best friend even though we took different tines at the fork in the road.

"Niecy," she said once I was out of the dress and sitting there in my girdle and struggling to unstrap my shoes, although I could hardly bend over. "Now I see why they call me a brides-*maid.*" She knelt beside me and undid the ankle straps. Glancing up at my face, she said, "That was a joke."

"I know," I said. "I just can't breathe well enough to laugh."

Her hands kneading my calves were strong and capable, so different from the way Joette touched me. She blew out a long breath that I knew to be a preamble.

"What, Annie?"

"I talked to her."

"Who?" I said, but I knew the answer.

"You need to know what's being said."

"Jesus," I said, reclining as best I could in the stiff undergarments that turned my body into a sculpture.

Annie tugged at her fingers, releasing each knuckle with a crack. "How you want this? Straight up or on the rocks?"

I wasn't even sure what that meant, when it came to information, but I said, "On the rocks."

"She told me the whole thing," Annie said. "At least I reckon it was the whole thing. It took three rum and Cokes and about forty-five minutes to tell it. Even if I don't know all of it, I am pretty sure I know more than the half."

I took two breaths, long and slow. "At La Carrousel? Why is she trying to ruin my life?"

Annie said, "She didn't tell nobody but me."

"Why is she talking at all?" Below my collarbones, rage mixed with shame. Who was Joette to share details so intimate to my cradle friend? And what kind of cradle friend was I to have held back such a secret? And while I was wondering, I had to add one more question: what kind of wife was I, harboring a full set of closet bones?

"She told me because she knows I'm the one in the room who is going to love you no matter what. She don't want to mess up your situation. She can't ruin your life without ruining hers back."

I painted fresh rouge on my cheeks and said, "So what do you want to say, Annie?"

Annie shrugged. "I ain't got nothing to say—to you or to anybody else."

"Annie," I said, "I never not once strayed off the path. The one time, Annie. The *one time* I fall in the bayou and it comes to bite me on my wedding day."

Annie reached behind her neck to scratch her back. "I didn't say you did anything wrong. Maybe you did something a little different, but it's not for me to say it was wrong."

Once she was satisfied with her scratching, she asked me to unzip her dress and she shimmied out, not having even bothered with a girdle. Then she rummaged in the stack of clothes on the floor between the double beds. Finally, she found a rayon swing dress and pulled it over her head.

"Before I go back down," Annie said, "I want to point out what you haven't said."

"Oh Lord, Annie. What?"

"You ain't said your fiancé's name one time."

"Husband. I'm married now."

"Whatever. You know what I'm saying."

"Annie, grow up. A wedding is a full-on production. Today is not about Vernice and Franklin. This is about the society page, his family, Spelman, Morehouse, Atlanta. Today is my wedding day, *tomorrow* is when I begin my married life."

Annie nodded in a way that said that she didn't believe me. "Mmm-hmm."

"Annie, we are not in Honeysuckle. This is not our mothers saying 'I do' after church."

"You know Hattie Lee never got married," Annie said.

"Oh, Annie, that wasn't what I was trying to say. I'm sorry."

She nodded this time and I knew that she was sincere. She took a sip from the water glass on the nightstand.

"Niecy, you got a big life ahead of you and I begrudge you not a thing. You earned that Union Army ring and what have you. But, Niecy, this is not how you are. You do right by people."

"Annie," I said, "what can I do? I just got married."

"You can talk to her. You obviously are done with all . . ." She flapped her hand in confusion. “All *that*, but she’s a person and you got to tell her to her face. You can love a person, but you can’t be with them. You could tell her that.”

“It’s too much,” I said. “This thing with Joette . . . I don’t know what she wants.”

“Well, that’s a lie. You know what she wants. She wants y’all to be together.”

I cut her off. “Two ladies married? Where they do that?”

Annie said, “Y’all could be like Mrs. Ola Mae and Miss Jemison?” But she was laughing just to think about it. “I can’t see you catching babies. But before now, I couldn’t see this other thing either. Is this how you been this whole time? You could have told me.”

“I’m not *like that* this whole time or anytime. It’s hard to explain.”

“You were lonely?”

“It wasn’t only that.”

Annie plopped on the bed and narrowed her eyes like she was doing long division in her head. “But you liked it, being with her?”

I thought about lying, spinning a sad story about me being lost in the city, just a country mouse, after all. It was tempting, the idea of denying my feelings and becoming the woman born to wear pearls stretching the length of my back and dividing me in two. The falsehood was poised for launch, but I swallowed it back. If I lied to Annie there would be no one in this world who knew me at all.

“I loved her,” I said. “But it’s over. Over, over, over.”

“Well, it ain’t over for her. Don’t you think she at least deserves a proper—”

“Annie, I don’t think ‘proper’ is what’s at issue . . .”

She tapped me with her elbow. “I was about to say a proper goodbye, but maybe that’s not what you want to say.”

“Annie, do you tell Bobo everything?”

“I used to.” She looked down at her lap, talking to her knees.

“Girl.” I put my arms around her broad shoulders. “Y’all are going to work it out.”

"This is not about me and Bobo," she said. She kissed the top of my head. "Get your house in order. Tell her what she needs to know. Tell Franklin what he don't want to know. Getting married on top of secrets is like spraying perfume without washing first."

"Do I have to do it today?"

She turned her mouth to one side. "Franklin don't need to know today. But you and Miss Lady need to have a word, right away."

"Where is she?"

"Crying into her lowball glass. Everybody down there thinks her fiancé is about to leave her."

"Oh Lord, they watch too much TV."

"You best be glad they do."

Annie didn't say much as I got myself into my traveling suit, as she was giving me space with my thoughts. Franklin and I weren't going any farther than the third floor for the night, but a bride needed to make an appearance, at least, seeming like she was on her way to her honeymoon.

A quiet Annie made me nervous. So I took the silence and broke it over my knee. "What is it, Annie Kay Henderson?"

"What about Franklin? Is he your one true love?"

"Annie, I don't know what you mean by that."

"Vernice, I can't believe that you would lie to my face after I paid all this money for an ugly dress, and had that wig on my head, looking like the chubby girl from the Supremes."

I smiled, because that was the Annie I knew. I was about to toss a joke back at her but she fell sober fast.

"I think you are asking the wrong question."

We were mercifully interrupted by a tap on the door. As Annie departed, Mrs. McHenry entered, glowing like the mother of the bride, despite the fact that her love was on the other side of the aisle. Her face was champagne flushed and triumphant.

"Sweetheart," she said, "I knew it from the day I met you."

"Me too," I said.

She dabbed her eyes, believing me, in the way that she wanted to.

"Mother," I said, trying the word out.

"Well, I am here, darling," she said. "I am right here."

Returning to the ballroom dressed in my traveling suit, I kept my eyes on my husband, rehashing the words of my vows. I hummed them like the lyrics to an old melody. In his ear I whispered them. To have and to hold. The words in my mouth were as sweet as God's own truth.

Joette was among the guests cheering for us as I accepted Franklin's kiss. His fingers on my chin were intentional but gentle. Over his shoulder my eyes landed on Joette's face. I was glad that I hadn't gone down to La Carrousel for one last emotional exchange. She knew me too well for me to lie to her, and the truth of my soul was none of her business. And besides, I already knew the truth of hers.

*Chapter 31*

# ANNIE

Bobo waited until after Niecy was good and married to quit me. He called himself being considerate, keeping me from being unescorted at a wedding. He used that word, "unescorted." I used the word "motherfucker," which wasn't like me at all. But it's the sort of word that, if you need it, no other word will do. I bet even Bobo couldn't think of a better way to say it, despite having the entire dictionary wedged in his chest, where his heart used to be.

The only reason he didn't Dear John me is that I came home early from work, as I was on my cycle and not feeling well. It was a Wednesday night, and business was slow at the Elektra. Because my skirt was spoiled, I wore my apron backward. When I opened the door, there was Bobo—seated at the table, gnawing on a pencil stub. With the terrarium as a paperweight, he frowned over a yellow notepad. He hadn't gotten any further than "My dear Annie Kay."

"You were going to quit me with a letter?" I asked him.

He tucked the little chewed-up pencil behind his ear. "Sometimes it takes pen and paper for a man to get his mind right."

"You just didn't want to have to answer any questions."

He shook his head like he was the one disappointed. "In all

the time we have been involved, have you ever known me to dissemble?"

"Just because I didn't know about it doesn't mean it didn't happen," I said.

"That's fair," he said, reasonable as ever.

He had all his things bundled up and ready to go. Leaning by the door was the leather valise he had brought with him on that fateful night when I climbed out my window believing I was about to be with Clyde. Next to it was a burlap bag stuffed with everything else he owned by himself and half of anything that we owned together. The far side of the sack bulged with the rectangular shape of his boar-bristle brush.

Despite my fuming, he was oddly calm as he listed his reasons. I imagined him as a boy, reciting a Langston Hughes poem for Negro History Week. I had never met his mother, but I could tell by the ease with which he was walking out of my life that she treasured him. People who are loved well always think there is more out there for them to enjoy.

Me and Niecy know better. We know that love is as fragile as good health or a nest egg. Because look at me. Look at my life. Look at my man. What did I do besides give him the best that I had? What did I ever do against him? What did I do besides chase my mother?

I was cramping so hard that I had to sit down. The pain was worst just behind my navel. It felt as though two strong hands wrung my womb like a dirty rag. With each twist, I felt a hot gush, thick with clots. My pants, pasted to my body, were heavy and sticky. "My monthly is hurting me so bad today."

I saw that little light of charity flicker in his eye before he snuffed it out. Then I saw the look of relief when a man understands that a woman bent over with cramping isn't a woman carrying a child.

"You want me to get you an aspirin?" he asked.

"No," I said. And that was when I used the word that wasn't like me. The foul language freed him to put on his hat, gather up his stuff, and wish me the best. Those were his exact words.

He wished me the best. That word-heavy heart of his, and that was all he had.

I tried to ask myself if I was lucky to have gotten home when I did, forcing him to leave me to my face. Even Hattie Lee had paid this courtesy to Granny. She didn't go climbing out a window in the middle of the night, like I did. Hattie Lee, so the story goes, unhooked me from her nipple and forked my bundled body over to Granny, who was occupied with a hunk of pecan candy. The overcooked sugar stuck Granny's back teeth together, so she could hardly open her mouth to protest.

On that fateful day, Hattie Lee had just rounded the corner of sixteen years old and I hadn't even finished up my first month. Granny must have been somewhere in the neighborhood of fifty, give or take. Hattie had worn her school skirt, although there was no more education in the cards for her. When she had been pregnant, her skin was clear, but in motherhood, the pimples had returned. Almost the same thing had happened with her hair. Before I was born, she must have grown five inches of curls plaited into thick shiny ropes crisscrossed behind her ears. Granny said was beautiful, like Queen Esther. But once I got here, it shed in curly black nests that somehow lodged in every corner of the house.

"Mama, I can't," she had said.

---

"Bobo, you can't," I said.

By this time, he had his hat on, so it was all over but the shouting. But I had to know. "You got somebody else? Are you replacing me?"

He pouted his lips a little bit, like it wasn't a simple yes-or-no question. Finally, he said, "I am not replacing you."

"Where are you going then?"

He did more thinking with his lips, and then he spoke. "There is someone who is anticipating my arrival, but she is not replacing you. She's . . ."

While he searched for the words, I thought of all the ways that he could complete his thought.

"Does she have a name, at least?"

He took his hat off and sat back in his chair. "Why do you insist on making things as unpleasant as possible?"

"Tell me her name isn't Annie. Tell me you are not getting another one just like the other one."

"No," he said. "Her name is Regenia. Her father is a professor at LeMoyne-Owen. She's studying there herself."

"You're going to be staying with her?"

"Of course not," he said. "She lives in a dormitory."

And that's when I knew that I was beat. My Bobo was taking a page from Niecy's book. He was going to "I do" his way to a better life. This was a girl who slept under an eyelet bedspread. She wasn't the kind of girl you bedded for the first time on a corn-husk pallet at a sharecropping whorehouse. This was a girl who genuinely was what Niecy had convinced everyone she had become.

As he departed, I listened to the drumbeat of his shoes. For a man so light on his feet, he made a lot of noise walking out of my life. I wouldn't have followed him even if I hadn't been bleeding like a stuck pig. Chasing people who don't want to stay is a waste of time on par with trying to put rain back in the sky. I stayed at that table for a good hour, just sitting in my own fluids, taking in the odor—musty and funky, like life.

*Dear Lulabelle,*

*Bobo has gone and left me. I know I am not the only person in the world that this has happened to. And he is not the only person in the world that has ever done this to me. As you know, my mother, Hattie Lee, scrammed when I was just a baby. But I don't think anything hurts less just because it has happened before. Anyway, I am just in pieces. I know you said you don't ever want to see me again, but I didn't believe you for one second. Please stop pretending you don't love me.*

*Bobo had the nerve to ask me to forward his mail. In other words, he had time enough to think of every little detail before tipping out to chase some siddity heifer. I didn't ask him, but I am sure that she is a knockout. She's intelligent. He did tell me that much. When they get married, it will be like having a full set of encyclopedias in one bed. I have been going crazy trying to figure out if he loves her or if she is just a serious step up. I can understand that, I guess. Most people want to get ahead. I don't, but there has always been something wrong with me.*

*Babydoll says that the only thing that matters is that he has picked Little Miss College as the one he wants to be with—love or no love. Ever since she and Clyde got married, she thinks she is the expert on men and women. Now, I believe that she wants to have a baby to sort of lick the envelope closed with her and Clyde. He runs around on her, but he always comes home. Bobo didn't run around, or at least I don't think he did. Babydoll says I am stupid if I think that the first time his eye wandered, he ended up in love. She says they have to kiss a lot of frogs just like we do. But I didn't kiss hardly any toads before I found Bobo. If you recall, I was a virgin when we arrived on your property. I was fresh as a sheet hanging on the line.*

*Please tell me that it is okay for me to come and visit. Please let me be your daughter for just a few days.*

*Love,*
*Annie*

---

*Dear Annie,*

*When you came to my place two years ago, it was cute to see a virgin walking around like it was the most natural thing in the world. It warmed my heart seeing a little colored girl, feeling like a girl, not having learned to be a woman way too soon. As you can imagine, I don't see much of that around here.*

*But these years later, it is time for you to grow up.*

*Here are three things for you to know: One is that the best way to get over a man is another man. This is true no matter your age, even if you are old and you get widowed. Find you another one and you will feel much better. Two, you need to count yourself lucky. You did not have kids with him so you don't have to see his eyes in the face of your child. This is why our mother never loved Lurelia and me. She had to look at that man in double. And three is that I do not want you around my place. I told you before but I will underline myself. Nobody ever comes back here for nothing good. When I say I do not want to see you, please take it in the loving way that it is intended.*

*Yours,*
*Lulabelle*

*PS: As you know, I am merely taking dictation for Mother. She talked very fast in an agitated fashion, but I believe I got down her every word. If I wrote it wrong, it is not incorrect in the spirit of what was said.—D*

*Chapter 32*

# VERNICE

As Mrs. Franklin McHenry, I didn't "have to work," which was Aunt Irene's wildest dream in a muffin tin. She had taken up with a new man up in Ohio, of course she had, but he didn't have the means to "sit her down." She wasn't doing laundry, praise Jesus. She said if she had to touch lye soap, she would just come on back home to Honeysuckle and live in a house that was already paid for. Why live on the distant side of the Mason-Dixon if you still suffered with peeling hands and a cruel mistress? In Dayton, she worked in the back room for a haberdasher, stitching fine wool into three-piece suits. Her boss was white but well-behaved. Aunt Irene said she didn't know if it was because he was an honorable man or if it was because she was getting old. She signed off by reminding me how lucky I was that I didn't have to be concerned with all of that.

What did I have to worry about? Dust. I knew it wasn't a problem worthy of sending a letter of complaint to Annie or Aunt Irene. After all, Annie had troubles of her own. Bobo had up and left her and she worked all hours of the night at that filthy nightclub just to make the rent on the hovel she had once shared with that man. Her letters were so full of sadness that even her penmanship was weighted down with the unfairness of it all. She knew more than she should have about the girl that Bobo had taken up with. I prayed to God that she wasn't out there being a colored Nancy Drew. Hers were real problems: Heartbreak. Bills. Loneliness. Dust was not a tragedy, although it was the bane of my existence.

After our wedding, Franklin and I moved in with my in-laws. It was a temporary situation, just a detour until our house on Lynn Valley Road was completed. The estimate for completion was six months and we were two months in. My mother-in-law, whom I thought of as the "real" Mrs. McHenry, was delighted with the arrangement. "It's lonely being the only lady in this house," she said. "And besides, domesticity is best learned by demonstration." And with this, I became her apprentice, a wife-in-training.

"Dust," she explained, feather-duster aloft, "is disgusting. What do you think it's made of?"

"Little pieces of dirt?" I said, understanding that I had been set up to give the wrong answer.

"If only it were that benign." She crossed the room to jerk the cord to open the jacquard curtains. "There's so much in life that's like dust. Banal but utterly revolting."

We were in the formal living room, which was so different from the cozy sunroom where she and I had first made our connection. This room was populated by furniture the color of homemade ice cream, a sort of beige-ish yellow. Pinstripes of yellowish beige gave the set texture without exactly providing a pattern. Thick carpet of a similar hue swallowed our socked feet. Here and there were mahogany tables topped with glass and decorated with ceramic figures.

"Dust," she began again, "is the residue of life. Dirt, tiny bits of dead skin, cigarette ash, carcasses of microscopic insects. I could go on and on, but it's too depressing. This is why we must drive it out."

The room seemed clean to me, but Mrs. McHenry frowned, surveying the scene. Squaring her shoulders, she took a pillow from the couch and motioned that I should do the same. I followed her to the back porch, where she placed the cushion on a clean wicker chair. From a matching chest she produced a bat. With her determined jaw, bent knees, and protruding rump, she resembled Jackie Robinson facing off against some racist pitcher.

When the bat connected with the pillow, an iridescent puff of dust belched from the padding.

"See?" she said. "Dust hides."

She gave the pillow a few more thwacks, each punctuated with an unladylike grunt. Panting, she passed the bat to me.

"Your turn."

I took the bat, but I didn't stick out my rear end as I gave it a swing.

"Harder," she said. "Think about somebody you hate."

I felt my lips pucker the way they did when I thought too hard. When I did this around my husband, he laughed and met my mouth with a kiss.

Mrs. McHenry chuckled. "You are such a sweet girl. You don't have anybody you hate? What about that cracker who threw you off the bus?"

In the years since, that incident had come to seem more like a fable than a memory. This is what I will tell my future daughter-in-law, in the way that Mrs. McHenry told me about her mother's mistress who didn't write her a check. Under her encouraging eyes, I tried to conjure the bus driver's face, but I could only recall his striped button-down shirt, filthy around the collar. But memories love company, so one recollection led to another. The right side of my face stung as I relived the slap from the gasman. He might have claimed that he hit me just to make it realistic, but he enjoyed it. When he tried to jump in my dress just a few minutes later, it was all of a piece.

"There you go," said Mrs. McHenry as I dislodged whatever filth lurked in the pillow. "Get it all out."

As I swung, I wondered if I was "getting it out" or if I was "digging it in." I imagined the grease monkey's face with each blow, but each blow made his sneer more vivid in my memory. The little particles of life found their way to my nose. Powerful sneezes that made my brain feel crowded in my skull forced me to put down the bat.

Mrs. McHenry's brow crumpled with concern. "Is it your daddy you're picturing?"

I shook my head. "No, ma'am," I said. "I never met him. I was a baby when it happened."

"Don't mean you're not mad. You miss your mama, don't you? You didn't need to know her to miss her."

"That's different," I said, wiping my snotty nose with the tail of my apron.

"You can hate somebody for what they've done to you, especially if you never met them. Probably if you knew the man, you might be conflicted. But since you never laid eyes on him, all you got is pure hate."

"No, ma'am," I protested, blinking against the dust. "I have never hated anyone in my whole life."

Now she bobbed her head and clicked her tongue. "You think that's something to be proud of. But I have never met a colored woman who didn't have somebody in her life worth hating. That's like somebody saying that they have never felt love."

It took all day to clean a house that looked just fine when we got started. But dust was everywhere if you knew where it hid. Balls the size of corn kernels clung to the floorboards. These Mrs. McHenry called slut's wool. We banished it with oil soap sweetened with orange peels.

Somehow Mrs. McHenry managed not to sneeze or gasp. A few rivulets leaked from behind the scarf on her head, eroding the pancake makeup that lightened her complexion. For my part, I was soaked like I had just run a marathon. My hair was gritty with all the airborne dirt and spongy from the heat of my own body. From under my arms wafted a musty, nutty smell, but I didn't mind it. My breath was hot in my mouth and I was lightheaded from the chemical smell of a house so clean that you could eat off the lime-colored bathroom tiles.

My shoulders ached from all the dusting, mopping, and beating. I kneaded the place where my arm fit into its socket.

"Satisfying, isn't it?" she said.

"Hurts," I said.

"But doesn't it feel good knowing that all you have done is for the benefit of your own family? The bed you make will be the bed you make love on. Anything filthy is your own mess. Franklin has never in his life been able to pee straight, but when you scrub that floor, you do it because you love him. Anything you do for love is a pleasure."

When we were done, Mrs. McHenry and I visited each of the four bedrooms, then made our way down the hallway, checking the seams in the wallpaper for separations. When I touched the heavy door to the basement apartment where I slept with my husband, Mrs. McHenry shook her head. "Keep that private."

We ended our workday in her sunroom. Before she sat down, she placed two ice cubes into a small flowerpot, where a twig hosted a half-dozen purple blooms. Then she settled herself on the low divan. She kicked her shoes off, one at a time, revealing girlish ankles. "My throne room," she said.

She pointed at a clump of slut's wool in the corner. "Dust is wily," she said. "But I am not touching that broom one more time today."

"Want me to get it?"

She shook her head. "We are done until the men get home. Anyway, they never come in here." She puckered her lips and added, "They know better."

I knew that my "throne room" in the house that Franklin and I were building wouldn't be so grand as this, but I looked forward to selecting a rocking chair and lamp. I could imagine a petite shelf where I would alternate poetry and the ceramic bells I had received from my wedding registry. I wondered if Franklin would mind if I added a record player. But as soon as the idea came to mind, I chased it away. The whole point of a throne room was to have a nook where what my husband minded was beside the point.

Mrs. McHenry tuned the radio to WAOK. Ray Charles sang about having Georgia on his mind. She sang along in her glee club soprano. I slid my alto underneath, and we made a joyful noise from that longing song.

"Franklin is seeing the architect today," she called over her shoulder as she poured us each an ounce or two of orange liqueur.

"Did you know that his wife left him?" I said, ready to gossip. "Who up and leaves an architect?"

"Somebody whose daddy is an architect, too."

I considered that for a moment. The architect was an upright man, at least from what I had seen. Except for his profession, he was as ordinary as a pan of cornbread. His wife was a woman that I didn't know well, but I knew she was a soft-foot who finished Spelman a few years before I arrived.

"She puts me in the mind of your little friend Joette." Mrs. McHenry sniffed. "When people grow up with the best of everything, nothing is good enough for them."

The mention of Joette made my stomach cramp. "Well, I'm not like that. I am nothing like Joette at all."

Mrs. McHenry licked a splash of orange liqueur from her knuckle. "Of course you're not. That's why I picked you. If the architect had let his mother pick his bride, he wouldn't be in this predicament. He insisted on moving through the world penis-first. Bet he won't do that again."

I couldn't help adding my chuckle to hers, imagining the cornbread architect tapping through a crowd using his Johnson like a blind man uses a cane. But as soon as I grinned, I felt guilty. By all accounts, the architect was devastated and humiliated.

"Ooh," I said, electrified by an idea that bounced me off the divan. "What about Annie?"

"Annie?" Mrs. McHenry was puzzled.

"My friend from home. Annie!"

"Oh. What about her?"

"She's back on the market. One hundred percent unattached. We could introduce her to the architect. She could certainly appreciate him."

Mrs. McHenry rose to refill her tulip glass. Between the radio and the revolving fan, the room was full of sounds, but without her voice, the space was overlaid with an eerie silence.

“What?” I said.

My mother-in-law took my hand before pressing it to her lips. “There are so many things I love about you, little girl. At the top of the list is your generous nature.”

“What?”

“You want to share your blessings with your friend. I had the same impulse when I was just married. I thought it would be cute if my little sister could marry a McHenry, too. We could be sisters and sisters-in-law. I mentioned it to my husband and it took all his self-restraint not to laugh.” She chased the cruel memory with her sweet drink. “It was our first fight. And let me tell you. It was a row.”

She ran her pinky around the inside of her empty glass and sucked it clean. “Here’s what I didn’t understand.”

She lowered her voice, forcing me to lean over to catch her words.

“Like you, I was a newlywed with a tight little waist and comfortable for the first time in my life. Naturally I wanted to share with my baby sister. She was sweet as a Christmas apple but without schooling or manners. She was a good girl, but nobody had taught her to be a lady. In Atlanta, people try not to be prejudiced against where you come from, but they reserve the right to judge you for where you are. Do you understand?”

“But Annie is my friend. She’s . . .”

Mrs. McHenry spoke over me as I rattled off everything I loved about my cradle friend.

“My sister was *my sister.* And while I didn’t leave her behind, I couldn’t take her with me.”

Sitting in silence, I could only say, “I love her.”

“I know you do, honey. You will come to understand. Not today or tomorrow. But you will. Now, drink up.”

I took my drink slowly, enjoying the burning stickiness of it. I had barely taken three swallows, but my mother-in-law refilled my cordial glass. “And here is another trick of the trade. You always want to be a little loose when your husband comes home. But let him think that it is natural.”

I nodded, adding this to the long list of her commandments.

"And be pretty," she said. "Make him feel like he has stumbled into heaven."

When the men came home, they found us wearing dresses cut from the same bolt of green gingham. Mine was sleeveless, A-line, and short, while Mrs. McHenry was full Dinah Shore with a pinched waist and circle skirt. Loose curls rested on her shoulders. My poor hair had not recovered from the work of the day and had required a fistful of bobby pins and a generous dollop of pomade.

Franklin was a few paces ahead of his father, managing his cane despite the rolled paper under his arm. When I waved, Franklin smiled as though he had, indeed, just limped through the pearly gates. Mr. McHenry seemed tickled by the spectacle of his wife having an apprentice, but he didn't act like he thought this was God's antechamber.

"Martini?" he asked.

Franklin, still learning, said, "Same for me."

Mrs. McHenry snagged a fifth of gin and headed toward the kitchen. I picked up the slender bottle of vermouth and followed her. This evening ritual was one I had mastered. Fill the shaker with a half-tray of ice. Pour enough gin into the shaker for the bottle to glub twice. Carefully add just a few drops of vermouth. "It's a gesture," Mrs. McHenry explained. Mr. McHenry liked two olives held together with a metal toothpick. Franklin didn't care for olives themselves but appreciated the briny juice. Once the drinks were ready to go, I refilled the ice tray from the tap and slid it back into the freezer, which I had learned to stop calling an "icebox." As I did this, Mrs. McHenry provided me with a splash of vodka, which was supposed to leave no trace on the breath. To be on the safe side, we shared a sharp lemon wedge.

As Franklin took his cocktail, I peeked over his shoulder at the page unrolled and clipped to the pedestal table. It was the layout for our new home. On the first of the year, we would move a full mile away from his parents. I knew it wasn't far, as the crow flies, but mentally it was like relocating to a neighboring planet. The house would be a beauty, and it would be ours. As our first home, it wouldn't be terribly large but would be up-to-date in every way imaginable. Situated on a dead end, there would be virgin forest on two sides. Split-level was the trend, but we would live in a single-level, so my husband could be spared the hassle of stairs. For the first time, I would sleep in a space untouched by anyone else's memories.

"Come see," Franklin said to me. "You too, Mother."

Hip to hip with Franklin, I looked down at the table. Suddenly, I felt sheepish for only at that moment understanding the term "blueprint." I had heard it thrown around, mostly when Mr. McHenry discussed strategies for civil rights. *Up north*, he often said, *they work from a whole different blueprint.*

The paper was the very same color as Franklin's card—deeper than robin's egg but lighter than navy. White marks separated the space into rooms. My husband looped his arm around my waist and squeezed. The jilted architect had dropped it off just this afternoon. Taking the martini, Franklin offered me a magnifying glass.

I was a little loose, as instructed by my mother-in-law, so I made the mistake of having an opinion out loud. "I don't see a sunroom. I was supposed to have a sunroom, remember?"

Franklin opened his mouth before he had decided what he wanted to say, leaving him open-lipped but silent like a fish. I reminded Mrs. McHenry. "You said that I should make sure I have a little space for myself."

She was looser than I was, yet her giggle sounded uncertain. "Did I say that?"

Mr. McHenry's chuckle was deep as his orator's voice. "Oh, my wife. She's obnoxious, but I love it." He patted her hip before he continued. "You'll get your sunroom, don't you worry. But my wife didn't tell you that she had given me three sons and twenty years of marriage before she got her little lady-lounge. You've just been married three months. What you need from a first house is rooms for children!"

Franklin let his finger rest on a square toward the front of the house. "Two rooms right here for kids. They can share a bathroom."

"Jack and Jill," cooed Mrs. McHenry. "Very nice."

"What about right here?" I asked, picking out a good-sized square.

"Guest room," he said with a smile. "For when Annie comes to visit."

I returned the love in his eyes, imagining Annie unpacking a little suitcase propped on a wooden stand. On the bed table, a carafe of fresh water would rest beside a matching tumbler. "Okay," I said, tapping a smaller rectangle, enjoying the game of it all. "What about here?"

"Butler pantry," Franklin said.

"Where then?" I said, letting my eyes rove but finding no other unaccounted-for space.

Mr. McHenry all-out laughed. He patted his wife again, a little harder this time. The corner of her mouth twitched, activating her dimple, before she managed a wide smile and swatted his hand. "Franklin, honey, maybe Vernice could have a little sewing room?"

"You have this girl dying to have a space away from our son," Mr. McHenry said with a rattle. "Where do you think grandchildren come from? They need to be together."

Now everyone laughed, except for me.

"Don't worry, sweetheart," said Mrs. McHenry. "This is just your first house. You'll get your sunroom. Right, Franklin?"

"Of course," said my husband. "I just didn't know it was so important."

Mr. McHenry rocked an imaginary baby. "All things at their proper time."

"It will be beautiful," Mrs. McHenry assured me, covering her hand with my own. She guided my hand over the blue page. Her boozy lips grazed my ear as she whispered, "You will be lady of this whole house. They are all your rooms."

After dinner was eaten, the dishes washed, and the table polished, I joined Franklin in our basement apartment. Fresh from his bath, he sat on the edge of the bed, wearing only his underpants. His chest and arms were covered with fine hair that caught the light. His right leg was as sturdy as the rest of him, but the left was much thinner. He rubbed it and made a face.

"Lie back," I told him, squirting Jergens lotion into the cup of my hand.

He moaned with appreciation as I kneaded the withered muscles. "It was a harrowing day today," he said.

I clucked in sympathy as I pressed, squeezed, and rubbed. "You can only do what you can do."

"The lynching files always make my leg hurt. I can't explain it. I was working on that case I told you about."

"The mother?" I said.

"Yeah," he replied. "This woman is dead. Her kids are orphans. And I am just throwing paper at the situation. We all know who did it. The nephew of the mayor. And we all know what's going to happen—not a goddamned thing."

My fingers must have strayed to a tender place, because he called out.

"Oh, baby," I said. "I'm so sorry."

Once the spasm passed, he said, "I am the one who should be sorry. You don't like the house."

"No," I assured him. "I love the house."

"Even without your sunroom?"

I didn't answer with words. I let my hands pass over his body until he could take my teasing no longer and pinned me to the soft mattress.

"I am going to fill you up with babies," he said. "Then we will fill that house up with babies. You'll be a beautiful mother. The whole house will be full of babies and love."

"You promise?"

"As long as whatever I give you, you give me back, you will have everything you want."

Knowing him to be a man of his word, I gave as good as I got. Maybe even better. We lay there tangled in the damp sheets; it crossed my mind I would have to wash them in the morning.

Franklin inched near and clamped me close with his healthy leg. "I know I'm not the first," he said.

I tried to keep myself soft and pliable, but my joints stiffened as my husband stroked my goose-pimpled arms.

"I'm not angry. I just don't want you to think you have a secret from me."

"Why would you even say that? Did someone lie to you?"

"Vernice," he said. "You don't make love like a rookie. You know what you want. You know what I want. Unless you're some kind of savant . . ."

He chuckled and I jerked away from him. It felt like people had been laughing at me since my wedding day. I couldn't do anything right. Mrs. McHenry told me that it was my job to make sure that Franklin was delighted in every way. She assured me that whatever happened in the marriage bed was blessed in the sight of God. "You should do everything; you just don't want to seem like a woman who will do anything."

I turned toward him and beat his chest with a heat that I had reserved for couch cushions and pillows. But fighting a man is a waste of time. You can't hurt him. And if he is a decent person, he won't hit you back, and fighting someone who won't hit you back makes you feel like a child. The only thing that would make it worse would be the very same thing that would make it better—crying. The pressure inside my head spread to my neck. My pulse banged against my voice box. My words were unsteady as a raft on the ocean. "You will not insult me. I am doing the best I can."

*Chapter 33*

# ANNIE

After ten days, I came to accept that Bobo was gone-gone, even though he had returned to the rooming house twice. Once to see Clyde—they were cousins, after all. The second time was to get his mail, and to leave me a few mangy dollars. "I wouldn't leave you high and dry." I am sure there is a word for the tone of voice he used for his little speech. When he popped in, waving that raggedy little envelope, I hadn't been expecting him, but I was put together, with lipstick on my mouth and cheeks both. This is what they call keeping hope alive. But when he said that thing about high and dry, I knew the candle was out. That night, I came to understand the second part about my new life. I was not meant to sleep alone.

As a child, I had my bed all to myself. Niecy did, too. To everybody else we knew, this was some kind of luxury, since they all slept so many kids under one roof. Mothers and grandmothers had them stacked up on a mattress like matches in a box. They complained about feet in their faces and the funkiness of it all. And I believed them. At that time, the only person I had ever shared a bed with was Niecy and when we were together, she migrated to the outer edge, as did I.

But when Bobo and I shared a pallet at Lulabelle's, I appreciated the heat of his body, even though summer in Mississippi is not what you would call balmy. In the country, even the breeze is gummy. But I found that I enjoyed the way the bed shifted when he got caught up in a dream. It was what I imagine it would be like to travel by boat, just letting the water carry you to someplace new. Even his soft snore that finished off with a little whistle was a lullaby to me. Now that he was gone, I found myself all night awake but with my eyes closed. I tried to explain to Babydoll that I was just on top of the sleep, not up under it where a person could get some rest.

We were out back at the Elektra. She wore a shiny button-up top that she tied just under her breasts to show off the smooth skin around her navel. Her nails were painted a color that Granny called "whore's red" but what the bottle said was "Candy Apple." Clyde's ring was shiny on her finger, because she cleaned the green from it every Sunday with baking soda and vinegar. She was such a pretty girl, just like Niecy. I wondered what it must feel like to be somebody that people liked to look at. This made me think about Bobo, because he used to enjoy watching me. Then big ol' stupid tears gathered like dust turning into bunnies.

"Dry it up," she said. "You don't need Mr. Wilson to see that you have a new malfunction." She tore a stick of gum in half and gave it to me. "You can cry when we get home."

The gum was clove flavored, spicy and sweet at once. I gave it a couple chomps before I stood up. It was Wednesday, and Mr. Wilson let me tend bar, which paid better than waitressing. I was grateful because Bobo wouldn't drop off sorry-money forever, and the landlady wasn't exactly sympathetic to my plight.

When I got back to the bar, Mr. Wilson was pulling a beer that was mostly foam. "Where you been, Spoken For? People want drinks."

I didn't know what people he was talking about. It was a Wednesday after all. Most everybody that wanted a nip had one.

"I don't see no order slips," I said. "And anyway, I ain't spoken for no more."

"Really?" he said slowly, drawing the word out before licking his thumb to separate a napkin from the stack. "You don't say."

The shift in him was quiet. He didn't develop a sudden interest in my astrological sign or opinions about the news of the day. Instead, Mr. Wilson just softened his eyes as I mixed the drinks. Rather than watch the jiggers to make sure I didn't overpour, he seemed to admire the movement of my elbows. This went on for nearly a week.

The following Wednesday, Babydoll wasn't on the schedule. She wasn't thrilled about losing the hours, but she was glad to spend the evening at home with Clyde. She had plans to cook pork chops and apples—a recipe she'd swiped from one of Niecy's Betty Crocker letters. It was the rare day that I was at work without Babydoll, who kept my sound judgment tucked in her back pocket. Not that I am blaming anyone. But this was the situation.

And yes, it was Wednesday, but it was the first of the month, so paychecks burned holes in many a pocket. To keep up, I lined glasses up six at a time, only eyeballing the watered-down booze landing on the ice. If they had a drink-pouring team in the Olympics, I could be right up there next to Jesse Owens. Since he had taken Babydoll off the schedule, Mr. Wilson himself served the drinks to the high-top tables.

At the end of the night, we were the only ones around. Mr. Wilson counted the till out three times and jotted marks in the ledger as I washed the dirty glasses, made sure the bottle openers, toothpicks, and paper napkins were all prepared for whoever was on the roster for the next day. He asked me for a Sazerac, which I was glad to mix since it reminded me of Mr. Daniel and The Den. And besides, what was at home but that lonely bed?

"Make yourself one, too," he said. "Then come sit next to me."

Pulling down the bottles, I apologized for using bitters instead of absinthe. "The barkeep in my hometown had some. That's the only time I ever made a Sazerac by the book."

"I wouldn't know the difference." He watched me work with such appreciation that I felt a little bit foxy.

When we were situated with our cocktails, he said, "I feel bad for Brother Bobo."

I set my glass down hard, hackles up, but he shushed me.

"I feel bad because he is missing out on you."

Bobo had said something similar, three years earlier when we were at Lulabelle's. The difference was that Bobo had been talking about Hattie Lee. The sameness of it touched me. In the half-light, Mr. Wilson wasn't fatherly, though he was old enough. A full-grown man, he took up space with confidence, not like Bobo, who pedaled his maturity with training wheels.

"Fix us another round. And teach me how you do it."

He followed me to the worker side of the bar. As I melted the sugar cube with the rye, he pressed his hips into the small of my back and kissed my neck. When he turned me toward him, my fingers were tight on the bottle neck, until he gently extracted it. I had expected him to kiss me, but grown men don't kiss for a while and call it quits. He hadn't hardly opened my lips before he was unbuttoning, unzipping, and hiking things up.

"You are sugary as a peach with the pit pulled out."

It wasn't his touch that made me call out. It was what he said while he was doing it.

I swear to God I hadn't seen it coming. Babydoll said, "I didn't say you were blind. I'm saying you are stupid." After that, I got mad at her since she had agreed that the only solution for lost love was a new love.

"But not our boss," she snapped. "You will have both of us out here unemployed."

---

The affair was short-lived. It wasn't just that Mr. Wilson wasn't Bobo. It was also that he was just so old. Before I could even read and write, he had been to Europe, fought the Germans, and come home just to get called out of his name while wearing his dress uniform. Every time he told this story, he added more details, like a striptease going in the opposite direction. The final time he told the tale, he admitted that the occasion for donning all his medals and the peaked cap had been his wedding day.

The mention of his wife made me feel dirty, and not in a sexy way.

He tried to smooth it over by tickling my bare belly with his chin, but where Bobo had whiskers, this man had bristles. And where Bobo had manners, being careful with wearing a rubber or getting out while the getting was good, this man was sloppy and inconsiderate. The whole affair had been a terrible idea and my despair was only deepened with every touch of his gold-ringed fingers.

*Dear Niecy,*

*There is nothing that makes my day like a letter from you! I have to admit that I don't know exactly what an architect is. That is the kind of thing that I used to ask Bobo about. I have to tell you that I miss him every day. I see him sometimes around town.*

*Babydoll, as you know, is super-religious. She drags Clyde to Mass because she wants to be married by a priest. They are Mr. & Mrs. now, but that's just in the eyes of man, she says. Poor Babydoll thinks she is living in sin now, more than when she was just living in sin the regular way. I try to feel sorry for her, but living in sin is way better than having to live by yourself.*

*But anyway, I went with them to St. Augustine. Did you know that Catholics won't let you take their communion unless you are one of them? So when everyone else was at the altar with their mouth open for the cracker, who do I see setting back in the empty pew but Bobo. His new girl, the one whose daddy is a college teacher, well, she and her whole family had him in a button-up shirt and a wide tie. If I had known that I'd see him, I would have fixed myself up a little more. What could I do but take comfort in the fact that I still looked like my regular self while he looked like he had been gotten by the body snatchers.*

*But let me stop talking about him because I am the one with the real trouble here. Niecy, it is so bad that I almost can't make myself put it on the paper. Nobody else knows but Babydoll and even she doesn't know the whole of it because the whole of it isn't truly known. Please excuse me for being so mysterious. I can't bring myself to say it. It is so terrible.*

*Niecy. I think that I have gone and gotten myself pregnant.*

*I went to the doctor and they took some of my pee and they will tell me in two weeks. Babydoll says that this was a waste of money and I should give her the five dollars and she will officially tell me that fat meat is greasy.*

*If you will recall, I told you that I had been on a couple of dates with my boss, Mr. Wilson. This was only partly true, as he didn't really take me anywhere. And since I believe that I have his baby, then you don't need the rest of the particulars. There are so many terrible details. The biggest one is that he has been married for almost as long as we have been living, so they are not a couple that can be shook. And he is not someone that I would want to be married to.*

*The second disaster is that Babydoll and I are out of a job. Mrs. Wilson came to the Elektra spitting mad. She mistakenly thought that Babydoll was the one that her husband had taken up with. You can't blame her. Babydoll is the ripest fig on the tree and her husband has a sweet tooth. So she comes to the Elektra and grabs Babydoll by the hair, calling her everything but a child of God. At this point, Babydoll could have just pointed her to me—the frumpy girl mixing rum and Cokes. Instead, Babydoll put up her dukes. She has been fighting all her life, so she whipped Mrs. Wilson's tail. Mrs. Wilson's dress rode up and you could see her old-lady drawers. I do not know why she wore a dress coming to fight somebody. But I also do not know why you would fight somebody without making sure you were snatching the right person. But there is so much that I don't understand.*

*Why did I get tangled up with Mr. Wilson? I needed my job. Bobo's little money is long gone. And now I am knocked up. It's like history is repeating itself. My daddy is likely a married man. And like my mother, I am definitely stupid. And Granny could see it coming from way across the street. She tried to warn me.*

*So now I am caught, but it is very early. Two weeks late is not very much. I tried to tell myself that I was just under the weather, but of course I knew what I had been up to. Mr. Wilson is not a gentleman like Bobo.*

*Niecy, I know that there are remedies that somebody can do about this, especially in a place like Atlanta. I am praying that you will help me. Whatever you loan me will be promptly repaid. Somebody will hire me because thirsty people are everywhere. Someone will also hire Babydoll because she is so foxy, and people want pretty girls around. Please say the word and I will come to Atlanta. Babydoll knows how to drive Clyde's car.*

*Your loving cradle friend,*

*Annie Kay*

*Chapter 34*

# VERNICE

One day, I will write a list of what I learned in the first six months of my marriage. I will make a little booklet and record the recipes for beef Wellington, chicken salad with golden raisins, and pie crust with lard. Maybe I will dedicate a few pages to the many uses for cream of mushroom soup. I will put it in writing that although fried chicken was a Sunday dinner meal in Honeysuckle, west of Beecher Street it should only be served ironically or at the most casual gatherings—like when my husband's brother came over to watch football or play pool. If invisible ink existed anywhere but in comics, I'd write a bedroom guide—how to be good, but not too good. And what to do when the two of you have been going at it like rabbits but you are as regular as the seasons. The final chapter of my little book would be about how there is etiquette for every occasion, relationship, or crisis.

"Protocol" is the word that Mrs. McHenry uses. She is a member of a ladies' group and protocol requires that they dress in "uninterrupted white" when they gather for their shadowy meetings. No silver buttons, gold belt buckles, or pale pink piping. And by "white," they mean usher-board white. No ecru, eggshell, or beige. In a year or so, she will put me up for membership—as soon as protocol allows. Besides church, I have never been a member of any organization. I was excited at the idea of formal belonging. Despite the violation of secrecy, Mrs. McHenry let me handle the delicate gold pin she received upon swearing her solemn oath.

When the mailman arrived, Mrs. McHenry scanned the envelope addressed to her with curiosity. "What do you think this is all about?" she said, waving the mysterious envelope. The return address read *Cunningham*, Joette's family name.

"Open it and see," I said.

"No," she said. "Not yet. Let us speculate."

She lay the envelope on the kitchen table between us and we studied it like a scientific specimen. The paper was ecru and thick, yet light enough that it required just one stamp. This meant there was no internal envelope or reply card. Adding to the mystery, the address was printed in block letters like a ransom note, rather than in the florid calligraphy that protocol requires for an invitation.

News involving Joette caused my lungs to seize, no matter how much I tried to assure myself that those months in our dorm room were nearly three years behind us, and meaningless. I had been young and confused. No one knew but me, Joette, and Annie. At least these were the only people that I knew about. Maybe she'd told someone else. The unwritten protocol is that every secret comes with a plus-one. But I had never known Joette to have connections besides Marylinda. And if Marylinda was her plus-one, then who had she gone on to share it with? The idea of a daisy chain of gossip threatened my stomach. Had I run to the bathroom to vomit, then Mrs. McHenry might think I was expecting and I would have to disappoint her.

As I rehearsed all the worst-possible-case scenarios, Mrs. McHenry slit the envelope with a silver letter opener. It had been a gift from one of her sisters in the secret organization.

The card was rectangular, a perfect fit for its envelope, and of course the fiber of the paper matched the envelope exactly. Centered was one sentence broken into four lines.

*Mr. and Mrs. Harold Cunningham II*
*announce that the marriage of their daughter*
*Joette Michelle Cunningham to Thomas Adolphus Donaldson Jr.*
*will not take place.*

Mrs. McHenry clucked her tongue. "I bet Albertina is fit to be tied."

She was not alone. I had taken a small comfort in the idea of Joette, like me, safely wrapped in the blanket of matrimony, back on the path of normal people. Once she was married, she could be put up for membership in the secret society. Since her mother was a member, they wouldn't even have to vote on her. We would stand side by side in uninterrupted white dresses and receive the gold pins together. We could tell everyone how we were once roommates and smile a private smile about our folly.

"My guess," said Mrs. McHenry, "is that the man couldn't go through with it. A girlfriend for every day of the week, then all of a sudden he pops up with a fiancée? They have a name for that. When you run into Joette, you tell her that she dodged a bullet."

"Limoncello?" I asked.

"When we get done with the dust mop," she said, flipping through the rest of the mail and tossing me an envelope. "You two girls exchange letters like lovers." She sighed. "That's how I used to be with my sister."

I put Annie's letter in the pocket of my apron to read after the floorboards were clean.

Our limoncello time was wrecked by the phone ringing so often that it fairly danced in its receiver. All the SWANs had received the announcement that there would be no Cunningham-Donaldson wedding—which Mrs. McHenry insisted on calling an "arrangement." Even I got a call, from Marylinda, who swore up and down that she found out in the mail just like everybody else, despite the fact that she was family.

While my mother-in-law gossiped, I enjoyed another limoncello and remembered the letter from Annie, tucked so carelessly in my apron pocket. I retrieved it, refilled my glass, and used my teeth to make a small tear in the corner of the simple envelope. Annie's letters were like a novel in serial form. Memphis was home to such a raucous cast of characters. Babydoll intrigued me. Despite being country-sexy, she was serious and sometimes even wise. I could see why Clyde had dropped Annie for her. And let's be honest, we can put that in the file labeled *Blessings in Obvious Disguises*.

When it came to Bobo, I think I was as offended as Annie was sorrowful. Who was he to stop loving Annie? When a woman comes to you clean with no track record, you owe her. If I ever found myself in his company, I was going to tell him about himself. Well, maybe. Because the only chance I would likely have to encounter that little man would be if he and Annie were pulling covers again. In that case, I would have to let bygones be just that.

By the time I finished this particular letter, I was soft-set like a Jell-O salad. Annie was pregnant by the old man she worked for? Or that she used to work for, because now she didn't even have a job anymore. In my mind, I leafed through all the letters she had ever sent me, and I couldn't remember one word about this Mr. Wilson person. How had she ended up in this dreadful, untenable situation?

I wondered if she should try to wrangle him to the altar, despite the complicated circumstances. Single girls are always told that married men "never leave their wives." However, every wife knows that men can, and do, change their minds.

The thing about forced marriages is some work out, and some don't. Occasionally young people want to be married, so they are careless in their love, leaving no choice but to make it permanent. They act all surprised, like they didn't know where babies came from. But sometimes the man feels like the girl clamped one of his paws in a steel-jaw trap. Sometimes he can gnaw off his own hand, chunking it on the counter, ring and all—baby or babies be damned. That's too bad but not uncommon. I see these one-handed men all the time. But other men—and my daddy was one of them—will marry you because they have to, then they'll kill you.

---

Mrs. McHenry returned to the sunroom flush with all the back-and-forth about the aborted royal wedding in the funeral world, yet she caught the distress on my face.

"What's the matter, baby?" She joined me on the love seat, hugging me around my shoulders.

Whenever she called me "baby," I felt all the love I never had as a child. I let myself lean on her and enjoyed the potpourri that was her signature scent. Gardenia soap, sugary liqueur, and just a whiff of the perspiration that comes from constant motion. She kissed my temple. "Tell me, baby. What's wrong?"

"It's Annie," I said.

I had shared with Mrs. McHenry many of the twists and turns of Annie's Bluff City adventures. She had been especially engaged by Hattie Lee's death and resurrection both. But those stories only asked for a patient ear and a few sympathetic clucks. I could tell she was eager for the next installment, ready for me to spin a yarn.

"She's expecting," I said, regretting my choice of words. Annie wasn't expecting, she was dreading.

"So, Bobo has returned! Did I not predict it?" She clapped. "Aren't you glad you heeded my advice not to speak against him? Now the challenge is to get him to the church in time."

I rocked in my chair, struggling to find a way back into the conversation. Once Mrs. McHenry got to talking, it could be like scratching a roll of tape to lift up an edge.

"It ain't Bobo," I said, letting my frustration warp my grammar.

"Oooh," Mrs. McHenry said like she had just stepped in dog shit in the yard. "Ooh," she said again, like she was wearing her best shoes when it happened.

"She can't keep it," I said. "She has lost her job and is in danger of being kicked out of her place."

"Adoption?" Mrs. McHenry's mind whirred. "I know that when little white girls get themselves in trouble, colored families will take in their cute little babies. Not to be crude, but how dark is the daddy?"

"Not adoption," I said, my voice barely a squeak.

"Ooh," Mrs. McHenry said. This time, her voice dropped a couple of octaves.

"There are doctors that do that sort of thing," I said. "Junior is a physician. Could he?"

"My son," she hissed, "is a pediatrician, not an abortionist."

"No, ma'am," I said. "I know he's not. But maybe he knows somebody that . . ."

My mother-in-law had finished her limoncello and reached for mine. "Listen to me, Vernice. I have tried to be compassionate with you on this subject, but I think now is the time to be more direct. You are from Honeysuckle, Louisiana. I am from Sunflower, Alabama. Isn't it charming how they name these dreadful little towns after flowers? But you and I both know that nothing blooms. That's why we are not there.

"Once you escape, you do not want to transfer the squalor of your childhood to your new life. Don't let other people's bad luck tarnish your chances. What happens back home is *country mess*. What happens on the other side of town is *ghetto mess*. Your goal, at all times, is to make sure there is a chasm between you and the mess—be it country or ghetto. You better build a moat and fill it with alligators, crocodiles, electric eels, and whatever else."

She covered her mouth too late to trap a sugary belch.

Too stunned to speak right away, I stared at Mrs. McHenry, watching her bosom lift her caftan with every drunken breath. Her rouged cheeks and mascaraed lashes were garish in the light of the sun that had given this room its name. I was grateful that there was no mirror nearby, because I had adorned myself to match and I probably looked like a clown right beside her.

"I know I sound harsh," she said. "It's only because I love you so."

"You sound cruel," I said. "I knew Annie when we rocked in a cradle together."

"But you are no longer a motherless baby."

---

Not understanding the way families work, I thought that if Mrs. McHenry wouldn't ask Junior for a name, maybe Franklin would. But he said no. Even when I pleaded. Even when I tried to ply him with sweet talk and sweet love.

"Annie could die," he said. "And Junior could lose his license."

"All I need is a name," I said. "Your brother won't even have to lay eyes on her."

"White people know how to connect the dots," he said. "McHenry is a big name in Atlanta. Especially after our firm fought the freeway so hard. There is nothing they would love more than to bring my father down."

We lay in bed, but the thought of his father's enemies had taken the contented glow off his face. "You don't know these crackers like I do. Did you know they watch our cars? If I even think of overstaying the meter, I have a ticket on my windshield like a declaration of war. One time, I parked against a yellow curb and they had my car impounded faster than you can say 'Fuck you, nigger, we don't care if you are on a cane or not.' So can you imagine what they would do to my brother if he got involved?"

I pounded his chest with my open palm. The smack underlined itself with an echo. "Do you care about Annie at all? She doesn't have a job. She doesn't have a husband. The man the baby is for is married. She needs help."

"Of course I care about her. She's your—what do you call her? Your crib sister."

"Cradle friend."

"I stand corrected," he said. "But would it be the end of the world for her to just have this baby and get on with her life? I mean, this situation is hardly unprecedented."

I got up from the bed and took all the covers with me, leaving him naked on the fitted sheet. That little hog gut lay sheepishly against his thigh.

"Vernice," he said, "can't you be an adult?"

"Franklin," I said, "can't you be something besides a pompous ass?"

With an annoyed sigh, he got up from the bed too. He stood there bare as the day he was born and still held court. I marveled at the way that men are so at home with their bodies.

"Annie got herself in trouble. I hate it for her. But we can't roll the dice on everything my father built. I do care about her. But I don't love her. You do. It's your job to be unreasonable. It's my job to have some sense.

"Now come on back to bed, Vernice," he said. "I'm cold." And I could see that the hog gut appreciated his little speech.

"Please, Franklin. For me?"

"I can't," he said. "I would say no even if I wasn't an attorney."

"But—" I protested.

"No," he said. "Now come here."

I returned to the bed. He held me fast, but I didn't kiss him back.

---

In the end, it was Marylinda, with her bandage-colored skin and so much to prove. Before I could finish the story, she tore a page from her daybook and wrote down a phone number and address, from memory.

The ripped page was precious the way that money is, although it, too, was just paper. The blue lines were all control, but her writing cut across in a rebellious diagonal. Each letter was the same size, with the flourish of calligraphy. The edge was rough-torn but purposeful somehow. "What's the doctor's name?"

"Just tell them you know me."

I tucked it into my bra, remembering that when we were in college, we used to call her the Conductor.

*Chapter 35*

# ANNIE

When Babydoll and I shut the doors on Clyde's battered Packard, I knew that I wouldn't return to Memphis. We had arrived in that city as a party of four. Two couples. Babydoll and Clyde were going strong, and there wasn't room enough to slip even a sheet of wax paper between them. Folks never asked them how they met because it seemed like they had always been together. Bobo and Clyde were first cousins and they fit together in the way that boys do when their daddies are brothers. I was the only one without somebody to connect with. Babydoll was my close friend but not my family. Besides Granny, the only kin I had in the world was Niecy, waiting for me in Atlanta with her arms wide open. Once I got there, there was no way she would send me away.

I had done all I could not to be a burden. Tucked into my sock were a few bucks that I had squeezed out of Mr. Wilson. The soft dollar bills had come straight from the till and smelled of beer. He had set them on the bar like he was too good to touch my open palm, despite having touched my everything else. I was glad to have the money, but I wasn't grateful. I thanked him out of relief, and habit.

When I exited the Elektra, Babydoll was waiting in the Packard with the motor running. At the filling station, she paid for the gas with coins from the blue embroidered pouch where she kept her tips. When I offered up Mr. Wilson's cash, she waved it away.

"I'll pay for lunch," I promised.

"Can't you just let somebody help you?" For the first time since Bobo burned rubber, I experienced the rush of love. And on the other end of the trip was my dear Niecy. She was going to help me.

"Help." It was such a simple, ordinary word. I knew what it was to give help, to be the help, and to call for help. But receiving help was akin to Favor. And once you have accepted true help, you know that whatever you do at work wearing a uniform should never use the same word.

Niecy called me on the telephone the day she got my letter. Long calls are not cheap, but she dialed the number and held on while the landlady came to fetch me, even though she was being charged by the minute.

"Come on down here," Niecy said. "I will take care of you."

Ever since this happened, I am so sensitive to words and what they mean, the same way I have become sensitive to smells. When she said that, the word "care" was comforting to my nose like bread in the oven. Bobo and me both held a strong regard for what people say. He was fascinated by ten-dollar words, while I liked to get to the bottom of the simple things we say all the time. Like "care." Like "help." I was going to get to Atlanta, and Niecy was going to help get me some care.

---

We made it, but barely.

"That ain't nothing but God," Babydoll announced. She wore sky blue from tip to toe, the way she did when she needed a little extra attention from above.

The car bucked and gasped as we came down I-20. Babydoll's grip on the wheel was fringed with her prayer beads. Somehow we overshot our turn and ended up downtown, nearby to the state capitol. The sun bouncing off the dome made Babydoll curse and flip down the visor. But I let the golden glow bathe my face until I felt fortified.

---

All the McHenrys waited for us. Franklin looked like married life was treating him well. His hair was longer and fluffed a bit, making him seem like a lawyer who knew how to have a little fun. His experiment with sideburns made him a little sexy, like Niecy was doing everything just right. The man looked happy as a pig in slop. His mother, on the porch, was anything but. Tugging her coat closed, she frowned at us like we were bad weather rolling in. After a few moments, she tipped down from the stairs and stood beside Franklin. Her hand on his shoulder was a mother's touch, one I knew because of all the ways I didn't know it. When she was near Niecy, she smiled, and it was real. The genuine love she had for Niecy flowed right through her contented son.

Niecy herself looked warm as hot chocolate with marshmallows. At first she was stock-still like she and her in-laws were posing for a photographer, but then she broke loose and bounded in my direction, hollering my name like the two country girls we were.

"We were so worried about y'all," she said, jumping into my outstretched arms. I leaned back as I held her, lifting her feet off the ground. When I put her down, the whole McHenry family surrounded us, including the daddy, who had appeared out of nowhere.

"You remember Babydoll," I said, nodding in her direction.

"Ruth," she said.

Mr. McHenry took our bags, the same cases we had run away from home with. Everyone followed him like a flock of ducks, but Niecy and I trailed. She held my hand, stroking my knuckles with her thumb. "I won't let you down," she whispered.

I know that this was meant to reassure, but it frightened me. She wouldn't have said that if the situation wasn't crooked. All the comfort I got after her long call dried up like mist in the sunlight. My throat swole up and threatened my air. I squeezed back.

"Shh," she said, like she was comforting a baby.

Feeling the vibes, Babydoll glanced over her shoulder. I gave her a little wave to say that everything was going to be all right. Her lowered brow let me know that she didn't agree.

"You okay, Annie?" Niecy whispered.

"Not sure," I said.

"Don't worry. I got somebody to help us."

At breakfast, I wasn't sure who knew what. The six of us gathered at the kitchen table that was made to fit four people. The ones who lived in that nice house used the chairs that matched the table, made from wood that was more gray than brown. The men's seats were fitted with armrests. Babydoll and I used folding chairs like the ones they used for revival, when so many sinners showed up that the pews couldn't handle it. Niecy and Mrs. McHenry wore aprons printed with hearts and other reminders that Valentine's Day was right around the corner. Both of them blinked with mascaraed lashes, even at six in the morning. Franklin and his daddy were all about business, with their initials embroidered on the cuffs of their shirts. Babydoll and I had been sound asleep fifteen minutes ago, and we looked it.

The pancakes were fluffy like air, polished with butter. I peeked my eyes at Babydoll because the pancakes we were accustomed to had a little more weight to them, the flour mixed fifty-fifty with cornmeal. What the McHenrys served made you see why they were called pan*cakes.* The maple syrup—I knew what it was because it came from a bottle shaped like a leaf—was thin as a player's promise, and even sweeter.

"You have some Karo?" Like me, Babydoll preferred the dark corn syrup we were all trained up on.

"Course I do," Niecy said, popping up from her chair and rummaging through the pantry, raising up on her tippy-toes.

"Karo?" Franklin asked.

Niecy said, "Here it is."

She plunked it on the table like a trophy. The cap was crusted on with sugar crystals.

"So," said Mrs. McHenry in a songbird voice, "what do you ladies have ahead of you for the day?"

My hand, headed for the Karo, froze in mid-reach. Babydoll's fingers fluttered like she held her prayer beads. Niecy laughed like a three-dollar bill.

"Shopping," she said. "Maybe go get this hair tamed." She touched her perfect pageboy. Although many things had changed about my cradle friend, she still couldn't lie worth a damn.

Mrs. McHenry struck me as the sort of person that even an experienced hustler couldn't get over on, let alone an honest soul like Niecy. "Is that right? Maybe I should come with you. I have a meeting at one, but after that . . . ?"

Mr. McHenry looked over the top of his newspaper. "Let the young people go out and do whatever they want to do."

"I'm just being a proper hostess," she said. "Annie and her friend are new to town."

"Let's split the difference," said Franklin. "I'll take a half day, come home for lunch, and then I shall squire these ladies around."

"We're adults," Babydoll snapped, as I just sat there with my hand in the air, the syrup just out of reach.

Back in the guest room, Babydoll and I stood on opposite sides of the large bed and tucked and folded until the sheets were military tight. Niecy gave a polite tap on the door before walking in.

"Your husband knows, don't he?" Babydoll said.

"No," I said. "Niecy wouldn't do that."

Niecy turned her palms up. "Franklin and I don't keep secrets."

"Don't you?" Babydoll said, which made Niecy look at me, wondering what all I had shared.

This is why friendships work best in pairs. Miss Jemison had taught us about equilateral triangles, but when you get three people together, there is always a power play. Niecy was my person and I was hers in return.

Babydoll knew how to wave a question like a switchblade. "Did you tell the whole damn family?"

Niecy sat on a bow-legged chair and then popped up again in order to pace the floor. "I went to my mother-in-law first. She is a woman, after all. But she couldn't help."

"That bitch," said Babydoll.

"That's not fair," I said. "Maybe she didn't know anyone."

"Ladies like her can get anything you want," Babydoll said. "If I told her I needed a rhinoceros tusk, she could connect me with somebody just back from Africa. I know a stone-cold bitch when I see one. Annie, she wants you to sleep in the bed you made. Like she never spread her legs before she got that ring."

Niecy said, "Could you please lower your voice."

I laid myself on the army-tight bedspread. This wasn't the daily sick that got me first thing every morning since Mr. Wilson's seed had taken root inside me. This was the nausea that came from being disgusted with myself. I could picture Mrs. McHenry in front of a vanity mirror, pulling a paddle brush through her shiny hair, muttering the word that I never wanted applied to me—"trifling."

The church teaches us that our body is merely the vessel where our spirit lives on this earth. Granny clung to this promise, so eager to shed her skin so she could go be with the Lord. This last month had taught me that the body wasn't just a place for my soul to dwell. It had its own plans and aims. This body of mine wanted to grow a baby. Mr. Wilson sent his seed and my womb said, *Come on in.* This body that I had known all my life was a traitor, welcoming an uninvited being to share my blood.

Niecy and Babydoll bickered in hushed tones until they noticed me. "Oh, honey," Niecy said. Babydoll made a shushing sound. My friends joined me on the bed, one to the front, the other to my back. Their bodies were warm and fragrant against my clammy skin.

*Chapter 36*

# ANNIE

Franklin owned a two-door hardtop Coupe deVille. Black roof, the rest the nearly-white of pearls. A pair of fins on the back gave the impression that the car could fly, if things came to that. It had been a wedding gift. Niecy explained that his father and brother drove the exact same make and model, but the paint jobs reflected the men's personalities. Mr. McHenry's was all white like God's upholstery. The doctor brother painted his the dark green of a Georgia pine. Franklin accepted his just like it was on the car lot. "My husband isn't boastful," she promised. But there's no such thing as a humble Cadillac.

The three of us sat on the front seat, hip to hip, like we couldn't bear to be apart. Before we left, Franklin kissed Niecy's lips.

"Shopping," he said. "Just shopping."

"Davison's," she said. "Your mother said I need a dress. Uninterrupted white, remember?"

He nodded but squinted at me like he didn't trust me and Babydoll any farther than he could throw us. "Be safe," he said, leaning in to kiss her again.

"We're just going to the store," said Babydoll.

When we pulled away from the curb, he stood in the driveway, leaning on his cane, watching but not waving, until we couldn't see him anymore.

Who was I to say whether someone is a good driver or not? After all, I had never operated as much as a bicycle. That said, Niecy moved the Cadillac like a drunk after last call. Lurching. Whenever an unusual word popped into my mind, I knew that Bobo was the one who put it there. I turned my face to the glass so nobody would see my quivering lips and misunderstand my sadness, and turn the car around.

Babydoll gasped as we almost sideswiped an old Packard that was almost the same as Clyde's. Niecy jumped on the brakes, sending all of us toward the dashboard. The person that we almost hit cussed us out with just his horn. Niecy did something with her feet and pulled the lever behind the steering wheel. The car made a grinding sound.

"Niecy," said Babydoll, "are you trying to get us killed so we don't have to go where we are going, and do what we are doing?"

"I'm nervous, that's all," Niecy said.

---

A better person would have called the whole thing off. A better woman would have just reaped what she had sown. What kind of friend would have Niecy out in her husband's new car and maybe getting us all thrown in jail? I was selfish. I guess I had been this way all my life. It was greedy of me to even insist on being born. I imagined myself inside Hattie Lee, stealing half of every bite she ate. I pictured myself making her ill, making her tired, making her weepy. Hattie Lee had been in the very same situation as me, sucked it up, and weathered the storm. Mrs. Ola Mae, right around the corner, could have helped her.

Hattie Lee, no matter what people said, wasn't trifling. She left me because hatching me had been plenty to give.

Maybe it was payback, the way the one inside me was so stubborn, hanging in there no matter how hard I tried to clean myself out. Soapy douches had left my private parts so riled up that even the rub of my soft underwear was offensive. Castor oil vacated my bowels. But my period did not come.

"I tried, Niecy. I wouldn't bother you if I hadn't tried everything I knew how to do."

. . .

The journey from Veltre Circle to the address on the scrap of paper was about nine and a half miles. Niecy said that she was taking us on the "scenic route." She pointed out the sturdy brown building where her brother-in-law took care of ailing children. A couple of blocks up was an office where the Bronner brothers had made themselves into millionaires with pomade and hair spray. To the right was Paschal's, where Niecy had been presented as Mrs. McHenry. We crawled by the Herndon Home, which was outfitted with Scarlett O'Hara columns, the whole nine.

"And to think that Mr. Herndon was born a slave," she said. "Now they throw wonderful parties on the terrace."

There was a lot of luck in life, and they seemed to keep it all in Atlanta.

Babydoll raised her hand like a teacher's pet and said, "With all due respect, Niecy, why the hell are we sightseeing? Don't we have somewhere important to be?"

"I know," Niecy said. "I just thought since we were a little bit early . . ."

"Five minutes early is late," Babydoll snapped. "Ain't that what rich people say?"

The torn-paper address belonged to a busy laundromat. We didn't pull up right in front because Niecy didn't know how to park between two other cars up against the curb. She said that Franklin would teach her that part soon. Babydoll said she could, but Niecy said that she'd rather just leave the Cadillac somewhere else. We left the car near a large church that resembled a fortress, with a gray stone front and tube-shaped towers, like the one they locked Rapunzel in. At the tippy-top, near the steeple, a blue neon sign promised JESUS SAVES.

Babydoll clucked her tongue. "AMEs do way too much."

As a Catholic, she was one to talk, but this was no time to argue. Besides, she had knotted a blue scarf into a bow, to flag down the Virgin Mary, which was very nice of her.

Niecy checked the car doors twice to make sure the Coupe deVille was thoroughly locked. And then we walked the two blocks in the direction of another neon sign. This one said LAUNDERETTE, like it was a girl's name. The cursive *L* was almost flirtatious. A window sign, in no-nonsense print, read 30 CENTS WASH, 10 CENTS DRYING. The steamy air was heavy with the odor of clean clothes. Powder soap smelled different than the bars I had grown up on. Still, it brought back every memory I ever had in my whole life.

At Lulabelle's, the soap was spiked with peppermint oil because it could cut through blood. That memory locked my knees and jaws both; I couldn't will my feet to cross the threshold, nor could I will my mouth to explain why. Niecy and Babydoll nudged me inside.

---

To those who knew what was what, our business must have been obvious, as we were the only people there without dirty clothes. With our arms pretzeled, we made our way toward the back, bordered by washers the color of lemons on the verge of turning. Women's chatter competed with the sound of wet agitation. Against the back wall, a few dryers tossed sheets, but most people saved the dime and took their clean clothes home wet, where they could air-dry for free.

A woman behind the counter wore a green turtleneck sweater. She favored Mary McCleod Bethune with her dark skin and heavy body. Rhinestone earbobs, shaped like stars, winked through her cloud of white hair. As we advanced, she tracked us with narrowed eyes.

"What can I do for you ladies?" she said in a way that wasn't unkind but wasn't exactly welcoming, either.

Again, my mind went to Lulabelle. And again, I went rigid with fear. I wanted this to be over more than I have wanted anything, outside of finding Hattie Lee. But I was afraid. Ladies died getting this done.

Babydoll rubbed the place where my back disappeared into my britches while Niecy did the talking.

"Good afternoon," she said. "I called seeking medical assistance?"

"You need a hospital? Grady takes colored around the back."

"I'm the one that called," Niecy said.

"Who are you, again?"

"My name is Niecy," she said.

The lady grunted. "We don't use names in here. I'ma call you polka dots after your skirt, and you can just call me Miss Ma'am."

"Yes, ma'am, Miss Ma'am," I said.

She nodded slowly and fed herself two jelly beans from a Dixie cup. "Who you talked to?"

"Xavier," said Niecy.

Miss Ma'am looked skeptical. She chewed the candy, releasing a scent that I knew was meant to be cherry, but it smelled like chemicals.

"Which one of you has got the problem?"

"It's me." I took a step forward. "I'm the one."

"How you know to come here?"

Niecy said, "We're friends of Marylinda."

At that name, she smiled. "It's just twelve thirty. You too early. Your slot is not 'til one, and he got a little white girl in there now. You won't go in until two at least."

"That long?" I said. "What are we supposed to do 'til then?"

She shrugged, letting her shoulders lift and lower her large bosom. "CP Time."

We sat down on metal chairs to wait. I watched the women sort their clothes. I wondered which ones of them were doing the work for their own families.

---

"Babydoll, when was the last time you saw Bobo? I miss him."

Babydoll shrugged at Niecy and explained. "He's my in-law, you know."

"Have you met his other girl?" Niecy asked the question that was my wondering.

Babydoll nodded. "She's nice, or what have you. One time we invited them to go get a fish sandwich on Friday, but she didn't want to be around all that grease smoke." She snapped in the way you do when the perfect word comes to you. "She's the kind of girl that makes you keep sniffing up under your arms to make sure you smell right."

Niecy laughed. "I know women like that."

Babydoll said, "You better be careful before you mess around and become one of them."

Niecy stopped laughing and looked a little hurt. I don't know why Babydoll kept taking shots at her like that. I offered my cradle friend my hand and she held it in her lap.

Miss Ma'am, light on her feet despite her size, set down a wicker basket that smelled damp and musty. "You can't sit here like this is some kind of waiting room. Put this on to wash. You got dimes?"

I didn't but Babydoll did.

Grateful for something to do, I dumped the clothes onto a table and set about sorting them. The men's drawers were large and dirty enough to stand up by themselves.

Niecy was trying to decide if emerald green should be sorted as light or dark when Babydoll said, "Hail Mary, full of grace."

I looked up from our work to see three Atlanta policemen storm through the glass door. By instinct, all the women backed up and pressed themselves against the banks of machines, clearing the way for the white men with guns. Two wore the flat-topped hats with gold braid over the brim, but the one in front covered his head with a round helmet. As they passed us, I smelled traces of cigarette smoke.

Niecy punched Babydoll in the arm to get her to shut up with all that praying. "Stop being so conspicuous."

And of course, words like that made me think of Bobo. I wished that the baby in me was for him and it made him want to marry me and we'd be in Atlanta starting up a new life instead of me being here with my friends in a crowded laundromat, so scared that my ankles could hardly hold up the weight of my legs.

"Take us to the back room, Maybelline," the helmet cop said to the lady we called Miss Ma'am.

"We ain't got no back room," she said like Amos and Andy's

neighbor. "Lessin' you want to see the supply closet. That's all we got here."

He smiled like he was on *What's My Line?* and she had said just what he wanted to hear. To the cops in the flat-tops, he said, "Bring in the ram."

One of the officers acted like he had gotten the battering ram for Christmas and hadn't had a chance to use it yet. The other one seemed like he wanted to be at home listening to the radio.

The one in the helmet called us all out of our names. It didn't happen often, white men with their lazy accents speaking that word, slippery with cottonseed oil, but it happened enough that you never forgot that it was possible. Each time, it reminded me of the first time, when Niecy and I were just girls. We had walked to town with Granny to check the mailbox. Some white folks walked in our direction, having just left the post office themselves. A little boy, smaller than us, he tried the word out, like the first time you successfully pucker your lips to whistle. He said it, and looked proud of himself. "What did he say?" Niecy had asked. I didn't tell her so she didn't have to feel what settled in my gut.

But we were not kids anymore. And the man speaking with centuries of disgust wasn't eight and very small. The word from his lips was worse than a threat, it was a promise.

Niecy threw the smelly clothes to the floor as Babydoll guided me through the throng of frightened women. We were frazzled, as was everyone else, but we were not confused. As we fled, three more cops entered. One was a Negro, pushing through the crowd of women and baskets with his baton snug in his fist.

*Chapter 37*

# VERNICE

They already knew. We emerged from the Cadillac, ready to recite the lies we had rehearsed, but it was clear that there were no more cats in the bag. Every resident of 455 Veltre Circle gathered in the living room, seated on sofa cushions that got the dust beat out of them every Monday. I was a grown woman, married, and with some real education under my belt, but I was vulnerable as a child. That was the underside of being a soft-foot, along with wearing girdles, sweeping away slut's wool, and perfuming myself each day at 5 p.m.

It must have been the underside of other lives too, because Annie slumped, as hurt as a kicked dog. Babydoll twitched like she wanted to fight but was unsure who to punch.

On Franklin's face, relief mingled with anger. His energy was like I imagined a father's. Loving rage. Mr. McHenry also simmered, but untempered, like hot whiskey uncut. Mrs. McHenry was furious too, but hers was streaked with sorrowful frustration. She cocked her head and gave three unhappy shakes.

"Did I not tell you?" she said.

Sitting in the corner, as though she were in the dunce chair, was Marylinda, her bright red face cast toward the door.

As best as I could put together, Marylinda had received word about the raid and had zoomed over in her father's car, hoping to catch us before we left. Mrs. McHenry had opened the door and pried the story from her before summoning the men. Franklin and Mr. McHenry had connections with law enforcement but all they heard was that an interracial cluster of men and women had been arrested. They were a doctor, his nurse, two other women, and a man who tried to fight the cops with a broom. The lady who had been spread on the table was at Grady hospital. Everybody else was up under the jail.

Mr. McHenry had one question. "Did they see the car? Where did you park the car?"

"We put the Caddy over by the big church with the beer sign for Jesus," Babydoll said. "Damn. Y'all need to settle the hell down."

Franklin's face jerked into a quick smile until he was able to flatten it behind his hand.

Mr. McHenry didn't acknowledge Babydoll. Instead, he turned his attention to his wife like she was the one in charge of wayward girls. And Mrs. McHenry, for her part, shone her spotlight on me like I was a small creature that could grow up to be any kind of animal. Marylinda, for her part, never looked up. I couldn't tell if she was ashamed before us or my in-laws.

"What did you want us to do?" I said.

Mrs. McHenry said, "I believe I told you what you should do."

Nobody would ever accuse her of speaking with a forked tongue.

In her nervousness, Annie had unraveled one of the braids that traveled down the side of her head, and it made her appear younger than she was, and less loved. "I'm sorry," she said.

Franklin rose and leaned hard on his cane.

"Listen," he said. "No harm, no foul. Everyone is home safe."

"But think of what could have happened," Mr. McHenry said. "This is recklessness."

Franklin put some bass in his voice. "'Could have happened' is not admissible in this conversation."

"Oh," said Mr. McHenry. "Are we in court now?"

Annie rose. "Please stop," she said. "I have never really had a family, but I know that it's not supposed to be like this."

Marylinda and Babydoll, tickled by some joke I could not decipher, both began to laugh. They crowed like their hearts were breaking.

*Dear Annie,*

*Friend, I feel like I haven't taken care of you in the way that I promised. Time is running out.*

*Marylinda slipped me the name of another doctor, but I don't think that you need to fool around with anyone else in Atlanta. It has been made very clear that if I am a McHenry, I must act like one, and the first step is to protect the name that I so "happily added to my monogram." This is exactly what my mother-in-law said last night. Like you, I always wanted a mother and I guess I have one now. And having a mother involves letting her down, or so it appears.*

*My main regret is that I have put Franklin in a difficult position. If being a daughter is 25 percent being a disappointment, then being a son is about double that. He went into the law to prove that he is good enough, despite the polio. And he is a very strong attorney. I keep a scrapbook with every news clipping. But he will never be the whole son that the other McHenry boys are. And now I have embarrassed him. This is foreign to you and me both. How it feels not only to be a son, but to have a father at all.*

*My father's people were right up the road in Eloe, but I never made any effort to connect with them, nor they any effort for me. Aunt Irene says that he shot himself in the chest because he wanted an open casket. She kicked him in the face when she found him, hoping to derail that train, but you know that Negro funeral directors can be miracle workers, especially in the South, where they sometimes have to be.*

*This is part of why I feel so blessed. I know that the McHenrys might be siddity and what have you, but they are nice people and they are a family that I can be proud of. I never knew how weighted down I was about my history until I was able to untie it from around my neck. With this ring, this name—for the first time in my life, I am not anybody's "poor thing."*

*Life has never been fair. You and I have always been on the opposite sides of the table. In cards the person across from you is your partner, and I am yours. I will always be. You know my heart and I know yours. So please do not take what I am saying as a rejection.*

*You and Babydoll must leave before my in-laws have a stroke. I wish that this whole thing was happening in April, when I'd be the lady of my own home. Then there would be room for negotiation.*

*You need to go to Lulabelle's. She is mistress of her own kingdom and can handle this. She has no good name to protect. A person who has no shame can be your greatest ally, or your worst enemy. Franklin says that if he was making up an army, he'd want at least one battalion of shameless whores.*

*Take the Cadillac. Your Packard cannot make the journey and the last thing you need is to be stranded in some backwater with the clock running and no help available until it is too late. Franklin keeps the keys to the Coupe deVille on the THIRD PEG. Please do this before morning light. When we wake up and find the car gone, I will be* Casablanca *shocked, but I will make sure there will be no action taken against you.*

*You will notice the money in this envelope and you know what it is for. I have also included three pinches of dirt from my yard. It will bring you back to me.*

*Love and prayers,*

*Niecy*

*Chapter 38*

# ANNIE

This was not how I intended to return to Lulabelle's. As we turned that two-tone Caddy onto the property, whores peeked out from their shacks with curious eyes. A dog barking in the distance shut up when he got a good look at the hubcaps. Babydoll chewed a wad of gum with sass, enjoying her place behind the wheel of a car that cost more than these girls would ever make if they laid up under sirs all day, every day for the rest of their lives. I, on the other hand, was eaten up with dread.

My dream had been to come back with Bobo, a ring on my hand. I wanted Lulabelle to see me in one of those maternity dresses decorated with a stiff bow to make you seem like a virgin despite the jutting belly. I would bring her all the gifts that I had in mind for Hattie Lee. She'd open them and, with ribbons torn and strewn every whichaway, give us her blessing. Maybe even a party.

But no. Here I was riding in a car that made it where I had no choice but to tell the whole story. Of all people, Babydoll was with me. Her and Lulabelle went together worse than sand and collard greens.

---

In the years I'd been gone, somebody had been busy. The shacks had been treated to a nice coat of paint in shades of peaches and cream. I wondered who had provided the labor and how it had been paid for. The only one that had not been improved was the broke-down building nearby to the rose garden, where Bobo had crossed paths with a haint that sent him right into my arms. A puff of air, like your breath against candlelight, would turn it into kindling.

The Gibson girl, Delia, stood on the porch of the Jim Walter house, like she was expecting us. But I guess that in this business, you can expect anything at any time. She might have had the same *Oh, there you are* expression if we were little green men carrying an elephant in a hammock.

"Mama be down in a minute," she said, looking to me, then to Babydoll. "I thought you would be here with your man, not her."

Babydoll popped her gum. "I would have thought that, being a whore, you know how to mind your business."

"I ain't no whore," Delia said.

"Not yet," said Babydoll.

"Y'all," I said. "Come on."

Delia didn't ask us in, as it wasn't her threshold. It was noon and the sun was straight ahead, but we were cold inside our jackets. I was depleted in the way that only pregnant women can be. I sat down on the porch swing, hoping to soothe myself with the back-and-forth, but it only made me queasier.

The woman who emerged from the house clutching a rake surprised me. She wasn't decked out, like the Lulabelle I remembered. Instead she wore a bulky felted coat over trousers. Her hair was frozen into even rows of curls that had not yet been loosened by a comb. A gold cross dangling from a chain was the finishing touch.

Behind me, Babydoll whispered, "Lulabelle done got saved."

At this, I felt my shoulders slump. If Lulabelle had changed her life, she probably wasn't calling up doctors in Meridian to help women who needed what I needed.

She smiled, despite a face full of suspicion. "What can I do for you?" she asked.

"It's me," I cried. "It's Annie!"

She puckered her lips as she tried to recall who I was. And just when I was about to burst into tears, another woman pushed her way onto the porch. "Lurelia! Why do you like to do people like that?"

Here was my Lulabelle, dressed for gardening in an outfit specially designed for this activity. The color was orange, crossed with brown, with a little cap to match. Through her azalea-pink smile, the gold-framed dogtooth caught the light. She had accused her twin sister of playing games, but I knew she was a woman who liked to make an entrance.

"Jesus Christ," said Babydoll. "I forgot there were two of them."

Said Lulabelle, "If it ain't Ruth Ann."

I don't exactly know why, but calling Babydoll's given name seemed to put her in her place.

Now that Lulabelle was finished with swordplay, her face softened and she turned her attention to me. "Annie Kay," she sighed. "Didn't I tell you not to come round here again?"

Lurelia said, "Don't make the child cry."

Lulabelle said, "It's not me that's making her cry. Whatever brought her back is what's turning her inside out."

Lulabelle wanted to talk in the rose garden, across from the run-down shack. She carried pruning shears and heavy gloves. Her sister brought a box of baking soda, a jar of cooking oil, and a bottle of Palmolive soap. Babydoll and I lugged a bucket of water made tart with vinegar. Winter in Mississippi is colder than in Georgia. There's a wetness in the air that invades the bones. Making our way across the property, I said as much, as Lulabelle's sister laughed at me.

"Poor Mississippi," she said. "It's like God put us here to make the world feel better. Whatever people got in any other state, they can hold their head up and say, 'Least it ain't Mississippi.'"

Lulabelle said, "Well, how do you know it's not the truth? You have never been anywhere but here."

Lurelia said, "Not true. We both been to Tennessee."

Lulabelle said, "Tennessee is just North Mississippi."

"We went to Alabama for a funeral."

"East Mississippi."

Handing us rags, Lurelia informed us that the little house-type thing in the garden was from the Jim Walter catalog just last year. It was known as a "gazebo." As always happened with me when I learned new words, I remembered Bobo and my face slackened. And as always when my eyes went sorry, Babydoll tried to distract me. "Roses without blooms are just sticker-briars," she said.

In summer, the rosebushes were wild with yellow, pink, red, and white. Some crawled up trellises, and others just stood independent and heavy with blossoms. The odor was so thick you could spread it on toast. And then there were the bees, lumbering around like pregnant women, parting the petals like curtains, until they made their way to the yellow cores. But in February, all that remained were grayish stalks, barbs, and knobs.

Once Babydoll and I had cleaned the gazebo with the vinegar water, Lulabelle and her twin beckoned for us to join them in the thick of the garden. My lips were numb from the cold and my toes hurt. In their warm clothes, the women settled their knees on pads made from folded newspaper.

"Can we just explain to you why we're here?" Babydoll said. "Or do we need to freeze to death first?"

"I know why you're here. Girls don't have but two reasons to come here and from that new Caddy, I don't reckon that you need the work. And that green ring on your finger says you're not the one that needs the help." Lulabelle grunted and went after a bush with her shears.

"We do this for our mother," Lurelia explained, using gloved hands to gather the stalks. "The garden is a tribute."

"Although she don't never come over here," Lulabelle griped.

"Your mother?" I said. "I thought she passed."

"Been passed," said Lulabelle. "Been dead longer than you been living."

Babydoll bowed her head to show that even she had respect.

"Be merciless, Sister," said Lurelia. "Half a prune is the same as none at all."

We worked together for what seemed to be a long time but couldn't have been because the sun was the same height in the sky when we were done as it had been when we got started. But some days are like that. You work yourself weary, but the hours don't move.

The roses didn't appreciate our efforts. The thorns more than did their share to protect the sleeping plants. Our arms were lumpy with welts and bumps, but we kept snipping and pruning until Lulabelle was ready to hear my plea. In a strange way, earning her attention gave me a sense of worthiness.

The labor completed, the four of us went to the gazebo, sat upon wrought iron benches, and admired our work.

"Summer will be here before you know it," Lurelia said.

In the daytime, you couldn't even tell that this was a whorehouse. With the fresh paint on all the shacks, it didn't seem like a sharecroppers' farm either. It just looked like land with small spaces of refuge and shelter. The ladies who popped out from one house to another merely appeared neighborly.

"How's Clyde?" Lulabelle asked with a little vinegar.

"He's doing very well, thank you," Babydoll shot back.

"He working?"

Babydoll shook her head. "Not at the moment."

"You know he is never going to hold a job, not long-term, at least."

"Doesn't mean he's not a good man," Lurelia added.

"Spoken like another woman whose man don't work."

Lurelia nudged her twin on the arm. "You speak like a woman who ain't got no man."

Turning her attention to me, Lurelia said, "You sure this is what you want to do? How come you don't want to just have the baby and let your grandmother help you raise him?"

"No," I said. "It's nothing worse than knowing that your mama didn't want you."

Babydoll said, "Niecy might like to take the baby. That's the only thing she doesn't have yet."

Lulabelle stamped her foot. "What makes you two think that you have anything to say that she hasn't already thought about? Nobody comes all the way to Mississippi, in a car they clearly stole, because they are on the fence." She pointed at Babydoll. "You are a contrary human being. And, Lurelia, you are just stupid on purpose. I don't understand, but I am used to it."

Lurelia was quiet because maybe she was accustomed to being insulted by her twin. And Babydoll was quiet, maybe because she didn't want to fight Lulabelle and ruin things for me.

"Like I was saying." Lulabelle steered the conversation onto a road that suited her better. "This garden is for our mother. Her name was Hortense. We grew up right here on this farm. Our daddy was here with us. All of us. Tobacco, rice, sugarcane. Don't let Lurelia's little apron fool you. She could cut cane like a man."

"Had to," Lurelia said.

"But look at us now. We own the land our daddy was beat on. We own the land our mama died on. First thing I did was get rid of all the crops. If I never see another stalk of cane for the rest of my life, I'll die happy." Lulabelle's voice was colder than the whole month of February. "I don't even use Karo. I'll eat my hoecake with honey, or just have it dry."

Lurelia took her sister's hand. "It's Mama's birthday," she said, explaining the scene in front of our eyes.

From our time at the Elektra, Babydoll and me knew that liquor was at play.

"It was our mama that Bobo saw that day," Lulabelle said. "Her spirit likes that lean-to, and I just don't know why. I planted this garden so she could have somewhere nice to be, but she just wants to roam around that nasty little room for all eternity."

"I don't believe in haints. Our mother is with the Lord," said Lurelia.

"That's because you have never seen her. If you saw her you would know that it was Mama."

"The devil wears many disguises."

"You just mad because she didn't come to you, Lurelia."

"Because Satan knows better than to mess with me."

Babydoll stood up. "Ladies. You both just miss your mama. Let's not quarrel on her birthday."

We were quiet again. The wind stung my ears. The sun hurt my eyes.

"You'll call the doctor for me?" I asked Lulabelle. "We got the money."

Lurelia piped up. "It's dangerous, you know."

"We know," Babydoll said. "We were laundry girls here three summers ago."

In the trees, squirrels chattered and played while we just gazed out pondering mothers, death, blood, and life.

"Birthing a baby is dangerous, too," Lulabelle said. "One of our little brothers killed our mother, trying to get born. They were twins, like us. The midwife refused to tell my daddy which, but whoever came out last was a born murderer."

Lurelia shook her head mournfully. "They are both passed now. Couldn't live with it."

*Chapter 39*

# VERNICE

I confessed before breakfast that Annie hadn't stolen the car. Partly it was because I loved Annie too much to let them think of her as a thief. And secondly, I treasured my new family too much to give them the cause to say something that I could not love them in spite of. Besides, I have never been a liar.

Mr. McHenry was vicious, a side of him I had never seen. "You are just determined to help her kill that baby, aren't you?"

Mrs. McHenry glared at him. "Rich, grow up."

Franklin didn't give a damn about whether or not what Annie had gone to do met the legal or moral threshold for murder. His face was hurt, in a straightforward, uncomplicated way. It reminded me of Joette on the first day I came home wearing Franklin's grandmother's ring. There was no arguing with cloudy heirloom diamonds. Just as there was no contesting the empty space in the garage.

The world wanted so much from me. Love required so much betrayal. Sometimes of myself. Oftentimes, everyone with a heart ended up devastated. This is what I wanted to tell Joette. I needed her to understand that it had torn me up to walk away from her. I couldn't say for sure if I loved her or not, but I could say that I missed her. She was well acquainted with the real me.

I didn't have secrets from her because she was my secret and I was hers. She knew me in ways that even Annie did not. But of course, Annie knew me like no one else could.

But where was my husband in this math of love? Didn't he also bear witness to an aspect of me that was unknown to the others? We had been married only months, but the vow we had sworn at Danforth Chapel was binding. He offered me his name and I took it. He offered me his mother and I took her. He offered me monthly security tucked into envelopes and I took them. He offered me his imbalanced body, and I took that too, with the enthusiasm with which I embraced the rest. Last night, I had made my way up that twisted leg with my lips, and the sensation brought tears to his eyes. "Love" was all he could say, and I wasn't sure if it was a command, a description, or maybe a name for me.

This had been only a few hours before, and now he gave me those Joette-hurt eyes. "You gave her my car?"

In my palm, I bounced three quarters. Annie had left them atop the guest-room dresser with a note. *Keep these for me. They are precious to my soul.*

---

Annie was three days gone with the Cadillac when the phone rang. I was zipping Mrs. McHenry into her dress of uninterrupted white for her meeting of this club that she was so pleased to belong to. The preceding seventy-two hours had been tense as the Last Supper, but in the way of people with money, we resolved to behave as though it weren't happening.

To prepare for her special afternoon, Mrs. McHenry wore a full suit of armor. Long-line girdle, cone-cupped brassiere, sweat pads, stockings and garters. A tight dress would have revealed her to be an aging pinup. But the dress she wore for this event was fit for a lady—flowing but nipped to flaunt the discipline required to be so lean, despite the three sons, despite the daily limoncello. Her waist spoke of eating little, even though she could afford plenty.

I had just joined every hook and eye when the phone jangled in its cradle.

"McHenry residence," I said, just as I had been trained to do.

"Can I talk to Niecy?"

"It's me," I said. "It's me."

Somebody named Delia said a few words before passing the phone to Annie. Her voice was strong, but her words were slow.

"You got my quarters?" she said.

"In my jewelry box."

"Keep them safe. Please, Niecy. I need to have those exact same coins."

"I will. Are you okay, Annie?"

"They say the fruit don't fall far from the tree." Her voice held a desperate tone. "You know how they say that? But it's a lie. Look at you. Married to somebody nice. Franklin is not going to kill you. And look at me. I am not going to run off on a daughter. We're not apples."

Then a new voice got on the phone.

"This here is Lulabelle Simms. I gave her a pill. That's why she's talking crazy."

"Thank you, Mrs. Simms," I said.

"No Mrs. here. I'm just too old to be a Miss. But I let her call you to let you know that she made it through all right. She and that fast one are heading your way. Is it true they stole your car?"

"Annie would never steal from me."

"Not her," said Lulabelle. "The other one."

"No," I said. "I lent it to them."

"Well, they will be your way middle of the night."

"Tell her I said to go on and ring the bell. They can spend the night here."

"Good for you," she said. "Up on your hind legs. I'll tell her."

"Thank you," I said. "For taking care of her."

*Chapter 40*

# ANNIE

I never told this to anyone, but she came to the Elektra on a hopping Saturday night. This was just two weeks or so after Bobo left. I didn't see her arrive because I had long let go of my habit of looking for her. Ever since I had taken on my new role as Mr. Wilson's special girl, I was always behind the bar, where he could keep an eye on me and where I could feel like I was receiving some reward for what I did after the drawer was counted and all the tables wiped clean. I glanced up from a screwdriver and there was Hattie Lee, posted up on a stool like a canary on a perch.

Babydoll passed behind her, none the wiser. The gentlemen beside her glanced in her direction and went back to their glasses. The two youngbloods across from her argued about politics the whole time and never even turned their eyes. I wondered if it was my turn to be visited by a haint. In all my days, the dead had not called upon me, but it happens to all of us sooner or later.

I turned my back, to gather myself, but Mr. Wilson spun my shoulder and pointed at my mother, who held a dollar bill. "Get her order," he said.

"Ma'am," I said, "what can I get you?"

"Coca-Cola," she said, the country way. Co-Cola. Like how Granny said it.

"Yes'm." I reached for a shapely bottle and set it before her. "You want a glass?"

"Your name Annie Kay?" she said. "It is, ain't it?"

"Yes, ma'am," I croaked.

Mr. Wilson, behind me, patted my hip as he made his way to the peanut barrel and received my sharp elbow in reply.

"You know me?" she said, her fingers resting below her chin.

"Isaiah and Sweet told you I was here?" I asked.

She nodded. "I wanted to know."

"What else do you want?"

"Just to lay eyes on you. Why are you here in Memphis?"

"For you."

She sucked the Coke from the bottle, ignoring the glass. Her face was scarred from the life she had led, but her throat was long and beautiful. It was a neck that called out for pearls. When she finished, she patted her bosom to settle the fizz.

"Don't waste your time on me," she said. "Everything can't be fixed, you know."

"But how can you tell the difference?"

She smiled with a mouth of teeth that were stained but even. "Oh, you'll know."

There were seventy-five cents left of her dollar. She transferred them hand to hand before leaving them behind.

"Tell my mama I love her."

"Me too," I said to her back.

When I collected the shiny coins, they were warm from her touch.

*Chapter 41*

# VERNICE

Ruby Falls is in Tennessee, a couple hours outside of Nashville, if you are traveling from Atlanta. Miss Jemison once took Mrs. Ola Mae there. She told me that story on my way to college and I had mostly forgotten about it. It's an underground waterfall. A river crashes from a cliff that you can't even see from the woods just above it. Everything seems placid and calm as a prayer. And underneath, a violence of water.

Mrs. Ola Mae told me because she wanted me to learn to cry like regular people, to wail, holler, and beat my chest. She was worried because I had never really mourned my mother. But maybe it was normal not to grieve a stranger. Yes, I had a loneliness in me that had her name all over it. And if I ever had a daughter, custom said to call her Arletha, and I would. It is sad to not have a mother. It is sad to be incomplete. But sadness is one thing. Grief is another.

Mrs. Ola Mae meant well, but she went on too long about the truth of women's emotional composition. She should have told me more about the workings of these fragile bodies we are cursed with. Why did she not tell me that someone could bleed to death from the inside and never shed a drop of blood on the slate-gray sheets I'd ironed the day before? She could have mentioned that my cradle friend could tell me she loves me and thank me for the envelope of money, despite grave danger hidden deep within her body. Grinning, Annie asked me if someone like her could go to college. She wondered if we each have one true love and if the person doesn't love you back, does that mean he's not your true love? So tired that she could hardly hold her eyes open, she said that somebody should write a reverse dictionary where you could look up what you were feeling and then it would give you the word. No one, not one person, ever mentioned that it was possible for Annie to go to bed full of questions, lay her head over three hot quarters, and all the while be bleeding to death because real doctors don't work for pussy at Mississippi whorehouses.

## *Chapter 42*

# ANNIE

When I ran away, Niecy thought that I had died. She was scared, but she went into my room to shut my eyes. She undid her hair, ready to loop a ribbon around my jaw. Finding my bed empty, she left the length of green grosgrain on my pillowcase.

In her letter, she wrote that one of us was going to have to bury the other one. I said I hoped it was her and she wrote back that she prayed it was me.

*Chapter 43*

# VERNICE

It was a sin. It was a shame. It was a scandal. Annie Kay Henderson was the daughter of Hattie Lee, who wasn't cut out *for* mothering. She was the granddaughter of Irvina Henderson, who couldn't cut out *of* mothering. Her great-grandmother was named Persephone because in slavery times, they called you any old thing. All this was in their Bible. All this Annie has memorized. What wasn't on the record was that Annie had been told that her great-grandmother was called Michaelene. This is how Annie knew her granny couldn't read. Her granny had touched that long name beginning with P and said, "My mother, Michaelene." Annie repeated after her, "My great-grandmother Michaelene."

---

This is who was lying dead in the guest room. Dear Annie. Kind Annie. Annie who had been in love and in trouble. Annie who kept three quarters close. Annie who missed Bobo. Annie who chased her mother clear across the South. Annie who gave me the name that people call if they really know me. Annie who thought that life was about to give her another chance. That's who was lying cold in my in-laws' house, clothed in my nightgown, atop sheets washed by my own hands.

Joette could trace her family on her father's side, going all the way past Daufuskie Island to the ones who could talk in another tongue. She told me this when we knew each other, when she talked about the death business like it was only about dignity and equality. When her people had been yoked on a South Carolina island, they boiled indigo flowers in piss to make dye. In those days it was the women who cared for the dead, sprinkling quicklime and ensuring the body faced east to get back home. There was no money in it. Just self-respect. She knew their names. She recited them like a spell, when she didn't join Marylinda in the Movement. She said that her father's line had done their duty just by helping folks get to heaven with their heads held high.

She and I talked so much in those very very young days. Only three years ago? A thousand or so nights? How had we been so green, so recently? In those tender days I had somehow lost track of the fact that someone had to be dead to buy the dignity that her family was selling.

Now I needed to purchase some. Because it was a sin and a shame and a scandal, what happened to Annie, what I had given her money to do. The McHenry home was not the site of scandal. Sin and shame happened from time to time. What could you do when a man had that much money and had not one, not two, but three sons? Sin was going to happen. And wherever there were women, there was shame. We are born ashamed.

But scandal. Absolutely not. Not ever. Not in the McHenry house.

---

There were other mortuaries in Atlanta. Sellers Brothers could make you so pretty that people would think it was your wedding, not your funeral, but the embalmers gossiped. The Haugabrooks were capable, but they were not in our circles. That left Cunningham & Sons.

"If Harold Cunningham were an honest man, he would admit that he is in our debt," Mrs. McHenry said. "And if his wife were less of a bitch, she would push him toward what's right."

I nodded, wondering how I breathed since the waterfall of tears inside me roared so hard that my ears popped. If you could bleed to death without a drop, then couldn't I drown despite my face being so dry that my lips chapped and split? There were too many questions in this world without answer, just gaping like manholes waiting for someone to slip through and be trapped in the sewer forever.

Mrs. McHenry snapped at me, "There will be plenty of time for misery. Whoever said it endureth for a night is a goddamn lie. You will grieve this forever. But right now, we have to protect our name, because it, too, is yours for the rest of your life."

In answer, I showed her my dry face, which prompted her to nod in approval.

"We have to go through the daughter," she said.

"We" was me. The daughter was Joette.

---

Cunningham & Sons used Gordon Street as its address, but the front door was on Peeples Street, in the West End. Like all of the other structures on the block, it was a grand Victorian, built after the Civil War. Tara was burned to the ground and these ornate mansions sprang up in its place. Joette's grandfather bought the place in 1907 and they shredded the mortgage the year that Joette was born. The idea was that the funerals and viewings could be held on the ground floor, and the family would live on the upper level. Down in the basement, they performed the services that no one liked to think about. They lived this way, commingling with the dead, until her grandfather was laid to rest in a coffin from his own inventory. The very next week, Joette's parents moved the family to Venetian Hills.

Besides that, not much had changed about the family business over the years, except for the fact that Cunningham & Sons was now Cunningham and his one daughter. Joette's younger brother wasn't the undertaker type. Burly but squeamish, he went away to Virginia for college and never claimed his birthright. He married into a solid family up there and worked for his in-laws as a mediocre accountant. I believe the company was called Johnson & Sons. And since her brother had escaped, Mr. and Mrs. Cunningham were uneasy but didn't block their daughter from standing in his stead. They did what they had to do even if it meant she would likely never marry, especially now that she had thrown off the Donaldson boy, the only suitor not put off by her proximity to the graveyard.

All this, Mrs. McHenry explained to me as I dressed for this agonizing errand. In the mirror my face stared back at me with eyes red, not from crying, but from dryness. I pulled a comb through my hair, but I didn't look put together even with every strand in place. When I reached for my lipstick, Mrs. McHenry advised against it. "They need to see that we are going through hell."

---

When I arrived, I tripped up the stone stairs, tearing my stocking and knocking my knee. As a blob of blood oozed from the wound, I marveled at how bright it was. From my purse, I unfolded a tissue and pressed to stop the bleeding. As I sat on the steps, a cluster of mourners watched me from the curb.

"You need some help?" asked a man wearing pinstripes.

"Annie is dead," I said.

"Condolences," said the woman beside him, holding a baby.

As they crossed through the arched doorway, they looked over their shoulders and whispered. I ordered my legs to rise, but they refused. Another dark-dressed family passed me, and then another. Finally, Albertina Cunningham found me and offered a helping hand. She was stronger than she appeared, pulling me to my feet despite the utter uncooperation of my legs.

"Do you want to speak to my husband?"

"No, ma'am," I said. "I need your daughter."

---

Joette sat in a dark-paneled office, behind a desk that stretched nearly the width of the room. Bare but for a silver tissue box and an elegant lamp covered with a stained glass shade. It felt wrong for anything to be as lovely. It felt wrong for me to notice.

"Country Mouse," Joette said from behind the impressive desk. I couldn't tell if she spoke my old nickname to be affectionate or cruel. "Country, Country, Mouse."

"It's me," I said.

Mrs. Cunningham lingered, as though unsure of her role.

"Go on, Mother," Joette said softly. "Please let us talk alone."

Her mother took two steps deeper into the room, almost spoke, but thought better of it, before she swiveled and left.

---

"It's Annie." I knew that a normal person would have been crying and pulling tissues from the silver box. But I wasn't normal people. My sadness was an underground waterfall. "It's my Annie."

"Oh, Mouse." This time there was affection in it. "What happened?"

"I can't fix my mouth to say it."

But she knew, just like she had known what happened to my parents.

"I saw on the news that there had been a raid, but folks said that the girl that died was white."

"That wasn't Annie. She went somewhere else."

Joette rose from the desk, and for a moment, I thought that she would touch me. I closed my eyes in anticipation, but that comfort didn't come. Instead, she clicked across the hardwood floor to the window. Twirling a rod, she opened and closed the heavy wooden shutters, blocking the sun and then restoring it. "I hate that," she said. "It happens more than you know and I hate it every time."

She settled on letting the light in and returned to her desk as the sounds of an organ floated in from the parlor. *Let the work I've done speak for me.* Joette tapped in time with the melody and hummed a couple of bars. Finally, she asked, "Where is she?"

"At my in-laws'."

Joette leaned back into the luxurious leather chair. "Oh," she said. "I see. I'm assuming that Patty McHenry is losing her mind."

I rocked in my chair, grateful that I didn't have to explain. Even now, even though—Joette understood me, and my life.

"You are seeking discretion," she said.

"You know I have the money." I fumbled with the latch on my bag.

"I know you do," she said. "But."

"But what?" I asked, stricken. "I need your help so bad, Joette. For Annie."

"Annie," she said softly, "does not care. We service the dead to take care of the living."

"So won't you help me?"

"You have to pay."

"I told you."

Joette shook her head. "My daddy won't want any part of this. He and your father-in-law fell out over the property I believe you are building a house on. I'm afraid it will take a little more than money to get what you need."

"What do you want?"

"What do I want from *life*, or what do I want from *you*?" Her mouth curled up on the left side, a gesture I remembered, a little bit mocking and a little bit loving.

"What do you want from me?"

"I wouldn't say that I *want* anything from you. But you need to do something for me."

I looked down at my busted-up knee and pulled the nylon, blood-pasted to the sore, disturbing the delicate clotting. I envied my wound and how easily it wept. "Just tell me what to do."

---

"This is a story about my grandfather," Joette said, opening the desk drawer and rummaging around. "My grandmother played the role that my mother does now, providing comfort, coffee, and so forth. First Lady, helpmeet, etc." From the drawer she produced a tarnished oyster fork and handed it to me.

"In Grandfather's office—that's now where Daddy is—I lay on the carpet coloring. Grandmother brought in a young couple in distress. The young lady's hair was divided into four, like a child's. I'll never forget it.

" 'Our baby woke up dead this morning.' She was just crying, crying. Then the fellow joined her. My grandmother added her tears to the mix. I was about five years old and the whole thing shook me up. I crawled over to Pawpaw so he would pull me onto his lap."

She shook her head at the memory and I could imagine Joette as a child, surrounded by so much sadness. She'd never mentioned the weight of it, all those years ago, when she went on and on about dignity.

"Anyway," she continued, "my granddaddy just asked them outright how they planned to pay for the services. And listen. You thought there was crying before. Now it was moved up to all-out wailing. The boy started in about what all he ain't got. But Pawpaw said, 'Come back tomorrow, and bring me what you have.'

"What he had was a Timex watch, two rolls of nickels, and that little fork you have in your hand. Pawpaw inspected every piece, even fitting a jeweler's loupe over his eye as he examined the silver. 'That's all?'

"The fellow patted his pockets like maybe there was some last treasure hiding in the folds. When Pawpaw didn't seem impressed, the young man removed the coat from his back. He didn't have on anything underneath but shirtsleeves.

"When they left, my grandmother was through, I tell you. Through.

"She said, 'Now the boy is hungry and cold.'

"Now, Mouse, here is the part you need to listen to."

"Okay," I said, a bit resentful for this whole story time. She had me where I had no choice but to listen, but I wouldn't hang on her every word.

"Mouse, I'm trying to help you." Her voice dropped to an authoritative rumble. "Pawpaw said, 'More than he needs the clothes on his back, he needs to know that he is the one who buried his son.' "

I sat there, confused and irritated. She was playing with me, like I really was a mouse and she a hostile cat. With the oyster fork, I tore at my stocking. "I told you. I have money."

She ticked her tongue against the top of her mouth. "You are hardheaded, Mouse. I know I can't make a horse drink orange juice, but I am going to try one more time."

She was up from the desk and kneeling before me. Taking my hands, she pressed them to her breastbone, allowing me to feel the organ churning there as the organ in the sanctuary ran through "I'll Fly Away."

"If I talk to my daddy, you will owe me a favor. Any money you give me belongs to your husband. Can't you see? Annie doesn't need dignity. You do."

She released me, straightening her face as she rose.

"Please." I slid out of the chair and landed on the carpet with a thump. "Is this what you want? I am on my knees." I dug into my purse and found the three coins, the significance of which I would never know. "Take this money. This is mine. Not my in-laws'. This is every penny that belongs to me."

Joette shook her head. Folding my fingers over Annie's money, she whispered, "Get up, Mouse. I don't want you to beg."

I stayed there, a crumpled ball at her feet. "What do you want, then? Just say it and I will do it."

"Tell your husband," she said. "Tell him."

"Why?" I wailed. "Is this payback? I know I did you wrong, but I didn't do you this wrong."

"Mouse," she said. "My Mouse. You know I'm not like that. You're acting like you don't know me."

"Think about it," I said to her. "I can't tell him about me without telling him about you."

"I don't care," she said. "My folks know."

"You told them?"

"They found out. I wish I had told them. Don't you wish you had sat in the white section on that bus on purpose? Then you would have been kicked off with dignity. It's the dignity that makes it worthwhile."

I shrank at the memory of the valor I had claimed but hadn't earned. "I never lied to anyone."

"But you let people believe you were some kind of hero."

"Not you," I reminded her.

"Mouse, I never needed you to be a hero."

"Yes, you did."

She considered this before she spoke again. The privacy of the office felt like the sheltered dark of our dormitory. "I thought maybe together we could be brave for each other."

She crossed the room but not toward the window. Stepping out into the hallway, she held her hand up to advise me to be quiet. After a few long moments, she was satisfied that we were alone. She returned to the leather chair behind the manly desk. She offered me a tissue that I didn't take.

"The short version is that my father discovered a perfumed note from a friend of mine, and there was hell to pay. At least I can be proud that I didn't deny it or tell them her name. It's not enough. But it's something. For nearly a week, they forbade me to cross their threshold. I lived here, downstairs. The dead don't mind company. But finally, my parents took me back. You know why?"

"Because you are their daughter and they love you," I said.

Her scoff was so abrasive, it could have taken the paint off the walls. "Spoken like a true orphan. Blood alone can't give you kinship, Mouse. No, no, no."

Mrs. Cunningham peeped into the room. "Is everything all right?"

"Get out of here, Mother," Joette said. "This is a personal conversation."

Mrs. Cunningham scurried away, as though she were afraid of her own daughter.

"I'm so angry," Joette said. "I'm just so angry."

"Me too," I said. "About so much."

"They took me back," Joette said, "because they couldn't very well explain to anyone why they had put me out. Besides, who would take over the business? It was too complicated to disown me. Finally, my daddy just asked me what was the word for a lady-faggot. He said, 'Just answer me that.'"

From my place on the carpet, I gazed up at her strong but quivering chin.

Nodding yes to an unasked question, she seemed to remember that I was on the floor. She extended her hand. "So, Mouse, you can see that I am not anxious to speak to my father on your behalf."

"But you will?" I asked, climbing to my feet.

She plucked the oyster fork from my limp hand.

"Don't you want dignity?" Joette asked. "There's no life without it."

---

Babydoll waited on the porch, still wearing her nightgown of uninterrupted white cotton. "Did you make arrangements?" she asked. "I can't go back in there until you find somebody to come get her."

"I'm working on it," I said. "It's complicated."

Babydoll pushed back on the porch swing with an angry creak. "What's the point of marrying somebody like these people if you can't even get your best friend into the ground?"

---

I found Franklin seated at the kitchen table, dressed in his undershirt and a pair of slacks. With a pencil, he jotted notes on the blueprint. Even with Annie dead down the hall, life went on. There were houses to be built. Lawsuits to file. Strides to be made.

The house was full but not busy. From the dark-paneled den wafted the sweet smell of pipe smoke. From the sunroom came the delicate tinkle of ice in a crystal glass.

"I need to talk to you," I said.

He motioned toward the chair where I usually sat, but I shook my head. "Not here."

I followed my husband downstairs into the room that we slept in but was not our own.

"Are you leaving me?" he asked with alarmed curiosity.

"No," I replied, shaken.

"Let me put it another way. Do you want to leave me?"

"That's not what I need to talk about."

He paced in his three-legged way. Leg. Cane. Then the other leg.

He closed his hands over a Spanish figurine that had not been on my registry, but someone had given it to us anyway. It depicted a pale ballet dancer balanced on her toes. He placed it back on the shelf, but facing the wall.

"You told me one time that your aunt raised you but never mothered you. Remember that?"

I did.

"And you told me how lucky I was because my mother loved me so completely. And do you remember what I said next?"

I nodded, recalling the conversation. Franklin had given a dry smile and said, "She loved me so much she found me a wife."

"I wasn't joking. Sometimes it feels like this marriage is a back-room deal between you and my mother. I get to play husband and you get to play daughter. And other times, I think that maybe this was between you and Annie. Whoever gets safe first will take care of the other one."

"No," I said. "No, no, no. It's not like that."

"Not all the time," he agreed. "Sometimes I feel like I am touching you. Like we are touching each other. There are days when I think you love me. There are days when I think you are *in love* with me. And then there are days . . . moments, really. Flashes, but I think about them for days. It's as if you go off somewhere, leaving me in my bed alone."

"I would never . . . ," I said.

"You are not the first woman in my life. One, I loved, but she couldn't get past the leg. Then there was another one, and we liked each other, but she was in it for the money. I'm not rich, but we have more than a lot of people. I didn't blame her, but I couldn't marry her." He breathed. "And then there was you."

He lay back on the soft bed with his arms stretched out to show me either that he was unarmed or that he wanted to embrace the entire universe.

I did love him, this tender man with this ruined leg, bright mind, and sincere eyes that told the story just as well as his lips. His face bore the pain of what he had just told me yet was set with the satisfaction that must have come from having no daylight between what he felt and what he had said. There was a solidness he had about himself that no one else in his family was blessed with. I thought of his parents upstairs, each in their own private space, with their separate thoughts.

When Mrs. McHenry had told me that I reminded her of herself, maybe this was what she meant. Not the obvious overlaps that made people smile at the wedding and say, "She is so much like Patty!" Maybe what she recognized in me was the nearly undetectable coat of secrets, thin and transparent but visible in the right light.

"I don't want us to be like your parents," I said.

"What does that mean?"

"I don't want to be lonely in my own home. With Annie gone, I will be so lonely. She knew me. Now, nobody knows me."

Franklin tore the undershirt over his head, like he was suddenly feverish. He spoke with echoes of the night we met, but now, he was half-clothed and a little wild, like this time he was the one trying to snatch the devil.

"I can't know you if you won't let me see you." He picked up the ballerina figurine again and examined it from every angle before he set it down gently, as though it were alive. "Vernice, you have to want it." He imbued his voice with quiet urgency that raised ghost hairs on my neck. Each word was simple and precise, like he was in court, but his tone was just for us. "You have to want this marriage."

"I do." The phrase was an echo of our altar vows, but without the spectacle of things old, new, and blue.

In response he lay back again with those open arms that could have meant so many things. As I closed the space between us, Franklin stroked my hair. "Just tell me. Just tell me who you are."

---

Victoria Falls is one of the seven wonders of the world. When Eleanor Roosevelt stood on its bank and witnessed the mighty Zambezi hurling over a cliff, conjuring mist enough to nurture an entire rain forest, she could only say, "Poor Niagara." This is something that Bobo told Annie, who told me. I have never seen a waterfall. But you don't have to see a thing to know what it feels like.

Franklin begged for my secrets because it was not dignity he craved, but the truth. I told him, not to honor the pact I'd made with Joette. I told him because I couldn't bear the desertion of being unknown in the world. Fear was merely undignified. I could endure that silent humiliation, but not loneliness. I could not be alone in a world with no more Annie.

Franklin was patient as I gathered myself.

"I am not brave," I said.

"But you can be," he promised. "Love requires courage, but it fortifies you at the same time. I don't know anything else in the world that yields the exact same treasure it demands."

"I do love you," I said. "I do, I do, I do."

"Show me," he said. "Let me see."

My words were not eloquent or florid. If they were tangible, they would have been made of gray stone like the ghost stairs at Piedmont Park—built to last, not to decorate. "Yes," Franklin replied. Sometimes asking for more, sometimes indicating that my disclosure was enough. My husband held me in his arms and in his wide heart as I revealed every truth that language allowed.

And after the words, a soft silence preceded the waterfall. So strong was the current—sharp, briny, destructive, yet cooling and cleansing as the sea.

*Chapter 44*

# ANNIE

The doctor said he was going to write down Lulabelle as my next of kin, just in case something went wrong. Lulabelle told him not to bother because nothing was going to go wrong, that I was special, and nothing better not go sideways. Babydoll pointed out that forms were stupid anyway because this was illegal and if something did go wrong, he wouldn't want his name nowhere near anything.

"Ladies," he said, "I am a professional." Next of kin was part of being a doctor, he said. Even his brother, the dentist, had to ask.

"We're her next of kin," said Lulabelle, "and we're right here."

I was naked from the waist down and the room was a little drafty. The doctor looked like Dennis the Menace in the funny papers, except older. Lulabelle had watched him scrub his face, hands, and forearms with Lava soap, and then she mopped him all over with rubbing alcohol. Babydoll fiddled with her praying pearls, wrapped so tight that her fingers were a little purple.

"Wait," I said again. "Give me a second."

"I'm waiting," he said. "But I can't wait all day."

"Why," I asked, "do they say 'next of kin'? Is there a second next? A last of kin?" Bobo probably knew the answer. The thought of him made my lips shake. When I was on the other side of this, when my body was healed and my spirit mended, my love would be the next thing to repair. I imagined it like a bolt of flowered fabric, silk maybe, but on sale because of a rip. I could line the blossoms up just right and use stitches so tiny that they'd vanish into the pattern. That is what I would do. I had never asked him to come back, not with words. To my way of thinking, my distress was plea enough, but a man of words needed to hear my language.

"Ma'am," the doctor said, and I wasn't sure if he offered this respect to Lulabelle or to me. The money had been mine, but Lulabelle was the one who would provide the girl. That's why Babydoll didn't like Lulabelle. Her mama had been like that. I had no idea what my mama was like. I hoped she was good to her new Annie.

"Next of kin," he prompted.

"Not my mother," I said.

"Well, technically," he began, "it's her."

"Not Hattie Lee," I said with some bass in my voice. "Not her."

"Then who?" the doctor said.

"Mrs. Vernice Irene Davis McHenry. Her mother was Arletha."

"You got that?" he said to Babydoll, who was the one holding the pen.

Babydoll mumbled all of the names under her breath, making sure she was getting it down right. Cross, Lulabelle corrected her. Hearing all of my friend's names in the air brought me comfort, even in the wrong order. But the list was incomplete.

"Just write Niecy. I'm the one that gave her that name," I whispered. "It's what I called her when we were just two babies."

# ACKNOWLEDGMENTS

With every book I write, I am reminded anew that I found my voice at Spelman College, a historically Black college for women in my hometown of Atlanta. On that hallowed campus, I earned the courage to call myself a writer. Upon discovery of *A Mighty Justice* by Dovey Johnson Roundtree (C'38), I discovered new reasons to be proud of the powerful lineage of Spelman women. I hope I have done justice to experience of the undaunted alumnae who led the way with their bravery, rigor, and heart.

While writing is a solitary act, living is not. I am endlessly grateful to my kin—some by blood, others by love—who lifted me up in the seven years since my last novel. Pearl Cleage (C'71), Wanda Lloyd (C'71), DeAna Jo Vivian (C'83), Nicole Avery (C'91), Jill Ashton Hughes (C'91), and Taneika Jenkins Edwards (C'03) demonstrated the role of courage in the word "encouragement." Dolen Perkins Valdez knows all there is to know about Memphis, and no one writes about love better than Amy Bloom. They are generous with their expertise, and for this, I am grateful. Derrick Scretchen and Jeffery Murray are good brothers and good men. Behind every great woman is an even greater group chat. Marla Frederick (C'94), Beverly Guy Sheftall (C'66), Evelynn Hammonds (C'76), Paula Giddings, and Lisa Coleman held me down one text at a time. And to my parents, Mack and Barbara Jones, I am forever grateful for reasons too numerous to list.

As we face stunning cuts to arts funding and books themselves, I am blessed to have been supported by the John Simon Guggenheim

Memorial Foundation, the Fox Center for Humanistic Inquiry, and Emory University College of Arts and Sciences. Time is the greatest gift to any artist.

My dear Jane Dystel is my agent, confidant, and friend. We've been together my entire adult life. Jordan Pavlin is a wonderful editor; I am certain that Lindy Hess is smiling at us from heaven.

## A NOTE ABOUT THE AUTHOR

TAYARI JONES is the author of four novels, most recently *An American Marriage*, which was an Oprah's Book Club selection and also appeared on Barack Obama's summer reading list. One of the *New York Times* 100 Best Books of the Twenty-First Century, it won the Women's Prize for Fiction, the Aspen Words Literary Prize, and an NAACP Image Award and has been published in two dozen countries. Jones is the Charles Howard Candler Professor of Creative Writing at Emory University and lives in Atlanta.

## A NOTE ON THE TYPE

This book was set in Janson, a typeface long thought to have been made by the Dutchman Anton Janson, who was a practicing typefounder in Leipzig during the years 1668–1687. However, it has been conclusively demonstrated that these types are actually the work of Nicholas Kis (1650–1702), a Hungarian, who most probably learned his trade from the master Dutch typefounder Dirk Voskens. The type is an excellent example of the influential and sturdy Dutch types that prevailed in England up to the time William Caslon (1692–1766) developed his own incomparable designs from them.

*Composed by North Market Street Graphics,*
*Lancaster, Pennsylvania*

*Designed by Casey Hampton*